RUNAWAY MAGIC

FOREST GUARDIANS BOOK 1

ALI INGS

ALI INGS

CONTENTS

For Ulrika, passed on but never forgotten. You were my main inspiration for Charger, with your gentle nature and your kind heart.

Dedication from the 1st Edition:

For Ariel, a pony just like Leya, and every bit as loyal and opinionated.

To Trend, my old boy, a special dog and faithful companion. You kept me company as I wrote the original version of this book. May you also rest in peace.

CHAPTER 1

TIME TO GO

The bushes trembled. A thundering rumble drowned out the birds chirping. The herd of wild ponies crashed through the bushes, darting around trees, their small hooves shaking the ground. She clutched her pony's mane, balanced perfectly on the pony's wide back, clinging with her legs as they swerved around the trees and galloped with the herd.

Water splashed, spraying, as the ponies charged through the stream. She laughed. The cool water was refreshing. Her pants soaked through below the knee, and were damp higher up, just like her pony's back. This was freedom. Nobody expected anything of her out here, and there was no one to disappoint, just her and the ponies.

She turned her face to the sun. The heat felt welcome, and the gentle breeze kept her from feeling hot with the exertion of their run. Her fingers stayed secure in the golden mane, helping her balance as they galloped.

The trees thinned out. She smiled at the wild meadows ahead, bright green in the spring, and dotted with wild-flowers every colour of the rainbow. The ponies slowed to a lazy walk, staying among the trees as they skirted the meadow. Her pony snorted and blew hot air from her lungs, cooling herself with each breath.

Ponies ambled along, grazing on the succulent grasses along the meadow's edge. Birds chirped and flitted about above her, searching for nesting materials and food. She watched them dart about. It wouldn't be long, and she'd be watching their offspring taking flight for the first few times, learning to use their wings.

Aili knew the animals of the forest. She grew up playing in these woods, knew its seasons and cycles. She learned which plants were edible and what grew in each month, and how plants changed as winter approached. She saw animals be born, grow old, and die. Out here she felt at home. Out here, she could forget.

She turned her gaze to the undergrowth. The ponies browsed through the grasses at a slow walk. Aili was close to a spot where a particularly rare herb grew. It only grew in the shelter of a certain bush species, where it was protected from the weather and shaded from the hot sun. She slid from her pony and kneeled beside the bush.

Aili slipped the cloth bag from her shoulder. Inside, she selected the sharpened trowel. She dug around the roots, feeling the damp soil cling to her fingers. Ilia would appreciate her efforts. The plant was already in bloom, and they would waste no part of it.

Ilia was a Master Herbalist and had taught Aili how to harvest each herb she needed. Aili knew how to protect each plant, whether to leave roots behind, or how to pick flowers and leaves, and how to make sure the plants would regrow and stay strong.

She pulled a cloth from the bag and wrapped the plants inside. The cloth was spelled to preserve and protect the plants Aili harvested, made by Ilia herself. Aili could flatten these flowers, but she didn't want to crush and damage them.

With the plant collected, she refilled the hole, lightly packing the dirt around the remaining herbs. She wiped her trowel off in the grass and tucked it back in the cloth bag. Aili slung the bag over her shoulder again, leaving it in front of her chest to protect the herbs inside. She walked back to Leya, her pony, and kneeled beside her.

"Time to go back, girl." She patted her pony's neck, the soft hair gleaming in the sunlight. "We'll deliver these first."

Leya bumped Aili's leg with her nose. She blew a soft breath over the girl.

Aili sighed. "I want to stay, too." She ran her fingers through the coarse pale mane. "Let's go. You can have an apple when we get back. Only one, though." Why couldn't she stay here forever?

Leya snorted. She nudged the girl. Aili set her hand on the grass for balance.

"I know. Hurry up, you say." Aili laughed and rose to her feet. "At least you have a reason to go back."

She sprang onto Leya's back, landing gracefully behind her withers. A light squeeze with her legs and Leya walked. The pony headed for the city, a marching walk that covered the ground. Aili was certain she knew the word apple, and a pony always knows where the treats are kept.

The woods were peaceful. Nobody was out here, just her and the animals. Aili looked up through the leaves, smiling at the way the light filtered through, dancing in a speckled pattern on the forest floor. She inhaled deeply. This air didn't smell of people, it carried the scent of plants and damp soil.

City noises slowly replaced the birdsong, at first a distant background noise, growing louder as the pony walked. She left the sound of the breeze rustling leaves behind and passed into the wild fields around the forest. Aili knew where the roads were, even if she didn't use them in the forest. The path back into the city was just up ahead.

The white towers of the Magic University dominated the skyline, standing high above the manor houses and other buildings. Out here, near the edge, she could see the smaller houses and merchant's shops, just visible over the thick stone walls that bordered the city.

Leya slipped in among the traffic, the carts that magically followed merchants, and mages going about their business. Leya grew up here with Aili and knew the way as well as the girl did. Congested city streets didn't bother the pony at all.

Aili steered Leya away from a larger horse ridden by a noble. Leya's pinned ears promised mischief that Aili would rather avoid. Some nobles preferred to ride, her father did, but most residents walked or used the self-propelled carts instead.

She guided her pony by shifting her weight or pressing lightly with her legs, taking Leya down side streets to Ilia's shop. Her hooves clattered on the cobblestones, getting lost in the noise of cartwheels and merchants shouting about their wares.

Stone buildings loomed over her, two and three stories high. Aili kept Leya pointed towards the University, visible from anywhere for a great many miles. She left the shops and merchants behind as she entered the heart of the city.

The lone wooden building was visible up ahead, tucked in among the public buildings. Ilia once explained that wood didn't obstruct magic the way stone could and was better for herbalists to work in. Maybe Ilia was so old that she moved in while this area was still forest, and the city simply grew up around her over the centuries. She had always been here, and nobody remembered a time without her.

Leya turned into the alley and wandered behind the shop. Aili stopped her at the small shed with a feeder for the pony. Aili filled the feeder with some hay Ilia kept there for her. The pony stuffed her nose in and crunched the sweet hay.

"I'll be right back." Aili tied her rope bridle to the shed at the feeder and gave Leya a scratch on the neck.

She stepped from the shed. A little white fence protected the herb garden back here. Aili slipped through the gate and latched it securely behind herself. The paths led between pots and garden beds, bursting with colourful plants and flowers. Most were tempting tasty treats for hungry ponies.

Aili took the short path to the back steps. The inside door was open, only the screen door keeping insects from her shop. Aili opened the door and slipped inside, as quiet as a spirit.

"What has my favourite herb collector brought me today?"

Despite her shaky voice, Ilia still sounded strong. Aili smiled at the cauldrons bubbling with brightly coloured mixtures and the spoons stirring without being supervised. The smell of herbs being crushed in mortars and pestles filled the room, the stone tools lightly clacking as they worked by Ilia's magic.

She stepped through the curtain and into the front shop. Ilia perched on a stool behind the counter. She spread dandelion leaves and roots on the counter in front of her, and Ilia was sorting and bagging them without magic. She looked up and met Aili's gaze.

Ilia beamed at her. "I smell the Balic plant." Her grey eyes sparkled with an energy Aili seldom saw in anyone.

Aili grinned. "The patch is doing well. It was flowering again."

She eased the bag from her shoulder and set it on the counter beside the dandelions. Ilia pulled it closer and opened the bag, her delicate hands steady and strong. Aili waited in silence as Ilia pulled the cloth out and unwrapped the plants. They were nearly perfectly preserved, still a brilliant green with purple flowers, and not crushed.

"You did a great job." Ilia held the flowers to her nose and inhaled. "You're my best harvester. Your ability to find plants at the peak of their potency is like magic."

Aili stared at her shoes. Swallowing felt difficult, like she had a large rock stuck in her throat. "If I had magic like everyone else, I wouldn't be escaping into the forest and collecting herbs. I'd be studying or working and contributing to society."

Ilia slid from the stool and wrapped her bony arms around Aili. Her hug was tight, nearly bone crushing. She squeezed Aili's shoulder with her hand. "There are more kinds of magic than the foolish University Mages know. What you do for me is every bit as valuable as anything else you might be doing. Do you know how many people I have healed, people sometimes on the verge of death, using these herbs you bring me?"

Aili smiled, ignoring the tears that rolled down her cheeks.

Ilia wiped Aili's tears away. "Here, I made a salve for the ponies. This will heal the skin and stop the itching." She pressed a jar into Aili's hand. "Here's the recipe. You can make this over a campfire in the woods, if you want to try." She tucked a folded paper into Aili's pocket.

"Now, here's a treat for your greedy little friend, who is trying to unlatch my garden gate." Ilia handed Aili a carrot.

Aili dashed through the curtain and darted through the workshop. She nearly flew down the steps and along the path. Her feet skidded to a stop at the gate, which bumped into her legs as it swung in. Aili stared at Leya with narrowed eyes. The pony nudged her hand, lipping at the carrot. Aili laughed at the hot breath blowing over her skin.

"You little sneak." Aili stepped through the gate, pushing Leya back.

She latched the gate behind her, holding the carrot out of reach. Leya followed her back to the shed, her eyes on the orange prize. How did Ilia know? Aili smiled as she broke the carrot into pieces. Ilia always knew somehow.

Leya snatched the carrot from her palm, her agile lips grasping the sweet treat. Could Ilia hear the loud crunching from inside? Aili fed her the carrot piece by piece. She scratched the pony under her mane, letting her finish her treat.

Aili leapt onto Leya's back and picked up the reins. Leya carried her down the alley and back into the street. She headed towards the nearby University, dodging scholars and students. Most manors were just past the school, Aili's family home among them.

Leya marched up to a massive metal gate. The stone wall towered over Aili, hiding her family home behind it. She slipped from Leya's back and pushed. It took little effort to open the gate, the metal hinges noiseless despite the gate's age and weight.

Aili walked Leya down the stone driveway. The large manor house stood ahead of her. The lawn was perfectly manicured. Aili preferred the wild ivy that grew up along the outside walls, climbing for the sun. There was something about it that even the best Earth Mages couldn't fully tame. She glanced at the copper roof, spelled against tarnish or lightning strike.

She turned to the stables and smiled. Board fences surrounded grassy paddocks in front of the stone stable. Aili opened a gate and Leya wandered into a paddock, her nose diving for the grass as Aili shut the gate again.

"Something you want?" Aili smiled at the pony.

Leya raised her head and stared at the girl, her mouth full of grass. She stuck her nose over the top fence board and snorted.

"I'll be right back with that apple. It's not nice to manipulate me with your cuteness." Aili rubbed Leya's cheek.

Leya sighed, blowing a breath over the girl. She closed her eyes and leaned into Aili's touch. Aili gave her golden hair a pat. Time to keep her promise. She turned to the stable and walked to the main door, a skip in her step.

A couple of younger stable hands unloaded hay bales from a massive wagon, levitating them into the nearby storage shed. Aili stopped and watched for a moment. She'd read about the magic they did, learned the theory, but her heart ached to try it.

A snort pulled her from her thoughts. Aili headed inside the stable. She inhaled deeply, taking in the smell of clean horse, fresh hay, and leather. The windows let natural light inside, giving everything a warm glow from the sunlight. Aili wandered down the aisle to the feed room.

Darik stood with his back to her, lifting bags of grain and dumping them into a container spelled against rodents. He slit the bags open with a knife and heaved them up in his arms. Aili often saw him work with no magic at all. Was that why he wasn't bothered by her lack of magic?

He wasn't from the city, but he never told Aili where he grew up, or what he did before coming here. What kind of past did this mysterious man have? All Aili knew was he was like a second father to her, spending time with her as she grew up. Just being around him, even like this, her heart warmed.

Ilia was the other person in her life that worked without magic. She explained once that magic can affect some potions and salves. She mixed them without magic, or with tools that were specially spelled.

"What grand adventures did you two have today?" Darik glanced over as he slit another feed bag open.

"Oh, nothing much. Monsters to slay, treasures to find, the usual." Aili grinned back at him. She pulled the small container from her pocket. "Ilia gave me this. Use it on Linna's skin condition. It'll speed the healing."

Darik took the little jar from her. "As much as you love those stories, you should focus on making a life here in the real world with us. Find your place. You have one, you know."

"This says otherwise." Aili fingered the metal band around her neck, still a dull bronze. "I have no status and no place in a magical world. All I have is my pony." With a trembling hand, Aili grabbed an apple from the bucket and marched from the room.

"You have me."

Aili froze in the doorway, the whisper barely reaching her. She blinked back the tears; her head tipped back so they wouldn't fall. She left without a backwards glance. It hurt to swallow, and she wanted to be in the sunshine.

She took a few slow and deep breaths, slowing her steps as well. Darik had always been there for her, no matter what. When the other kids teased her, Darik would tell her stories and cheer her up. When they wouldn't play with her, he would teach her more about ponies and spend time with her. She hadn't forgotten him, and now he thought she had.

"Here you go." Aili held the apple out in her palm. "Just like I promised."

Leya snatched the apple away and crunched it between her teeth. Aili stayed beside her pony, running her fingers through Leya's pale mane. What should she do now? The kids her age were in magic lessons or out working already, helping society and advancing magical knowledge.

Aili had nothing to contribute. She wiped another tear from her face, another one of many, and surely not her last. Leya rested her head on the fence beside Aili, her nose touching the girl.

She wandered behind the stable, out of sight of the house. The small stack of hay bales still sat there. Darik forbid anyone from moving them. Aili reached beneath the top bale of hay and pulled out the wooden practice sword he kept for her.

This sword was their secret. She ran her fingers along the edge of the wooden blade, nicked and barked up from him sparring with her. He taught her in secret, helping her hone her abilities and polish each movement to perfection. She still felt he was holding back with her, but occasionally she could surprise him now.

Aili felt the wood grain against her palm. He mentioned it was time to get her the next size up, now that she was bigger again, but he was busy with some fencing improvements here. Aili moved to the shade the stable gave, protected from view by the high stone wall and the hay shed.

She stood still, stretched tall, her breathing slowing as she settled her mind. Aili felt the weight of the wooden blade and focused on her surroundings. With an exhale, she raised the sword and stepped, sweeping the blade around her.

Her breathing matched her movements, flowing through the pattern slowly. Breathe in and draw back, step out, and thrust on the exhale. She knew the moves by heart. Aili didn't pause once, didn't falter, and settled back into the quiet stillness that began and ended each form.

The next two forms followed, one after another, with a moment of stillness between. He promised to teach her the fourth form soon, and spar with her more. Aili trembled at the thought. He often had to sneak her sessions in at night, after the workday was done, but he made time for her every day. Aili was a good sneak, and nobody ever noticed the girl with no magic.

She rolled her shoulders, feeling the muscles move freely. Her body felt better after practice, loose and balanced again. It helped her centre her mind and focus on the moment. Aili tucked her sword back in the hay. She felt calm again, ready to face lunch with her family.

Aili stepped around the stable and looked up at the house. Maybe she could go live in the forest and forage for her food. Aili had done that for camping trips, and Darik taught her all about bushcraft. No, her parents loved her and did their best for her, but Aili felt that pit in her stomach every time she came home.

She forced her feet to carry her to the back door. It was the superior looks from the servants, the constant reminder she only had the rights of a small child without magic, that's what she hated the most about being home. Technically, her bronze band meant she needed to listen to anyone with a silver band or higher, which was everyone over five, pretty much. No servant would boss her around for fear of her father, but they all knew they could. Her stomach churned.

The scorching sun had dried her pants already. Nobody would know where she'd been or what she'd been up to. She snuck in through the door. She knew where everyone would be this time of day and could go unnoticed, like a stealthy assassin she once read about in an old storybook.

The back halls and passages were empty. Aili could hear the occasional conversation on the main floor as she headed for the back stairs. Her father's library was nearly as impressive as the one at the University and he allowed students of all levels to come and study here. There were always strangers in the front part of the ground floor. She kept to the private halls, where only their noise could come.

Aili climbed the steep back steps, seeing by the light of small windows spaced far apart. The servants would simply cast a ball of mage-light, which would hover along with them and light their way. Aili didn't need it, though. She knew the way. This was also much simpler than climbing trees.

There was no sound outside the hidden door. Aili stepped into the hallway near the large main staircase. She glanced down at herself. Her pants and shirt were fine for playing in the forest, but her mother would frown if she showed up for a meal like this. Only workers wore pants.

She turned down the hall to the bedrooms, the thick carpet muffling her footsteps. Heavy tapestries gave the hallway some colour and hid the stone walls behind them. Aili crept towards her room at the far end.

A maid's cart sat in the hall just outside her sister's room. The door was cracked open.

"I just think it's a shame that a perfectly healthy young woman has nothing to do all day." Mora's voice carried into the hallway. "She may not be good for anything, but at least she could make herself useful, instead of disappearing all day. She shows up for meals like a boarding house guest."

Aili stood frozen, their words making her chest feel tight. It wasn't her fault she was useless. The best mages, those most revered, worked to make life better for everyone. Aili would never be one of them.

All she could do was read and study theory and science. She knew more about magic than most mages. She just couldn't make any spells work. Aili could never try the spells she had memorized. Sure, she could use science, but that would only take her so far.

"Imagine how her parents must feel. Such a high-status family, and they have an unmarriageable daughter with no future."

Aili growled to herself. She never cared much for Lalu, the head maid. She balled her fists. Her arms shook. No, Aili didn't need to hear anything else. She slunk down the hall to her room at the end, closing the door behind her.

She stared blankly around her room, the conversation still running around her brain. Darik taught her a meditation that helped. She'd try that first. Aili settled on her bed cross-legged and took a deep breath. She focused on her body, on what she felt right now. There was no breeze in the room, and it was comfortably warm. Aili slowed her breathing. Her heart slowed and her muscles relax.

Aili opened her eyes again. Her family would wait for her. She pulled her formal robes from her dresser and changed. Sorry, comfortable clothes. Society calls.

Aili straightened up and held her head high. This was her family home, and she belonged here. Aili swung the door open and stepped into the empty hall. She walked down the hall and to the stairs, mimicking the confidence of a Master Mage.

She passed the stairs and headed down the opposite hall. The first door was the small dining room they used every day. Her parents' voices came from inside, and they hadn't closed the door fully. Aili reached up to push it open.

"Any news about Aili, dear?"

Her fingers trembled at the sound of a sharp breath. Aili rolled her eyes. Her mother was fretting again. She waited, the silence stretching out painfully long.

"I'm exploring a few possibilities."

Aili frowned. He sounded so tired. She hated being a source of stress for him, especially when she enjoyed spending time with him so much.

"I have a friend who will take her on as a maid. I might find her a place at a stable. She's unusually skilled with horses, and she could teach children to ride."

Aili's hand dropped to her side.

"I wish I could do more for her." She almost didn't hear his whisper.

Aili pressed her hand to her chest. Was her heart being crushed, or did it just feel like it? Could words actually wound someone? Aili was the first person born in her country without magic in centuries. Her existence was an embarrassment to her family, especially with her father on the Council of Mages.

No, she had no intention of becoming a maid. Aili was happy to work without magic, and she could do a lot more than clean up after someone. Ilia taught her well. She could study more herbalism or go into the forest and do research. Maids specialized in cleaning magic and decorating. They had a passion for it Aili just didn't share.

Footsteps pulled her from her thoughts. Aili ducked around the corner to the back stairs. Her feet carried her down, out the door, and to the paddocks. She leaned on the paddock fence and watched Leya graze, gasping for breath.

Leya ambled over and pressed her nose against Aili's shoulder. Aili rubbed her smooth and wide forehead. Her muscles relaxed, and Aili smiled sadly.

"Well, Leya, they're deciding my future. I have skills. We can move through a forest and never get lost. I can fix nearly anything with twine from a hay bale, and I can train horses. It's time we make our way in life. We'll choose for ourselves where to go and what to do."

Leya blew a hot breath over her. Aili grinned. Ponies had a simple view of life. All Leya worried about was where the next treat was coming from and where the best grass was.

"Should we spend some time with the wild herd before we settle down somewhere?"

Leya poked her nose through the fence and tugged at Aili's pockets, her lip catching the loose fabric of Aili's robes. Aili laughed and pushed her nose away. She and Leya could do this together, she was certain.

"I'll get you a treat before we go. After that, I need to pack."

The hay wagon was gone, and the yard was empty. Her thoughts turned to Darik. She would miss him so much. Aili blinked back her tears. She could cry later. For now, she needed all her courage. Besides, how could she thank him for everything he ever taught her, everything that would let her thrive in the forest once she left?

Aili slipped quietly into the feed room and snatched an apple from the pile. She ran back out, putting her fear and worry into each step. She could run off her emotions for now.

The apple disappeared from her palm, Leya's whiskers tickling her skin. Aili smiled at the contented crunching sounds, Leya's jaw breaking the apple into pieces and chewing. Leya lifted her lip and stared at Aili, searching the girl for more treats.

"That's all there is for now. I'll be right back."

She darted across the yard and to the back door. Sneaking like a common thief, Aili returned to her room and closed the door. Her parents would have started eating without her. Her sister would be there by now, and she was more interesting. She was a prodigy with Illusion Magic. Nobody would notice Aili's absence for a while.

Aili pulled the rough canvas bag from under her bed. She used it for camping trips, and she already stocked it with essential tools and supplies. She'd need clothes, so Aili grabbed her favourite shirts and pants. No need for robes out there. Her brush and hair ties joined the pile in the bag.

The book Darik gave her on outdoor survival was on her night table. He got it for her ages ago, when he first started taking her into the woods. She added the notes Ilia gave her on herbalism, nearly another book worth of loose pages Aili tied together with string.

Her hand hovered over a picture of her with her parents. Her stomach flopped around. If she tried to say goodbye, they'd keep her from going. Darik or Ilia had spelled her book and notes against tearing and being soiled, but the photo hadn't been. Aili left it on her desk.

She changed back into her forest clothing, a dark green shirt and pants that let her blend into the background. Aili folded her robes and left them on her bed. A last glance around and she checked her bag once more. That should be all she needed.

Aili slung her bag over her shoulder. Time to look ahead now. No going back. Her family was better off without her. Aili crept back down the stairs and out the door. Once she got Leya ready, she would be on her way.

Leya stood at the gate, waiting for her. Aili frowned, her steps slowing as she came around the house. Darik stood beside Leya, saddlebags over his shoulder. Leya leaned into his scratch, her lip curled, and her head stretched out. Aili's saddle and equipment were on the fence, ready to go.

"Darik?" Aili stepped beside him and set her bag down.

"It's time to go, isn't it?" He smiled, but the lines around his eyes tugged at her heart.

Aili opened her mouth and closed it again. It felt hard to breathe. "I think so."

"I packed you some food and supplies for your trip." Darik draped the saddlebags over the paddock fence. "You've never done more than a week, and I didn't want you to forget something important. Where are you going?"

Aili sighed. "I'm not sure. Maybe I'll go where there is no magic, and I can be like everybody else."

"It's a different world out there. You won't find it any friendlier than here. You can always come back, and I'll help you. You're not as alone as you feel right now."

She blinked back her tears and stepped into the paddock. Leya's brushes gave her something else to think about, the smooth wood handles familiar in her hand. She pressed the brushes against the pony, falling into the familiar routine. If Leya was going to carry her any distance, Aili had to be sure she stayed healthy. She wouldn't fail her best friend.

"Thanks for everything," Aili whispered. "I couldn't even try this without everything you taught me."

Darik nodded, his eyes on the ground. He picked up her saddle and set it on Leya. A slight wiggle and the saddle shifted into the right place. Aili fastened the girth and Darik tied the packs behind the saddle, balancing them for Leya's comfort. Too much weight on one side could make Leya sore. Aili slipped Leya's rope bridle over the pony's head.

He held the cheekpieces of her bridle and looked the pony in the eye. "You take care of her. Don't let her get lost."

Aili pressed her hand to her mouth, choking back a sob or a laugh. She wasn't sure which it was, but her throat ached. "I'll miss you, too."

Darik opened his mouth and closed it again. He brushed his hand over his eyes and blinked rapidly. Aili pressed her hand to her heart. She swung herself up into the saddle and picked up the reins. The rope felt soft and light in her hands. She didn't really need the bridle, but Aili didn't want to stand out from other riders on the road.

Darik swung the gate open and stepped aside. "Safe travels."

Aili gave Leya a light squeeze with her legs. The pony strode from the paddock. She rarely got to go out again so quickly. Did Leya know what was going on? Aili didn't look back as she passed through the manor gates, away from her family home and the man who watched over her as she grew up.

CHAPTER 2

A New World

Mages moved through the streets, some dashing past while others strolled. Most were heading back to work after the lunch break, though some were going shopping. Aili slipped in among the crowd, just another person on the street.

She pointed Leya towards the nearest city gate. The main road would run right to it, past the University and another district of manor houses. Leya knew the way. Aili let her mind wander, ignoring the chaos and noise of the streets.

Leya took her northeast, following the road. She didn't come this way often. Her woods were to the west, but the nearest border with a non-magical country was this way. Aili brushed away her tears. She could live in the forest alone, foraging and spending time with the ponies, but she'd eventually get lonely. People who might accept her were this way.

Her thoughts turned to the border, a magical barrier that hid them from the outside world. She'd read about it before. Even though she didn't have magic, her father encouraged her to read everything she could on a variety of topics. She knew the border was patrolled and guarded and had multiple layers of magic for protection.

Leya stopped and leaned, shifting her balance. Aili clung to the saddle, her hands buried in Leya's mane and her fingers gripping tightly as she tipped forward.

"What's up, girl?" Aili looked around. "Oh."

How did they get to the edge of the city already? Leya stood at the crossroads outside the gates, grazing on the grass at the edge. Aili looked east, out at the crops and orchards as far as her eyes could see. Her forest was to the left, the far eastern edge of it, and another forest was visible ahead and to her right, way off in the distance. That was her destination.

She patted her pocket, the compass secure inside. It was a gift from one of Darik's friends. She'd never seen one before he gave it to her and had seen no one else with one, either. It worked on science, not magic, and had never failed Aili yet. She liked the shiny brass metal.

"This way."

With a shift of her weight, Leya headed east along a side path. The pony's hooves thudded against the packed dirt. Aili recalled the maps she studied as a girl. Maps fascinated her, places she never thought she'd see, and she had a memory for them. This one paralleled the main road and was used by the farmers.

The fields were empty of people, but the orchards had workers out tending the plants and fruits. Aili shifted her collar up over her neckband. The last thing she needed was someone calling the Defence Forces and for them to send her home. Harvest was weeks away, and the workers were busy inspecting plants. With some luck, Aili should make it. She hoped, anyway.

Her thoughts turned to the Border Guards as she let Leya carry her on. They patrolled the forest and the border and monitored the magic there. She also had to avoid magical alarms, set to prevent people from crossing anywhere other than on the roads. They'd never let her cross at the manned checkpoints. She'd need to be sneaky and hope for the best.

She'd give anything for a concealment spell right now. Aili felt exposed on the road, but she knew how to move through a forest without being seen. Act like you belong, Darik once said, and people won't question your presence. If you look suspicious, people will get suspicious.

A farmer narrowed his eyes at Aili. She waved as she rode past, giving him a smile. He raised his gloved hand and waved back.

She sighed when she finally slipped into the trees, disappearing into the forest. Leya let out a deep breath, her head dropping as she walked.

"I know, girl. Feels good to be in a forest again, doesn't it?" Aili scratched Leya's withers.

Tall trees scattered the light that made it down to her, casting deep shadows she could hide in. Aili scanned the forest as they moved, listening as well as looking, as she searched for somewhere with water and a spot she could camp. She had a tarp she could use for shelter from the wind. These trees were thick, much thicker than in her forest.

Aili listened closely and watched Leya's ears. She could hear running water. Leya's ears kept flicking to the bushes, so Aili guided her towards the welcome noise. A few birds chirped, darting between trees above them. The thick foliage seemed to absorb the sound. Aili smiled. She could use that to her advantage.

She slipped from Leya's back and grabbed her canteens from her pack. One was full, so she put it back. She had sipped from the one as she rode, so she dipped it in the water and filled it. Aili recapped the canteen and tucked it away. Leya took a long drink.

With just a quick look around, Aili identified four edible herbs and two berry species. She collected those and tucked them in a cloth. Now it was time to find somewhere to camp. They moved from the stream and into the thicker bush before Aili stopped for the night.

Aili untacked Leya, setting the saddle and packs on the ground. She took her brushes and went over Leya thoroughly from head to tail, massaging the pony's muscles. Aili looked for any bumps or swelling, any sign Leya had an injury starting, like heat in her legs. Leya felt healthy. Aili scratched her between her front legs. Leya stretched her head out and flapped her lip, leaning into the touch.

"We did it, girl. The border is close. Let's get some sleep." Aili kept her voice low. Were there people around? She didn't know.

She blended the tangy berries and the sweet herbs, setting half aside for breakfast. This close to the border, Aili didn't dare start a fire. Her meals would be cold until she was safely on the other side. Aili didn't mind. She ate her berry blend and watched Leya graze beside her.

Daylight faded and the shadows spread. Aili tucked her breakfast safely in her pack, where squirrels couldn't steal her food. She spread her bedroll out and curled up under the trees. Leya grazed nearby, the steady sound of chewing lulling her to sleep.

***

Light scattered over the forest, soft in the early hours. Aili stretched her body, blinking as she pulled herself from sleep. She eased herself from her bedroll and glanced around. Leya grazed just beyond her small camp. Aili packed up her bedroll.

Aili popped a berry into her mouth and scrunched her face. They didn't seem that tart last night. The sweet herbs blended in only helped so much. She took a long sip from her canteen and looked around again. The only sign she'd been here was the short grass Leya snacked on. "Well, girl, it's time to go."

Leya wandered over to Aili and her packs, snatching grass with each step.

"What do you think? We can make a run for it, and they may see us, or we can try to sneak, and hopefully avoid the magic traps." She set the saddle on her pony and snugged up the girth.

Leya shifted from hoof to hoof. Aili vaulted up, barely getting a leg over the saddle with how Leya danced around.

"Alright, we'll go fast."

She walked Leya back to the stream and let her drink. The walking would warm up her muscles and get her ready to run. The last thing Aili needed was for Leya to pull a muscle this early in their trip, and on this side of the border.

Aili turned Leya back towards the border, keeping her at a walk. They were only a few feet past their campsite when Aili felt the tingling, almost a buzzing. It felt like an incredibly slow pulsing, something she felt deep in her bones and nerves.

"We're almost there, I can feel it. Ready?" Her heart hammered in her chest. She gripped the reins tighter, her sweaty palms making the rope damp.

She grabbed Leya's mane. If they needed to dodge and weave through the trees, Aili didn't want to pull Leya off balance. Leya would smell or hear mages before Aili, and Aili trusted her to keep them safe.

Leya pranced, her steps high and her ears pricked ahead. Aili crouched low in the saddle. She squeezed lightly and Leya galloped. Hooves pounded on the soft soil; the sound absorbed by the ground. Aili shifted and moved with her, in perfect balance. The wind whipped through her light brown hair, loosening small strands from her braids.

Her skin prickled with energy. Aili closed her eyes and let Leya run. Pressure squeezed the air from Aili's lungs, like someone wrapped a hand around her firmly. She gasped for air.

The pressure was gone. Her skin calmed. The ache in her lungs eased with each breath. Aili was across. She felt the unease, a sense of not belonging. Aili read about this part of the magic once. It kept the non-magical folk from coming near the border. There wasn't any mention of the physical pain she felt, though. No wonder so few people left the country.

Trees loomed over her, casting dark shadows. Did each have a monster ready to leap at her, or was that just the magic, too? Clouds covered the sky, blotting out any direct sunlight. Aili glanced between the dark and the less dark shadows. Well, if she didn't do well in town, she could always come back and hide. The townsfolk shouldn't want to follow her into this magic.

No, people will be friendly, she was sure of it. She could make a new life and belong. Darik's words echoed in her brain. All she could do was prepare for the worst and hope for the best. Aside from the magic, this was a normal forest. Aili was at home in a forest. She'd be fine.

Leya slowed to a walk. The pony sweat freely, her breath hot and puffing. Aili wiped her forehead with her sleeve. She cast her mind back to the maps. The main road led right to a town. It should be south of her. Aili pulled her compass out. She wouldn't see the sun until she was away from the border.

She pointed Leya southeast and let her walk. If she turned south too quickly, she might run into the Border Guard. No, Aili wanted more distance, first. She should still reach the road and town if she set out in this direction.

Aili followed her compass through the trees. The shadows were less deep, and she could see fields ahead. A metallic clanging carried through the air and farm animals called to each other. Aili stopped Leya at the edge of the forest.

The town sat among fields of growing grains. A large vegetable garden was off one side, with people hunched over among the plants. The blacksmith's shop belched out black smoke. She'd done it. She was here.

Her mouth was dry. Darik worked without magic, but to be somewhere where that was normal, Aili almost couldn't believe her eyes. She took a deep breath. Could she do it? Talk to strangers? Aili gripped the reins tightly.

"Let's go, girl. We'll just do our best and hope for the best."

She skirted the edge of the field, careful of the crop. Leya carried her to the road, visible now without the forest in the way. Aili kept her gaze on the town. Maybe she'd see someone who looked friendly. Darik's friend spoke of inns, how even small towns had one. Would she know it when she saw it?

The stench turned her stomach as she rode past the blacksmith's shop and into the town. The man glanced up as she passed, his eyes dropping back to his work after barely a look. Small houses lined the street towards a central open area.

Two larger buildings sat at the end. Was one of those an inn? Nothing looked like the stone buildings she was used to. Aili rode to the buildings and slid from Leya's back. She looked between them. They looked the same.

A tall and muscular boy stepped from the shadows between the buildings. "That's some fancy leather you got there. A pony that well trained is worth some pretty coin, too."

She shifted closer to Leya, closer to her bush knife hidden in her saddle pad. Another boy hopped a fence on her right, moving towards her a single step at a time. More boys of all ages approached, appearing from shadows or buildings, forming a ring around her.

A man nodded at the boys. They charged. Dust rose behind them. Aili leapt into the saddle and gripped Leya's mane. The pony bolted through the boys, smacking one with her shoulder. He hit the ground with a thud, the dust rising to cover him. Rocks whistled past her, bouncing off the stone walls bordering the road or hitting the dirt past her.

She burst into the trees, back into the shadows.

Aili's hands trembled. "Easy, girl. Walk."

Leya slowed, her sides heaving with each breath. Aili slid from the saddle and walked beside the pony; her fingers twined in Leya's mane. Walking eased the tension from her muscles, and Aili sighed. She wiped the tear from her eye and looked around.

"Okay, girl, that will not be home. Let's get you cooled out and find you some water. Can you sense any?"

She glanced around again. The town was back that way, or was it that way? Leya sniffed the air and turned, heading deeper into the forest. Only a few dozen steps later and Aili heard the stream Leya detected. She sped up beside her thirsty pony.

The water ran fast and clean, wide and shallow. Leya stepped in and stirred the mud from the bottom. The sediment flowed swiftly beneath the pony. She dropped her nose and took a long drink.

Aili stepped into the stream. The water came up over her ankles and felt cool through her boots. She crouched and splashed cool water on her burning face. Aili pulled a cloth from her pack and dipped it in the stream. She rubbed Leya's sweaty spots, her neck and belly and rump.

"Maybe another town? We can always come live in the woods or keep moving along the border."

Her heart sunk in her chest. Being lonely was better than having rocks thrown at her. Was she cursed to be alone forever? Aili bent down and felt Leya's legs. She ran the cloth over her pony from the knee down, cooling her hot tendons. Running like that was risky. Aili had to protect Leya. She wiped more tears away with her damp sleeve.

With Leya taken care of, she tucked the cloth back in her pocket. She pulled her compass out and held it up. The needle spun one direction, changed directions, and bounced around. Aili stared at it; her eyebrow raised.

She looked up, seeking the sun. The clouds were back, so she must be close to the border, but which way? She'd need to walk and find a clear spot to see where she was.

Wait, she realized. There was another way. Aili led Leya from the stream and climbed back into the saddle. "Home. Apple."

Leya turned and marched into the forest. She climbed a rise and eased her way down onto a road.

"Whoa." Aili picked up her reins and pulled lightly.

Leya snorted.

Aili rubbed her neck. "I know. I'll get you a treat as soon as I can."

She scanned the road both ways. The trees bordered the road, thick and dark, the perfect place for bandits to hide. There was an intersection that way with a large signpost. It was more open, and the sunlight touched the road.

Aili kept her eyes on the trees as they headed for the road marker. Leya pranced, ready to run. Her ears swiveled side to side. Leya raised her head and her ears perked forward.

"People?" Aili scratched her neck. She stopped Leya and waited.

Soft footsteps approached. Aili strained to hear, and she could usually hear a mouse in moss. Leya tracked their approach. Her eyes and ears focused on the noise. Aili asked her to walk, guiding her wide around the corner, crossing to the opposite side of the road. She might see them before they saw her. She hoped.

Aili stared into the deep blue eyes of a man. He watched her; his expression relaxed. She tore her gaze from his and assessed him and his companion. The man stopped walking. With a motion of his hand, his companion stopped beside him.

They were taller than most mages and stood with confidence. Something about the way they moved pulled at Aili, a memory half-triggered. The sun glinted off their neckbands. Master mages, based on the platinum bands both men wore.

Aili pulled her collar up around her own neckband, but he already assessed her back. She just knew it. Would they walk past, avoiding her like everyone else? Would they drag her back and make her go home?

"How did you get so far from home?" He gave Aili a slight smile.

"We walked." He wasn't leaving? She fidgeted with Leya's mane, her fingers gripping the coarse strands, twisting them around her fingers.

His companion snorted. His black hair floated for a moment as he ducked his head, settling down again as his eyes met hers.

The man raised his hand a fraction and his friend fell silent. He met Aili's gaze again and smiled, a genuine smile that reached his eyes. "This road is dangerous. Why don't you walk with us?"

"I don't know you. I know how to stay safe in a forest." Her heart screamed to go with them, but her gut churned, warning of danger. She sat rigid in Leya's saddle. "Who are you? You move like Defence Mages."

He threw his head back and laughed. "Where have you seen or met a Defence Mage?" He ran his fingers through his dark hair.

"Darik, our stable manager, he introduced me to one once. That man taught me tracking." Aili clamped her mouth shut. Why was she being friendly? She didn't know them. Still, something about him and his easygoing manner, she felt calmer than she should around him.

"You're from the House Aldoni?" He raised his eyebrow. "How did you get out past the border?"

"We walked."

"It's really not safe for you out here. Come with us and we'll get you home." He held his hand out to her.

Aili's thoughts jumbled in her head, a mess she couldn't untangle. They were friendly. They might drag her home. She shook her head. "It's not home anymore. Safe travels."

She pulled Leya's rein, and the pony burst into the trees. Leya cantered over the small hill and back down towards the stream. Aili didn't slow her until they reached the stream, out of magic range. Was she crazy? She wanted to go back. She wanted to run. What did she want?

Leya glanced back at her.

"I know. You think I should go with them?"

Leya snorted and bobbed her head.

"There's no future for me there. There's no future for me here. Leya, I don't know what to do anymore. We're fine in the forest until we decide. We know how to live out here." She scratched the pony's neck.

Leya snorted and hopped her back end up, just a few inches, jostling Aili.

"I know you need friends. You're used to a herd. Why don't we go back to the wild ponies tomorrow? At least you'll be happy there, and I'll just have to avoid people."

Leya sauntered along the stream bank. She exhaled deeply, her sides heaving with the deep breath.

"I don't know what else to do." Aili let the tears roll down her cheeks.

Leya whickered, her nostrils vibrating.

"Thanks, girl. Let's get a drink."

Leya stepped into the water and dropped her head. Aili slipped from the saddle and landed, barely splashing in the shallow water. She crouched and scooped up some water in her hands. Aili froze.

A silver glint in her reflection caught her eye. It was distorted in the flowing water, but Aili leaned down. Her neckband had silver strands in it. No, this had to be a trick of the light. She blinked and looked again, her braids dangling close to the water. Her band was partly silver.

"What?" Aili fingered her neckband, feeling the ridges of the silver strands. "Leya?"

Leya nuzzled Aili's hand, dripping water over the girl. Her whiskers tickled against Aili's face.

"This isn't supposed to happen." She pressed her hand to her chest, over her heart. "It's not supposed to change colour like this, and not until they identify my magic. Magic I don't have. Why's it changing?"

Her heart pounded against her ribs. Now what should she do? She clearly remembered being paraded before Master Mages with other children. Master Mages identified their magic, a ceremony changed the colour of their band from bronze to the silver of a student, and they found teachers. Not Aili, though. Each time she went, her heart broke. Each time, she remained without magic. Her band stayed bronze.

Aili brushed more tears away. Nobody's bands changed on their own. Leya nudged her with her nose, throwing Aili off balance. She thrust her hands into the cold mud. Her world spun. Aili took some deep breaths. She needed help.

She stood and wrapped her arms around Leya's neck. Her muscles relaxed and Aili felt calmer, less like crying. Leya had always been there for her, no matter where their adventure took them.

"You're right. Food, shelter, and sleep. We can decide what to do in the morning when we feel better."

Aili crouched and cupped her hands, scooping up the water to drink. She scanned the banks for edible herbs, often found near running water. She remembered a berry bush they passed earlier, close to here, and Aili found some edible roots. Within a short time, she had enough for supper and breakfast, tucked in a cloth in her pack.

"You pick great campsites, girl. Where should we bed down tonight?"

Leya splashed through the stream and up the opposite bank, between thick bushes. Aili grinned and followed her pony. She pushed through after Leya, easing herself through where the bushes grabbed at her clothing, threatening to tear it.

Aili stepped into a grassy clearing, thick bush on all sides. She was hidden and protected and would hear anything coming through. How did Leya know? "Brilliant." She stepped beside the pony, already grazing in the middle, and scratched her neck.

The surrounding trees reached for the sky, young and strong. Branches hung over the clearing, shading parts from the sun. The grass was young and thick, and Aili could start a fire without risking it spreading easily. Aili grinned.

She pulled a chain from her pack, grasping the wooden handles on the ends with her fingers. Aili looked at the trees again. "That one."

Leya followed her to the edge of the clearing, where a tree lay partly in the bushes. The trunk poked into the clearing, about as big around as the length of her hand. Aili wrapped a rope around the trunk and tied the other end around Leya's shoulders, like Darik showed her long ago. With her pony's help, she dragged it into the clearing fully.

Once she freed Leya, Aili took her chain and set the saw teeth against the wood. She sawed at some branches, stripping them from one side. She cut the tree shorter. Aili grabbed the branches and dragged, moving the tree between two living trees near the edge. Leya pushed with her nose, pressing her shoulder against the tree as Aili hoisted it up to her waist level.

Aili lashed the tree in place and moved to the other end. Soon she tied it in place and Aili rigged the tarp. She had a space underneath that was protected from the worst weather she might see this time of year.

With shelter taken care of, Aili unsaddled Leya and set her packs aside. She pulled her brushes out and treated the pony to a thorough grooming, pressing hard and massaging her muscles with each brushstroke. She ran her hands over Leya and didn't find any heat or swelling.

Aili gathered rocks and built a firepit. She added some of the cut branches and started a fire with her flint. Once it was going, Aili set some roots on the rocks she placed in the fire. Her mind turned to her band. She ran her fingers over it. The ridges were more pronounced now.

Those men, both had been Master Mages. Even from a distance, Aili could see that, from the colour and the markings. A mage's rank determined so much about their life, how they acted around mages of higher and lower ranks, and what positions they could hold for an occupation. What were they doing out here? Master Mages could do whatever they want. Why be out here, over the border?

Did one of them trigger her magic, or detect it somehow? Why now, and not earlier, when she was presented to Master Mages in the city? They sorted everyone into a Magic school before they were seven, when their magic showed. Everyone but Aili. She didn't recall seeing crystals in her neckband, though. Those showed which magic school she belonged to, and she didn't have them.

She ran her fingers over the band again. Aili felt the flat plate in the middle that would display her teacher's name, but she didn't feel any letters on it. Even those who took classes at the magic schools had their school's name on the plate. Aili shrugged. Nothing else about her band was normal. She felt the clusters of crystals forming, still slight bumps in the metal band.

"I don't feel any different. Should I try something simple?"

Leya snorted. She dropped her nose back into the grass and tore some off.

"Right. Eat first and worry later." Aili grinned. How like a pony that was to put food before work. Leya had a point, though. New students could get famished after using magic until they built their strength up.

She pulled her roots from the fire and dropped them on a large leaf. Aili kicked her fire apart and took her leaf to her shelter. She settled on the grass and leaned back against Leya's saddle. The steam rose and filled her nose with fresh herbs and bitter roots, mellowed with cooking. Her stomach rumbled.

Aili crushed the cooked roots with the side of her knife blade and added some berries from her pack. The food cooled fast, mashed like that, and Aili scooped it up with her fingers. She wolfed down her meal and licked her leaf clean.

"Alright, now or never. Time to see if something changed in me."

She sat upright, crossing her legs. Aili slowed her breathing like Darik taught. Leya moved to the far edge of the clearing. She eyed the girl as she tore more grass and chewed it.

"Thanks for the vote of confidence." Aili smirked at the pony.

Leya snorted. She dropped her head and grazed.

Focus, Aili chastised herself. You've seen enough magic lessons. What did they say? Right, reach inside and feel for a pool of power down in the belly. Aili emptied her mind of thoughts and felt for her inner sensations.

No, she felt no power. She felt nothing different at all. Mages often described it as a warmth that swirled and tingled inside. Aili sensed nothing like that. She opened her eyes and sighed, flopping back on the grass.

Leya ambled over and dropped her nose to Aili's shoulder. She scratched her pony's neck and rubbed her broad forehead. What should she do now?

"Maybe my band is wrong?"

Leya breathed out, sending a blast of hot air over Aili's face.

"Stop laughing." She sat up.

What about the men? Might they know? They were Master Mages. They were supposed to know all about magic, right? Aili stood and brushed her clothing straight. What if they don't want me around?

"Well, I can't change what my band is doing, and I don't have magic yet, so let's go for a walk. We've got time before supper."

Leya raised her head and stared at the girl. Aili grabbed a handful of mane and vaulted onto her back. She didn't need the saddle or bridle for this ride. Leya passed easily through the bushes and out among the trees.

Aili kept watch, looking for food and for signs of people. She didn't need food now, but later she might, so she noted where it grew. There was no sign of any farms, no sounds of cattle or sheep, no hint another person had been here ever. Hopefully they were far enough from the border the guards wouldn't come looking, either.

Once back in camp, Aili slid from Leya's back. She prepared her fire but didn't light it yet. Aili pulled her long bush knife from her pack and moved away from the fire. She took a deep breath and stood tall, her mind on the first sword form.

She inhaled, standing still. On her exhale, she stepped out, knife held out to block. Aili stretched and lowered, slashed and stabbed, flowing through the form. She relaxed her mind, letting her senses pick out her surroundings, feeling for the imaginary opponent.

Her skin tingled, like when she felt magic around her, but not. It felt like the forest was vibrating, a quiet buzzing from every living thing nearby. Even her own body had a vibration, a rhythm all its own. Leya felt like a burst of energy near her, pulling at her inner senses somehow.

Aili settled into the closing position and let the feeling linger. Her breathing slowed, and the sensations slipped away, like a pleasant dream that faded as she woke. Aili stood still, staring at the surrounding clearing. What was that?

She slipped her knife back in the sheath and sat in the shade. If Darik were here, he'd tell her all about it. He taught her meditation and must know what happened. Her stomach growled. Aili breathed through the empty feeling in her belly, the ache of cramps from going too long without eating.

Aili struck the flint and got the fire going. Roots were more digestible when cooked. She popped a few berries in her mouth, sighing as her stomach cramps eased. Within moments, she coaxed her fire into a fierce blaze, adding more cut branches for fuel.

The bushes rustled. Her hand froze, roots still in her fingers. A large animal, right? People made more noise in the bush. It must be big, though. A bear? Leya raised her head, her ears perked towards the noise. Not a deer, Leya ignores those. Wolves would call. Did her food smells attract a bear?

Aili snuck to her pack and grabbed the knife, sliding it from the leather sheath. Leya moved beside her, head still pointed at the noise. Another snapping noise, and the bush shook. Aili wrapped a hand around part of Leya's mane.

Her heart raced. She tightened her grip on the knife, her palm sweating. She could handle this, she reminded herself. A shape pushed through the bushes, obscured by the leaves. Aili held the knife out, ready to strike.

CHAPTER 3

Unexpected Camp Guests

"We surrender. Don't attack." The mage from the road spread his raised hands out, palms open to her.

He stepped into the clearing, stopping at the edge, leaving room for his companion to step beside him. Aili blinked at him, still as a statue, knife held out. Leya nudged her elbow, jostling the girl. Right, breathe, she reminded herself.

Aili lowered the knife. What were they doing here? How did they find her? She had felt no magic. Actually the lack of magic around her was disconcerting.

He flashed a lopsided smile at her. "Permission to enter your camp?"

She tucked her knife back in the sheath and walked to her firepit. Aili settled, crossing her legs, and watched them.

They hadn't moved. His companion crossed his arms over his chest but hadn't come closer. Since when did Master Mages ask permission for anything, especially of someone like her?

"What are you doing here?" Aili set her roots on the hot rock.

"Your father asked us to check on you." He shifted, but remained where he stood.

Aili frowned. How could they possibly have reached her father, especially across the border?

"We came to make sure you were safe. Did Darik teach you all this?"

She glanced up at him and nodded. Aili gestured at her fire and the men walked over, lowering themselves to the grass opposite her. She turned her roots using a stick and a finger, letting go quickly so she didn't burn herself. The roots smelled sweeter. In a moment, they'd turn a golden brown. That was the best time to eat, and she would not miss it.

"You're incredibly skilled at bushcraft. Have you thought of becoming a Defence Mage?"

Aili sighed. "Not a mage, remember?" She fingered her neckband. The ridges were smoothing out. Was it going back to bronze? Had it all been her imagination, some hallucination brought on by fatigue or something?

"The colour change disagrees with you." He leaned back on his hands.

So, it was still silver, after all. It wasn't a dream.

"Do you know what it means?" she whispered. Aili focused on her roots, pulling them from the fire and setting them on the leaf. Her heart wanted to burst. All her life she dreamed of this, of getting magic, and it wasn't like this.

"You know what it means. I have identified your magic. You've met your teacher."

Aili looked up, her neck muscles protesting the quick movement. "Why? Why now? I wished all these years, suffering as an outcast, shunned. Why now?" She wiped her sleeve across her eyes. Why was it so hard to breathe?

Leya dropped to the grass behind her, folding her legs under her belly. She stretched her neck around, her head against Aili's side. Aili smiled and rubbed her head. She wasn't alone. Aili leaned back against Leya and wrapped an arm around her as far as she could reach. Her fingers disappeared into the soft hair. Leya's slow and deep breaths calmed Aili.

"Maybe it's because there's something different about your magic? The University Mages might not have recognized it." He leaned forward, his elbows on his knees.

Aili raised an eyebrow. "They research magic. Don't they know all about it?"

His companion snorted and looked down at the fire.

"They know all about spells. They know amazingly little about other forms of magic, because they don't use those forms of magic. There are field mages out in the forests who research magic in all its forms, and they know a lot more."

Aili pressed her fingers to her temples. Her father was in the Inner Circle of University Mages. With his influence, she saw the best mages in the city, so he assured her. They spoke with such certainty. As far as they knew, she was completely without magic. But her band changed, a little voice inside whispered. They were wrong.

"Do you speak?" She narrowed her eyes at the second man.

"Focus on your magic teacher, not me." He crossed his arms over his chest, his own dark eyes narrowed back at her, staring her down.

"I don't have a magic teacher." She rubbed her temples again, an ache forming under her fingers.

"That band says you do. Look." The dark-haired man reached into his pocket and pulled a shiny brass object out. He tossed it to her.

Aili caught the thing and turned it over in her hands. It was round, like her compass, and reflective. Aili held it up and aimed it at her neck. Her band was completely silver, no trace of bronze anywhere, but the nameplate was empty.

She tossed the mirror back. "No name. I don't have a teacher."

The friendly man smiled and leaned back against his hands again. "Allow me to introduce myself. I'm Andvari Aleyn, Third Mage of the Defence Forces. I lead the Scouting and Reconnaissance Division. You are a Nature Mage. I'll teach you to use and control your magic."

Aili stared at him, open-mouthed. The mirror landed in her lap. Aili picked it up and raised an eyebrow at the gruff man. He gestured to her neck. She aimed the small mirror again. The plate now had his name engraved, shining in dark lettering on the silver plate. The first crystal in each group of four glowed a brilliant emerald.

"This is too much." Aili pressed her hand to the ground and pushed herself up.

Leya grabbed Aili's belt in her teeth and tugged, dropping the girl on the ground.

"Hey," Aili growled. "You, too? You believe this? It's incredible." She slumped and buried her face in her hands. She'd almost given up on this dream. Now her heart ached. Could she learn to be a student after being cast aside like that?

Leya released her belt and lay her head against Aili. Aili knew that promise. Leya was with her, no matter what, no matter where she went.

Aili stroked her long nose. "You don't even know if we're going somewhere you can stay. I could get dragged off to magic lessons in some stuffy tower and have to send you home."

Leya sighed, her breath warm on Aili's skin.

"Can you hear her thoughts, or do you communicate another way?" Andvari stretched his long legs out and he eased his pack off his back.

Aili chewed her lip as she debated how to answer. Some mages could use spells to talk to animals, but only the most gifted Earth Mages would try. Even Darik didn't talk to them like she could, and he was amazing with horses. Did this man think she was crazy?

"It's more like I feel her emotions. I get vague impressions of her thoughts, but not like a voice in my head. It's more I know her desires and feel her moods." Aili scratched Leya's forehead.

"Does it work with other animals as well?"

"Not like with her. Horses are easier than other animals and I get more from them. Animals seem to know I won't harm them, and I kind of know their mood, but that's it." Aili rubbed her eyes, holding back the yawn.

"You've had a busy day. Eat and rest. We'll clean up and ward the camp." Andvari stood and stretched, his eyes on her.

Aili nibbled the cooling sweet root and berry mixture. Andvari walked along the edge of the clearing, his fingers and hand moving in a wavelike motion. He muttered under his breath. A shimmering dome formed behind him, stretching up over them. It closed over itself when he returned to his starting point.

"The dome will keep people out?" Aili stuffed more roots in her mouth.

"And in. You can see the dome?" Andvari sat beside her, his eyebrow raised.

She nodded.

He looked at his companion and scratched his chin. "Get some sleep. We'll talk in the morning."

Aili set her leaf down near the fire. She crept into her shelter under the tarp and tree frame. Leya followed and lay down across the opening, hiding the girl from sight. Aili rubbed her shoulders, massaging the pony's muscles as her mind wandered.

She knew all about magic, the theory behind it, how most mages used it, and more. These men did things differently. So did Darik, she reminded herself. Was this why they found her magic? Why didn't Darik? He was also an Earth Mage, just like this stranger. No, her teacher, she realized. She had a teacher.

The chants weren't what caused the magic, they were just how a mage focused their thoughts. The mind and body actually did the magic, but chants were a memory tool. Fire was caused by speeding up molecules and making heat. Objects could be floated by altering density, either of the air or the item to be moved. Anything more than basic spells took a good grounding in science, and most people only learned spells they'd need in their daily lives.

These men, though, they were different. Darik was different, too. They used hand motions like most mages chanted. The one time Aili saw Darik do powerful magic, he also used gestures. Was he once a Scout?

She rolled over and peered out at the men, barely visible around Leya's rump. His companion set bedrolls out without magic, while he placed some food in a pan over the fire. They were both large and strong, like Darik. What was it he once said? Right, our power comes from us. If we're strong, our magic is potent.

Aili wrapped her blanket around herself tightly and closed her eyes. She curled up against Leya's back, smiling at the warmth her pony gave off. She could hear Leya's heart, steady and slow. The chant for a healthy hay crop rolled through her mind, following the cadence of Leya's heart as she drifted off.

***

"Good morning."

What? Aili blinked. People. In her camp. She rubbed her eyes and tried to sit, but her muscles protested with aches and stiffness. The dragon in her dream, she was running from it. It wanted her to do magic, or it would roast her alive. She swore she couldn't. She had no magic–right, magic. Her teacher. She had guests.

Aili rubbed her eyes and forced her body upright. Her eyes wouldn't focus at first. Leya grazed outside her little lean-to, the grass crunching in her teeth. Aili crawled from her bedroll. She stretched as she looked around, taking in the quiet campsite.

Her stomach growled. Fresh smells surrounded her in the faint morning breeze, straight from the campfire. She loved basil. Fresh bread? The first recipe she learned to bake with Ilia was herb buns, useful for restoring health and magic, and tasty.

"Kyson is getting water. You have a few minutes to relax before the food is ready." He sat by the fire, his attention on the pan. What was his name? Come on, Aili, you could do this. Andvari. Right.

Aili took slow steps, stretching her legs and moving her arms around. No, after her dreams last night, she just didn't feel rested. Aili moved closer to her shelter, where she had more space, and stood in silence.

She closed her eyes and settled her breathing. The morning sun was behind her, warming her back. Aili breathed out, turning and bending, lowering her body slowly. She flowed through the morning pattern Darik taught her, stretching her muscles as she stepped and shifted. It got more challenging from start to finish. Aili kept her eyes closed until she settled back into her starting position again.

Kyson, the gruff man, stepped through the bushes, two canteens in his hands. His eyes were on her. He sat the canteens in the cooking area and settled beside Andvari.

Aili kneeled beside the fire across from them. Andvari slipped a tool under a pancake and flicked his wrist, sending the pancake into the air. It flipped and fell back into the pan, right in its spot around the others. The golden-brown pancake steamed, sending fresh smells to tease Aili.

He stacked the pancakes and slipped them on plates. Kyson took the plates and added a mashed mixture of berries and nuts, drizzled across each steaming pile of pancake deliciousness. The berries warmed and their aromas added to the already teasing delight of fresh pancakes.

"Enjoy." Andvari handed her a plate. He passed her a knife and fork once she balanced her plate in her lap.

"Thank you."

She stuffed the pancake into her mouth, wiping berry drippings from her chin with her fingers. Aili smiled and licked her fingers clean. She would not waste any of this. If being a student meant waking up to a hot meal like this, maybe it wouldn't be so bad? Not fetching cold water first thing was a treat, as well.

At least they were quiet. She cleaned her plate in peace, eating every crumb and scrap. When she gathered the plates and washed the dishes, Aili smiled at the warm water. Of course, the canteens sat near the fire, she realized. They cleaned the pots and pan. Aili smiled to herself. At least they did not expect her to clean up after them. Some students got stuck doing chores like that, as part of their training in discipline.

After she set the clean cutlery on the stack of plates, Aili wandered back to her little shelter. She settled onto the grass, leaning back against her saddle. Her eyes were on Leya, grazing nearby, but her mind was on last night.

"What's on your mind?" Andvari settled on the grass nearby, facing her.

Aili opened her mouth and closed it again. She took a deep breath and let it out, counting in her head. Calm. I'm calm. "So many things." Aili scrunched her face, her chin resting in her hand, her elbow on her knee. "My band insists I have magic. Why can't I feel it? It's supposed to be inside me, right?"

"I've been thinking about that. Are you ready to try some things?"

She stared up into his eyes. He was asking? She nodded. If this is a magic lesson, it's not at all what she expected.

"Come sit here, cross-legged, and relax. You know the sitting meditation?" Andvari pointed at the ground in front of him.

Her body felt numb, her limbs heavy. Could she do this? Give up her freedom for the one thing she always wanted, and never thought she'd have? Aili forced her body to move, crouched and stiff, until she settled where he pointed. Her gaze fell to the campfire, a few tendrils of smoke rising from the hot ashes. She straightened her spine and folded her hands in her lap.

"Meditate like a magic student, or the other way?"

He shifted beside her, turning to face the fire as well. "However you feel more comfortable."

She closed her eyes. After so many years of practicing, her body calmed and breathing slowed automatically. She could sense him beside her, hear his breathing, slow and steady like hers. His hand rested on her back.

"Keep going, like he taught. Let your focus relax and feel the world around you."

He was still there, beside her, a calm presence she didn't mind. There was a bit of a hum, a vibration, something unlike her surroundings. The ground beneath her rumbled so slowly she almost didn't feel the pulse. Leya burned brightly in her mind, tugging at her heart. Aili smiled at the warmth she felt around her heart, all from her pony. Her attention slipped, and the feelings faded.

She relaxed her focus again, open to that calm feeling meditation brought. No thinking, she chastised, letting her remaining thoughts fade. The vibrations pushed at the edges of her awareness, getting stronger as she breathed. Even the air felt fresh, less a breeze and more like a breath. Was air a living thing?

The grass grew with vigor, full of life. The places Leya had grazed, Aili could sense a difference there. She could feel the grass sealing off the damaged ends and repairing. She turned her attention to it, focused closer, and the sensations faded. Aili backed off and relaxed into that detached interest. The world around her popped into focus, a tapestry of energy before her mind.

Snap! Aili's attention ripped her from the meditation. The energy faded.

"Sorry." Kyson held a pack in his hands. The gear strap was snug around the bedroll, holding it for travel.

Aili braced her hands against the ground. What did she just feel? Could she do it again? For a moment, she felt like part of the entire world, part of nature and the circle of life. Being yanked from that peaceful place, back into reality, it felt like stepping from a warm house and into a fierce blizzard.

"Did Darik teach you the fighter's meditation?" Andvari lowered his hand from her back.

"He made me learn before he'd teach me the sword forms. He taught me every form of meditation I know. How do you know him?" Aili shifted, turning to face him.

"He was a Scout. He didn't mention it?" Kyson snapped the strap around the second bedroll, snugging it for travel.

"He doesn't talk about his past." Aili held Andvari's gaze. "What did I just experience?"

"Have you ever meditated in a forest before?" Andvari raised an eyebrow.

"Well, yes, just not the fighter's meditation. I only did that one in our training space behind the barn, usually with him there." Aili scratched her chin. So many memories flooded her mind, years with him as he taught her to fight, all passing in seconds.

"The fighter's meditation opens our awareness to our surroundings. We calm our bodies so we can react quickly in a battle. It can let us sense what our opponent is about to do. I guessed, since your magic works differently, that it might open your magical senses as well as your physical senses."

How can he stay so calm? Her heart pounded against her ribs, threatening to burst through. "Different how? What kept the smartest mages around from seeing my magic?"

"You've been right all along. You don't actually have any magic within you." He took her hand and held it between both of his. "You can channel all the magic around you and use it. We're limited to what we possess and our own inner strength. You are not."

"The magic in nature? Ilia talked about it." Aili stared around at the trees. "She never explained it, just mentioned it was there."

"Is that wonderful old woman still in her shop?" Andvari grinned.

"Wooden building that looks completely out of place in a city of stone? She sure is. How long has she been there?"

Kyson laughed. "She was there when my parents were small." He settled on the grass beside them, crossing his legs and leaning back on his hands. "She's probably older than time."

"She did a lecture for the Scouts I was at. She taught us basic healing potions. Ilia mentioned the magic of nature. All good herbalists learn about it and get a feel for its presence. They can't use it themselves, but they learn how it affects potions. Some plants interact well, others don't, right?"

Aili nodded. "She said it runs through every living being, and even rocks have it." Her last conversation with Ilia replayed, hazy, but those words came back to her. Did Ilia know Aili had these abilities? Why didn't she say anything?

Aili stood and paced, trampling the grass between the fire and her shelter.

"What that means for you is your ability to use magic is limited by your focus and by practice. Our focus and physical strength limits our magic. If you can keep your focus, you can probably move mountains. If you can focus." He caught her eye. "You'll need to practice. I hope you like meditation."

Aili sighed, pausing at the fire. She liked meditation just fine, but sitting still that long? Wait, Darik taught her many kinds of meditation, and not all were boring. "Darik showed me moving meditations. Would those count?"

Andvari shrugged. "We'll have to see what works. We're both in somewhat unmapped territory here, so we'll be doing some experimenting together. Why don't we pack up? There's somewhere we need to be."

"We?" Aili spun on her heel, her eyes up at the trees.

Andvari chuckled. "As my student, you go where I go. Your pony, too," he added, staring at Leya, who sidled to the fresh grass across the clearing. "Besides, if you have that much energy, a walk will be good for you."

Leya snorted and turned her rump to him.

Aili giggled. "Hey, you promised to stay with me, and you want me to learn. Going without eating for short bits won't kill you. I promise."

"Get your hairy little friend ready to travel. We'll pack up the camp." Andvari rose to his feet, graceful for a man of his height.

Leya snort and blew a breath at him. She walked to the saddle and packs and stood quietly, her eyes on Aili.

"Did the pony just sass me?" Andvari laughed.

Aili covered her mouth, tried to hide her laugh, but she couldn't. She hunched over, hands on her knees. "Yes, she really just did."

"She understood me." Andvari stared at the pony, standing over her saddle.

Aili shrugged and moved beside Leya. "She understands more than she should. I always guessed it was because I talk to her. Maybe she learned over the years."

"We'll explore that, too. It's possible your Earth Magic abilities have always been active. The crystal is already glowing. You might be connecting with magic and just never knew it. It doesn't explain why she understood me, though." Andvari scratched his chin, his eyes on the pony.

She pulled out her brushes and gave Leya a quick grooming. Aili picked up the saddle and settled it on Leya's back. Darik gave her the saddle and packs, special light-weight equipment she could easily lift and move. Aili slid her hands under each strap, flattening the hair and smoothing the skin. Leya didn't need rub marks from ill-adjusted gear.

Kyson stepped beside her. "Are you fit to walk with us?"

Aili nodded, craning her neck to look up at him.

"If your hairy little friend doesn't mind, she can carry our packs and you can walk with us. She'll have less weight to carry, and we can all travel lighter." Andvari waited for Aili's response.

"Sure." Aili rubbed Leya's forehead as they strapped their gear to her saddle.

They balanced each item, spreading the weight across the saddle. Aili scanned the campsite. She dismantled her shelter. They spread the campfire out, cool ashes that posed no fire danger to the forest. Other than the short grass where Leya grazed, there was no sign anyone had been here. Did they use magic? Would she have felt it? She should have, but Leya had her full attention at the time.

"You two do a lot without magic." Aili pulled Leya's rope bridle on, sliding it over her ears.

Andvari led the way through the bushes. Aili felt the tingle as the bushes parted, watched him spread his hands in front of him. They passed through and the bushes sprang back in place. Something tugged at her heart, a little sense of loss. Her first bit of actual magic happened here. This place felt special now.

"You may not have seen it yet, but there are places where magic is less effective." Andvari slowed and let Aili step beside him. "That, and when we're outside the country, we may want to pass unnoticed. We can't do that if we're chanting and waving our arms about."

Aili grinned. She'd seen the University mages get together for a renewal spell on a tower, a mass magical working of many mages. They stood around the tower, chanting in unison, moving as one. It helped them keep the spell together and strong, but also made a spectacle for anyone watching.

"All Scouts learn to do everything both with and without magic."

"Wait, places where magic is less effective?" Despite a childhood of reading and learning about magic, she'd never encountered that idea before. What else didn't she know? A book on cities and civic issues did mention magical interference, and to consider it when choosing a site, but only in a single paragraph.

"In places where Earth Magic and the magic in nature are exceptionally strong, like the Western Wood, it can be harder to control spells. Spells take more concentration to cast. It's not impossible but drains us faster. Why use a spell when a compass works just fine?" Andvari led her out onto the road, Leya still beside her.

Aili pulled her compass from her shirt pocket and opened it. The little dial pointed north this time, no longer spinning wildly around. A Scout gave it to her. Wouldn't he need it?

"Darik?" Kyson glanced at the compass over Leya's neck.

"No." Aili snapped the lid closed. "A friend of his."

Kyson grinned at Andvari.

"So, that's where he 'lost' it." Andvari chuckled.

Her skin prickled. They were getting close to the border, though she couldn't see it yet. "Why Earth Magic?" She tucked the compass back in her pocket.

Andvari wrinkled his brow. "I'm not sure what you're asking."

Aili rubbed her temples. That wasn't meant to be out loud. Her face burned. "Only one of the four crystals is glowing, and it's green. It's glowing brightly, like I've mastered Earth Magic, even though I haven't."

"Well, if you've been using Earth Magic passively all this time in the forests and to talk to Leya, you may have some level of control already. If so, I only need to teach you how to use it deliberately. That might be why." Andvari gave her shoulder a light squeeze.

"Why one in four, though? Yours all glow with Earth Magic, and his with Air Magic. That's normal." She wrinkled her nose and stared at Andvari's neckband.

"We'll just have to be patient and see. We'll figure it out."

Maybe she shouldn't have been so quick to avoid reading about neckbands. Aili didn't want to learn she was defective or something, but now she had no idea what was going on. Then again, neither did they, and Master Mages were supposed to know this stuff, weren't they?

Her bones felt the vibrations. The border was just ahead. The shimmering curtain between her world and this place danced before her eyes. Her body ached and her lungs felt tight. Her steps slowed, her legs heavy and stiff. Leya rested her head against the girl.

"I'm fine," she whispered. Aili scratched Leya, draping her arm over the pony's neck for support. "I can do this."

"Is something wrong?" Andvari held her elbow, steadying Aili. He slowed his step for her.

She clung to Leya's mane. Aili took a slow breath, but the ache continued. She shook her head. "Magic tingles, usually. Powerful magic like this feels like walking through a lightning storm." Another deep breath helped, the extra air letting her feel her body better.

"You can feel magic, too?"

"Can't everyone?" Aili raised her eyebrow at Andvari.

Kyson laughed, slowing so they could catch up. "What other surprises does your student have for us?"

Andvari stopped, a hint of a smile on his face. He lifted his hand, a signal to stop. His brow furrowed and smoothed out again. "Can you walk through without being harmed?"

"Yes. It's just incredibly uncomfortable. It feels like being crushed, but I'm not actually hurting, I don't think." Her voice was barely a whisper now, her head aching.

He frowned down at her. Her fingers twisted in Leya's mane. She wasn't disappointing him already, was she? What a way to start as a student, she sighed.

Andvari reached into his pocket, pulled out a leather pouch, and opened it. He slipped a medallion out, untangling the chain. "Wear this while we cross. See if it helps."

Aili stood still and let him slip the chain over her head. The medallion hung down over her chest, near her heart. It was heavy for such a delicate looking thing. Sun reflected off the gold metal disk, a crystal in the middle. Aili cradled it in her hand and examined it. "Magic Be Gone–Physical Strong?"

"And she reads Ancient." Kyson raised an eyebrow at Aili.

"I had a lot of time to read." Aili let the medallion rest against her body again. It felt hot, but she no longer felt anything magical. No tingling, no vibrations, just her physical senses working as normal. "That's amazing."

"It should cancel all magic that touches you, like a personal barrier spell. It won't stop the border, but hopefully you won't feel it." Andvari tucked the leather pouch back in his pocket. "There are downsides, so you don't want to wear it long, but it should help in situations like this."

"It's never been used in situations like this," Kyson muttered.

Andvari grinned. "Okay, good point, but it seems to work. Ready?"

Leya bumped Aili with her nose, pushing the girl on. Aili straightened up and marched forward, towards the shimmering curtain. She didn't feel a thing, not even as they passed through. Marvelous. Did he have any books about this medallion? What else could he tell her?

"How do you usually use this?"

"Mostly we use them when doing a fugitive capture. Any magic they try to use against us won't work. Our magic won't work, either, but we train for that. We get the advantage, since most mages depend so heavily on their magic." Kyson stretched and turned his face to the sun, visible again on this side of the border.

Andvari nodded. "That, or if we're going into an area with strong nature magic, like parts of the Western Wood, we can wear it if we feel disoriented. Some of that wild magic can be disruptive, even making us ill."

Aili played in those woods since she was big enough, and never once felt anything like that. Maybe her unique abilities protected her? Maybe she just felt the magic like any other magic, a background noise in her body she was used to, living in a city full of mages.

"That's why that Scout could teach me so much," she mumbled, her fingers rubbing Leya's neck. "City mages are too lazy."

"Our health and fitness limits our magic. We can stay strong and fit by working without magic, though we need to use magic to keep our abilities up."

Aili glanced at Kyson. "That's—complicated."

Andvari laughed. "Not really. It's built into our training and daily routines. We patrol and protect ancient places, so we get plenty of practice without magic, and in camp and on regular patrols, we use magic like any other mage. You'll see. So, how was it?"

"I didn't feel a thing. It was amazing."

He held his hand out. Aili slipped the medallion over her head and dropped it into his palm. Andvari tucked it back in his pouch. She felt the faint prickling on her back, but nothing she couldn't handle. Within a few steps, the sensation faded.

"Did my ward at camp feel like that?"

"No." Aili shook her head. "Your magic is powerful, but I've felt nothing like this before, not even at the University."

The forest thinned. Sunlight beamed down on her, warming her through. Wildflowers bloomed in the fields beyond, surrounding a large settlement with wooden buildings tucked among the rolling hills.

"Is that it?"

"It sure is. That's a base camp for both Scouts and the Border Guard. We both protect the border here. There's even a place in the stables for Leya, and someone to look after her when you're busy."

She walked along the road, straight for the settlement. They arranged everything in a circular plan, around an open space in the middle. Aili didn't hear any noise from it, not even the ringing of hammer on anvil from the blacksmith's shop. At least Leya will be with me, she thought, still clinging to her pony's mane.

CHAPTER 4

A NEW HOME

Aili barely saw the shimmer of the ward around the camp, though she felt the buzzing in her bones. Not nearly like the border, just enough she knew she passed through a potent magic. Noises reached her ears now, talking, hammering, horses snorting and calling to friends, the sounds of life.

There was something about this place, a warmth the stone city lacked, and Aili loved it. He led her into the camp and down the paths towards the tallest building, a three-story wooden structure that overlooked everything else.

People sat outside a workshop and spun cloth. Others stripped hides and prepared leather. Despite the slight ache in her heart, Aili knew they only harvested leather from animals that died naturally or were taken for food. Cooking aromas from the kitchens, filled with warm spices, let her know the latter was more likely. Another group was making furniture, carving the wood to shape.

More people moved boxes, crates, and other supplies around. Aili stayed close to her teacher. She didn't want to be in the way. They passed some people practicing with swords, going through the familiar patterns she knew well, and some she didn't. Still others sparred with a partner, swords flashing in the light.

Wait, nearly all of them are working without magic, she realized. Small spells were being used, bigger magics added after most of the work was done, but the carving and spinning and such were done by hand, just like she did things. Do I really belong here, maybe?

"We'll get Leya settled first, and then settle you in." Andvari headed for the massive building. "We have a message to send, too."

She gripped Leya's mane tighter, her fingers twisting in the hair. Aili's heart pounded in her chest. He was really going to call her father. Leya nudged her, shoving her free of her frozen state. Aili gasped and stumbled, catching herself. It felt better to breathe again. She righted herself and stroked Leya's nose.

"Thanks, girl."

Leya snorted.

Kyson walked up the steps and disappeared through the large double doors. Andvari stopped in front of the steps, waiting for her to catch up.

"The stables are back here." Andvari led her around the building.

Grassy paddocks stretched out back here, around a small stable. Horses grazed in the paddocks, calm and content, their tails swishing the occasional fly away. A couple of nearby horses lifted their heads and called to Leya. Leya bellowed out a whinny.

Aili covered her ear, wincing. "Later," she scolded. "I get you're excited, but wow, that was loud."

"This way." Andvari led her into the stable, the corners of his mouth twitching into a partial smile.

Stalls lined the walls, each with a window to let in fresh air. Further along, Aili saw the enclosed rooms, usually a feed room, tack room, and office. Everything was clean and bright, the floor was tidy, and a rack of halters lined part of a wall, each labelled with a name.

Andvari opened a stall door and stepped aside. "She can stay in here for now. We'll arrange a permanent stall and space for her gear later."

The stall was bedded with clean golden straw and large enough for a massive draft horse. Leya almost couldn't see over the half-wall. She'd need to lift her head high to see out. She marched over to the feeder, walking past Aili, and stuffed her nose deep in the hay. She'll be a while. Aili smiled, seeing how much hay was there. They must mostly have larger horses here.

Aili removed her saddle and picked up her brushes. Andvari took the equipment from her and set it on a rack outside the stall. She brushed the pony while he collected their packs, unfastening them from the saddle.

"You look good, girl." Aili patted Leya's rump. "I'll be back later. You have new friends to meet. "

The horses on either side of Leya were sleek and fit, their hair shining in the light. She nodded to herself. Those two were well bred and are in excellent health. Leya should be safe here, and cared for, when I'm busy.

Leya ignored her new neighbours, her attention on the hay instead.

Andvari handed her the saddle bags and her bedroll. The Scout packs were over his shoulder. "Ready to go?"

Aili nodded. She followed him back into the sunlight. He took her back around the extensive building and up the steps. The wood was worn, countless people passing over it for who knows how many years, but it was cared for and in good repair.

She touched the door frame as she passed through. The wood glowed and welcomed her. If ever a building had feelings, this one seems happy, she thought. How old was it? She could see the fresh oil rubbed into the living wood.

When she was young, Aili devoured a book on trees and harvesting living wood. Mages would harvest wood, freely given from trees that still lived. The mages would tend the trees and aid them in growing strong again. It was a living partnership, and they cut no tree down just for lumber.

"Coming?" Andvari stopped at the bottom of another set of stairs, his hand on the railing.

"Yes, sorry." She shook herself free of her thoughts and followed him up this wide inner staircase.

This place is like Ilia's workshop, Aili realized. It has the same feel to it. Almost like it's pulsing slowly with life. She climbed the stairs behind him, avoiding more people going up or down, though most were headed to a room off the entryway.

He turned at the top and walked down a long hallway, with no hesitation at all. He belongs here. Will she ever feel that at home here, too? She jogged to catch up. He didn't stop until he reached the last door at the far end, near a large window. Aili glanced out and saw a hay shed.

Andvari swung the door open and stepped aside. "Go on in. This is my room. Well, our room, now."

Aili walked inside. The room was large, with two massive windows overlooking the stable and paddocks. His bed was between the windows. His desk was to her right, a large mirror above it. Funny, he didn't strike her as the type to stare at himself and fuss about his looks. Beside his desk, a door led to a bathroom. To her left, the room was mostly open and empty.

Andvari set his supplies on the floor beside the desk. "I'll have the Quartermaster furnish that space for you today." He nodded at the open area. "I used to exercise there, but you need the space more. It might not be what you're used to, but we'll make it as comfortable as we can for you."

Aili laughed. "We just spent a night on the forest floor, and you're concerned I'll find a bed uncomfortable? I'll be fine."

"Welcome back, Sir."

Aili spun at the gravelly voice. A large and hairy man leaned against the door frame. He wore work pants and a plain shirt, like nearly everyone else in camp, but his were plain brown. Scouts seemed to wear green, and the Border Guard wore green and brown. So who was this man?

"Thanks." Andvari greeted him with a smile. "That was quick."

"I had a spare moment. What can I do for you?"

Andvari waved at the corner. "My student needs a bed-room."

"Is that all?" He threw his head back and laughed. "When are you going to challenge me?"

"You can sit on my bed while he prepares your room. I have some reports to file while he does this. Take your boots off and leave them there." Andvari pointed at a boot tray beside the door.

Aili kicked her boots off and set them on the tray. She dropped the saddle bags and pack beside her boots. The floor was smooth under her socked feet. Aili moved to the bed and sank onto the thick mattress.

The big man assessed the space. He glanced at her and smiled. Was this the Quartermaster? He raised both hands and chanted, the words low and inaudible to her. His hands moved through the air in front of him, as if he were drawing a bed. A bed with a sturdy wooden frame materialized in the room's corner, complete with pillows and blankets.

His hands moved around like he was forming a chest from invisible clay, and one appeared at the end of her bed, a thick wooden trunk she could store her things in. A night table materialized, with a little oil lamp full of oil and ready to use on top.

He held his hand out over the floor, palm down, and waved it in horizontal circles. An area rug formed beside her bed; thick fibers woven together to keep her feet warm on bitter days. He reached up and pulled his hands down, like he was drawing a blind over a window. Curtains appeared around her space, translucent at first, and turning a deep blue, like the shirt she wore. They solidified and made her new space private.

He poked his head around a curtain. "Does it suit you?" The big man grinned at her and wiggled an eyebrow.

Aili giggled and nodded. "Yes, thank you. I've never seen magic like that before. How do you do it?"

Andvari folded a piece of paper into a little bird shape and tossed it into the air. It flew from the room. "You're going to learn about all kinds of magic you've never seen. He was using spells, but not like they use at the University. Those spells don't always work—"

"Where natural magic is strong," Aili finished with him.

"You learn quickly." Andvari chuckled.

"Let me know what else you need." The big man headed for the door.

"Thanks. I will." Andvari's quill sped across a piece of parchment, his attention on another sheet of paper before him. "Once I finish this, we'll contact your father. After that, your magic lessons start."

Aili shifted from the bed and retrieved her saddle bags and pack. She slipped through the curtains into her new room. His back was still to her. Aili set them on her trunk and slid her feet into her boots. He hadn't turned. Aili eased through the open door and down the hall. Her stomach flopped around. What would her father say?

She descended the stairs. There was an alcove she didn't notice coming in, right there beside the main door. A statue filled the space, a woman in robes, her hair blowing in the breeze. Aili walked over to it and looked closer. The statue was marble, smooth and shiny. In some places, the marble was so thin the light was almost visible through it.

Aili headed out the door and down the steps. Guards and Scouts were everywhere, moving between buildings or practicing with weapons in the grassy area nearby. Support Staff worked in front of buildings, making things the camp would need. People glanced at her, but nobody stopped to talk or paid much attention to her. Right, with a silver band, she was just another student. She saw a couple of other students here, darting between buildings.

Act like I belong. Nobody will question it. That's what Darik once said. Aili headed around the building and to the stables behind it. The stable doors stood open, letting the light and breeze in. A familiar whicker called to her. Aili grinned and sped up, heading for the stall with her pony inside.

She rested her elbows on the stall door and looked down at her pony. Leya lifted her golden nose and nudged Aili's elbow. She sniffed the girl, her little nostrils trembling with each inhale.

"Nice to see you, too. I only have a little left."

Aili pulled the herb from her pocket and lowered her hand over the door. Whiskers tickled her palm as Leya lipped the herb from her hand. The pony chewed the herb, releasing a fresh minty smell.

"Can you believe it all?" Aili stroked the pony's smooth forehead. "It doesn't feel real yet, does it? I'm waiting to wake up and find its all been a dream."

Leya swallowed the herb and nudged Aili's arm again.

Aili laughed and pushed her nose away. That's all I have, you greedy thing. Too much is bad for you."

Leya sighed. Aili scratched behind her ear on her muscular neck. She looked around, now that she had time. The stalls were all in good repair, no chewed boards or rough metal anywhere. Natural light flooded in from windows on both sides of the building, all protected with a mesh grill, and each stall having a view outside.

About half of the stalls were occupied. The horses were sleek, well fed and fit looking. Whoever cared for everyone here knew what they were doing.

Wait, something wasn't quite right.

Aili walked slowly over to a stall at the end of the stable. A large farm horse stood near the back wall, his head low and his eyes partly closed. His legs shook. Was he going to collapse? She'd seen this before. Could she help?

She slid the latch back and stepped into the stall. The straw was deep and cushioned the floor for him. She pulled the door mostly closed behind her and walked over to him, her steps slow.

"Easy, big guy. I think I can help you. You'll be okay."

His ear flicked towards her once, before going still again. Aili kneeled beside his head and looked into his eye. He didn't move or react. She shifted beside his shoulder and ran her hands through his thick hair. No, not on his legs. She felt his belly, but that was fine. Wait, there it was.

Aili stretched the skin behind his front leg. A tick was buried in the hair in a fold of skin. It must have been there a while to be so full like that.

"Aha," she whispered.

"What did you find?"

Aili twitched. She glanced back up at the voice behind her. The gelding stood still, not even flicking an ear at her sudden movement. Aili frowned at him before looking back up at the dark-skinned man behind her.

"He's got a tick. They can carry the paralysis, and I think he's got it. I don't have tweezers with me."

"I can take care of him now." The big man stepped into the stall and kneeled beside Aili.

She glanced at his gold neckband as he leaned towards the tick. His band had the emerald crystals of an Earth Mage. Aili shook her thoughts free and turned back to the tick.

He let out a low whistle. "It's been there a while. No wonder the big lad doesn't feel well."

"May I use this as a teaching opportunity?"

Aili whipped around at Andvari's voice, her heart racing. She tumbled to the hay and gripped the big man's sleeve. How did that man sneak so effectively? Aili took a slow breath and calmed her heart.

"You may. I'm watching to make sure he's cared for." The big man steadied Aili as she shifted back into a crouch.

"I felt it," she whispered.

"Felt what?" The big man tilted his head to the side.

Aili shook her head. Was that out loud? "I felt the tick. It was a little bundle of wrongness on him, and I felt it."

"She's a healer?" He looked up at Andvari.

"She's new and unknown." Andvari stepped into the stall and kneeled beside her in the hay. He set a hand on her shoulder. "We'll get rid of that for him. Focus on the tick. See if you can convince it to let go. Use your mind, not words, and make it drop into his hand." Andvari moved his hand from her shoulder to her back.

Aili stared at the tick. That tick was going to let go.

No, it's nice here. This host is strong, and I can feed for a while.

Aili blinked at the impression in her mind. Was that the tick's feelings? No, you will let go. She stared at the tick with all her might, her demand in her mind. Let go.

The tick shivered and dropped into the big man's hand. He smiled and nodded. "Well done. You got the whole thing, jaws and all."

"Thank you." Aili grinned. Her first deliberate magic, and she did it. She couldn't stop smiling. "Does it always work that way?" She looked up at Andvari.

"With animals, it should. We have to use different techniques for plants and inanimate objects." Andvari frowned down at her. "Why didn't you stay like I told you to?"

Aili squirmed. His frown made her want to curl up and hide. "In fairness, you didn't actually tell me to stay. You just said we'd contact my father when you were done."

The man snorted. "Good luck with this one. She's smart." He pulled the horse's skin taut and examined where the tick had been.

"Aili, meet Jordi. He's in charge of the stables and looks after or oversees all the animals in Scout care. He'll look after Leya when we're busy. Don't worry, he's excellent with horses."

"It's nice to meet you." Aili smiled.

"And you. Where did you learn about ticks and paralysis?" Jordi waved a hand, and a small jar flew over to him. He dropped the tick inside and sealed the jar.

"Ilia. The Master Herbalist. She taught me when a farmer brought a goat in with it. She taught me how to make a salve and remove the ticks with tweezers. I learned all about the disease, including how different farm animals react to it." Aili patted the big gelding's side.

Jordi held the little jar up and looked at the tick inside. "I know that salve. I keep some here. It's good for a variety of skin ailments." He stood and scratched the horse's withers. "Bring her back regularly and I'll help you teach her more about animal care and magic."

"Yes, please." Aili bounced on her toes; her hands clasped together in front of her. Healing with magic, like Ilia and Darik? She dreamed about that. It took her days or weeks to help an animal heal with potions and lotions, and magic sped the process up.

Andvari chuckled. "We'll arrange some lessons. However, you left when you knew I wanted you to stay. As your discipline, I'm assigning you chores to help you remember."

"The back stalls all need mucking, if you're looking for ideas." Jordi gestured to the far end of the stable.

"Where's the muck fork?" Aili stepped from the stall and looked for the tools.

Andvari laughed. "I was thinking about chores she wasn't actually excited about, but that'll work. As soon as you're done and he's satisfied with your work, come back to our rooms. You remember how to get there?"

Aili nodded. She selected a muck fork from the tools hung on the wall. The wood handle was smooth, and the tines were in good condition.

"I'll leave her under your supervision." Andvari passed Aili and headed for the door.

"I've got her." Jordi waved after him.

Aili looked at the muck bucket. It shimmered and felt charged. "Have you spelled this to repel flies?"

"Of course." Jordi walked over to her side. "That one also empties itself automatically when it's full, right into the muck heap out back. Normally I make students use the non-magical buckets when they're being disciplined, but since you helped the big guy, go ahead."

Jordi pointed at the first stall. Aili took her tools and stepped inside. Mucking was easy. She'd been doing it since she was big enough to hold a muck fork. She slid the fork into the bedding and scooped up the waste. A quick shake and the clean bedding fell through. Aili tipped the muck into the bucket.

Aili worked quietly, surrounded by the comforting sound of horses chewing hay and the smell of fresh straw. This was the life. Her, her horses, and peace. Aili got the obvious waste before hunting around in the straw for the rest. She smiled when she looked at the straw and the stall was clean. Time for the next one.

The room was empty when she returned, horsehair still clinging to her clothing. Aili opened her saddlebags and unpacked them. She didn't have much, mostly a change of clothing and her camping gear. It all fit neatly in her new trunk. Aili brushed her fingers over the varnished trunk lid and smiled.

She changed into her clean clothing. Where could she get more? Father would send her money, but was there anywhere to shop nearby? Aili folded the dirty clothing and left it on her trunk. Where would she wash it?

The door creaked. Light footsteps crossed the room. Aili peeked out from behind her curtain. Andvari stood at the window, looking down on the horses in the paddocks below. She stepped from her little room and walked to the window.

Andvari shifted and looked down at her. "What do you need?" He smiled at her.

Aili glanced up at him. "How do you know I need something?"

"Scouts learn to read body language and expressions. It gives us a better idea what's going on, especially if we're observing people at a distance. We can better judge who's a threat and who needs help. Now, what's on your mind?"

She smiled and looked down at her boots. Aili lifted her gaze to meet his. If he could read her as easily as she could read Leya's body language, she was in trouble. Aili hesitated, her fingers playing with the hem of her shirt. "This is my only change of clothing. Where do I wash the others, and how do I get more clothing?"

"I'll have more for you by the end of the day. You're my student, so I provide for you, or arrange for what you need. That includes lunch, which is being served any moment. Come. You won't want to miss this." Andvari pushed away from the wall and headed for the door.

Aili raised her eyebrow and smiled. Not cooking? She didn't mind that at all. It left more time to explore and have adventures. Then again, moving into an unknown place, away from the city? This just might be the biggest adventure she's ever been on. Aili followed him from the room.

"Who's this?" Aili pointed to the statue at the main doors.

Andvari walked over to the alcove and stopped. He placed his fingers on the base of the statue and closed his eyes for a moment, his head bowed. "We call her the Green Lady. She was a powerful Nature Mage who lived hundreds of years ago. She lived in this area and protected this part of the border and the surrounding forest."

"A Nature Mage like me?" Aili's heart raced. "She wasn't in the Book of Great Magics I read a few years ago."

"Were there any mages in there that didn't use spells?" Andvari raised his eyebrow.

Aili searched her memory. "No. I've never heard of magic being used any other way before, except Ilia. Not in all my time at the University with Father."

"I'm not surprised." Andvari set a hand on her shoulder. "She set many of the protective spells at the border. They've been added to many times over the years, but it's mostly based on her work. She founded this outpost for protecting the forest."

"Did people pass freely between countries before that?" Aili tilted her head and stared at the statue. There was something about her smile and her eyes that pulled at her.

"Stories say they did, many years ago. There was plenty of trade and people exchanged ideas and culture. This was all before the outside world fell to the Dark Ages. People were better educated then and didn't fear magic or dismiss it like they do now. Their skills with trades and crafts were astonishing, and they taught us many things. We gave them magical artifacts in exchange, and both groups benefitted."

Aili wrinkled her nose. "What caused the Dark Ages?"

Andvari frowned. "War. Not with us, but with another country. We sent Scouts to retrieve the artifacts, so they wouldn't be used or lost. That was the original job of the Scouts. Since then, we still observe the outside world, but it's in our defence. All artifacts are back or they were confirmed destroyed."

"I never read about this in any books," Aili mumbled.

Andvari chuckled. "I bet there's a lot you haven't read about yet. Not all of our records are public. Now, how about some food?" He smiled and nodded at an archway nearby.

Aili walked with him through the archway into a long hallway. Voices echoed down the hallway. Aili turned and looked back. It had been so quiet on the other side of the archway. Now it sounded like a huge mass of people ahead, like being in the University cafeteria. Aili forced herself not to cover her ears.

"You have a question?" He leaned against the wall, waiting for her.

Aili spun and frowned. "Are you going to know every time I'm thinking of something?"

He laughed, adding to the noise. Andvari wrapped an arm around her shoulders and steered her down the hallway. "Yes. Now, was that the question?"

Aili scowled before grinning. He was too easygoing to be mad at. "No. Why doesn't the noise go past the archway? Wooden walls shouldn't stop noise that easily."

He guided her around the corner and into a massive dining hall. "Noise dampening spells. We can have a meeting in the rooms above and not hear a thing. We can sleep in our rooms, even with a party raging in here with music, and we won't be disturbed."

Aili's stomach growled. Tables full of food stood along one end of the room near a kitchen. Some trays were still steaming, loaded full of various foods, and Aili knew most by smell. Andvari led her over and handed Aili a plate from an enormous stack. He took a plate and scooped ladles of food onto it.

"There's plenty, so have as much of anything as you want. You can eat an entirely plant-based diet here if you like. You're not the only one." Andvari took a buttered bun and set it on his plate. Another bun appeared in the serving bowl to replace the one he took. "You've seen this kind of magic before?"

She nodded. "The University has it, too. I've read about how the food moves from one tray to another." Aili loaded scoops of rice, vegetables, and beans onto her plate. She grabbed a bowl of fruit for after.

He led her along the wall, past rows of long tables with benches, to the far end of the room. She walked up a few steps onto a raised area, where a long table filled the space. It was quieter up here. Aili smiled. She could feel the magic here, buzzing in the background.

Fewer people sat at this table, and they were all older, like Andvari. He walked to the middle and sat facing the room. He gestured for her to join him, and she set her tray down. Aili lowered herself to the bench and looked around.

There were maybe around thirty people here, scattered among the tables, though the room held more than twice that many. Most were at the long tables below them, wearing the green of Scouts, the brown of the Border Guards, or the clothing of support staff.

"There are more students here than I expected." Aili nodded at a table to one side, where younger mages gathered, their heads low and together as they whispered about something.

Andvari turned and glanced down at her. The man across from them smiled. Aili buried her face in her hands, her cheeks burning. Was that out loud? Would she have to watch that now, with other people around?

"Maybe a quarter of the residents here in the camp are students." The man across from her took a sip of tea. "I thought you were across the border. New student?"

"Aili, meet Broso Lito. He helps lead the Border Guards here. Everyone at this table is a high-ranking officer, or the student of one." Andvari picked up his teacup and smiled. "I met Aili in the forest."

Broso laughed. "Fate. Only you could go into the forest, far from any town or village, and find a student."

Aili scooped up some rice and ate, glancing around as she did. Broso's face had the lines of someone who spent a lot of time in the sun, but he smiled freely. The people at the other tables all seemed familiar, greeting each other, even as they sat in smaller groups. People must not arrive often, based on the way people glanced at Aili.

The room was comforting, though, with golden wood and dark metal fittings. It felt alive, warm, and like a home should. Actually, it reminded her of Ilia's workshop. If Aili knew places like this existed, she'd have left the city long ago.

Most of the students she saw were younger, nearly all between maybe eight and fourteen years old. They acted like long-time friends, giggling and chatting easily. Her heart ached. What would it be like to have friends like that? Would it be easier to make friends now, since she had magic?

Aili blinked back the tears and focused on her food. Whoever was in charge of meals was excellent at their job. They blended herbs and spices to complement the foods, sweet for the bitter veggies, and savoury for the sweeter foods. Aili tore into her roll and let the bread melt in her mouth. The herbs inside gave bursts of flavour, and Aili loved the dried fruits mixed in.

"What is it?" Andvari smiled at her.

"Would you stop doing that?" Aili dropped her fork.

Andvari chuckled. "What's your question?"

Aili grinned and pinched her nose. "If I'm eating here without you—?"

"You can still come eat up here at this table. You can also take a plate to our rooms or the stable, as long as you get it back promptly. If you don't, the kitchen staff might hunt you down and retrieve it, with much scowling." Andvari nudged her lightly with his elbow.

Broso covered his mouth and snorted. "Yes, that Niral is a tyrant about dishes and utensils. Forest forbid you ever lose a fork or something. Niral is head of the kitchen."

Aili turned back to her meal, savouring each bite now. The rice with dried berries and nuts was possibly her favourite, though the broccoli with mustard and honey was amazing as well. Still, after so many meals in the quiet forest, Aili felt crowded here.

Andvari rested a hand on her knee. "If you're done, you can put your dishes in those baskets. Go to our rooms and get ready for a ride. We're going into the forest for a magic lesson this afternoon." He picked up his roll and tore a piece off.

She smiled. "Thank you," she whispered. Aili took her tray and slid from the bench.

"Wait for me in the stables if you're ready before I am. Groom Leya and get ready to go."

"Sure." Those were instructions Aili didn't hesitate to follow.

She took her dishes to the baskets and put her tray away. Aili raced from the room and darted up the stairs. The room felt like home already. Aili wandered to the window and opened it. She leaned out into the breeze. Smells of horse and hay reached her, even up here. The sun warmed her face. Aili smiled.

Well, time to get ready. Aili had no idea where in the forest they were going, how long they'd be, or what she'd need. If it was his job to provide, would he bring anything? Aili looked around and shrugged. He didn't say to change, so she must be dressed okay. Aili left the room and headed for the stables.

Leya stuck her nose over the stall door and nudged the cat balanced on top.

"You made a friend already?" Aili smiled as she walked over.

Leya snorted. She bumped the cat with her nose, sending it flying across the aisle. The cat yowled and hissed. It arched its back and ran off.

Aili chuckled. "I guess not. Ready for a ride?"

Leya perked up, her ears pointed at Aili. She took the brushes from the little shelf outside the stall and joined her pony. Aili rubbed Leya firmly, hair and dust rising from the golden coat. Leya lifted her head and rolled her eyes back. Aili picked her feet out and set her brushes back on the shelf.

Andvari appeared beside her and glanced at Leya. "Don't tack up yet. We have a date with the Communications Officer."

Aili scowled. Her stomach did somersaults and plunged towards the floor. Andvari placed a hand on her shoulder and walked with her down the barn aisle. He guided her between two stalls and through a door. The main building was just across the grass. Andvari took her through a door, down a short hall, and into a new room.

People wandered around the room, moving between mirrors, bowls of water, crystal balls, and every method of magical communication she had ever heard about. Some people were having conversations with someone far away, others monitored messages, and others were on typing machines that sent their messages to another machine somewhere else entirely.

"You're ready?" A slender woman appeared beside them.

Aili jumped and stepped back into Andvari.

He steadied her with a hand on her shoulder. "Finally." Andvari smiled at the woman.

The woman glided across the room to a large mirror on the wall in a corner. The surface swirled with a mist. She placed her hand on the frame and the mirror glowed. "Sorry for the delay."

A familiar face appeared in the mirror, a little larger than he was in person. The woman stepped aside and guided Aili in front of the image.

"You're safe. We were so worried."

Aili sighed. Her shoulders relaxed. No lecture about running away, no speech about being disappointed, just concern. Aili nodded. She struggled to swallow, and she wasn't sure she could speak.

"She's starting her education already and doing well." Andvari stepped beside her. "We've got her room all set up, and she's settling in."

"Earth Magic." Her father beamed down at her. "It suits you."

Aili grinned. "Thanks." A memory flashed through her mind of being little and sitting on his lap, reading Earth Magic spell books with his help.

"Her apprenticeship probably won't follow the normal path. She's a Nature Mage, not a spell caster. We're both learning as we go." Andvari smiled.

"I'll see what I can find in the private libraries, since I have access to scrolls most people don't know exist. I'll send copies of anything relevant I find." Her father gazed down at her. "You work hard and study well. Learn everything you can. We have so much to talk about when you come visit next."

Aili twisted her fingers together in front of her. "I don't know when that will be." Her throat tightened again. This was home now. She was a student now. Everything changed.

"It'll be awhile, unfortunately." Andvari shrugged.

"No matter. I know you're well, and the forest hasn't swallowed you whole. Your mother is worried, but she'll relax now, knowing you're alright."

Aili looked up into his dark eyes. "I'm sorry," she whispered. "You were going to get rid of me anyway, so I didn't think you'd care." She stared down at her boots. Aili scuffed the toe along the small carpet they stood on.

"We never meant to give you that impression." Her father frowned. "We were worried about your future."

Aili raised her gaze and met his eye. "My place has always been in the forest. It always will be."

"Then you be the best forest guardian you can be." Her father nodded to the woman.

She placed her hand on the mirror frame and Aili's father disappeared, the mirror turning back into a mirror and reflecting the room at her.

"Just like him not to say goodbye," Aili mumbled. She blinked back a tear.

"He didn't want you to see him cry." The woman took Aili's hand and gave it a squeeze.

"How do you know?"

The woman wiped the tear from Aili's cheek.

"Communication mages specialize in various forms of communication, including emotions and non-verbal messages." Andvari gave Aili's shoulder a gentle squeeze. "Thank you. Aili and I have somewhere to be."

He guided her back through the doors and into the stable.

"I'll just tack up Charger and we'll go."

Aili paused outside Leya's stall. "Will I need a saddle?"

He gathered his brushes and stepped into Charger's stall. "Do you often ride at speed without one?"

She grinned. "Yes."

"Your choice, then. We're not going far."

Andvari groomed his horse and tacked up. Aili took Leya's simple rope bridle from her hook and slipped it over the pony's head. She didn't need it, but it made people more comfortable, so she used it. Aili stroked Leya's broad forehead.

He led Charger from the stall, tacked up and ready to go. "Mount up."

Aili followed him from the stable. He swung up into his saddle. Aili vaulted onto Leya's back, landing softly. She loved feeling Leya's muscles move under her as the pony walked, a gentle rocking motion, smooth and familiar.

She followed him through the camp. People moved aside for the horses. They left the packed dirt paths of the camp and headed out into the wild fields.

CHAPTER 5

TIME TO FOCUS

Andvari turned Charger south. Aili held the reins loosely, letting Leya follow on her own. She gazed out at the wildflowers, little bursts of colour amidst the deep green grass. Aili turned and looked back at the camp occasionally, watching it appear and disappear as they passed through the rolling hills.

"Ready to go faster?" Andvari guided Charger beside her.

Aili gripped Leya's mane and straightened up. "Bring it on."

Charger sped past Leya in an easy canter. Aili squeezed Leya's sides lightly. Her pony surged ahead, a speedy canter to catch up to the bigger horse. The woods were just ahead now. Aili smiled at the sound of the breeze in the leaves. Songbirds flitted about in the trees, hiding from the hawk soaring high overhead.

He slowed before the trees. Charger relaxed and lowered his head as he walked. Leya's sides heaved with each breath as she walked beside him. Aili felt the heat from Leya's muscles through her pants, her backside damp with the pony's sweat.

They stopped at the edge of the forest and Aili slipped from Leya's back, dropping into the long grass. Andvari slid from Charger's saddle and patted his horse. Charger's head dropped to the long grass, and he tore a mouthful up, grass blades sticking out from either side of his mouth.

Aili patted Leya's thick neck. "Don't go far, okay?"

Leya pressed her nose to Aili's shoulder. Aili stroked the sleek golden nose. Leya dropped her head to the grass. Aili chuckled at the tearing noise as Leya made quick work of the long grass. Ponies and their appetites, Aili smiled.

"That's a strong bond you two have, for her to stay like that." Andvari kneeled down and strapped hobbles around Charger's front legs. He unfastened the saddle and leaned it against a tree nearby.

"I was there when she was born. We've been together for a long time. Most of my life, and all of hers." Aili scratched her pony's neck, up under Leya's mane.

Andvari gestured to Aili's pants. Leya's sweat dried and her pants felt fresh.

"Thank you." Aili grinned.

"Wet pants are no fun to sit in. What's the point of being a Master Mage if I don't use my skills occasionally?" Andvari pointed at the grass. "Have a seat." He pulled a bag from his saddlebags.

Aili lowered to the grass and crossed her legs. He sat across from her. Andvari took a flat dish and a canteen from the bag, setting the bag aside. He uncapped the canteen and poured water into the dish, filling it until only surface tension kept the water in.

"We're starting with Water Magic today. Since you manipulate the magic in things that are already there, instead of using your own magic, you may not conjure water like a Water Mage. However, you should be able to use anything you find around you."

Aili leaned closer to the dish. The blue sky reflected clearly back at her. She touched the water with a finger, sending little ripples surging around the dish. The ripples bounced against the edges, making patterns on the surface. Aili smiled and shook the droplets from her finger.

"It means you'll need to be smart about how you use magic, but you also might have more possibilities. If we're beside a lake, and you focus well, you might use the entire lake. If all you have is a puddle, though, that might limit you."

Aili ran her finger around the rim of the dish. "You're starting with this, so I don't have some kind of accident and drown us, aren't you?" She grinned up at him.

He laughed, and Aili relaxed. Andvari leaned back against his hands. "Something like that. Until I know how good your focus and control are, I don't want to let you flood the countryside, or something like that. Darik taught you meditation, so you'll have some focus already. Your mistakes might be bigger than normal for a brand-new mage."

"How do we begin?"

Andvari raised his eyebrow. "We start by you not touching the water."

Aili grinned sheepishly and tucked her hands in her lap.

"Try this. Imagine the dish is calm, the water so smooth you can see like a mirror. Just look at the water and see that in your mind."

She took a slow breath and let it out. Each breath got longer and deeper. Aili focused on the dish. She pictured it clearly in her mind, calm and still like before she touched it. The sky was that deep blue, she reminded herself.

"Your focus is good."

His voice pulled her from her mental image. Aili blinked up at him, her brow wrinkled. The water stilled, just like she pictured it. The sky reflected clearly in the dish.

"Look up." Andvari pointed above her.

Aili leaned back on her hands and tilted her head up. Yup, the sky was that bright blue, except where the clouds—oh!

"How could the clouds roll in so quickly?" Aili watched the wispy white clouds hovering above her.

Leya snorted. Aili jumped at the deep rumble. Her heart raced at the sudden noise.

"What?" Aili glared at her pony. "Suddenly you know everything?"

"There were no clouds. You put them there."

Aili glanced back at him. He watched a cloud drift past, slow and lazy.

"How, though? I didn't mean to. I didn't even know it was happening."

Andvari smiled. "Through your imagination. We're working with water, so you were tuned into water around you. You must have called the water vapour together, maybe by imagining clouds in the reflection. There's not a lot of water vapour in the air today, which explains why the clouds are so light."

Aili lay back in the grass and stared at the sky. "I really did that. How can I do that? I wasn't even trying?"

"You thought them into existence. I saw them in the reflection before they appeared in the sky. It wasn't a long delay, though."

She sighed. "Am I going to have things like this happen every time I try something?" Aili covered her eyes with her arm.

"Almost certainly, as you first learn how to control magic. You'll make mistakes and mess up, sometimes dramatically, and you might even destroy things. That's why we left camp."

Aili sat up and narrowed her eyes at him. Andvari smiled and touched the water, tapping it and letting the ripples surge around the dish.

He met her gaze and smiled. "Besides, causing clouds to form, especially those wispy little things, it's harmless. Way better than burning down a forest or striking yourself with lightning, right?"

She pressed her hand to her chest, over her heart. "I could do that?"

"Maybe. I don't know what you can do yet." Andvari shrugged.

Aili dropped her head in her hands. "You're being awful casual about me destroying things," she mumbled. What if she destroyed a forest? Most new students struggled to call a ball of mage-light at first, and she was making clouds without knowing how? What else might she do by mistake?

"Do you want to learn to work with nature and help it? Nature Mages can heal plants of parasites, or help crops thrive. I'm betting Ilia loved the herbs you harvested for her."

She smiled. So many memories rushed back, Ilia's beaming face when Aili appeared with a collection bag full of herbs. "She said I could find the herbs at their most potent every time I harvested."

"How did you know which ones to pick? How did you choose?" He rested his chin on his hand.

How? Even Aili wasn't sure. "I guess I just felt it? Wait, if I can work with water vapour in the air, can I work with it in other things, too? Plants have moisture in them."

"Most likely, once you learn how. Now, if you remove water from something living, like a plant or person, you'll affect them. You could call water from a blade of grass, but it might die. On the other hand, you can help farmers cure their hay and dry it out like that. Magic isn't good or bad. It's how you use it that matters. You can help or harm. Remember that."

"I can help," she whispered. Even thinking about destroying a forest made Aili shake, but knowing she could help? It was worth the risk of learning, if she could help. I'm no monster. I can do this. I'll learn.

"You can help in ways people will really need. You will probably be able to do things we don't even have spells for yet. You might even inspire new spells. If you really want to help, we'll look for ways you can assist people, if it interests you most."

Aili stared into his deep blue eyes. He sat so calmly, like he did this every day. He wasn't afraid of her, her abilities, or what she might do. "Thank you."

Andvari raised an eyebrow. "Ready to get back to training? How tired are you from that?"

She sat straight. "I'm ready. I'm not tired."

"Get Leya. We're going somewhere nearby. We'll try something practical for you." Andvari picked up the dish and let the water fall to the soil.

Aili got up and wandered over to Charger. He'd shuffled over to a patch of short and sweet grass. She took his reins and removed his hobbles. Charger followed her back over to Andvari. He tucked the bag back into his saddlebags.

"Thanks." He lifted the saddle onto Charger's tall back.

Charger's hair tickled her fingers as she rubbed his broad chest. He leaned into the scratch, stretching his neck up.

"Hey, silly." Aili pushed against him. "You're too big for that. I know it feels good, but stop it."

Charger sighed. Andvari muffled his laugh in his elbow, his head turned away. He took the reins from her, and Aili stretched her hand out to Leya. Leya stepped beside her, and Aili vaulted onto her back. She settled into place on the sun-warmed hair and gripped Leya's mane.

"Yes, you're still my favourite." Aili scratched Leya's withers.

Leya whickered, her nostrils vibrating.

Aili guided Leya along the edge of the forest behind Charger, through the low shrubs. Ever since that meditation session in the forest with him, she could feel the energy in things if she focused. The forest buzzed with a slow energy. It was in everything, from the plants and trees to the birds and animals. The trees were especially strong in energy.

Andvari stopped at a berry patch at the edge of the forest. Bright red berries covered the bushes. She slid from Leya's back. Andvari dismounted and tethered Charger to a tree where he could graze a bit.

She followed him into the berry bushes. Aili plucked a berry from the bush. It slid free without resistance, ready to eat and full of juices. She popped the fruit in her mouth and smiled. Sweet berry juice flowed over her tongue. Perfectly ripe right now. Aili smiled.

"You'd think we didn't eat recently." Andvari chuckled. "We're going to harvest a small quantity of berries for the lesson. Don't eat them all right away, or you'll have nothing to practice with. Lessons, remember?"

Aili stuck her berry-stained tongue out at him. She threw a berry at him. Andvari ducked, and the berry sailed into the trees past him. Aili helped gather a large handful of berries and placed them on a cloth he held.

"We'll sit on the grass near the horses. I'll be right there."

Aili gathered the corners of the cloth and carried the berries to the grassy spot. She laughed at the large patch Leya had already grazed, shortened by pony teeth, and settled in the middle of it. "Someone's been busy."

Andvari took the bag with the dish and canteen and brought it over. He set the dish between them. Andvari took the cloth and dropped the berries into the dish. He tucked the cloth back in his pocket.

"You're going to dehydrate the berries. Use magic, and focus. Try and gather the water from the berries and let it settle on the dish instead. If you can learn to do this, you'll always have food you can travel with, and an emergency water source."

Aili raised her eyebrows. "Great." She scrunched up her face and stared at the berries. "How do I do that?"

"We'll try different things until something works. Maybe imagine the berries dehydrating, and the water gathering in the dish?" He rubbed his chin.

She crossed her arms over her chest and glared at the dish, focused hard on the ripe red berries. This was it, real deliberate magic. Could she do it?

"If that doesn't work, try to feel for the water and coax it from the berry. Dehydration spells draw the water out through the skin and collect it together."

Aili frowned at the berries. Feel for water. She could do that. Aili closed her eyes and took deliberate, slow breaths. Feel. There, in front of her, she could sense the berries. They were like a tasty beacon calling to her, full of life and seeds and potential.

The dish felt like a void below the berries, easy to sense from its plainness. She could feel the clay they made it from, but all life and energy were long gone. Aili felt for the water with that relaxed openness she now had. There it was, right in front of her, in the berries. She coaxed it together and moisture gathered on the dish.

"What about the juice? It's all mixed in with the water." Aili glared at the juice.

"It's not poisonous, so you don't have to worry about it right now. We want to focus on dehydrating the berries, and we can drink the juice when you succeed." He tapped the side of the dish.

"You have a lot of faith in abilities I don't know I have," she muttered.

"Hey, when you're practiced, you can pull water from plants or the groundwater, purify it, and use it to clean wounds or something. You're just beginning, so you're not there yet, but we all struggle with new things. We all get better."

Ilia purified water for wound cleaning that way. It would be great to help her, and not just by gathering herbs.

Aili smiled. "Okay. I'll try again."

He chuckled. "Good. Just focus on what you want."

She felt for the berries again, closing her eyes this time. It worked with the clouds, so why not? The ripe fruit was full of moisture. She sensed the berries and explored the skin. There was a weak spot, an opening where the stems were. Aili pulled the water to the stems and let it ooze from the weak spot. This was a lot like coaxing a stubborn pony from a feed room. Aili smiled. The juice flowed faster.

Aili wiped her forehead with her sleeve. She flopped back on the grass. Dare she look and see how she did? Could she handle it if she failed?

"Giving up so soon?"

"I need a break," she whispered. "That was hard. I'm seeing the world in a whole new way, and it's exhausting, focusing through the new."

His fingers peeled hers open, and he placed a berry in her palm. "Here. You had a great start."

Aili opened her eyes and held the berry up. It was shrivelled and dried, just like the dehydrated foods Darik used to bring into the forest. Aili sat up and smiled.

"Not bad for a first try, don't you think?" Andvari smiled and leaned back against his hands.

She popped the berry into her mouth. It was sweeter, like it should be. "I guess not." Aili smiled to herself.

Aili glanced at the dish. A third of the berries were dehydrated. Another third was partially shrivelled, but still somewhat moist. The last third she hadn't affected at all.

"Remember, most people start lessons as small children, and they learn to see the spells they want to cast. You're starting now. Give yourself time to practice and build your skills. Ready to head back?"

"I'm ready for a nap." Aili sighed.

"Here." Andvari divided the berries, giving her a larger share.

He handed her the canteen and Aili downed half of it. It grew heavy in her hand as it refilled from somewhere wherever the magic connected to. Aili ate her berries. Her energy returned with the fruit sugars.

"There're herbs in the canteen."

Andvari nodded. "They'll help you recover while you learn to use magic. When we get back, I have some duties to attend to. There's a stack of books on my desk for you. Set aside any you've read and start on any book you'd like. If you've read them all, you can always help Jordi in the stables."

"Alright." So far, being a magic student wasn't bad. It's not what she expected, but Aili was grateful. Students in the city didn't get to practice magic outside like this.

They rode back together and took care of the horses. Aili filled their hay racks and checked the water buckets as he untacked Charger. They returned to their rooms, and he unpacked his saddle bags. Aili sorted through the books on his desk, stacked neatly in a pile.

He stopped in the doorway. "If you need anything, see Jordi. He'll help."

Aili smiled, her attention still on the stack of books. "I'll be fine."

His footsteps faded as he left. Aili picked up the two books she hadn't read yet, leaving the others where she found them. She wandered to the window and opened it, letting the gentle breeze flow into the room. It brushed over her neck as she sat on his bed in the sunbeam, the books in her lap. Aili opened a book. She could hear the horses below, gentle snorts to clear their lungs as they grazed.

She propped herself up against the headboard and selected a book. Aili got into the book quickly, always ready to soak in more knowledge. To her surprise, it wasn't a magic book, not really, but a book on nature and science, and how magic is used for conservation. She devoured each page, speeding through the first few chapters.

Aili blinked. She just read that paragraph four times. Her brain ached. She rubbed her temples. The book fell from her lap to the bed. Time for a break. She closed the window and set the books on her night table. Aili slipped her boots back on and headed down the stairs.

Leya's stall was empty. Charger wasn't there, either. Aili walked down the stable aisle, heading for the paddocks. She grasped the door handle. Wait, was that what she thought it was? Aili let go of the door and walked to where the tools hung on the wall. A wooden practice sword hung on a large hook, tucked behind some muck forks in a corner.

Aili glanced down the aisle. Nobody was around. She picked up the wooden sword and ran her fingers over the dents and nicks. Was it Jordi's? It was big and heavy enough to be his. Would he mind?

Another glance showed she was still alone. Aili darted from the stable and around to the hay barn. They stacked hay in the back half, leaving the front part clear. The open front faced the edge of camp, away from any weather that might spoil the hay. No one would see her here.

Aili stood quietly in the middle of the open space. The floor was littered with hay, but it was soft to walk on. She gripped the wooden sword hilt, her fingers barely able to circle the wood. Aili closed her eyes and settled.

She opened her eyes and raised her hands, lifting the sword. Aili exhaled and moved her arms, flowing through the first pattern Darik ever taught her. She stretched and slashed, stepped and turned, swinging the sword slowly through each movement as he taught her.

The form ended and Aili settled again, her mind quiet and her body full of energy. She felt it easily. This time, her energy flowing through her when she did the form. Aili pressed a hand to her heart. What was Darik doing now? Did he miss her, too?

How would she keep learning? Would she keep learning? Would she have time to practice on her own like this? What if Andvari found out and said no? Could she sneak away and practice anyway? Would he teach her more? He was already so busy; would he have time for her? Maybe Jordi would teach her?

Aili snuck back to the stable and stashed the sword on its hook. She turned at the whinny. Leya's nose poked over her stall door.

"Hey girl." Aili took the herbs from her pocket. "Here you go. I got these for you earlier, you greedy little thing."

Leya lipped the herbs from her palm and crunched them between her teeth.

"Welcome back." Jordi led Charger down the barn aisle, and into his stall beside Leya. Charger's hooves thudded on the floor. "Done your studies already?"

"As much as I could. He must be stuck in meetings. Want any help?" Aili rubbed Leya's forehead.

"Sure. I'd be foolish to say no to willing and experienced help. It's time to groom them once they're all in." He stepped from Charger's stall and latched it behind him. Jordi hung the halter on the hook. "Use those brushes. They're spelled against disease, so you can use them on anyone safely."

Aili picked up the brushes from the shelf he pointed at. "Where should I start?"

"Well, you did these two earlier, so start with Trickster there and work your way down that wall. I'll get the others in and do this side." He pointed at a big black gelding beside Charger.

She slipped into the stall with Trickster, brushes in hand. Aili greeted the black horse, holding her hand out for him to sniff. He blew a hot breath over her hand before turning back to his hay net. Aili reached as high up his neck as she could and started brushing. She pressed firmly, sweeping loose hair from his coat.

Sure, they could spell brushes to groom a horse, Aili thought, but they can't check a horse for issues. She examined Trickster as she groomed him, checking for lumps or swellings, heat, or any other sign of an injury or illness. Magic can't do that without a mage to monitor it and actually do the spell. She smiled to herself. Even as a tiny child, Aili knew how to brush and care for a horse.

Trickster was done and Aili moved on to the mare in the next stall when Jordi brought the last horse in. He also grabbed a set of brushes and worked across the aisle from her. Aili hummed softly to herself as she relaxed into the steady rhythm of the brushes.

She worked her way down the aisle, greeting each horse as she went. Aili was in the last stall, Jordi a couple of horses behind on his side, when the gelding she was brushing raised his head and turned. Aili perked up at the sound of human footsteps. Was he finally free of his meetings?

"Have you read all those books already?" Andvari leaned against the stall door.

"No. I read until I couldn't anymore. My brain got tired, and the words stopped making sense." Aili rubbed the brushes together, sending dirt and hair into the stall bedding.

Jordi stepped from the stall he was in and came over. "She's a hard worker. Took me half the time it normally does. That, and she knows what she's doing, so I don't have to watch her."

Andvari smiled. "It's nice having a student I can leave un-attended and not have to worry about what they're getting into. Time to wash for supper."

He opened the stall door. Aili gave the gelding a last pat and gathered her brushes. She left the stall and held the brushes up.

"You can leave those on the hay bale. I'll put them away. Here, let me help." Jordi rested his hand on her shoulder and muttered under his breath.

Warmth flowed over her skin and clothing. Jordi waved a hand down in front of Aili as he cast the spell. Dirt and hair fell from her skin and clothing, landing in a pile between her feet. A broom and shovel floated over to her. The broom shooed her, and Aili leapt back. She watched the broom sweep up the dirt, and the shovel carried it to a muck bucket. With the dirt disposed of, the tools hung themselves back on the wall.

"It's nice to see you don't just randomly use magic for little things." Andvari chuckled. "Thanks, though."

"Hey, she can come and help any time." Jordi grinned and shrugged.

"Supper. Come." Andvari turned and headed for the door.

Aili smiled. She turned and followed Andvari down the barn aisle, stopping to give a last wave to Jordi. They headed back to their rooms, going the most direct route, weaving through the camp residents, each heading for supper like she would soon.

"You know how to use the sinks and such, and warm up the water?" Andvari gestured at the bathroom.

She smiled and nodded. "Sure do."

"I thought you might, but I thought I'd check. Go wash."

Aili filled the sink and warmed the water up. She splashed water over her face. Her body felt heavy, and her eyelids wanted to close. The bed looked awfully inviting. No, she needed supper. Aili dragged herself down behind him. She appreciated once again how quiet their table was compared to the rest of the dining hall.

She startled awake, her elbow slipping off the table at some random noise. Aili bumped her empty plate, sending it skidding across the table. She didn't remember eating, though her belly was full. Her eyelids wanted to slam shut.

Andvari grabbed the plate for her. "Go rest. I'll clean up. You're falling asleep here."

"Thank you."

Aili shuffled her way from the dining hall and up the stairs. She kicked the door closed behind her and slumped down on the bed. Her curtains were open to the rest of the room, but Aili didn't care. She wiggled her boots off, and her head hit the pillow.

Sounds pulled her awake when Andvari returned, the window closing and soft footsteps. She sat up and looked out the window. The sun was setting in the distance, the reds and golds blanketing the land around her. He sat at his desk, his back to her, going through papers.

She eased from the bed and walked to the window. Her socked feet were nearly silent on the smooth wooden floor. Aili leaned against the window frame and stared out at the nearly empty paddocks below. Was there a polite way to interrupt him?

"Do I have to ask?" He turned in his chair and smiled.

Aili shook her head and smiled. "Please, don't. How did you even know? Your back was to me and everything."

Andvari shrugged. "I just knew. What's on your mind?"

Aili sank to his mattress and crossed her legs. "Do I get free time to explore and relax on my own?" She shifted to the end of his bed and sat on the trunk, closer to him. Aili let her fingers glide over the varnished wood and explore the metal fittings.

He smiled again. "You're as wild as the nature you manipulate. Here, I have something for you."

Andvari reached into his pocket and pulled out a small mirror, just like the one Kyson handed to her when they first camped together. He held it out to her. Aili took the heavy brass mirror and cradled it in her palm. Despite the golden metal, the image reflecting to her was like a normal mirror, the colours true to life.

"Normally, magic students don't get unsupervised time like you want until they've been students for years. You're not a normal magic student, though. I know you can survive on your own and not blow things up, so you can have as much free time as our schedule allows, as long as you work hard in your lessons."

He pulled his mirror out from under his clothing, where it hung on a chain around his neck. "Hold that between your hands like this. It'll feel hot and then go cold again." Andvari held the mirror between his palms to show her.

Aili rested her hand over the mirror like he did, with it snugly between her palms. The metal cooled her palms, but warmed quickly. She pressed her lips together. No hotter, please, she pleaded. Aili sighed when the mirror cooled just as quickly. She raised an eyebrow at him.

"You just imprinted it on you. These let us communicate, no matter where we both are."

She opened her hands and examined the mirror, turning it over. Her name appeared, engraved along the top back edge by magic.

"If you want to contact me, hold the mirror up like this. Picture me clearly in your mind. The magic is in the mirror, so you won't need a spell. Try it." He held the mirror in his palm, up at eye level.

Aili raised her mirror and saw her reflection staring back at her, clear and undistorted. She focused on the shiny surface, imagining his face. Aili took a slow breath and kept the image of him in her mind.

His mirror glowed brightly. Aili glanced at it, losing her focus. Movement in her mirror pulled her attention back. He smiled at her, his little image on the surface of her mirror.

"Once the mirror knows which mirror to connect to, it will keep trying, whether or not you focus after that. It won't care if you get distracted."

She blinked. Hearing him twice, once from the mirror and again with him right across from her, it almost echoed.

"Close a call like this." He placed his empty hand over the mirror, just like imprinting it, and his image disappeared.

Aili's own reflection stared back at her. "If you call me, how do I respond?"

"Hold it up. Look at your reflection. Just think that you want to talk to me. It'll connect." He tucked his mirror back under his shirt. "In an emergency, you can think about the mirror and who you want to contact. The call will go through, whether or not you're holding it normally, as long as it's in contact with your skin. That's why we wear them on chains under our shirt."

Andvari held his hand out. Aili passed the mirror back to him. He took a thin silver chain from his pocket and threaded it through the ring at the top. She sat still as he moved behind her and fastened the chain around her neck, closing it with a quick muttered spell.

"You can take it off at night if you want to, but most of us sleep with them as well, especially in the field. If you're out and get hurt, just think of me, and I'll get an emergency signal. I'll come right away."

The metal felt pleasantly warm against her skin, even through her shirt. Aili traced the rim with her fingers.

"Now, wash up properly and get to bed. The morning is yours while I work." Andvari stretched his arms up, nearly touching the ceiling. "I start early. You can sleep in, or not, as you choose."

"Yes." Aili bounced to her feet and darted across to the bathroom.

"We work twice as hard later to make up for that time, though." His voice was slightly muffled through the bathroom door.

"Sure," she called back.

Aili filled the sink and washed up. She brushed her hair slowly. I have magic now. The one thing I never thought would come, and it's mine. Leya's here with me, and we can stay together. He's kind and patient, unlike so many mages at the University and schools. I have it all, but why now?

She set her brush down and wandered to her bed. Aili closed the curtains with a gesture and pulled her blankets back. Morning comes early, and I'm not wasting a moment of it.

CHAPTER 6

PLAY TIME

Aili woke early. She smiled and eased herself from the bed. The morning was hers, and she wasn't about to waste any of it. Aili changed into clean clothes from the new pile on her trunk and opened her curtains.

Andvari sat at his desk, his back to her, absorbed in his paperwork. "Have some breakfast before you go." He pointed at a plate on the corner of his desk.

Three sandwiches appeared on the plate. He picked one up and took a bite, his attention still on documents spread across his desk. Aili shivered. Was the kitchen watching? Was it his gesture? How did they know to send food just then?

She took a sandwich and sat on his trunk. Aili smiled to herself as she bit into the sandwich. He might get upset if she dropped crumbs on his bed, but here she should be fine. Hmm, beans and vegetables, pressed together with

127

spices. This should give her energy all morning and was delicious. Do all the Scouts eat this well? She thought back to her last meals. Yes, they did. Aili finished her first sandwich and snatched the second one from the plate.

"When you're ready, go have fun. Be safe, answer if I call on the mirror, and come back if I tell you to, alright?" He finally looked up from the papers, his deep blue eyes holding her gaze.

"I will." Aili squirmed.

"Go." He grinned and nodded at the door. "Say good morning to your little friend for me."

Aili darted across the room and slipped her boots on. Freedom. She eased the door closed behind her until the latch caught with a small click. Aili dashed down the hall, took the stairs two at a time, and ran for the stable.

Leya perked her ears and whinnied. Her mouth full of hay muffled the noise.

Aili skidded to a stop in front of her stall. She rubbed Leya's smooth forehead. "I'll just be a few minutes, and we'll go." Aili glanced around. She smiled. There was no one around her.

She took the sword from the wall and snuck towards the hay shed. Aili ducked into the feed room to avoid a stable hand coming back with an empty halter in his hand. His footsteps receded, and Aili ran for the side door. Within moments, she was at the hay shed.

The hay shed was dim in the early morning sun, but Aili could see well. She settled in the middle of the front area, the sword in her hand. With a slow breath, Aili moved, her body flowing through the pattern Darik taught her.

With each slow breath, her awareness stretched out over more of the camp. Aili could feel people moving around, walking between buildings and going about their day. She turned her focus back to her own body, and how each movement felt. Her muscles loosened, and she stretched with ease.

Someone approached the hay shed. Aili dived behind the hay bales; the sword clutched to her chest. She felt them, she realized. She really felt them. Aili smiled and peeked around the hay. A stable hand came with a cart, loaded a hay bale, and left again. She sat quietly and let her heart slow again, her back to the hay bales behind her.

After a long minute, Aili returned to her practice spot. She sat for a couple minutes of quiet meditation. With her body settled, she stood. Aili flowed through the last two sword forms she knew, slow and easy. With a nod to herself, she left the hay shed. Aili slunk back and returned the sword to its hook.

Aili leaned on Leya's stall door. "Ready for an adventure?"

Leya snorted and stuffed her nose deep in the hay feeder. Aili took her brushes and joined the pony in the stall. She took a deep breath, inhaling the smell of fresh straw and clean horse. Perfect. She started grooming Leya, pressing firmly with the brushes, and checking her pony for issues as she groomed her. Leya looked good.

She set the brushes back on the small shelf on Leya's stall front. Aili opened the stall door. "Come on, then."

Leya looked at her and snorted. She looked back at the feeder. Aili tapped her foot. Leya wandered over to her and followed Aili down the stable aisle. Aili stopped at the large map and examined it, her fingers combing through Leya's mane absent-mindedly.

The map detail was amazing. It showed the entire country. Aili touched the mark where the camp was and the map zoomed in until the map of the camp and countryside filled the space. She frowned at the detail. Where should she go, with so many interesting things to see?

"Where are you off to this morning?" Jordi stepped beside her and stared at the map.

"I don't know." Aili shrugged her shoulders. "I have all morning to explore, so I thought I'd see what's around."

"I'd recommend the falls." He touched a spot on the map, and it appeared in more detail in the upper corner. "They're beautiful, magical, and quiet."

Aili grinned. It was easy to get to, just a brief ride into the trees once she reached the forest. "Thanks." Aili vaulted onto Leya's back. "See you later."

Jordi opened the door and Aili rode Leya out. She guided her from camp, through the paddocks and into the fields beyond. Leya strode out at a peaceful walk. Being in a stall all night, she needed a chance to stretch her legs. Aili would have taken her to the hay barn during her practice, but the pony was a little glutton, and Aili doubted she could explain how quickly Leya could eat.

The camp noises disappeared as she passed through the shield. Aili felt the tingling in her skin, like static electricity, but less startling and strong. She pointed Leya north and gripped her mane.

"Ready, girl?"

Leya snorted and pranced, her muscles tense.

"Go." Aili leaned forward slightly and gave Leya a squeeze with both legs.

Leya shot forward at a gallop, her hooves pounding as she charged through the long grass. The wind whipped Aili's braids and clothing. She crouched close to Leya's neck for balance, the white mane blowing against her face. Warmth filled her heart. This was more like it.

They sped over the hills and through the grass. Aili sat taller as they approached the trees, and Leya slowed down.

She let the pony walk. Leya's sides heaved with each breath. The cool morning air made Aili shiver, and she pulled her cloak around herself tighter.

At the edge of the trees, Aili slid from Leya's back. They walked together towards the sound of running water cascading down rocks. The air was thick with moisture. It was close. There was real energy here, too. Aili felt the vibrations of power all gathered in one place.

"This way, girl." Aili turned towards the power and led Leya into the trees.

The trees grew thick and close together, a blend of evergreens and deciduous trees. The shadows were a little less thick, so Aili walked towards that spot. There was an opening between the trees and bushes. She passed through the gap and towards the sunlight ahead.

They stepped into a clearing with a large pond. Water crashed down the rocks and into the pool below, sending ripples through the otherwise clear water. Lush, green grass surrounded the pond. Mist saturated the air. Even the birdsong was hard to hear over the crashing water.

Leya stepped to the pond and sniffed the water. She took a long drink. Aili walked along the pond's edge. This whole place buzzed with magic, old and powerful energy that felt warm and comforting, like a hug from a friend. Her thoughts flashed back to the forest near the city, where she played so long as a child.

Aili sat on the grass and leaned back against a rock. The water flowed over the cliff above and tumbled down the rocks. She slowed her breathing and meditated with her attention on the water. It flowed like a single thing, one cohesive being, but it wasn't. It was millions of little individual droplets. No, it was both. Aili let the essence of water flow through her as she experienced it in a whole new way.

A boulder part way down the falls caught her attention. It projected out from the rock face, and the water flowed over it, spraying out and down. Aili kept her attention on the boulder and the surrounding water. Could she move the water?

She pressed her will on the water, as she did with dehydrating the berries. The water ignored her, flowing on, untouched by her desires. Hmm, was it like a pony? Ponies hated being told what to do, but she could coax them into listening. Was water the same?

Aili touched the water again, feeling deep inside herself. Maybe just shift a little, yes, just like that. How about a little more over here? This was a lot like working with Leya. Aili smiled to herself. She nudged and guided, pushed and prodded, and the water gave way.

Now she could see the boulder, and how it was embedded in the cliff. The water diverted around it, exposing the wet rock to Aili. She grinned and sighed. The water crashed down again, with her attention relaxed. It flowed back over the boulder, through the path of least resistance.

Her heart raced. She did it, and on her own. Her body was heavy, and her eyelids drooped despite the excitement running through her. Aili curled up on the grass and closed her eyes. She listened to the sound of Leya ripping the grass loose and chewing it.

Her chest felt warm, right over her heart. What? She dragged herself from her nap and sat. Aili pressed her hand to her heart and felt the mirror under her shirt, hot through her clothing. Right, the mirror. She pulled it out and cradled it in her hand. The metal glowed, casting shadows around her. Aili dashed into the trees, away from the noise of the water, and answered the call.

"There you are." Andvari frowned at her, his forehead creased. "Are you okay?"

"I'm fine." Aili smiled. "We went for a ride and stopped at the waterfall. I fell asleep. What's up?"

"Were you using magic?" He raised an eyebrow.

Aili frowned. "Was I not supposed to?"

He shook his head, his eyes up at the sky. "I'm done with my meetings, so come on back. We'll discuss the rules more thoroughly. After lunch, we're working with Jordi and the horses again, so more Earth Magic."

"Be right back." Aili closed the call, her hands shaking. She whistled and Leya darted over. Aili leapt onto her back. "Let's go."

Leya carried her through the trees and back to the grassy fields. She cantered back towards the camp, a relaxed pace she could do for hours. Aili let her walk the last half-mile or so. She took Leya back through the paddocks, avoiding the busy camp trails. They stopped at the stable doors and Aili slid from her back.

Jordi stepped from the building. "Charger and Trickster are in the far front paddock. She can join them. She needs more time in the sun."

Leya whickered and bobbed her head up and down. Aili laughed.

Jordi smiled. "She's also too smart for her own good." He turned and disappeared into the stable.

Aili walked with her to the paddock and opened the gate. Leya marched inside. Once she securely latched the gate, Aili returned to the main building. The sun warmed her through, chasing the chill of the mist away. She inhaled and smiled. This just might be her favourite place in camp.

She headed for their rooms. Andvari was at his desk, deep in paperwork again. He turned and looked her over. Aili squirmed. Darik used to give her the same look when she returned from her adventures, worried she'd gotten herself maimed or something while unsupervised. Aili froze in the doorway.

The corners of his mouth twitched. "Come in. Sit." He pointed to the end of his bed, near the desk.

Aili kicked her boots off and walked over. She sank to the mattress, her body stiff. Her heart pounded. Was she in trouble?

"Well, how did it go, and what did you try?" Andvari smiled.

She let out the breath she didn't realize she was holding. Smiling was good. She could work with this.

"Jordi suggested the falls, so we explored that." She twisted the hem of her shirt between her fingers. "I played with the water, made it move and stuff." Aili kept her gaze down at her knees.

"Did you move it? The water, I mean."

Aili glanced up and nodded. "I could move it a little if I was patient and guided it gently. If I didn't work as hard and let it happen, it worked better."

Andvari took her hand and guided her from the bed. "You must have learned something valuable while you experimented. Look." He stood her in front of his large wall mirror and pointed at her neck.

Aili stared, her mouth open. She saw the emerald crystals in her neckband, one in each group of four, but another crystal also glowed. Now she also had a deep blue crystal in each group. The last two crystals remained clear. Aili fingered the crystals as she stared at them in the mirror.

"Promise me you won't try Fire Magic without me present, agreed?" Andvari crossed his arms over his chest, though he stood relaxed beside her.

Aili grinned. "Agreed." Easiest promise I'll ever make.

Her mind brought countless memories up of Darik teaching her to light a fire in the woods, and her resisting each time until she finally gave in.

"I'm comfortable with you using Earth Magic alone, as long as you're careful and pay attention. I suspect you've been passively using it all your life anyway, and it comes so easily to you. Try not to use the others outside of lessons, so I can help if things don't go as you planned." The corners of his mouth turned up in a lazy smile.

Aili grinned. "Okay. Are there other rules I'm supposed to know already?"

Andvari laughed. "We're both learning as we go. The usual rules don't apply, since you're not following the normal path of magical learning. As long as I know where you are and how to contact you, we're probably okay. If you don't tell me where you go, like if I'm busy, at least tell Jordi."

"I can do that." Aili nodded. "So, tell people where I am, and Earth Magic only."

"Right." Andvari nodded. "We'll add or change rules as situations come up or we find we need to. Now, wash for lunch. I'll wait."

Aili wandered into the bathroom and placed her hands on the sink as it filled. The water responded to her and warmed. She sunk her hands into the white bowl. The dirt wiped off her hands and floated down, disappearing to whatever muck heap or wastewater site the sink was connected to.

She smiled at the warm water and left her hands in the sink for a few long moments. After gripping Leya's mane so firmly during their gallop, the heat eased any remaining tension in her fingers. Gently rubbing her hands together, she dislodged the last of the oils from Leya. It disappeared like the dirt had.

Washed and ready, Aili followed Andvari down the busy stairs and into the noisy dining hall. At least there were fewer people here with everyone's lunch breaks staggered a bit, but Aili still winced at the noise. From now on, I'll treasure every quiet meal in the forest, with birdsong to keep me company.

Aili joined the line at the serving table. Unlike the University, where teachers were presented with plates when they arrived, Andvari and the officers didn't mind waiting in line like everyone else. Other than the table at the far end where they ate, it was hard to see any privilege for them at all. Somehow it made them easier to talk to, more like regular people.

"What are you doing here?"

Aili turned and glanced down. A small girl stared up at her. She had the coldest pale eyes Aili had ever seen. Aili shivered. Unlike most children, who seemed to radiate happiness, she had a dull lifelessness about her.

"I'm eating." Aili gestured to the tables full of people eating their lunch. She turned back to the food table and took the plate Andvari handed her.

"Papa always said they should shut away older people with fewer magic skills to do menial labour, as that's all they're good for."

Aili kept her back to the girl but glanced up at Andvari. He shook his head slightly and loaded a last spoon of rice on his plate. Aili selected food and filled her tray as the little girl rattled on about all the things her Papa must have said, ever. She sighed and smiled when she left the line and followed Andvari to their quieter table.

"That was very diplomatic of you." Andvari set his tray on the table.

"This is why I like horses better than people." Aili set her tray down and sat beside him.

He chuckled. Aili glanced over at the girl. She sat at a table with other students, glaring at Aili.

"She's from a lesser house, the lower nobility, as you might have noticed from her band. Some of them are still prone to the pretentious thinking of status and position, trying to claw their way up the magic ladder to greatness in the University." Andvari tore his roll open, releasing steam.

"How'd she end up here?" Aili speared some vegetables with her fork.

"After an—incident—in their home city, it was hard for her father to find her a magic teacher. No one would deal with him. A guard finally agreed to take her as a student, and she came here. She's forgiven no one for it, for being here and not at the 'best magic school in the country.' Mostly, we try to ignore her attitude." He sipped his tea. "Her teacher is working with her on social skills, but it's been a challenge."

Aili glanced over again. The other students were ignoring her, talking among themselves, and no one was listening to her. "I can imagine."

"Don't tell me you've never worked with a problem horse before." He raised an eyebrow at her.

"Well, sure, but horses are only a problem when people make them that way."

"Children are the same." He took a bite of his roll.

Aili watched her for a moment, chatting away as if the others hung on her every word. Did she know she was being ignored? Was she lonely, like Aili felt for so much of her own childhood? Aili turned back to her food and focused on eating.

They put away their empty dishes and stacked the trays, before heading to the stables. Aili smiled and turned her face to the sun. She inhaled deeply, taking in that fresh horse smell. Could she bottle that and keep it with her forever?

"Ready?" Jordi leaned against the wall, waiting with his arms crossed.

"For ponies? Always." Aili grinned.

"Horses today." Jordi laughed. "Charger is ready. He rubbed his mane into a right proper mess."

Andvari rolled his eyes. "Of course he did. Show her the spells and we'll sort out what she can try."

"Alright, time to remove some tangles. I'll show you how I do it on a small section of mane, and you can fix the rest." Jordi opened Charger's stall door and stepped aside, letting her in.

The big horse stood at his hay net, nose deep in the food. Aili winced at the tangle of hair; his mane nearly completely matted. Jordi stepped beside Charger and held his hand over the tangle. He chanted out loud for Aili's benefit. She smiled as she watched, feeling for the magic. A small section of mane relaxed and slipped free of the bigger tangle.

"As I did that, I imagined what I wanted it to look like. If the tangle is bad enough, I may not follow it all with my mind, but I can encourage it to work itself free. The hairs want to be straighter. If I use both hands, I can do the entire mane at once. I thought I'd leave some for you to try." Jordi nudged her.

"Gee, thanks." Aili elbowed him back.

Andvari rested a hand on her shoulder. "Any thoughts on how you want to try this?"

Aili wrinkled her brow and focused. Imagine the result, huh? She could do that. Aili nodded. She closed her eyes and felt for the mane with her senses. Aili rested her hands on Charger's mane and took a deep breath.

The hairs were flexible and wanted to lie flat. They were smooth and strong. She touched the hair with her senses and imagined his mane hair laying straight along his neck, just that gentle waviness it had to give it body.

"That's one way to do it." Andvari squeezed her shoulder lightly.

Aili opened her eyes. The mane lay neatly against Charger's neck, looking freshly combed and shining in the sunlight through the window. "Oh?"

"You didn't unwind the hair like I did." Jordi held her gaze. "You caused the hair to pass through itself in some places, like you changed their molecular bonds temporarily or something." He smiled up at Andvari. "Think she can walk through walls?"

Andvari scratched his chin. "Maybe, but if she messes up, she dies. Nothing like materializing inside a wall to ruin your day."

Aili shivered. "Umm, I'm good, thanks. That's why people invented doors, right? Besides, I just put the hair back where it wanted to be. I didn't imagine it passing through itself."

Andvari glanced around. He stepped from the stall and picked up a metal bucket. Aili watched him set the bucket on a shelf. What was he doing?

He waved for her to join him. "See if you can make the bucket drop through the shelf."

Aili pressed her lips together. "Okay, I guess."

She touched the bucket with her senses. It was cold and hard and distant from her, not like hair and grass and natural things. "I can sense the bucket, but I can't touch it. The hair is natural and wanted to be straight. The bucket doesn't care about the shelf, if that makes sense?"

Jordi wrapped an arm around her. "Hey, amazing has limits. It gives me an idea, though."

Aili stepped into the stall and gave Charger a scratch while Jordi disappeared into the tack room. He leaned into her affection, lowering his head and blowing softly with his breath.

"His favourite spot is here." Andvari scratched Charger high on his hip, along his spine.

Charger raised his head and stuck his lip out.

Aili giggled at the horse. "You know each other well?"

"He's mine. Jordi cares for him and keeps him fit when I'm busy, and Charger carries me between camps and to the cities when I need to travel."

Jordi came back with a saddle in his arms and set it on a wooden rack outside the stall. "Dazzle me. We're going to tackle leather repair."

Aili left the stall and examined the saddle. There was a small rip in the leather on the seat. "No pressure," she teased, her finger running over the split. "That's a small tear, fixable by hand in minutes."

"Yes, but you'd see the repair. I have a spell that makes the repair invisible, so you might also learn to use similar magic. Look for the edges in your mind and knit them back together."

She set her hand over the rip and felt for it with her magical senses. Aili sunk down into the essence of the leather, feeling it like she did the waterfall. The tear was jagged when looked at closely. Aili pulled at the leather, matching the edges, and weaving the leather together at its essence. She smoothed down the edges in her mind, making the fix invisible.

Aili wiped her forehead with her sleeve. She took a breath and focused again. It was slow, but it was working. Aili could do this. She stayed at it, working the leather with her will and mind, until it felt like a single piece again.

She moved her hand and opened her eyes. The leather was smooth and solid again, just a slight colour change left where the tear used to be. Aili frowned at the spot.

"It's your first time. Don't worry about the colour. I can finish and treat it, and you'll never see it." Jordi smiled at Aili. "Now if you're out and your tack breaks, you can fix it safely without tools and make it back."

"Sit." Andvari guided her to a hay bale, and Aili sat. "I'll get you some juice."

Aili leaned back against the stall wall behind her. Andvari disappeared into a room, only to come back within moments with a bottle of juice. Did Jordi keep some juice around like Darik did? Was that a Scout thing?

"Here. Keep your energy up as you learn." Andvari uncapped the bottle and handed it to her.

Aili took the bottle and sipped the sweet juice. She sighed and smiled. "So far, I'm learning to do things I can already do without magic." She took another long sip.

"The little things let us experiment with how your abilities work." Andvari sat on the hay bale beside her. "It lets you get used to your powers and build up your control. Most mages start by calling a ball of light and might work on that for a month. It's only your first week, right?"

Aili nodded. "Do you know what kinds of things I can do? What are my limits?"

"We're learning that as you go. You are close to nature, so plants, animals, natural things should come easily to you. We have yet to see if you can influence processed materials like glass and metal. Now, if you feel up to it, get ready to ride. We're going into the forest." Andvari took the empty bottle and stood.

Andvari took his brushes and groomed Charger. Aili worked on Leya, keeping him quiet company. Something about the sounds of horses chewing contentedly on fresh smelling hay soothed her. Would he be upset if she moved into the stable? Aili grinned at the thought.

He led Charger from the stall, saddled and ready to go. Aili followed with Leya, who wore the rope bridle. They mounted the horses outside the stable and rode off into the fields. The forest was close here, and it wasn't long before they stood beneath the edge of the trees.

"Don't wander off." Aili slipped from Leya's back. She scratched the pony's withers.

Leya ripped a mouthful of grass up and chewed, ignoring the girl completely.

"Since you'll be coming with me on many missions, we're going to start on things you need to know to stay safe." Andvari removed Charger's saddle and set it aside.

CHAPTER 7

SNEAKING AROUND

Andvari headed into the woods, his green clothing blending in with the trees around him.

Aili followed, hustling to catch up. "What am I learning this time?"

"We'll practice how to move without a trace, and blend into shadows. I want to see if you can move silently. I can use spells, but you need to learn what works for you." Andvari stopped and leaned against a tree.

"Aili nodded. "Alright, where do we start?"

"To pass without a trace, you need to put the forest back exactly how you found it. Think you can do that?" He smiled at Aili.

She laughed. "Heck, yeah. I got this."

Andvari lowered himself to the ground, crossing his legs as he leaned against the tree. "I'll wait here with my eyes closed. You have five minutes to go for a walk and end up back here. For part of it, try jogging slowly. When you get back, I'll follow any trail you left."

Aili grinned. She turned and walked away. So many hours of her childhood were spent playing with Darik like this in the woods. She even got to test her skills when Darik's Scout friend came to visit. Now, think of the end result. I've got this.

She glanced back. He sat quietly, motionless. Aili picked a route between some bushes and headed deeper into the forest. She opened her senses and felt for the trees, for the familiar thrum of energy the forest had. Pass without a trace.

Grass bounced back where she stepped on it. Branches she brushed against went still once she passed. The trees were thick enough he was out of sight in a few yards. Now, what had she learned about anti-tracking? Aili circled back on her path and changed direction completely. It was nearly impossible not to leave sign when she jogged, but Aili still had to smile at using magic.

She came back to her starting spot, easily detecting him among the trees with her senses, and sat beside him. That was less than five minutes, but not by much.

Andvari opened his eyes. "How do you think you did?"

Aili rubbed her cheeks. "I guess I'll find out, but I think it went okay."

"Did you want to come, and see what I do?"

She leapt to her feet. "Absolutely."

Andvari rose to his feet and walked slowly around, searching the forest floor and trees. Within a few feet he stopped and touched a branch. "Great job on not leaving footprints. We'll work on the higher signs like this, though." He straightened the bent twig.

"You're tracking me with a twig?"

Andvari smiled and began searching ahead again. "A good tracker doesn't need much. A single broken twig or misplaced stone is more than enough, even without me using tracking spells."

He slowly walked in a zig-zag pattern, heading in the general direction Aili had gone. She stayed back and watched, following a few steps behind.

"I'm also looking for the most likely path you'd choose. You knew you were being tracked, and you had a time limit, so that would affect your choices. You'd stay away from heavier brush, and stick to more open paths, right?" He turned and glanced at her.

Aili smiled and stared at her feet, her cheeks burning. She nodded.

He followed her circular diversion, going around a thick cluster of bushes, and returned to their path. Aili waited as he cast about, looking for her trail.

"Aha." Andvari kneeled beside a small stone pushed out of place.

Aili raised an eyebrow. Had she moved that? She must have, it was on her path. There was so much to think about when being tracked. She followed him along her trail.

"You did well. If someone were tracking you with magic, they'd still take time, and you'd probably have made it to safety before they caught up." He pointed at another bent twig. "There's the next one."

It was almost twenty minutes before they returned to the start. Aili had a new mental list of things to look for when tracking, and to watch when making a trail.

"That was impressive. We have some things to work on, but I've seen new Scouts take over a month to get where you are now." He leaned against the tree.

"What is tracking magic like?" Please, show me, she willed silently. Aili turned pleading eyes on him.

He stared into the trees for a long moment. Andvari sank to the ground and patted the grass beside him. Aili settled in the soft grass, her chin on her hand.

"First, we track by detecting magic they cast along the way. Most people try to hide themselves with spells, silencing spells or leave no trace spells, and the like. Scouts developed spells to sense that magic. It's like a shining path through the forest for us to follow."

Aili scrunched up her nose. "I don't use spells. Would that work against me?"

He shook his head. "Probably not. If I know where you've been, I can cast a clairvoyance spell and follow a shadow of you. She'd move at your speed and do what you've done, so you would still have a head start on me. Would you like to see that spell?"

She bounced to her feet. "Heck, yeah."

Andvari grinned. He stood and moved to where the first twig was broken. Andvari raised a hand and muttered softly, his fingers moving as he chanted. A faded blue version of Aili formed before him, translucent and life sized, glowing in the shadows of the forest.

Her shadow walked along her path, confident and smiling. Andvari followed the spectre. Aili caught up to him and walked beside him. She rubbed her temples with her fingers. This was so weird. Her gestures and expressions, her movement, it all looked so unfamiliar, yet it was her. She moved gracefully, though. Aili smiled at the spectre. They reached the spot where Aili doubled back, and the spectre stopped for a moment. It grinned and turned.

Andvari chuckled as they returned to the same spot again. "You little sneak. We'll spend a lot more time on diversionary tactics and false trails soon, too. You've got a great start already, and a devious grin."

"Is this how you found my camp the first time?" Aili kept pace as her shadow moved on, staying beside him.

He shook his head. "No, actually. As my student, there's a deep magic that connects us. The bands react to it. Through that magic, I can feel roughly where you are, and when you're casting strong magic. I knew that first moment we met in the woods that we'd meet again, and I could sense you from that moment on."

"Interesting," she mumbled to herself. Aili watched her shadow self turn again and head for camp. "I can feel you easily out here in the woods, but in camp you get lost among the others."

"Most students can't sense their teachers at all." He raised an eyebrow. "This should make tracking games more interesting."

Her shadow stepped over to the starting point and sat, just like Aili had done. Andvari waved a hand and the blue form evaporated in a puff of blue smoke.

"You have three minutes to hide. I'll seek you without magic. Go."

Aili darted through the trees. Where should she hide? Aili opened her awareness to the woods. A hiding place, please?

She felt for anything to help, a cluster of thick bushes, a hollow, or anything.

Something tugged at her to her right, a sense or a feeling. She followed the pull, like a hand was guiding her, but the hand was made of air and transparent. A thick cluster of bushes ahead looked perfect. Aili touched the plants with her abilities and an opening appeared. She slipped through and settled on the soft moss as the opening closed again.

She pressed a hand to her mouth. She hadn't hidden her trail. Aili closed her eyes and took a few deep breaths. Her senses reached out to the forest, and she swept her path clear. It was slower than hiding as she moved, but she obliterated her path completely.

Her senses brushed against him; her path gone to that point now. Aili almost felt the grin she knew he had as her trail disappeared before him. Without magic to find her with, he had nothing now but what he could guess about her path. Had she zig-zagged enough? Would it be obvious to him anyways?

Aili followed him with her senses, though she heard the occasional soft step or the movement of a bush. She eased the brush around her open just a crack and peered out. He stood nearby, turning around as he sought any sign.

"I know you're here, but I can't see you or find sign. Well done. Come on out."

She crawled back out through the opening the bushes made for her. Aili straightened up beside him and brushed the dirt from her clothing.

"You were hidden before you remembered to hide your trail, right?" He chuckled.

Aili nodded, her gaze on her boots. Was he disappointed? Her cheeks felt hot.

He rested his large hand on her shoulder. "Once you remembered, you erased it completely. I only knew you were there because I felt you. I was guessing when I got close, and that's a job well done on your part."

Aili followed him back to the horses. "I didn't have to hide much in the western woods. Nobody else came close much, though I practiced when I could."

He saddled Charger and Aili vaulted onto Leya. They rode back together at a relaxed walk.

Andvari turned his face to the sun and sighed. "This is way better than paperwork. Having a student is better than I thought. I get to spend time outside again."

"Am I your first student?"

"Yes, you are. I've had apprentices before, new Scouts I've trained, but never a student as new to magic as you."

They returned to the stables. Aili filled the hay nets and Andvari checked water buckets. She picked up her brushes and started grooming her pony.

"After supper, I expect you to read more. I have some duties to see to, so if you need anything or finish early, you know where Jordi is." Andvari untacked Charger in his stall beside her.

"Any time you need me." Jordi waved as he walked a horse past in the aisle. "See you later. They want their supper, and you almost missed yours."

Andvari waved a hand over them, and the dirt and hair fell from their skin and clothes. He swept it up with a quick spell and gestured for her to follow. The sun was going down as they walked to the main hall. Her stomach rumbled at the smell of hot food from the dining hall.

"Normally we'd take the time to wash properly, but we got a little sidetracked out there." Andvari led her through the archway and down the hall to the dining room.

"You mean you got a little sidetracked. I'm just a lowly student, following my teacher's example." Aili grinned at his back.

He spun and swiped at her, smiling. Aili ducked and darted back.

Andvari shook his head and rolled his eyes. "Good reflexes."

He turned and rounded the corner into the dining room. This had to be the quietest Aili had ever seen the room. The low sun shone through the windows, magic keeping the reddish light from blinding people. A few people were scattered in small groups at the tables. A few dishes remained on the large food table, and all her favourites were there. Aili grinned and picked up a plate.

"They always have food here for latecomers, or people working unusual hours." Andvari picked up a plate. "The magic keeps track of who has eaten and who still needs meals, as well as who is on missions outside the camp. They know what we like and roughly how much we usually take, so there will always be plenty here for you."

Aili gripped her plate tightly. "So, I have no privacy, but I'll never go hungry?"

Andvari grinned. "That's one way to look at it."

"That's—disturbing, and yet, not. It's almost creepy seeing so few people here." Even at a whisper, Aili's voice sounded loud to her in the empty room.

"Would you rather eat in our rooms?" He loaded his plate with food.

Aili nodded. She selected her supper and followed him upstairs. Aili settled on his trunk while he ate at his desk. This was much better. Eating hunched over didn't bother her, it felt like camping, and the trunk was more than large enough for her and her tray. She smiled and stared out a window.

"What's the smile about?" He ripped his roll apart and tossed a piece in his mouth.

Aili tore her roll and breathed in the steam. "This place already feels like home." She chewed the fresh bread, tasting the herbs on her tongue.

"This is my favourite camp. I stay here as often as I can."

They ate quietly together after that, with Aili lost in her own thoughts. How could she be more comfortable here in this place after so little time than in her old room back at her parents' manor? Was it the wooden buildings? How close the forest was? Aili looked down and scooped up the last of her meal. Had she eaten that quickly?

"I'll take the plates back on my way." Andvari gathered the dishes. "Get reading."

Aili took the book from her night table and tossed it onto his bed. She opened the window as he left, letting the fresh air inside. Aili leaned out and inhaled. The hay barn was close enough to smell the fresh hay.

She settled onto his bed and picked up her book. The mage-light lamp on the night table gave her light to read by as the sun dropped below the horizon. Aili poured over the contents of each page, skimming what she knew, and absorbing new ideas.

Andvari came back hours later. "How did it go?"

"I've already read those." Aili pointed to the pile on his desk corner. "This one's not bad, but I preferred Lanikin's Mixture of Science and Sorcery. He went into a lot more detail."

Andvari crossed his arms over his chest and raised an eyebrow. "You've read Lanikin's book? It's considered very advanced."

Aili smiled and set her bookmark. "I had nothing to do but read when I was younger. With no magic lessons, when I wasn't with Darik or in the forest, I was with father at the University. I had free run of the libraries, including some of the professors' personal collections. I learned a lot about the theory of spells and magic. His book was one of the last I read before coming here."

Andvari let out a breath. "That's good, actually, although still frightening. Some mages study their whole lives and never reach that level of understanding in magic or science." He flipped through the pile. "When you're done that one, I'll have more sent. Wash up. It's bedtime."

She set her book on her night table with the other one she still needed to read. Aili headed for the bathroom and washed up in privacy. When she returned, he had lowered her curtains for her. Aili changed into her night clothes and lay in bed. Her eyes didn't want to close, and she rolled a few times.

"What's up?"

"Can we sleep with the window open? I miss the night noises."

"Curtains, too?"

"Yes, please."

Her curtains rose and he slid the window open again for her. An owl hooted in the distance. Night birds sang in the nearby forest, their songs quiet this far away. Aili smiled and closed her eyes. This was much better. This was home. Not home like her parents' manor, but home like the forest.

"Thank you, so much." She smiled.

Andvari reached for the mage-light lamp. "You're welcome. Now, get some sleep."

Her eyes closed and Aili settled within moments this time.

***

"Get your breakfast and meet me at the table. I have someone I need to talk to for a minute." Andvari headed for the table they usually sat at.

Aili picked up a plate and selected her breakfast. The cinnamon in the oatmeal smelled delicious, and she took a bowl. A dish of fresh berries joined the oatmeal on her tray. A bowl of steaming breakfast soup rounded out her meal.

"Shouldn't you be a full mage by now?"

Aili sighed. Her again. "You don't know anything about me." Her fingers gripped her tray and Aili clenched her jaw. Slow breaths, now. I can keep calm.

This kid was maybe twelve or so, no older for sure. She has no social skills. I can be polite. She'll outgrow this stage.

"Just how slow a learner are you? One of my friends became a full mage at sixteen. You must be younger than you look. Or maybe you're just not smart?"

Aili kept her back to the girl. She selected a couple pieces of toast and headed for the table. At least there no one would bother her. Being a student was supposed to make my life better. Not much has changed, though. Not really. I'm still being looked down on and underestimated.

She set her tray down and lowered to the bench beside Andvari. He was deep in conversation with a guard, so Aili focused on her food. At least she could eat here in peace. People actually welcomed her presence here.

Aili glanced at the girl. She sat with the other students again. They wore clothing not too different from Aili's, plain pants and a shirt instead of robes, and sturdy boots. Boots with laces, Aili realized. Leather. She knew how to work with leather. How would distance affect her abilities?

Andvari squeezed her shoulder gently. "I'll be right back."

She looked up and met his gaze. Aili smiled and nodded. He raised an eyebrow at her, before heading for the food table.

Aili turned back to the girl. Slow and steady breathing. That's it. Feel the leather. The leather laces were pliable, soft, and slightly warm. Loosen, she thought, as she felt deep inside the leather. That's it. Let go and relax. Now, up and together, around and through, slow and steady. A little tug, and that knot is snug.

"Not hungry?" Andvari set his tray on the table and sat beside her.

"Just lost in thought." Aili dumped the bowl of berries into her oatmeal and picked up her spoon. She dug into the oatmeal, cool enough to eat now.

The cinnamon mixed with the berries in each bite. How many times had she made oatmeal while camping? It cooked quickly over a fire. She could almost smell the smoke and hear Leya grazing nearby.

"Silla, let's go." A guard stood in the doorway, focused on the girl.

"Yes, Sir."

She gathered her dishes and picked up her tray. Silla slid from the end of the bench and went to step. Her bootlaces stopped her short. The girl tumbled to the floor; hands outstretched. The plate rolled away and hit the wall, landing with a clatter. The students laughed. Two helped her up. Silla's little face turned bright red.

Andvari set a hand on her shoulder and leaned close. "I don't know if I should punish you or be impressed," he whispered. "That was excellent control, but you could have really hurt her."

Aili shook her head, her expression as blank as she could manage. "I softened the floorboards as she fell. She may be annoying and immature, but I'm not heartless."

He snorted and hid a smile behind his hand. "So, that's what the second magic was. We'll talk about powers and wise energy uses soon. Once I eat, we go."

***

The noise of the camp faded behind them. The sound of muffled hoofbeats in the grass made Aili smile. "You ride well. Do you ride a lot?"

Andvari guided Charger north. "All Scouts can ride. Most only ride enough at camps to keep their skills up, though. I take Charger between the various camps regularly. We have other ways of travelling quickly. I'm sure you'll see them soon."

He eased Charger into a lazy canter. Leya sped up and cantered beside the bigger horse, her little legs going almost twice as fast.

Aili smiled, her gaze ahead at the forest. "Are we going back to the falls?"

He glanced over. "We are. That's observant. Are you sure you don't want to be a Scout one day?"

She clutched Leya's mane as she laughed. "I have trouble following orders, remember?"

Andvari shrugged. "If someone is highly skilled in other areas, like you're becoming, we'll spend more time and effort to help them adapt. It's not like the regular Guards and Defence Forces, where you work in large groups. We work in pairs a lot, and value people who can solve problems and handle the relative isolation. Just something to consider."

Pairs, like he and Kyson? They do seem incredibly comfortable with each other. "How long have you two been a team?"

"Me and Charger?"

Aili snickered, turning her head into her shoulder. "No, you and Kyson. You are partners, right?"

He laughed. "Yes, Kyson's my partner. We started working together in Scout training. We did so well together that we became a team when my apprenticeship ended. That was many years ago now." Andvari shook his head.

They slowed to a walk and let the horses relax. Andvari ducked under branches well over Aili's head. Leya headed for the lush grass at the edge of the pond, carrying Aili with her. She pulled Aili forward as she dropped her head and tore the grass out by the roots.

"Hey, greedy." Aili let go of Leya's mane and stroked her neck. "You'd think we never fed you, seeing you gorge yourself like this." Aili slid from Leya's back and stretched.

Andvari dismounted Charger and removed his saddle. He turned the big horse loose to graze. "She sure is dedicated to you."

Aili grinned at her pony. "Mutual attraction. She's my best friend."

"Come. Show me what you did. We may find new ways for you to work with whatever is around you." Andvari walked to the dry grass, back from the edge of the pond.

She wandered to the grass beside him and sat. Aili closed her eyes and opened herself to the land, feeling for the water. It was so familiar now, ever she sensed it that first time. She clenched her jaw. The water had so much power, it threatened to wash over her and drown her.

Aili opened her eyes and focused on the rock. Now, coax and guide, nudge and plead. There we go, a little at a time.

Aili could see more of the rock with each moment, as the water flowed to either side of it. She wiped her brow. At least it was easier than last time. At least she didn't need a nap right away. She let the water go and it crashed over the rock, flowing down into the pool below.

Andvari crossed his arms over his chest and stared at the waterfall. "I'm impressed you moved the water that much. There's so much magic in this part of the woods, especially the water in this pool, that most people don't even try. We can use magic around it if we focus, but it's harder than normal."

She ran her fingers through the grass as she watched the water cascade down the cliff. She could do something they couldn't. She was finally special for a reason besides her lack of magic.

"What does it feel like to work with the water?" Andvari leaned back against his hands.

She opened her mouth and paused. Actually, she'd never thought about it too deeply, she just did it. "I don't really have anything to compare it to. I can't talk to it like plants and animals, but I can, in a few ways. I can guide it, but that's about it. It wants to flow, and I can alter where it goes."

"I've seen you doing the first three barehand fighting forms. When doing those, you allow your energy to flow like the water, right?" He smiled at her.

He'd seen her? Right, when they first camped together. He wasn't spying on her in camp. Aili rolled her shoulders and loosened the muscles. "You think I should use the focus to try and move the water that way? Like my energy?"

"I have no idea, but it's similar in theory, right? Both want to flow. See if you can connect your intent and thoughts to the water. I'm here to help if something goes wrong." Andvari brushed the dirt from his hands and sat straight. "Start small, maybe the water in the pool instead. Try whatever feels right, or like something you can do."

Aili eased to her feet, her gaze on the rippling water in the pool. The forms were calming and meditative, and she wouldn't have to think about them. Okay, she could do this. Aili stood quietly, her hands by her sides. Now, slow and graceful, like a peaceful trickling brook.

She raised her hands, cupped like she was swimming. Aili circled her hands and moved them around her, slowly building and gathering the energy she wanted. In her mind, she touched the water and guided it with each gesture and movement. No force, just flow. Follow my path.

Her hand spiralled, pulling the water along in her mind. She raised her hands in an arc, sending the water up and over before letting it flow back into the pool. Through the pool and up, Aili thought, as she rose onto one leg with both hands in the air. She lowered the water again, using her own motions as a guide, and touched the flowing water to the start. There, a closed current of moving water, like art in her mind.

Aili opened her eyes. "Oh, my."

The water sparkled in the sunlight, shimmering and deflecting the reflected light around her. She walked under part of the water stream, flowing along the path she set. It meandered through the clearing, rising and falling, hovering in the air. The area was dazzling with the reflected light bending and scattering, landing on everything around her.

Andvari stood and stepped beside her. He reached up and touched the water over them. The water parted around his fingers and flowed on, following the path she set. He lowered his hand, and his fingers were dry. "How did you know to do that?"

"It just felt right, I guess. I followed the form."

He stepped around where the water flowed closer to the ground and peered inside the flow. His expression was distorted by the moving water, making him blurry behind it. "Are you using any energy to maintain this?"

Aili shook her head. "No, when I closed the loop, it just kept going. If I hadn't closed it, I think the water would have flowed along the path once and back into the pool. How do I know that, though?"

Leya snorted, lifting her head from the sweet grass.

Aili met her pony's gaze. "Because I feel nature like you do?"

Leya snorted and lowered her head. She tore more grass and chewed, her eyes still on Aili.

Andvari muffled his laugh with his sleeve. "Well, horses are part of nature, so it makes sense they can feel the magic in it. She might even understand it better than we do, or be able to express it better, anyway."

He walked around the water, following it back to the pond. "My student is talking to ponies, and doing things with magic I've never seen," Andvari whispered.

Aili splashed some water at him, flicking it from the column she made. "Is that a problem?"

Andvari wiped the water from his cheek with his fingers. "No, but they don't prepare you for this when you reach Master Mage. They teach you about spells and normal students. You're doing magic most students might only dream of, and that's if they have an exceptional imagination."

"You learn how to teach?" Aili walked under the water and joined him at the edge of the pond.

"Of course. How else can we turn out so many exceptional mages each generation. Actually, how much do you know about the levels of magic, and what students need to know for each stage?"

Aili dropped to her knees and dipped her fingers in the pond. "I've seen the exam guides, but that's it. Normally the teacher shares that, right?"

"True." Andvari kneeled beside her. "Your education won't look like that, and I'm not sure you even have levels, beyond Student, Mage, and Master Mage. You won't have exams, since you don't use spells. However," he reached out and touched her neck band, tracing the silver strands. "Your band is responding to your progress, so I guess I still know how you're doing, and what we need to work on."

"How will you figure out what to teach, if I'm not following the normal path?" Aili flopped back on the grass and stared up into the water, still flowing past over her head.

"I'm making it up as I go." He laughed and lay beside her, staring up at the water with her.

Aili narrowed her eyes at him, though she couldn't hide her smile.

"No, your band is helping. It's showing how you're progressing, right, so I know what areas you're still weaker in. Your last two crystals don't have colour in them, and we haven't started Air or Fire Magic, have we?"

Aili flinched. Her heart raced and she gripped the grass. No, not Fire Magic. Anything else, please. Bad things happen to careless Fire Mages. The smell of smoke filled her memory. She opened her eyes to escape the glowing flames.

The water sparkled above her, blue and calm and not on fire.

"Now, how would you stop this, and get the water back in the pond?" His fingers closed gently over hers and gave her hand a light squeeze.

Aili took a slow breath. No flames. She was fine. "I could cut it at any point, and the water would flow back in both directions. How do I know that?"

Leya's snort echoed off the rocks in the clearing, magnified by the cliff wall.

She glared at Leya. "That's enough from the cheeky pony. I get it, okay?"

Andvari muffled his laugh in his elbow, his shoulders shaking. He straightened up, a wide smile still on his face. "So, theoretically, you could take water from a water source and create a magical path to a new location, and it would keep following that path?"

Aili stared up at the water high on the cliff face. "As long as I can focus on the path the first time, and there's enough water at the source to maintain it, I think so?"

"Oh, the Civic Mages would love you for aqueduct development."

Aili shoved his shoulder. "Not an office job."

He resisted her push and stared out at the pond. "You stay with me until your magical education is complete. After that, you get to pick where you go, based on offers you get and recommendations I give."

She crossed her arms over her chest. "No office jobs. I mean it. If I get stuck in some stuffy tower somewhere, the next time you're somewhere incredibly public, I'm unweaving the fibres in your clothing. You'll be standing in your underwear in front of everyone."

He raised an eyebrow at her, still grinning. "Threatening your teacher, are we?"

"Consider it a prediction. Maybe friendly advice, if you prefer that term."

"How about you undo this, and we go back, before you get yourself into trouble?"

Aili waved her hand, her wrist rotating, and focused on snipping the magical path under the water. "I can do that."

The water flowed down and into the pond. It was so tempting to dump it on him, but he really had been good to her. Jokes could go too far. The water flowed one last time along the path, the end just a trail of water droplets, until it disappeared into the pool.

Except for the shocking amount of shorter grass, there was now no sign anyone had ever been here and played with magic. Aili touched the grass with her abilities and strengthened it while Andvari saddled Charger. Now it might even regrow fully before Leya comes back and decimates it again.

***

She reclined on his bed, belly full of lunch, and book propped up on her bent knees. The breeze flowed through the window, a lazy and calm wind carrying smells of horse and grass. Leya and Charger were in the paddocks, eating the lunch Jordi gave them. Andvari sat at his desk, his back to her, working on the endless stack of paperwork.

The mirror over his desk went cloudy, the reflection of the room gone. The frame glowed. Aili looked over as Andvari stood and tapped the bottom of the frame. A man in a Scout uniform appeared on the surface, in front of a forest background. She'd seen this man. He lived here in camp.

"Report."

The man saluted. "They're pushing closer slowly. There's some kind of camp forming just beyond the magical protection on their side of the border."

"Weapons?" Andvari ran his hand through his hair.

"None are visible, Sir. They have trunks and crates that could contain some. Orders?" The man stood at attention, waiting.

Andvari frowned and Aili's stomach did backflips. He seldom frowned. He rubbed his chin. "How strong is your magic?"

"Maybe four fifths of normal. I know it's weaker, but not enough to be a problem yet."

"Wait until it's safe, nightfall if needed. See what's in the crates. You have the All-Seeing Spell?"

"Yes, Sir. It still works if I'm close."

Andvari paced in front of his mirror. "Don't take chances. Find out what you can and get back right away."

"Yes, Sir." The man saluted again.

Andvari tapped the mirror frame and the room reflection appeared. He stood there, staring blankly at the wall. Aili fidgeted. Was something going on? What had this easy-going man so concerned?

He glanced over at her. "How's the reading going?"

Aili glanced down at her book. "Good. How do the mirrors work? I've never read about them before."

He sat on the end of the bed. "A special workshop makes them to order for the groups that need them. This one lets me contact any Scout or camp across the country. When my personal mirror is close, in the room, it sends the signal to the big mirror instead."

Aili stared at the shiny metal frame. "The one downstairs contacted the capital."

"Yes, that one is even more powerful, and can communicate with any other mirror, as long as it makes the contact first. Any Defence Force mirror can call it directly, no matter where the user is. The Council can call in, too."

The mirror turned cloudy, and the frame glowed. The words Western Woods floated on the surface.

Andvari sighed. "Back to work." He stood and walked to the desk again.

Aili turned back to her book, half an ear on the conversations, but it was all Scout administration. Boring. Aili focused on her reading again, glancing up occasionally to see him doing paperwork. Every now and then he'd fold a paper into a glider and toss it in the air. The gliders would speed out the window and into the camp somewhere. Other papers got placed in a basket with the label 'Out.'

She closed her book and leaned her head back against the headboard. His chair shifted against the floor, and it sounded like he stood. Aili opened her eyes and saw multiple people on the mirror, each in their own little space. She raised her eyebrow, peering over from her spot out of view of them all. Everyone was older, and not all were Scouts. Some wore robes of high stations in the governments.

"We're monitoring the situation. I'll know more soon. I have people out in the field now, checking on their activities."

Aili listened closely, staying as still and quiet as she could. Something was going on, big enough to involve people from the Council, and some of them looked worried. She didn't understand everything they talked about, but Aili knew so little of the ways of outsiders. Their world wasn't friendly, her experiences showed that, and this call confirmed it.

Andvari closed the call and turned to her. "Eat a light supper, something easy to digest. We can always snack later if you need."

Aili raised her eyebrow and nodded. He'd explain, he usually did, but maybe he had a lot on his mind. Her father would do this when accidents happened at the University and staying out of his way always helped him focus. Maybe it would help Andvari, too?

He was quiet through supper, talking in hushed voices to the Border Guards when he spoke at all. Aili sat quietly beside him and ate, looking after herself. They returned to their rooms as soon as they were done eating.

CHAPTER 8

MAGIC SWORDS AND MORE LESSONS

Aili reached for her book on her night table.

"Instead of reading tonight, you're going to join us for Drill."

She looked up at him, her hand hovering over her book. "Us?"

Andvari smiled, finally looking more like his usual self. "Wasn't it easier to move the water using a moving meditation than when you sat still?"

Aili nodded. "Yes?"

"You might find Wind Magic easier with movement, too. Since I know you know the first three bare hand forms, and some of the sword forms, you'll join us for the ones you know. When we work with the broadsword, you can do a sitting meditation instead, or bring a book to read, but you'll join us each night for Drill now."

He picked up a long and thin box that was leaning against the wall near the door. Andvari carried it to her bed and set it on the mattress. "Open it." He smiled at her.

Aili ran her hand over the smooth, lacquered wood. She slid her fingers to the silver latches and pulled until they released. The corners of the box were round and smooth, with no sharp edges anywhere. The hinges moved without a sound as the lid opened.

Light reflected up at her. Aili stared down at the thin sword, just like the wooden one she practiced with back home, but made from metal. She could see the sharpness of the blade, metal glinting in the light. The sword was small enough for her, with a wooden hilt and a metal guard to protect her hand.

"It's lovely," Aili whispered.

"Pick it up. Let it bond to you." Andvari sat on the end of the bed.

"Bond to me?"

"We don't tell people until they get their first official sword, but they bond to the user. It'll have a limited ability to come back to you, so if you drop it during a battle or get disarmed, you can call it back to your hand. If someone tries to use the sword against you, the blade will become like a mist and pass harmlessly through you."

She stared at him, wide-eyed. "That story was true? The one about the Scout who ran himself through with the sword and stabbed the enemy behind him, saving the woman? They said he was fine, not a scratch on him."

Andvari nodded. "I was there. I was too far away to help and dealing with my own adversary. He knew the blade would protect him. That's another thing, though. The blade is strongest when you're defending or protecting others. If you try to use it in anger or to harm someone for no reason, the blade might dissolve into dust."

Aili examined the blade, the metallic pattern almost shimmering in the mage-light. She'd seen blades like this in museums, but never had one she could touch before. Darik always used a plain metal blade, but he had a box just like this.

"Well, start the bonding process." He nodded at the sword. "Pick it up. Touch the blade with your bare hands. It won't cut you, but it needs to know you. Hold the hilt, too."

Her hands shook as she reached for the sword. She wrapped her fingers around the hilt and lifted the sword from the box. Aili cradled the blade in her hand and held it up. It was so light, lighter than she expected. Her eye stared back at her in the shining metal.

Warmth flooded through her body and electricity danced over her skin. Were those sparks bursting in the surrounding air? They exploded in tiny balls of coloured light, dissolving in moments. The blade warmed against her skin and the handle felt like it belonged in her hand. Aili smiled.

"Thank you. Why, though?" She met his gaze.

"I've seen you do form three, sneaking Jordi's sword without asking first. You do it well. I also know you can already channel your abilities through the bare hand forms. When a Scout masters form three, they're given their sword. Here it is."

Aili blinked at him. "I'm not a Scout."

"That's true." He raised an eyebrow. "You'll be able to channel your abilities through your sword. This is one more tool you can use to learn and practice with magic. These swords can even store magic for you."

She smiled at the sword; her grin reflected in the metal. "Is that how fire blades work?"

Andvari nodded. "A mage can store Fire Magic in the blade and unleash it when they need a boost in power. The blade fuels the flames and can do more damage, or be a light source, and so on."

"Does it work with the other magics? Earth Magic, or Wind, or whatever?" She ran her fingers along the blade.

The blade glowed with a soft white light where she touched it.

He shrugged. "It'll be fun finding out, won't it? There's a lot about you and magic that is—experimental." Andvari grinned at her.

She narrowed her eyes at him but couldn't stop the smile. Her own sword?

"You'll start with Drill with us. Get a feel for the blade and spend time with it. Use magic while carrying it. It'll feel different from that old wooden practice sword. Jordi doesn't know, does he?"

Aili's cheeks burned. She shook her head. "No. You knew?"

Andvari shrugged. "I'm your teacher. It's my responsibility to know."

She set her hand on her hip and raised an eyebrow. "How?"

He grinned. "I'm allowed to keep secrets from you."

Aili stuck her tongue out and scrunched her face at him. "You're not watching me bathe or anything, are you?"

He raised his hands. "No. I'm a Scout. It's my skill set to move quietly and observe without being seen. I checked on you occasionally while you were having free time in camp. Other than borrowing the sword, you've been fine, so I left you to do your thing. Now, we need to get out there, or we'll be late. I'm leading Drill tonight, and what kind of example would I be setting?"

Aili laughed. "True. Such a horrible leader."

He laughed and shook his head. Andvari took the smooth leather sword belt from the box and fastened the scabbard to it. "Back or hip?"

"Back."

Andvari slipped the belt around her shoulders and fastened it in place. He stepped back and nodded. "Sheathe your sword and draw it again."

Aili reached up slowly. This sword was just a smidge longer than the practice weapon she used to have, and she didn't want to stab herself the first time. The sword slid into the scabbard with a soft metallic hiss. She pulled it out, getting a feel for the positioning.

"Well done. Most people use the hip, because it's easier to draw."

She shifted the sword in her grip. "Darik started teaching me when I was as tall as a sword is long. I couldn't use my hip, not even with the little practice sword he made. I tripped and dragged it. He showed me this instead." Aili gestured to the sword belt around her shoulders.

"That sounds like him. Ready?" Andvari tilted his head towards the door.

Aili nodded. He grabbed his own sword from the wall hook and fastened the belt around his hips. She followed him from the room, down the stairs, and outside. She'd heard Drill before, while reading with the window open, but never seen it.

Everyone was gathering in the open area in front of the main hall, stretching, or standing in small groups and talking about and showing movements from the forms. Aili hesitated. Everyone here was older and knew what they were doing. Would she fit in okay?

"Kyson and I are leading tonight. I know you know the forms, so follow as best as you can. If you get tired, take a rest, but do as much as you can." Andvari stopped at the edge of the grassy area. "You can work just over here in your own space if you prefer or join the group." He pointed to a spot nearby.

Aili darted over to the spot he pointed, near the others, but not among them. At least she had her own space and could focus on what she was doing. Everyone started lining up, gathering and looking so organized. She twisted her fingers together. No, pretend it's just like the old days, Darik calling moves, and me following along. I got this.

Kyson and another Scout walked over to the group, the Scout joining the others in the lines as Kyson stood near Andvari, facing the group. Andvari called out the warmup, and Aili followed along. She smiled. Darik taught her these. She stretched and folded, moved and followed. Her muscles felt warm, and she was just a little out of breath when he called to stop.

"Alright, bare hand one."

The Scouts all stood still with their hands at their sides. Aili settled herself into position, waiting. She knew the commands. She could do this. He called out the familiar commands and Aili moved, reacting without thinking. She flowed through the form, keeping up with the group.

Everyone moved into the last position and Andvari nodded to her. "Full speed." His voice carried through the still night air.

Full speed? Uh oh. How fast would this be? Andvari called the commands, and everyone started moving, more than twice as fast as the first time. Her heart raced. No, calm and controlled. Aili slowed down a hair, letting the others go ahead, and kept up as quickly as she could. Form before speed. Speed will come, his voice echoed in her head.

She settled and smiled. Only a few seconds behind, and she kept her form. Aili opened her eyes and Andvari smiled at her.

"Bare hand two."

Aili took a slow breath and calmed her heart. Bare hand two was all about balance and was slower than form one. She could do this. Aili let her mind relax and flowed through the form. The cool air felt good against her hands and face. She relaxed and let her senses out as she moved.

She followed through form three, keeping up, and rested during the fourth form. Darik mentioned starting it soon, but she left. Would Andvari teach her? It was more advanced. Did he think she was ready? Aili watched every move, examining them all to guess how they worked in combat.

"Water break, then sword." Kyson waved a hand, and everyone dispersed, moving to grab canteens from the edge of the practice space.

Andvari handed Aili a canteen. "You're doing great. What's it like, practicing with the sword on your back?"

Aili took a long sip of water. "It's new. I only ever had it on for sword practice, so my skin isn't used to it."

"I have a salve for that. I'm pleased with how you're doing. If you fall behind, do as you did, and focus on yourself. They've been doing this for years, and you're new. Just finish strong. Are you tired?"

"A few muscles are, but I'm okay." Aili stretched down to touch her toes, moving slowly and focusing on her leg muscles.

"We'll be doing the same thing with the sword forms. Once we've gone as far as you know, rest." Andvari took the canteen and downed the water.

He handed it back and Aili had a few more long sips, the cool water feeling good on her parched throat. The sun dropped in the sky, turning the camp a golden red. The air cooled. Aili paced slowly to keep warm.

"Gather up." Kyson moved back to the front of the group.

Aili shifted from foot to foot. She grinned. Aili settled and waited for the command to start. She flowed through the forms, her blade reflecting the light from the setting sun. She matched their movements perfectly. Even at full speed, Aili kept up.

The sword was light. It moved like an extension of her arm. Her energy flowed through the blade with an ease the wooden swords couldn't give her. Aili smiled as the sword flitted around, responding to the slightest flick of her wrist.

"Form four." Andvari looked over at the group.

Aili left her sword sheathed and slowly paced, stretching her muscles and moving her arms. She watched every move they made. To think she could have ended up somewhere where she wasn't able to practice anymore. No, here she was with her own sword, practicing with a group of people.

Form four was for sword masters, yet everyone here but her seemed to know it. They moved as one, from the smallest Scout to the largest, though most Scouts were bigger to begin with. Everyone here but her was a highly skilled fighter, fast and agile. Would she be like that one day?

"Great work, everyone." Andvari wiped his brow with his sleeve. "Dismissed."

The group broke up and everyone relaxed, talking and laughing. There was no sign of the discipline Aili watched just moments ago. She smiled. These were the friendly people she ate with, nodded to in camp, and was getting to know. Not that scary group of fighters she saw moments ago. No wonder everyone was so confident.

Andvari passed her the canteen, heavy and full of water. She took another drink and handed it back.

"Did this refill while we were working?" Aili peered into the canteen.

"The blue ones do. We take green ones when we patrol near the border, in case we lose one and someone without magic finds it. For camp and work in Athia here, we like the ones that refill on their own." He smiled as she handed him the canteen.

Aili stared at the canteen. "Lazy. Smart, but Lazy."

He laughed. Andvari slung his arm around her shoulders, avoiding her sword. "Let's go. Time to clean up."

Aili held her nose and waved the air away. "Yeah, you could use a cleaning charm, for sure. You smell worse than the muck pile."

Andvari chuckled. "You're no flower patch either, stinky kid."

He walked with her back to their rooms. Aili unfastened her sword belt and eased it from her shoulders. Her muscles protested the intense exercise with aches and tension. Her skin burned over her shoulder.

Andvari hung his own sword on the hook. "Wash up and I'll treat any rub marks. Put on night pants and the robe, and it'll make this easier."

Aili hung her belt over the new hook by her bed. She grabbed her night clothes from the trunk and headed for the bathroom. The warm air soothed her muscles. Aili carefully peeled her shirt off, being gentle with the rubbed skin. She dumped her sweaty clothing in the basket.

She turned and looked over her shoulder at the mirror. Red marks showed where the belt hung over her shoulders. She could make a salve for that in minutes and had one in her kit. She'd even used it on ponies who hadn't exercised in a while, to prevent them getting sores under a saddle.

The water warmed her chilly hands. She plunged her hands deep into the basin. The water warmed up more, responding to her wish. She'd need to build up callouses for sword work.

The cotton night pants were soft against her skin. Aili pulled the robe over her shoulders and tied the belt. She held the front closed and stepped from the bathroom. Andvari stood at the desk with a tin of salve in his hand.

"Sit there and let the robe loosen so I can check your back." He pointed at the end of his bed.

Aili lowered to the mattress. She adjusted her robe and held the front closed, wiggling it from her shoulders. The skin ached as the cloth slid over it. She pressed her lips together.

His cool fingers touched the skin around the rub marks, shifting her robe down her back. "Stay still. This will help." Andvari uncapped the salve.

Aili inhaled the herbs. "Ilia's salve. I know that recipe."

"Of course." The salve cooled her skin as he rubbed it on the damaged areas. "Nobody does potions and medicines better in all the land. You think Scouts settle for second best?"

Alii giggled. "I guess not."

"There." He pulled the robe back up over her shoulders. "All taken care of. Let me know if it gets worse, or you have sore muscles in the morning. That reminds me—"

He placed his hand on her back, his fingers between her shoulder blades. His hand warmed up. Soothing magic eased her aches as he chanted softly, a spell Ilia had used many times on people. Her shoulders loosened, and the tension disappeared.

"Better?"

Aili grinned and looked back over her shoulder at him. "Better."

"Great. Get some sleep."

***

Sunlight hit her eyelids. Aili raised an arm over her face, and the discomfort eased. She smiled and rolled to face the window, and slowly uncovered her eyes. If the sun was up, it was time to get up. At least she got to sleep with the curtains open.

He was up and dressed, working at the desk. Aili marvelled at how quietly he moved, not disturbing her sleep in the slightest. A plate with breakfast waited on the corner of his desk. Aili lifted her nose and sniffed the fresh bread.

"Have something to eat. We'll be doing lessons this morning. I have important meetings this afternoon, so study, practice your sword work, and help Jordi while I'm busy." He turned in his chair and looked over at her. "How do the muscles feel? Are you sore at all?"

Aili sat up and rolled her shoulders. "What you did last night helped. I'm not sore at all. Thank you."

"You're welcome." He turned and pulled another piece of parchment in front of him.

The salve soothed and healed her skin, but that spell to soothe muscles was incredible. Could she learn to do that? Aili didn't have a single sore spot or twinge. She bundled her clothing in her arms and headed for the bathroom. Once she washed and changed, she took the plate and ate quietly by the window.

"What are we doing today?" Aili set the plate back on his desk.

"There's a collection of farms in the hills north of here. They need an Earth Mage to help with something big, so I'm sending one of my best Scouts. We're going to help her." His quill made a scratching noise against the parchment as he scribbled orders and notes.

"Should I tack up the horses?"

Andvari straightened his papers and set his quill down. He smiled. "Leya gets the morning off today. We're going to use something faster."

"Faster?" Aili tensed and her fingers twitched.

What could be faster? In the capital, horses were the fastest way to get around. Massive trolley wagons rumbled through some streets, but most people walked everywhere. People lived close to where they worked, and every community had small shops. There were smaller wagons people could hire. Maybe that's what he meant? They provided comfort, not speed, though. Aili wrinkled her brow.

He shifted from his chair and headed for the door. "Let's go."

Aili followed him down the stairs. The building was quiet, only a few people were up and ready for the day yet. It seemed so deserted after how busy last night felt. Aili stayed close and followed him out the main door.

A woman waited outside, sitting on the edge of a large—something. It was a long box, but not a box. The sides sloped in a little, and the front was rounded and almost pointy.

"Sleep in?" The woman ran a hand through her black hair. Her skin was almost the same colour as the rich dark wood, and she smiled freely. "It's not like you to be late."

Andvari grinned and shrugged. "I'm ready now. Aili, this is Dinna. We're helping her today."

Aili smiled. "Hi."

Dinna straightened up and leapt into the box. "It's good to meet you. Let's go."

"You just want to get airborne." Andvari walked right to the box, no hesitation.

"Wait, fly?" Aili's mouth went dry. Her legs shook. She stuffed her shaking hands in her pockets.

"It's fun. Climb in and hang on." Andvari gestured at the space behind Dinna's control seat.

Aili forced her legs to carry her to the box. She gripped the edge and looked inside. It was a few feet wide and as long as Andvari was tall. The sides came just above her knees. Her legs didn't want to bend, didn't want to lift over the edge.

"You're fine." Andvari placed a hand on her shoulder and gave it a squeeze.

He bent down and scooped Aili up in his arms. She squeaked and clung to him as he lowered her in the box. Aili curled up and huddled behind Dinna, staring around with wide eyes.

Andvari eased into the box behind her, folding his long legs and crossing them. "She's our best flyer. Hold on here, though." He pointed to a set of railings, one on either side of her, down near the floor.

Aili gripped the smooth, oiled wooden rails. The box rose into the air. Her fingers ached. She looked up to see the buildings disappear below her. The box sped off over the fields faster than any horse she'd ever ridden. The wind whipped at her hair and braids. She huddled lower in the box.

She peeked over the edge. Fields gave way to forests, the treetops far below her. Her fingers went numb. Camp faded behind her, disappearing among the hills. The sun sparkled off the water at the falls, the top visible from above like this. Camp was back there, and the falls were there, she recalled, pulling the image of the map up in her mind. She hadn't looked this far from camp, though.

Aili straightened up and loosened her grip as she watched the river flowing beneath her. It headed for the falls and stretched north, before turning northwest across the open farmland. It crossed the fields like a winding serpent. Ahead, many irrigation channels fed the farmland, carrying water to the local farms.

The area was all rolling hills, with stands of trees between the fields. Herds of deer darted in and out of sight as they moved from the forest to the small tree stands scattered about the fields. The box dropped slowly down, and Aili could make out farmers in the fields. Most walked beside planting wagons, self powered with magic, with their large bins that held the seeds the wooden roller planted in the ground.

Dinna sped towards a cluster of farm buildings. The box dropped lower the closer they got. It touched down lightly, gliding to a gentle stop beside the houses on a packed dirt road.

Andvari stepped from the box. He held his hand out to Aili. She placed her trembling hand in his. Would her legs support her? Aili gripped the edge of the box with her other hand and heaved herself up. Oh, solid ground, how marvellous you are. She stepped from the box, clinging to him for stability.

Andvari slung his arm around her. He guided her along behind Dinna. A solid-looking farmer stood by a yard gate. The farmer waved at the small group.

"That's probably the head of the farming cluster," Andvari whispered to her.

"Greetings, Mervin. Same hill?" Dinna waved to him.

"The same." He pointed north to the large hill over the settlement.

It looked more like a small mountain to Aili. It was rocky and barren, not covered in trees like the other smaller hills around here. Aili glanced up at Andvari. The hill seemed different somehow. It made her heart race and her palms sweat, though Aili couldn't tell why.

"What are you sensing?" Andvari met her gaze.

Dinna turned and watched Aili.

Aili closed her eyes and focused on the hill. What was she even looking for? "It feels hollow inside. It's like it could collapse at any moment, where it hasn't already."

Dinna walked over and kneeled in front of Aili. "You can feel that?" She glanced up at Andvari, her eyebrow raised.

"I'm still learning what she can do. That's why we came. You're our top expert in geo-stability and reinforcing magic." Andvari shrugged.

"Come, then. We'll get closer." Dinna stood and headed for the box.

Aili walked back to the box with him on shaking legs. She survived her first flight, so maybe it wasn't so bad? The view was incredible, even she had to admit. Aili managed to climb in on her own this time.

Dinna guided the box into the air and over the settlement, towards the base of the hill. She touched down on the small rise at the bottom, in the long grass. Aili threw herself over the edge and back to solid ground.

Andvari kneeled in front of Aili. "Are you okay?" He took her hand.

Aili nodded. "I can't feel the energy of the planet the same way when we fly. It's disorienting."

"Take a moment and reconnect with the soil. We won't begin until you're ready." He squeezed her hand lightly.

Aili closed her eyes and took slow, deep, meditative breaths. The energy from the soil flowed up into her, reconnecting her with the land she loved. Within a minute, Aili felt normal again. She opened her eyes and nodded. Andvari handed her a canteen and Aili took a long drink.

"Okay, I'm ready."

"Keep your focus on the hill. I can create a link between you and Dinna, so she can feel the land through your senses. It'll make her task easier."

Aili stood and faced the hill. It towered over her.

"Can you still feel the emptiness?" Andvari placed his fingers on her temple.

She felt him join her in her mind, let him touch her senses as she opened herself to the hill. "It's easy, this close to it."

Another presence joined her, distant and not right in her mind like he was. She could feel where Dinna's focus was, even sense her active thoughts, but she wasn't as close as Andvari was to her senses.

'This is weird.'

'Focus,' Andvari's voice sounded in her mind. 'You need to focus for her to see with your magic.'

'Can we start at the base? We'll work our way up.' Dinna's presence in her senses almost echoed.

Aili turned her attention to the hillside, down at the bottom. Tunnels crossed inside it, weaving around above and below each other. Some were already sagging; others had partially collapsed. One section was a landslide waiting to happen, the rocks loose and ready to tumble down on the settlement below.

'That's great. Focus on those places, and I'll strengthen them.' Dinna's power flared in Aili's senses, a bright flash among the rocks.

She probed the hillside for the weak places first, starting down and working her way up. All Aili had to do was look, and Dinna cast spells anywhere she felt would need it. Aili watched with her senses, exploring the spells while trying to focus on the hill. Her focus wavered about halfway up the hill.

'Time for a break.' Andvari moved his fingers and Aili was alone in her head again.

Aili took a deep breath and sank to the ground. She closed her eyes and lay back in the grass. She just had other people in her head. They couldn't see her private thoughts, could they? Aili pressed her lips together. She focused on the hill, so that's all they saw, right?

"Have a drink and stop worrying." Andvari sat beside her and held the canteen out to her. "We only detect active thoughts. We're not diving into your mind and invading your privacy."

Aili pressed herself up to sit and narrowed her eyes at him. "With you reading my thoughts just now, how can I be sure?" She took the canteen and drained it. It grew heavy in her hand as water flowed back in, refilling the canteen for her.

Andvari laughed. "Most people freak out about that the first time they encounter the linking spells. It's not mind reading, what I just did, it's knowing people."

She pressed a cool hand against her burning cheeks. Andvari dropped a tablet in the canteen and the smell of fresh herbs wafted up to Aili.

She took another drink and felt energy rush through her. "What are the spells you're using?"

Dinna sat on Aili's other side. "I'm using spells to reinforce the tunnel walls. I've been using all purpose spells, since I couldn't see into the rock as you can. Now I can actually heat and fuse the rock properly, with you helping me feel the rock directly like that. This fix will last years, instead of a few seasons. Maybe next time we can work together and fix it for good."

"We'll practice moving rock somewhere safer. An unstable hill over a settlement is not the ideal spot for your first attempt." Andvari gestured to the farmers below, working the fields near the buildings.

Aili smiled. "I appreciate that."

She capped the canteen and downed the energy bar he gave her. They turned to the hill and Andvari reset the link. Aili found the spot they stopped at, and she focused on her task. Dinna followed her senses and strengthened the weak areas Aili found.

'Back here.' Aili guided Dinna to the far side of the hill. She focused hard, as it was at the edge of what she could feel.

'Good catch. I'd have missed that.'

Dinna worked on the spot and Aili waited patiently. Once she was done, Aili went over the hill one more time. It was fascinating, watching the spells Dinna used take shape before her senses. She used heat and pressure to fuse the rock, just like the volcanic rocks Aili read about.

Aili nodded. They got every weak place she could detect. Andvari broke the link, leaving her alone in her head again.

"Thanks." Dinna smiled at Aili. "You sped that up for me. Normally I'd be here most of a day, and you found places I wouldn't have seen."

Andvari wrapped an arm around her and hugged Aili. "She learns fast. Ready to go back?"

Aili held her belly as she stared at the box. Please, snack, stay where you belong.

Dinna took Aili's hand and squeezed lightly. "Not a fan of flying? I love how free I feel. I can go places most people never see."

Aili wrinkled her nose. "You can have it. I like to feel the ground beneath my feet."

"Come on." Andvari steered her to the box. "One last trip back, and you won't have to fly for a while. I don't do it often, either."

She forced her wobbly legs to carry her back to the box. Aili clung to the sides and lowered herself back to the wooden floor. Andvari slipped in behind her, moving with an ease she envied. She rested her head against the side and took slow and deep breaths, her eyes closed so she didn't see the ground speeding away below her.

Within moments, the box touched down again, the familiar sounds of the settlement in the background. Aili opened her eyes and rested her chin on the edge of the box, watching as Dinna talked to the farmer nearby.

Andvari's hand radiated heat against her back. Magic flowed into her, soothing her, and her stomach calmed. "Tell me when you're unwell."

Aili nodded. She blinked back tears at the sharp edge in his normally calm voice. She didn't mean to make him upset with her.

"You're fine. I just can't help you if you don't tell me what you need." His voice was soft and caring again, and Aili relaxed.

Dinna bounced over to the box and leapt inside, settling lightly into the control seat. The box lifted off and sped back to camp. With the sun up overhead now, the land was no longer tinted pink and red, but shone green below her, with dazzlingly blue rivers and ponds. Both were beautiful, Aili decided.

"Let me find a landing site." Dinna slowed and passed over the camp.

People bustled around below them, passing between buildings or working outside. Leya, Charger, and Trickster grazed in a large paddock near the stable. Aili smiled at her pony, chasing the bigger horses from the patch of grass she wanted.

Andvari chuckled. "She sure settled in quickly."

Dinna lowered the box into an empty paddock near the horses.

"If there's food, she'll be friends with anybody. As long as she gets the best stuff, anyway." Aili laughed.

She sighed and smiled when the box rested fully on the grass. A slight bump was all she felt as it landed. Aili leapt over the side and stumbled a few steps away. She regained her balance and stood, hands outstretched, as she connected with the stability of the soil.

Dinna grinned. "I don't think she trusts my flying."

Andvari shook his head, smiling. "It's not personal. She's very much an Earth Mage."

Dinna stepped closer and clasped Aili's hand. "It was a pleasure working with you. I hope we get to work together again in the future."

"That sounds fun. Let me know when and where, and I'll meet you there." Aili grinned.

Dinna threw her head back and laughed. She let go of Aili's hand and returned to the box. With a last wave, she vaulted in and lifted back into the sky.

"Now, lunch, and then it's reading time for you." Andvari gestured at the main hall. "I've got meetings and paperwork, so you can check out the next batch of books I got and finish that one you're almost through already."

They returned to their rooms and washed up before having a quick lunch together in the dining hall. They were a bit early, so the hall was quiet. A few Border Guards and a couple of Scouts were here, all talking in pairs or small groups as they relaxed after the early shifts. A few looked as tired as her, drooping over their trays or sitting half-asleep as they focused on eating.

Aili glanced at the pile of papers on his desk when she returned. Was it getting bigger every time he walked away? She opened the window and grabbed her book. Aili settled on his bed in the gentle breeze. Andvari settled into his desk chair and got to work.

She read steadily, stopping to stretch occasionally. Now and then she'd look up and see who he was talking to in the mirror. The sun crossed the sky overhead, changing the light from the window. Finally, the words seemed to blur together. Aili rubbed her eyes.

"Go for a walk or something, if you like. Your concentration is improving, but we all need breaks now and then." Andvari stared down at his own paperwork. "Go see your hairy little friend. She enjoys your company, and you're happier around her, too."

"Thanks."

Aili closed her book and set it on his desk. She'd start a new one next time. She headed for the paddocks first. The sun warmed her face, and Aili smiled. Leya raised her head and whinnied. Aili met her at the fence. Leya nuzzled Aili's pockets.

Aili scratched Leya's neck. "It's great to see you, too, but I don't have anything."

Leya snorted.

"No, I'm on a break. I didn't sneak out." She rubbed the golden forehead. "Mind if I join you?"

Leya moved beside the fence, her head down as she snacked on the grass. Aili climbed the fence and slid onto Leya's back. She gripped the mane lightly, relaxing as she settled behind Leya's withers. Leya ambled along, snacking as she wandered through the paddock, until she reached a nearly consumed pile of hay.

Aili closed her eyes and took a deep breath in. That smell of horse and freshly cropped grass was the best smell in the world. She turned her face to the sun, her eyes still closed.

Leya's muscles supported her, solid under her. This was home. This was where Aili belonged.

"Is that your pony?"

Aili raised an eyebrow. She knew that voice. Too content to be irritated, Aili glanced over at the girl. What was she even doing here? "Yes, she is."

Silla stared at Leya, her lower lip between her teeth. "It must be nice to have a friend like that."

Aili smiled. Leya was easily her oldest friend, aside from Darik and Ilia. Still, she also knew loneliness, and Silla often looked dreadfully lonely. Aili always had her horses and ponies, so the loneliness never lasted. She had never been as alone as she sometimes felt.

"Don't you have a friend, or someone you can go to with anything?" Aili tilted her head and waited.

Silla shook her head slowly. "I don't know how to have friends. My teacher is helping, but he's not a friend, he's a teacher. No one else really wants to talk to me." She took a slow breath, still staring at Leya. "He says it's because of how judgemental I was when I got here, and first impressions matter."

"Most people start magic training around six or seven. How long have you been here?"

The girl scuffed her toe against the ground. "Two years. I started late."

Aili's heart ached just a little. "Would you like to pet her?"

Silla looked up at Aili, her eyebrows up and her body tense. "Can I?" She bounced on her toes.

She looks so different when she's happy or excited, Aili realized. "Yes, but you need to learn to speak pony. Let me help?"

Silla froze. "What do I do?"

Aili smiled. "Take a slow breath and let your body calm down. Ponies don't like it when you move unexpectedly. It can scare them." She slid from Leya's back and stood beside her pony's shoulder. Aili scratched Leya under her mane.

The girl took a slow breath. Aili waited calmly, watching her go between nearly vibrating with excitement and being calm.

After a few more breaths, Aili nodded. "That's better. Calm like that."

Silla grinned, beaming at Leya.

"Now, walk slowly. Come and stand beside me. You can climb over the fence. Just do it slowly."

She waited patiently as the girl scampered up the fence and landed on the grass in the paddock. Silla stopped and took a breath, calming herself again. She walked with hesitant steps to Aili's side.

"Ponies say hello by sniffing, so hold your hand like this to greet her." Aili held her own hand out, palm down, her fingers relaxed and curved.

"Like this?" Silla thrust her hand out, palm up.

Aili patted Leya. What a good pony, not spooking at her. Was the girl this inattentive during lessons, too? What was teaching her magic like? Andvari's words echoed in her head. Just like ponies, children react to their surroundings.

Leya snorted and blew a breath out at Silla. Silla leapt behind Aili, clutching Aili's shirt as she peered around at the pony.

"Slowly. Leya's a good girl and doesn't scare easily, but other ponies and horses might startle. Try again." Aili held her hand out again. "Palm down like this, so she doesn't think you have food. Stay still while she sniffs you. She won't bite." Probably, Aili added to herself.

Silla crept around Aili. She held her hand out, copying Aili this time. She gripped Aili's shirt as she reached out. Leya turned her head to the girl and sniffed her hand.

Silla giggled. "That tickles." Her voice was almost a whisper.

"She uses those whiskers to find food and explore the world around her."

"Can I—?"

"Can you what?" Aili smiled at her.

"Can I—sit on her?"

Aili rubbed her chin. "I don't know if she'll let you. I'm the only person who ever rides her. We can ask my friend who runs the stables if there's someone you can sit on, though."

Silla beamed up at Aili, her eyes shining with hope. Aili's face ached in sympathy at the wide grin on the girl's face.

"Sure, but I expect you to help around the stable," Jordi called.

Aili turned.

Jordi stood at the paddock gate, halters in his hand. "Can you brush a horse?"

"I can try," Silla whispered. "We don't have horses back home."

Aili nodded at the halters in Jordi's hands. "I'll bring Leya in."

Silla stood frozen, quiet and uncertain. She glanced between Aili and Jordi.

"Sure. I'll bring Charger and Trickster." Jordi stepped through the gate and walked towards the bigger horses, grazing nearby.

"Do you want me to bring someone? Leya will follow me." Aili held her hand out.

He passed her a halter. "Get Charger."

"Can I come?" Silla's fingers twisted around in front of her.

Aili stepped beside Charger and slipped the halter over his head. "Sure, but you have to listen if we tell you to do something, and walk slowly and quietly with us, okay?"

Silla nodded furiously, her head almost a blur. Jordi gave her a sharp look, and she stood quietly.

He smiled widely. "There. That's better. Come here."

Silla stepped beside him.

Jordi lifted her up onto Charger's back. "Hold on to his hair, it's called the mane, and relax. He's got a big step, but this lad's a gentle giant. Enjoy the ride and don't squeeze him with your legs."

Silla nodded.

"Leya, we're going. Come and you'll get an apple."

The pony walked to Aili's side; her ears perked at the girl. She nosed Aili's pockets.

Aili pushed her nose away. "I don't have it yet. We have to go inside first."

Jordi led Trickster to the gate and opened it. Aili waited as he passed through with the black horse, before following with Charger. Leya pranced along beside her, still nosing Aili's pockets.

"You're not using a strap to lead her?"

Aili glanced back at the girl. "It's called a halter. I don't need to. She's been my friend for a long time, and she stays with me willingly."

Silla crouched low on Charger's back as the big horse walked beside Aili, her fingers gripping his mane so tightly they were white. Her grin was wide, and she looked around at the world from her perch on the big horse. Aili took the big horse into the stable and to his stall. Leya marched past him into her own stall and stuffed her nose in the feeder. Aili stopped outside Charger's stall.

Jordi closed Trickster's stall door and hung his halter on the hook. He walked over to Charger and held his hands out to Silla. "Time to come back to the ground with the rest of us." He smiled up at her.

Silla reached out to him, and Jordi lowered her back to the ground. Aili led Charger into his stall. Leya whickered at Aili, her nose pressed to the stall bars.

"I'm coming, girl." Aili slipped the halter from Charger's head.

"Does she really understand you?" Silla stood at Leya's stall, watching the pony.

Aili shrugged. "She understands more than she has any reason to. She's incredibly smart."

Leya snorted.

"And sassy. Sassy ponies don't deserve apples."

Leya snorted, her ears pinned.

Silla laughed. "Can I feed her?"

"Sure, but we'll use a bucket." Aili stepped from Charger's stall and hung the halter on the hook.

Aili led Silla to the feed room and showed her the bucket with apples. She grabbed a bucket from the stack in the corner.

"Charger can have one, too." Jordi's voice carried from the barn aisle.

Aili dropped an apple in a bucket and handed it to Silla. She tucked a second apple into her pocket. They returned to the pony's stall. Leya eyed them over the stall door, her whinny echoing down the barn aisle. Her nostrils vibrated as she sniffed the air.

"Grip it firmly. She's going to want that a lot, and she's strong," Aili warned.

Silla gripped the bucket firmly in her tense arms. Aili opened the stall door and led her inside, shoving Leya back. Leya reached her head around Aili and stuffed her nose in the bucket. She tore into the apple, jostling Silla with her enthusiasm.

"She's very strong." Silla giggled.

"She's also rude." Aili nudged the pony.

Leya snorted in the bucket. Silla giggled.

"Here." Aili got Silla from the stall, retrieving the bucket as Leya tried to steal it with her teeth. "Charger is more polite. You can give this to him from your hand."

She showed Silla how to hold her hand flat and balance the apple on it. Aili guided her in front of Charger's stall door. The big horse leaned his head out and lipped the apple from Silla's hand. Silla laughed as his whiskers brushed over her palm.

"He's less pushy," Silla whispered.

"He's just a big softie who likes people." Andvari appeared beside them. He scratched the big horse, still chewing his apple.

Silla jumped back into Aili. Aili saw him coming, but the little girl hadn't. She craned her neck up at the tall man and his massive horse. Andvari scratched Charger under his chin. Charger touched his nose to his person.

"Is he yours?" Silla's eyes were wide. "He's big like you."

Aili pressed her lips together and covered her mouth with her hand.

Andvari chuckled. "Yes, he is. Your teacher is looking for you. You should go find him."

Silla skipped down the barn aisle, all energy again. She stopped and turned at the door. "Can we do this again?"

Aili nodded. "Sometimes. I have studies, too, but if we both have a break we can play with the horses."

"Great." Silla thrust her fist in the air. "See you later." She raced through the door and was gone.

Aili shook her head, smiling widely. She glanced up at Andvari. "What?"

He leaned back against the stall and laughed, his arms around his belly. "Considering the last time you saw her, you played a prank on her, it's surprising you're spending time with her now."

"Horses are wonderful for troubled people." Jordi stepped from his office and leaned against the door frame; his arms folded over his chest.

"I'm glad you think so. She might be here every free moment she has now." Aili grinned at Jordi.

Jordi shrugged. "There's always saddles to clean and stalls to muck. We'll see how much she really likes horses."

Andvari chuckled. "You're evil. Now, they need their supper, and we need ours. Drill tonight."

Aili raised an eyebrow. "So soon?"

"Every night." Andvari smiled. "When main Drill is done, I'll begin teaching you form four with both sword and bare hand."

"Yes!" Aili thrust her fist in the air and bounced on her toes. She ignored their laughter. She was going to learn more.

CHAPTER 9

WIND AND WILLPOWER

Aili ran her cloth along her sword, leaving a light coating of oil on it for protection. Andvari sat at his desk, his own sword out on his knees and his cleaning kit spread out. It was a week since he started teaching her the fourth forms, and Aili was getting it.

He even started getting her up early for extra practice sessions. Aili liked the quiet of the morning. There was no one around to watch her learn, so she could fail and try again without being watched. Andvari never gave up on her, not even when she struggled. They'd go to the hay barn and work under mage-light in the cool air.

The sun shone through the window, rising high enough to shine directly in. They'd just returned from an early session, and Aili appreciated the warmth in the room. This last week had been pretty amazing, with more tracking games, which might be her favourite kind of lesson. She was learning to use her powers to connect with the world in ways she never thought possible, like finding the smallest trace left after someone passed by, like a single hair or thread from clothing.

Every day she had magic lessons, not just tracking, but healing minor wounds with magic instead of potions. Aili got to meet the camp healers and more of the Scouts. Learning to banish parasites from plants and animals was both fun and gross. The practical magic was her favourite, as she could help people and animals and make their lives better.

She wrapped her fingers around the sword hilt. Whatever was going on that he'd been worried about was getting worse, though. She heard the conversations while she was reading. Plants were shrivelling up and animals were deserting the area. She didn't understand everything they said, but this place wasn't too far from the camp.

"Ready for inspection?" Andvari sheathed his sword.

Aili glanced down at her sword, balanced on the cloth over her knees. The red sunlight reflected off the blade and onto the wall. "I think so."

"My troops answer me with Yes, Sir." Andvari teased.

"And I'm sure you're proud." Aili giggled. "Good for morale. Especially yours."

He grabbed a roll from the breakfast tray on his desk and whipped it at her. Aili shifted, rolled, and swung her sword up. The roll sliced in two and flew past her.

"I might need another moment with the polishing cloth." Aili brushed crumbs from her shirt. "Didn't your mamma teach you not to play with food?"

"I was brought up bad. Consider it a surprise exam on your sword skills. You passed, by the way."

Aili wiped the crumbs from her blade. Andvari snapped his fingers. The roll zipped into his hand, the two halves resting on his palm.

He held the roll up and examined the neat slice, right down the middle. "Nice aim. How's the sword looking?"

Aili held the blade out on the protective cloth. Darik didn't let her use metal swords often, so she was learning how to care for the blade. Would he think she did a good job?

Andvari smiled. "Excellent. Put it away and take your plate. Lessons start right after that."

She sheathed her sword, the blade sliding in with a metallic hiss. Aili hung it back on the hook and took her plate from the tray. She settled on his trunk to eat, folding her legs under her, and set her plate in front of her. "What are we doing today?"

"Ready for wind magic?"

Aili tore her roll in half. "Maybe. What's it like?"

He shrugged. "I don't know yet." Andvari smiled at her. "Your magic is so different that we'll need to find out."

She chewed her roll. Earth Magic came so easily. It wasn't hard to imagine the result in her mind and influence nature around her. Water had a flow to it, that also made it easy to manipulate, as long as she asked and didn't demand. What would wind be like? She couldn't see it, or grip it in her hand, though it could touch her. Could she 'see' the wind? Maybe in her senses?

Aili set her empty plate back on the tray and grabbed her warmer cloak. It was one thing to stay warm during sword practice, but she didn't move near that much for magic lessons. Aili shivered just thinking about the cool air.

"Why don't I have anything like that?" Aili pointed at Andvari's thicker pants and shirt.

He pulled his own cloak on. "I'll get you some as soon as we're back, and the tailors are awake." Andvari moved to the desk, wrote a quick note, and threw it out the door. "For now, there's this."

Andvari rested his hand on her head and chanted under his breath. Warmth flowed down over Aili's body, like she was standing under a sun-warmed waterfall, but she remained dry. Within moments, the warmth covered her. It was like being snuggled in a wool blanket without the itchiness.

"Heat spell. It'll keep you comfortable while we're out. You might do something similar by blending Air and Fire Magic one day."

Aili glanced down at her warm self. "Like create a layer of warm wind around me?"

"Maybe. We'll get a sense of how you use wind today. We'll start with the basics. Let's get the horses ready."

He led her to the stable through the busier hallways, and they got the horses ready to ride. Leya perked up when she saw Aili and stood quietly for her grooming. Soon they were out riding through the rolling hills, towards the forest.

Aili sighed and rolled her shoulders. Flying gave her an amazing view, but this was way better. She'd be happy to never fly again. The grass rustled in the gentle breeze as they rode towards the trees.

Andvari stopped at the forest's edge and dismounted. He tied up Charger's reins and let the big horse graze. Aili hadn't been the only one in lessons this week. She spent some time teaching Charger to come on command for Andvari. Now the big guy could graze with Leya. She turned Leya loose as well.

"I chose the forest so we can see the wind as you manipulate it. We should see the leaves move, at least." He gestured at the foliage around him as he walked deeper into the forest.

The leaves hung from their trees, barely moving in the slight breeze.

"Perfect. A nice and calm day. What a beautiful day to not cause a hurricane by mistake."

Aili crossed her arms over her chest and narrowed her eyes. "Is this going to be another 'don't destroy the forest' kind of thing? I'm not thrilled about all these warnings you give me."

Andvari smiled. "It's good to be aware of what can go wrong. You're not limited by your own strength, only by your focus. However, you've trained hard in martial arts, and your focus is excellent. You might do actual damage. Besides, if I was that worried, we'd be much farther from camp. You'll be fine."

Aili placed her hand on a tree trunk. Nature was beautiful and full of creative powers, but could also be fierce and destructive. She'd read about forest fires in the old books of legends, and how far and fast they travelled back then. Aili shivered.

"All you'll do is take this tiny little breeze and make it bigger. Not a lot, just enough to make me cold. Don't blow the forest down." Andvari stood across from her and waited.

Aili grinned. Challenge accepted. His heat spell was welcome, but he had warmer clothing. Aili closed her eyes and felt for the breeze. She slowed her breathing and sensed the wind on her skin, slight though it was.

The wind moved in ribbons like water, but not in a contained way like a river. Okay, she could do this. Start small and build as she could. Aili grasped the wind with her mind and aimed it at his shoulder. She wrapped it around his body, winding it like a thin cocoon over him. She sensed the turbulence where the wind brushed against him and used that to keep powering the rest of the wind.

Andvari shivered. "Excellent. Now stop it."

Aili let the wind go, releasing her focus. Unlike Water Magic, the wind kept circling him. She swallowed hard. Her heart sped up. She snipped the wind, let the source go, but it kept circling him.

"Focus." His voice remained calm; his expression relaxed. "What's the problem?"

"The wind is independent in a way water is not. I can bend and shape it, but it keeps the shape when I let go, even when I don't want it to." Aili frowned.

Andvari crouched and stepped from the wind cocoon, his hair blowing around as he passed below it. Once he stepped aside, the wind untangled itself and Aili felt it flow again, as if he had never been there.

"Weird." Aili stepped to the spot and stretched her hand out. The wind flowed normally, quiet and calmer again. The leaves barely rustled.

"It looks like you'll be able to make wind shields. You can protect people or structures with them. They might even last as long as the wind does, since buildings don't move. There's so much for us to explore still." Andvari rubbed his chin.

"So, if I want to use the wind for or against people, I need to keep directing it to follow them." Aili reached out and touched a leaf.

"Looks that way. While it will take more focus to use, it'll stop as soon as people move, so you don't have to undo it if you want to let it go. It'll undo itself for you. Besides, what you learn now might change as you get more skilled." Andvari leaned against a tree.

"What's a wind shield?" Aili pinned him with her gaze.

"We can try one now. There are two main kinds. The first is a pocket or disc of air that is completely still, and it redirects the wind around it. That'll protect us from wind, even a windstorm. The second kind is creating a moving breeze that can deflect projectiles, swords, and even push people back. Warriors can use it on the battlefield."

"Hang on then." Aili paced slowly; her gaze unfocused on the ground. "I moved the wind around you by using you to change how it flowed. I could place a dead air space between you and the wind to protect you?"

"Yes, in theory. If it's windy when we camp, Kyson can make a dead air space around parts of the camp to keep us warmer."

"May I try?" She looked up and met his gaze.

Andvari smiled. "That's why we're here."

Aili felt for the surrounding wind. It wanted to move, even as slow and lazy as it was right now. She grasped it with her mind, but it resisted and flowed around her grip. Fine, if it was that set on moving, she'd make it move. Aili spun the wind around, forming it into a disc. She stretched it out, spinning it faster, until it was between them. The leaves behind him hung limp, no breeze left behind the shield to move them.

"Yes, that's the second variety of shield. You can also use the wind like a stream or a ribbon between two fighting forces to move one side around." Andvari reached out and touched the spinning wind disc.

"I couldn't do the first kind. I tried, but I don't know how to work with the absence of wind."

Andvari stepped around her shield and set a hand on her shoulder. "Give it time. It's your first day with wind magic. Can you undo this one?"

Aili gripped the edge of the shield with her mind and hung on. It unspun itself and flowed on in a thin ribbon until the extra power she added was gone. Within moments, there was no sign she ever made the shield.

"It's harder than Water Magic." Aili's shoulders slumped.

Andvari rolled his eyes. "Most people only fully master one school of magic, two at the most for exceptional mages. My student is disappointed that her third kind is tricky?"

"Wait." Aili stared at him. "Only one?"

He nodded. "We can use other magics, but we're strongest in one. My Earth Magic is powerful. I can use Wind Magic, but I'll never have Kyson's skill, no matter how much I practice. He won't have my skill with influencing the surrounding land, either. We complement each other, but neither of us can do it all."

"Water and Earth Magic feel easy to me, but Wind Magic sure doesn't." Aili pressed her lips together.

She walked with him through the forest, back to the horses. Both Charger and Leya were near the trees, snacking on the shorter grasses below the bushes. Charger lifted his head and walked over to Andvari.

Andvari stroked his long nose. "You were a good boy. Thank you for not running off."

Aili smiled. "He considers you as his herd. You're his leader."

Andvari scratched the big horse's chest. "You can tell that?"

She laughed. "We spend two days just on communicating with animals, and he asks me if I'm sure?" Aili rolled her eyes. "I'm sure."

"As far as magic goes, you're still a baby mage." He swung up into Charger's saddle. "As a mage, you're a few weeks old. Most people at that stage are still struggling to call a ball of light. They're not healing people and animals, creating water sculptures, and scanning mountains for weaknesses."

Aili leapt onto Leya, and they followed him towards camp. "Overachiever. I can't help it."

Andvari smiled and shook his head. Aili grinned. Being around him was like being with Ilia or Darik. So many teachers weren't approachable, but strict taskmasters, like at the University. She'd never really thought about what having a personal teacher might be like, but this was better than she hoped.

Camp came into sight among the rolling hills.

"Read as long as you can after lunch. The day is yours after that until Drill."

Aili perked up and Leya pranced under her. "Yes."

"I still expect to see you at meals. I'm supposed to make sure you're still alive, and you haven't blown anything up or anything." Andvari glanced down at her.

She held her hand up. "I promise." Aili burst out laughing.

Andvari laughed. "Let's get these guys put away so we can eat."

***

Aili gazed at the stars, twinkling brightly in the sky. The window was open, and the breeze reached her on her own bed tonight. Andvari slept soundly nearby, his fingers twitching as he dreamed. At least he doesn't snore. Was he dreaming of casting a spell?

She stretched as she contemplated her new life. Her routine of magic lessons, meditation, and sword practice was more fun than she expected, and she had so much free time. Most students spent their waking hours studying, but it's not like Aili needed to memorize spells or anything.

What would her life be like if she could cast spells? She'd be missing out on all this. Her father would have found her a high-status teacher in the city. They would have been highly skilled, but so were the Scouts. Nearly all were Master Mages, after all.

She smiled to herself. So many ways to use magic and she never considered most of them, despite the spell books she'd read. Here, there was no 'right way' to cast spells. Any method that didn't harm people worked. How much did the University mages really know?

Sleep pulled at her, and she finally closed her eyes.

CHAPTER 10

SOMETHING WORTH FIGHTING FOR

"Since you'll be coming with me when I go out on Scout duties, I need to teach you some Scout skills as well. Today, we'll be practicing the most important hand signals. We use these anywhere we don't want to be heard."

Aili jogged behind Andvari, hustling to keep up. His long stride was impossible to match. She breathed deeply as she followed him up the hill. He never slowed once, no matter if he was walking uphill or not.

Andvari stopped on the hillside just west of the camp. He turned around and surveyed the land before turning his attention on her. Aili forced herself to stand upright and control her breathing. Already she was fitter than she'd ever been, but she had more work to do if she wanted to keep up.

"You and I will go for runs together." Andvari placed a hand on her shoulder.

"Aren't there rules about torturing students?" Aili doubled over with her hands on her knees and panted.

"Yes. We need to do it regularly, so they don't get cocky. We'll start tomorrow morning after sword practice. You can sit. We'll start with the easiest hand signals first." Andvari folded his legs and lowered himself to the ground.

Aili collapsed on the ground in a heap. She crossed her legs and propped herself up on her elbows.

Andvari shifted in front of her. "We use hand signals any time we don't want to make noise. Sometimes we may not hear each other, like in a storm."

He showed her the hand signals one by one. Aili struggled to memorize each one. He took his time, going over each one and answering her questions, repeating as often as she needed. Some were obvious, like 'look over there,' but others weren't, like 'set up camp.'

"Are these written anywhere? I'm going to need to study them a lot more." Aili massaged her temples with her fingers. "I'm getting serious brain ache."

"I'll give you a Scout's Handbook. It'll have everything you need to know as a new Scout inside. You can study them in your reading periods if that helps."

Aili smiled and flopped back on the ground, her hands under her head. "Have you ever been on a mission where you needed a lot of these signals?"

Andvari moved and lay in the grass beside her. He stared up at the clouds with her. "Actually, I have. Kyson and I once were tracking a man on the other side of the border. He kept getting closer than we liked. It was an escaped criminal, and he was more afraid of them than the magic protecting the border. We spent three days following him, using only hand signals to communicate."

"What happened?" She turned her head to see him.

He watched a small grass seed float past, the little white puff ball keeping it aloft as it passed over his nose. "We scared him off with stronger spells Kyson had. He turned and ran right into their law enforcement. We haven't seen him since."

She gazed back up at the clouds floating past overhead.

"Since we're being lazy, let's try a more passive and relaxed type of magic." Andvari sat up. "Time to sense life energy. You've mentioned you can feel me in the woods, and I haven't snuck up on you lately in camp. You don't feel me separately from other people, though, right?"

Aili nodded. She pressed herself up with her hands.

"This is a chance to see how sensitive you are, and how far away you can detect life. It'll be like that first day, but you're stronger now. Let's see what's changed." Andvari eased behind her. He set his hand on her back, light but firm. "Breathe. Open yourself to the world around you."

Aili settled into a slow meditation breathing pattern, her body still and her mind open. The grass grabbed her awareness first, a steady hum or vibration of life that nearly filled the background of her awareness. The trees vibrated slower, but in harmony with the grass, a complimentary feeling to relax her muscles.

Flecks of colour overhead pulled her eyes up. Birds flitted about, little spots of colour that spun and darted about above her. Tiny mice raced through the grass, little bright green dots streaking past as they dodged the little weasels chasing them. A sleek weasel moved past, a bright red shadow that pounced.

Andvari glowed red behind her. Down the slope she could sense the camp, mostly red shadows of people moving around, along with a few green ones like her. The horses glowed green as they grazed in the paddocks, their tails swishing at the flies she couldn't quite sense from this far away.

"You glow green, but nearly everyone else shows as red. Why?" Andvari's fingers twitched against her back.

"Maybe because I don't eat meat? I'm green like the horses and other herbivores."

"Your range seems to be about a mile or so. It's fuzzy that far away, and only larger animals show up."

Aili focused lazily on the herd of deer at the edge of the forest behind her. There would be an abundance of birds, mice, and insects, but she couldn't sense them this far away. She turned her attention to the soil near her feet, and little insects tunnelled and crawled along in her senses.

"It seems little things need to be closer."

"Now you know. If you're helping with an ecology study, you'll know how close you have to be to detect each type of life."

Aili wiggled, her leg falling asleep under her. "Ecology study? Who does those?"

"We do, mostly. When we're not guarding and protecting the forest, we're monitoring how healthy it is, and how plants and animals are doing. We also watch for imbalances between predators and prey. A few mages get our help for advanced studies on species or ecosystems, but it's mostly Scouts."

She rubbed her leg. "Maybe being a Scout is more interesting than I thought. That sounds like fun."

"We even have Earth Mages who come to us for help and help us when we need. It's another thing you can consider for your future. I'll see about getting us on some studies soon, so you can try it for yourself."

"Oh, yes, please," Aili whispered. Her chest felt warm, a hope she hadn't felt in a long time welling up inside her.

"Now, hand signals one more time, and then we have lunch. After lunch, study time while I work. Free time after that until Drill."

He showed her all the hand signals, one at a time, until she saw them all again. Aili tried, she really did, but she hung her head. She got maybe half at most. Her cheeks burned.

"It's your first day, and many people struggle with this. Be patient." Andvari offered her a hand and helped her up.

They kept practicing on their way back to camp, walking slowly for her, and focusing on the ones she missed. It's easy for him to say it's fine, but Aili expected better of herself. She'd memorize them all, even if she had to study by mage-light at night.

"Rest your brain." Andvari led her through the archway to the dining room. "I don't expect you to learn everything the first day I show it to you. You have more important things to study."

Silla dashed up to her as Aili entered the dining room, bouncing on her toes and vibrating. "Can Aili come sit with me today?" She turned pleading eyes on Andvari. "I have so much to tell her about the horses."

Aili grinned. Andvari raised an eyebrow, and Aili nodded.

"Have fun. Meet me in the room for study time after."

Aili gathered her tray and selected her meal. "Have you been to the stable often?"

Silla nodded vigorously. Aili's neck ached just watching the girl.

"Yep. Jordi's been teaching me all kinds of things." She bounced along and led Aili to a regular table near the edge of the room.

Aili set her tray on the table and lowered herself to the bench. She glanced over and Andvari grinned at her. Aili smiled back. "How's that going?"

"He's giving me riding lessons," she cheered. "I got to sit on a small horse and direct it all by myself. It was amazing."

"Tell me about it." Aili picked up her roll and tore it into pieces. Enthusiastic people irritate her, but this was horse enthusiasm. This was different. Aili remembered being this bubbly as a small child learning to ride.

Silla told her all about learning to saddle a horse and how to groom them, leaving nothing out. Aili got to hear every little detail. Silla helped him lead horses to and from paddocks, and today was her first solo ride, where she wasn't being led. Memories flashed through Aili's mind as Silla talked, her and Darik and Leya together. Darik used to lead her around on Leya, too, her little fists gripping the golden mane as she laughed.

"That's amazing. Is he letting you ride more?" Aili picked up her teacup.

Silla nodded, bumping the table with her knees as she bounced on the bench. "My teacher talked to him, and they've set aside regular times every week for me. Thank you so much."

Aili grinned back at the girl. What a change, seeing the life and enthusiasm in her now. More horse time would help her calm down, but Aili could relate so much. "I'm glad you're having fun. I love my pony time. They've been my friends through everything."

Motion in her peripheral vision drew Aili's attention. She looked up and noticed Andvari approaching. He held his tray in one hand and gave her a hand signal she recognized now.

"I have to go. It was fun having lunch with you, but I have to study now." Aili gathered her dishes and picked up her tray.

Silla grinned and nodded. The girl fidgeted and went back to eating. Aili eased herself from the bench and joined Andvari at the doorway.

"Hard to imagine that's the same girl, huh?"

Aili nodded. "She's happy now, and much friendlier. Not the same snotty little girl I first met."

Andvari snorted and ducked from the room. Aili followed, smiling. They returned to their rooms and settled down to work, Aili on the bed and reading while he sat at his desk. His mirror turned foggy, and the border was red this time. Andvari's head shot up and he touched the frame.

She tried to focus on her book. The places they mentioned, she didn't know them. Something inside her sensed a problem, like a pit in her stomach that wouldn't go away. It was harder to breathe, and Aili wrapped an arm around her belly.

Aili closed her book and set it on his mattress. She opened her mouth to ask.

"Sir." A fist hammered on the door.

Andvari was at the door in two strides and swung it open. "Report."

"There's been an incursion. They're calling for all available troops." The Scout saluted.

"Let's go." He nodded at the Scout. "You, too, Aili. Stay with me and do as I say." Andvari strode to his sword and grabbed it from the hook. He buckled it around his waist.

Aili leapt to her feet and stuffed her boots on. She grabbed her sword and jogged out the door behind him, down the stairs, and out the front door. Andvari marched over to the gigantic building beside the Main Hall.

The large doors stood open, and wagons were being wheeled out. They had massive wheels for cross-country transport and were large enough to carry a lot of goods or people, though they didn't have side walls. People leapt up and sat, and the full carts sped off towards the forest.

"This one." Andvari led her to a cart with other officers. "Get on and move to the middle. Hang on."

Aili gripped the cart, and he boosted her up. She scooted into the middle and grabbed a rope handle threaded through the wagon floor. The rope was rough against her palms. People moved around, yelling orders or discussing tactics. Instead of covering her ears, Aili gripped the rope tighter.

Andvari settled beside her. "What's the situation?"

A Border Guard shifted in front of him. "They've weakened the barrier enough to approach. We've got them held off, but they're still pressing against our forces."

Andvari nodded to Aili. "Hold tight. We're going."

The wagon rolled through the thinning crowd and down the paths of the camp. It picked up speed as it reached the grassy fields, speeding up over the rolling hills. The enormous wheels carried them over the ground, though it wasn't the smoothest ride. Aili got jostled around. Andvari wrapped an arm around her, and Aili leaned against him. She closed her watering eyes against the breeze on her face.

Her stomach rolled. The cart slowed, and Aili opened her eyes. They were at the edge of the trees. Metal clashed against metal and people yelled indistinct noises in the commotion. Mages had their arms raised, sending wind and water at people in the trees.

Andvari dropped off the cart and held his hand out to her. Aili took his hand, leapt down, and followed him into the trees. Her group rushed forward, swords drawn and hands high, spells ready on their fingertips. More metal striking metal, the noise ringing in her ears. Why wasn't the magic overpowering them? She glanced up at Andvari.

"Something has been draining the magic around here. It's affecting us, too. How do you feel? Are you still strong?" He glanced down at her.

"I feel normal." Aili raised her voice to be heard over the commotion.

"Wind shield. Thin braid. Drive them back if you can." Andvari drew his sword.

"I'll have to focus." Aili gripped her lip between her teeth.

"I'll protect you. Just focus and feel. Do what you can." He stepped between her and the advancing forces.

Aili closed her eyes. At least now she couldn't see the blood and fighting. She slowed her breathing. Focus, Aili. Focus. Wind magic. Move with it. It wants to flow.

She drew her sword, flowing into the first sword pattern. Aili matched her breathing to her movements, sending her awareness out. Her body calmed to the familiar motions, and she felt for the world around her. There's the wind.

A nearby Wind Mage called more wind into existence. Aili grabbed that power and spun it into the breeze she collected. Another Wind Mage called more wind for her. Aili braided the wind together and threaded it between the fighting forces, her mind like a darning needle guiding her wind thread along. She headed for where the noise was most intense, the sound of swords striking against each other pulling her closer.

She parted the combatants, the wind slithering like a serpent, pushing the attackers away. Aili snapped the wind with her mind, flinging men back through the bushes. She kept moving in the sword form, using the motions to focus her powers, each gesture of a hand giving more force to her magic.

Aili shoved at a group of attackers with her wind. Their swords blew from their hands and they flew back into the bushes across the border.

Dust lifted into her breeze and blew at the attackers. A Scout fell nearby, his wound calling to her senses. His attacker stepped over him and raised a sword. Aili shoved the wind at him, pulling more Wind Magic from other mages, and sent the man sailing into a tree. His sword dropped to the grass.

Mages fought beyond her. The attackers were faltering. Aili rushed back along her wind ribbon, hitting attackers who had recovered already. More Wind Mages loaned her power, calling breezes she could weave in, and Aili made a high barrier between the groups. She pressed forward, slow steps with hands and sword raised, shoving them back through the trees. The border was close. Aili kept pressing.

"Close the gap. Close it now."

Mages rushed to the border and cast spells. The border grew stronger again, vibrating Aili's bones now. She whipped the last few attackers back like a slingshot, across the border and away. Her wind faltered. Aili's legs shook, and she sank to the ground.

Andvari slipped an arm around her waist and lowered her gently. He sheathed his sword and kneeled beside her. "Open your eyes. Look at me."

Aili forced her eyelids open, despite how heavy they felt. No, try again. You can do this. Aili fought her body and focused on his face.

"That's it. How do you feel?"

"Tired," she slurred. "Okay." Her eyes slammed shut.

"Here." Aili didn't know that voice.

"Drink." Andvari held something to her lips. He propped her up against him.

Liquid trickled into her mouth, a little at a time. Aili swallowed the sweetness. Her aches eased, though her body still didn't want to respond.

"A little more now. You did a great job. We can go back now."

He lifted her in his arms. The smooth rocking motion of his walk lulled her into the comfort of sleep.

CHAPTER 11

A New Problem

Knocking pulled her from the quiet rest. Where was she? The door hinges creaked in that familiar quiet way. Come on, brain. Wake up.

"How is she doing?" She'd heard that voice before. Where? During the fighting. Right. Fighting.

"She's still resting." Andvari's voice had that minor tremor that made her chest feel tight.

Aili fought to open her eyes. Good, that's a start. Now for the rest of her body. She took a deep breath and focused on her arm. Her fingers wiggled and her elbow bent, lifting her hand from the bed. Good.

"How do you feel?" Andvari sat in the chair beside her bed. He took her hand.

"Like I ran from the capital," Aili mumbled. Her throat ached from dryness. "Okay, though."

Andvari chuckled. "You and I use the word okay different-ly. Here, can you sit?"

He shifted and kneeled beside her. Andvari slid a hand under her back and lifted, easing her up. Her body was sluggish, but she could sit on her own.

The man took a cup from the desk and handed it to And-vari.

Andvari took the cup and brought it to her lips. "Sip this. It'll help."

Aili managed a smile. When she was small, Ilia cared for her like this when she was ill. She'd prop little Aili up and give her cups of tea and potions, and care for her until she was well. Aili blinked back a tear. Even the spice blend in the tea was the same. She sipped the comforting tea.

"Who chose the herbs?" Aili glanced up at him.

Andvari smiled. "It's a recipe I learned from someone," he teased.

"There's a Master Herbalist in each camp, and they make all the potions and lotions Ilia from the capital would, right here from a copy of her recipe book. You know the blend?" The man raised his eyebrow.

Aili nodded.

"She knows the herbalist." Andvari set the empty cup on her nightstand. "She came with a lot of knowledge already. Makes my job easier, as I can focus on her magic training."

"Well, you made a difference in that fight. Later, the Scout you saved would like to come and thank you. He's being healed and should walk on his own by the end of the day." The man folded his arms over his chest.

Aili smiled, though her jaw trembled. She'd never seen fighting like that before. Nothing in her life prepared her for an actual battle. The legends didn't mention the blood and yelling and smell of fear. Still, she saved someone. That mattered.

Andvari peered into her eyes. His forehead wrinkled. "She needs rest, and time to process it all." He held her eye contact.

"A field report just arrived. I'll have a copy brought for you. We need to act soon. Oh, and Orlo Mindar from the University is still missing."

Andvari looked up at him. "Is he?"

"If anyone knows about magic like this, it would be him. He was last seen days ago." The man smiled at Aili. "Get some rest. I'll see you both later." He left the room, closing the door behind himself.

Aili watched the door swing closed and heard the latch click. "Who was that?"

He gave her hand a gentle squeeze. "You're so good in the bush, I keep forgetting you're not actually a Scout. The crest tells you." Andvari tapped his shoulder, where his rank patch rested. "That's Sildan Monis, the First Mage of the Defence Mages, and overseer of the Border Protection Group."

"How's Leya?" Aili fidgeted with her blanket, her fingers rubbing against the soft cotton.

"She's fine. Last time I checked on her, she convinced Jordi to give her an apple, and was crunching it happily."

A laugh burst from her. Leya could use those big brown eyes to manipulate anyone, even a big and intimidating man like Jordi. At least she was okay, and well looked after while Aili rested.

"I have something to show you. Look." Andvari pulled his mirror out and held it in front of her, aimed at her neckband.

Aili angled the mirror for a better look. Her jaw dropped. The emerald and deep blue crystals glowed like they had been, and the next crystal glowed a light blue, like Kyson's did. The last crystal remained clear. Aili blinked and looked again. A single strand of gold intertwined with the silver in her band.

"I suspect you're going to be equally strong in all four magic types."

Aili touched her band, still staring at her reflection. "Gold so soon? I'm not ready," she whispered.

Andvari rubbed her back. "Don't worry about that right now. Rest. You won't be a full mage overnight. Interesting, though, isn't it?" He took his mirror and tucked it back under his shirt. "Get some more rest. Let the potion work. When you wake, we'll go see your hairy little friend."

Aili smiled and eased herself back until her head rested on the pillow. The tea was working, and her eyelids felt heavy. Aili rolled onto her side. Andvari tucked the blanket around her. Sleep pulled at Aili, and she gave in.

Sunlight on her eyelids pulled her awake. Aili stretched. Her body was less heavy. Her limbs listened this time. She opened her eyes.

Andvari was bent over his trunk, going through the contents. He glanced over as she shifted. "How are you feeling now?"

She relaxed at his warm smile. His worry lines scared her earlier more than the battle had. "Almost normal. What happened?"

He walked to the chair and sat beside her. "You used more power than I've seen you use yet, and longer. Not to mention channeling magic from at least seven other Master Mages at one point." Andvari crossed his arms over his chest. "You simply overloaded your body's ability to handle power."

"Am I good now, if I feel normal? Well, normal-ish."

He shrugged. "Your guess is as good as mine. Better, because you know how you feel. I want you to tell me immediately if you feel worse or more tired again. Today we're going to prepare."

Aili raised her eyebrow. "Prepare for what?"

Andvari rubbed his chin. "Something happened at the border. We've been watching it for a while, but it's getting worse, and fast. The magic in the area is weakening. When we're there, our magic is weaker as well."

"Weakening? How?" Aili pushed herself up to sit. "What does that mean?"

"It means the closer we get to the border, the less effective our magic becomes. You seemed completely unaffected. You used more magic than I've seen you use yet." Andvari rested his chin on his hand.

"Could we walk while you tell me about it? After being in bed for who knows how long, I want to stretch my legs." Aili eased the blankets back.

"Two days." Andvari stood and moved his chair to give her room.

"Huh?"

"You've been in bed two days."

Aili's brain froze. She paused with her feet part-way to the floor. Two whole days? Shouldn't she be a lot stiffer?

"Let's walk. I'll share what I know. I'd like to hear your thoughts on it, since you've read so much advanced magic theory." Andvari dropped her curtains for her.

Aili changed into her day clothing. She took it slowly and stretched her body lightly. Her balance was okay, at least. Aili pulled the familiar green Scout clothing on and smiled. She may not officially be one of them, but wearing this felt right, somehow. Aili raised her curtains and sat on her trunk as she pulled her boots on.

Andvari waited at the door for her. She gripped the railing as she walked down the stairs, taking her time. He walked quietly beside her, letting her set the pace. Her muscles freed up as she walked, and each step was easier.

Leya's piercing whinny echoed down the barn aisle. Her nose poked over the stall door. Aili sped down the aisle to greet her. She slid back the latch and stepped into the stall. Leya pushed her with her bony nose, sniffing the girl thoroughly.

"It's great to see you, too." Aili rubbed her forehead. "Were you a good girl?"

Jordi laughed. He leaned against his office door behind her. "Except for the time she busted out and tried to climb the stairs to see you." He wandered over and stood beside Andvari in front of Leya's stall.

"What?" Aili laughed. "Really?"

Andvari nodded. "It's true. She made it through the front door and to the top of the stairs, headed for our room to see you."

"I had to magic her down and put a ward on her stall and paddock to keep her wherever I left her." Jordi eyed the pony. "Sneaky little thing."

Andvari reached over the stall door and patted Leya's neck. "She was worried for you, too." He turned his attention to Aili. "We can walk outside of camp, and you can bring her, if you like."

Aili nodded. Jordi dispelled the magic on the door as Aili swung it open. Leya followed her from the stall, and they walked beside Andvari to the back stable door. Aili threaded her fingers through Leya's mane.

They passed through the paddocks and out into the sunny fields. Andvari had that quiet, thoughtful expression, where his gaze seemed so far away. Aili left him to his thoughts. He'd tell her when he was ready. She gazed at the surrounding land, her face turned to the sun. Her body filled with energy.

Andvari pulled himself from his thoughts and looked at her. "Are you gathering energy from the sun?"

"Maybe? I feel better when it touches my skin."

He shook his head. "Your rested more peacefully when I left the curtains up, and the sun shone in. I've almost never heard of this before."

"Almost?" Aili arched her eyebrow.

"I'll tell you about it later. First, there's something important going on. We need to talk about it." He stared off over the fields.

Finally. I might get to know what's been happening lately. Everyone in the camp seems on edge.

"Something started a few months ago, just over the border somewhere. Magic is being drained by something. The magic at the border is weakening, too. Not the oldest magic, placed By Ethala Minis, but the spells added since for privacy. They also give us extra protection. Understand so far?"

"Magic draining, border spells weakening." Aili nodded.

"It's affecting us, too. Just a little at first. Maybe we need to concentrate harder, but the longer we're in the area, the worse it gets. I've sent Scouts to investigate, but they can't identify what's causing it. The last two went missing." He looked down at her. The lines creased on his forehead again.

But she just got magic. It can't be slipping away, not now. Aili shuddered. Her magic was untouched, as far as she knew, but what if she was wrong? Even if she wasn't affected, could she stand by and let her friends lose something so deeply a part of them? What if it gets so bad, even she can't use magic anymore?

"This is the first time in a few centuries non-magical folk have crossed the border in a group, especially a hostile group. Our magic was less than half what it should have been. If we didn't train in physical combat, they'd have overwhelmed us."

Aili gripped Leya's mane. Swords clashed in her memory; men flew back as she hit them with her wind. So much yelling. Her head ached. Her knees wobbled. Aili pulled herself against Leya.

Andvari rested a hand on her shoulder. "You seemed unaffected at the battle, magically speaking."

She took a slow and deep breath and focused on Leya's mane. Her warm body soothed Aili. The battle is done, and I'm safe now.

"Your power was stronger than all of ours combined." He wrapped an arm around her and held her up.

"What happened to the Scouts? The ones across the border?"

He shook his head. "We don't know. Both were reporting in regularly, and just stopped one day. One mentioned people gathering in the northeast, around the mountains, and that was the last we heard. Since things are getting worse, Kyson and I are going across the border to check it out."

Aili's heart ached. He was her teacher, and she learned so much from him already. What would she do when he was gone? What if something happened to him, too? She couldn't pull air in for a breath.

He brushed her tear away with his thumb. "You're coming with us."

She perked up. Her body was strong again. "When do we leave?" Aili could breathe again.

Andvari laughed. "I tell you we're going somewhere dangerous, that two people haven't made it back, and your first question is when we leave? Aren't you worried?" He held her gaze.

Aili shook her head. "Whatever happens will happen. It has to be better than not having magic and becoming a maid, hidden in someone's manor somewhere. That was going to be my fate. Danger is better than boredom. Besides, maybe I can help?"

"Once we cross the border, we'll be working without magic most of the time. I'm not sure our magic will work, though your abilities might be as strong as ever. You can help. Even without magic, I know you'll be okay."

Aili smiled. "I'll help with anything I can. You changed my life for the better."

Andvari stroked Leya's neck. "We'll be riding. Do you want to bring Leya? If you don't want her in danger, I can arrange a Scout horse for you."

Leya snorted at Andvari and pinned her ears.

Aili giggled. "She says she's coming."

He rolled his eyes. "Who am I to argue with a pony? Less attitude, miss. If you don't behave like a normal pony, you could give us away. Stealth mission, understood?" Andvari stared Leya down.

Leya nuzzled his pockets, sniffing. She bumped his hip with her nose.

"See, that's more like it. I don't have any treats." He pushed her nose away.

Leya nipped at him, missing his clothing by a thread.

Aili pulled Leya's nose to her. "Be good and I'll get you an apple. Bite him and you won't get treats for a month."

Leya pinned her ears. She shuffled to Aili's other side, away from Andvari.

He turned and headed back to camp. "Today, we'll pack and get ready. We leave at first light tomorrow. I'll show you how we pack and get you what you'll need."

They returned to camp and got the horses settled. Aili gave Leya the promised apple. With that taken care of, Andvari led her to one of the large warehouses. The building was long and low, spacious inside, with mage-light illuminating rows of shelves and bins of equipment.

"Time for the big mission?" The gruff, hairy quartermaster pulled a list from the wall.

"Sure is. Myself, Kyson, and my student."

The Quartermaster picked up a piece of slate and made chalk markings on it. Aili watched the people moving around the warehouse. They pulled small slate tablets from their vests and read whatever appeared there. The workers retrieved the equipment from the shelves and bins, setting it on carts. Some people floated items from tall shelves, lowering them down to within their reach. The carts followed the workers to the desk.

"Standard cross-border spells?" The Quartermaster looked over the carts, checking the equipment.

Andvari nodded. "Please."

Aili's skin prickled. The Quartermaster chanted and circled his hand over the gear. His spell blanketed the gear and magic within came to life.

"Will the spells keep working?" Aili whispered.

Andvari shrugged. "Maybe not. Even if they're weaker, the spells will give us an edge in comfort and concealment. Without the spells, the gear is still high quality."

The Quartermaster placed everything in a box with And-vari's name, rank, and mission on the label.

"After lunch, we'll come by for the clothing and anything else."

"It'll be ready for you." The Quartermaster clasped hands with Andvari.

Aili followed him to the dining room. Camp noises faded around her as she got lost in her thoughts. Camp was now like her home. Aili belonged here with them. She had friends, and her room was no longer a refuge, but one more comfortable space among many.

Still, if he was leaving, she'd rather go with him than stay behind. Weeks ago, she wouldn't have cared about magic disappearing. Now she could influence magic and had friends she wanted to help and protect. Now her friends needed her, and she could make a difference. How could she say no?

Andvari ate beside her, just as lost in thought as she was. What was he thinking? Was he worried about the mission, or her presence on it, or thinking about something else entirely?

They returned to the warehouse after their meal. A pile of clothing sat on the large table beside the desk. Two pairs of boots were lined up behind the clothes. The box had more items in it now, full almost to the top.

"This should be everything you need." The Quartermaster waved at the piles and box. "Check that it fits well. If the magic fails, you still want the clothing to fit properly. There's time for the seamstresses to alter it if you check right away. Try the boots on here."

Andvari handed her the small pair of boots. Aili kicked her boots off and slipped the new pair on. The soft leather conformed to her feet like a second skin. Durable and thick leather soles would protect her well while letting her move quietly. Aili nodded.

He tried on his own new pair and smiled. "The cobblers keep notes on everyone's sizes, yours included. They took those measurements yesterday. The clothes should fit just as well. They know what size clothing I gave you and can keep track of how the magic adjusts the fit, if it needs to."

The Quartermaster set the clothing in another box and handed it to Andvari. At a nod from him, Aili picked up their old boots and tucked them under her arm. They returned to their room with the clothing, where he sorted two piles and handed her one.

"Try it all on. If it doesn't fit perfectly, we'll have it altered. You don't want any chafing or rubbing on a mission." Andvari waved and her room curtains dropped for her.

Aili slipped into her room and set the pile on her bed. The clothing was mostly soft cotton, with a thicker and tougher jacket and cloak. It fit perfectly, letting her move easily without being baggy anywhere. Aili changed back into her regular day clothes and refolded the pile.

"How does it all fit? I'm done," he called.

Aili raised her curtains. "It's great. Like they made it just for me," she teased.

He smiled and rolled his eyes. Andvari grabbed saddlebags from near the door and handed them to Aili. "I'll show you how to pack the Scout way."

He showed her all the compartments in the bags and how to pack, with a place for everything she might need. Aili blinked at the amazing amount of gear and clothing that fit, and all without magic to help. She picked up the bags. It was still light and balanced between the sides.

"Okay, that's impressive." Aili set the saddlebags down on her trunk. "That's a lot of stuff."

"We've had plenty of time to figure this out over the decades."

Kyson came in with the box in his hands. He set it on Andvari's desk. Aili sat and waited, watching, as they went through it all again. They compared each item to a list. Nothing was missing. They decided who would carry which items, so everyone had some of the group items in their packs. Aili usually camped with a knife, tarp, and rope. So much of this equipment was new to her.

"Oh, right. I also have this." Aili pulled a thin leather carrying case from her night table.

Andvari made a space on the desk, and Aili opened the case. Inside, straps held little rows of vials securely. Each contained a potion or a lotion, all shimmering with magic and glowing different colours. A small compartment held scissors and tiny tools for medical care, like tweezers and a probe.

"As long as the magic is active, these will refill directly from Ilia's supplies. I know how to make it all over a campfire if we can't restock it with the magic. We don't have to worry about running out." Aili waved at the case.

Kyson leaned over and peered at the vials. "Some of these are incredibly rare." He pointed to a vial of potent anti-dote. "You can make these?"

"If it's in here, I can make it. I don't even need a lab; I can get what I need from the forest."

"Bring it. Where do you usually carry it?" Andvari picked up the case and looked closer.

"I have a leather strap I wear under my shirt. It goes around my shoulders and the case is slim and discrete." Aili pulled the strap from her trunk and showed him, threading the case on it.

"Perfect." Andvari handed her the case back.

"That looks like everything." Kyson glanced at the equipment one last time. "We're ready for tomorrow."

"We'll get an early night and be off first thing." Andvari turned to Aili. "If you have any trouble sleeping, tell me right away. You need rest, so we can use a light sleep spell to help."

"I will," Aili promised.

"Wash up. We're eating here tonight in the quiet. After supper, we meditate. We're skipping Drill. Hurry. Supper is on its way." Andvari pointed to the bathroom.

Aili set her medical kit with the saddlebags. She closed the bathroom door behind her and filled the sink. The warm water left her feeling refreshed as she washed. Aili glanced in the mirror as she cleaned her face. Her first mission with him. At least she'd be camping again.

She returned to the room. They stood at the desk, examining maps. Aili settled on his bed in the breeze. A nap sounded good. Did she have time? She lay back across his bed, staring up at the ceiling. Her eyelids drooped, and she relaxed.

The knock on the door startled Aili up. She blinked a few times and stared at the door. Andvari opened the door. A tray of food hovered outside, waiting for him. Aili tilted her head and watched him grasp the tray. Odd. He carried the tray to the desk, where it just sat where he placed it, being a normal tray now.

Kyson held his hand out, palm down. He gestured with his other hand, tracing the shape of a chair in miniature. The air shifted and moved with his gestures, forming a chair large enough for him to sit on, though it was translucent and delicate looking. It looked like it was glass, though Aili could feel he entirely made it of air. She rubbed her chin.

"Would you like one?" Kyson waved at the chair. He sat.

Aili held her breath. He didn't fall. This chair that shouldn't exist was holding him in place, solid and stable. Aili pointed, mouth open, but no words coming out. She narrowed her eyes at the chair.

"Surely you've seen things like that at the University." Andvari grinned at her.

Aili shook her head. "I've seen more new ways of using magic here in a few weeks than I have all those years I followed father around there. Here it's all practical magic, too."

The men smiled at each other.

Kyson laughed. "Here we call it the School of Life. Need drives more magic creation than any other reason, and life in the University is comfortable."

Aili couldn't argue that point. Servants handled daily needs at the University. Academic mages taught commonly used spells and debated magic theory. Field mages discovered most magic outside the University, and later brought in.

Andvari handed Aili her plate. "She likes to eat where the breeze blows over her. She's fine there."

He and Kyson ate at the desk, still going over the maps. Aili listened as they debated routes and places they should look first. Andvari marked places the Scouts were, and where they were last heard from. Aili paid close attention as she ate. When she was done, she set her plate on the tray and leaned over the maps.

"Have a good look. Ask anything you want." Andvari set his empty plate on the tray. "We'll take copies of these, including a non-magical version, in case the magic fails."

Aili memorised the map. Northeast meant going around the cliffs. Mountains got steeper north of those, easing into rolling foothills to the east and south. A few roads crossed the border and headed for major cities deep in the country, and away from their probable path.

"Has Darik taught you the recovery and restoration meditation?" Andvari stood and stretched.

Aili nodded. "I know it."

"Get comfortable wherever you like. We'll start in a few moments."

She settled on the bed with her legs crossed. Kyson clapped his hands above the chair, and it disappeared, the air flowing out the window. He carried the plates to the hallway and tossed them, and they sped down the hall as he closed the door.

Aili blinked. Did she really just see that? How could she spend time in the University, supposedly the most magical place ever, and not see things like this? She shook her head. No, this place was far more magical than anywhere else she'd been. So many new things for her to see, and all in the few short weeks she'd been here.

Andvari sat on the bed beside her, legs crossed and back to the headboard. Kyson chose the desk chair. She closed her eyes and slowed her breathing. They taught most mages to focus on an inner pool of magic inside them, but Aili didn't have one. Instead, she recalled an image in her mind, a way to focus her thoughts and relax.

At first, the old pond came to mind, a place she played as a child in the western woods, and her favourite place to camp. Her thoughts turned to the waterfall nearby, the power flowing through the area, and Aili let the image settle instead.

Darik flashed before her mind, standing beside the pool. Aili smiled. She'd never seen him there. She let her thoughts wander. Darik nodded to her, smiling widely, the expression of a proud father looking at their child. He taught and guided her, advised and helped her, just like her actual father. Darik faded from the scene. Aili focused on the water flowing over the falls, and the feel of the air in her lungs, and finished her meditation with them.

"Have trouble settling?" Andvari stretched.

"No." Aili shook her head.

He stared at her, that amused smile on his face.

"Maybe a little." She shifted on the bed. "I thought of Darik. He always seemed to know things. A bit like you but different. Did he know I'd need all the meditation and the other skills?"

Kyson stood and stretched, his fingers nearly brushing against the ceiling. "Probably. For an Earth Mage, he had a rare gift with Air Magic."

Aili curled up and turned to him. "What do you mean?"

Andvari stretched his legs along the bed. "Darik learned and developed skills in magical foresight. It's a specialized field of Air Magic, and most mages never learn it, not even Air Mages."

Aili pressed her hand to her heart. "He knew it was time for me to leave. He had my gear ready for me."

Kyson leaned against the desk. "He could see possibilities. Most of us need a mirror or bowl of water, something to see the scenes in, but he could see them in his mind. He could also tell what was most likely to happen, where we just see what might be. Foresight isn't helpful for most mages. Even Darik had limited control."

Andvari pushed her leg with his foot. "Bedtime. We'll have plenty of time to discuss magic later. Tonight, we all need sleep."

"See you in the morning." Kyson straightened up and left the room.

Aili got up and went back to her own side of the room. She lay clothing out for the morning. With a nod, Aili went and washed up, with her night clothes under an arm. While the sink was draining, Aili perked up at the sound of voices in the other room. She changed into her night-clothes and opened the door.

A man hobbled to the desk chair, Andvari and a woman helping him move. Both new people wore the standard Scout casual clothing, though the man's pant leg bunched up above bandages wrapped around his leg.

"I remember you." Aili grinned and waved.

He lowered into the chair, eased down by the others. "I'll always remember the mage who saved me, too." The man smiled at her, his bright and clear brown eyes meeting her gaze. "Thank you for saving me."

Aili stifled her giggle. Someone was thanking her? That had never happened before. How was she supposed to respond? "It was the right thing to do."

The woman nudged his shoulder. "If you hadn't saved him, I'd be finding myself a new partner right now. Those are so hard to break in properly." She brushed her blonde hair back from her eyes.

The man shifted and sucked in a breath; his face scrunched in pain.

"Aili, this is Hildon." Andvari sat on the trunk near the man. "You'll be okay?"

Hildon nodded. "In a few more days. The healing spells are working, and I'm not in nearly so much pain. It's not comfortable, having a large muscle and all the veins and such reattached, but I'll live." He turned to Aili. "I'll live because you protected me. Nali stopped the bleeding right away, and I'm here to be grateful to you both."

"How did you get hit?" Aili walked past to her own space and sat on the end of her bed, facing him.

"I was trying to cast magic and swing the sword at the same time. I know—" he grinned and held his hands up. "Lesson learned. He got a lucky strike while another opponent distracted me, and I collapsed. I was getting my sword back up when you sent them flying."

"Fortunately for you, Nali's amazing with healing spells." Andvari leaned back against his hands.

Hildon shook his head. "Yeah, she could reach me without the people trying to stab us." He rested his hand on hers on his shoulder. Hildon looked up at his partner and smiled.

"I'm glad you're safe." Aili nodded at his bandages. "I hope you heal well."

"Oh, he will. Or else. Now, off to bed with you." Nali nudged her partner. "You need rest. If you split that muscle before it heals properly, I just might leave you like that."

Andvari helped him up and walked him to the door. He closed the door and turned to Aili. She stared out the window. Nobody ever thanked her for something like that before. Not people she didn't know.

He sat on the bed beside her, the mattress sinking under his weight. "What's on your mind?"

Aili smiled, though her jaw trembled. "It was so chaotic out there."

"That was your first battle, wasn't it?" His hand covered her knee. Soothing flowed into her.

She nodded. A tear rolled down her cheek. "So much yelling," Aili whispered.

He draped an arm around her shoulders and pulled her close. Aili leaned against him, her head over his heart. Tears streamed down her cheeks, soaking into his night shirt. Fear surged inside her, memories of the noise and people running and blood on the ground. Only the moving meditation let her keep going out there.

Aili clung to his arm as she wept. He rubbed her back and held her. How was he so calm after all that? How many battles had he seen? Could she handle being in another? Aili cried until no more tears came.

"Time to sleep." Andvari shifted and pulled her blankets back.

He guided her along the bed until she was laying with her head on her pillow. She rolled to her side. He pulled the covers over her, tucking them around her shoulders.

Andvari placed his fingers on her forehead. "Sleep," he whispered.

Her eyes closed and her breathing evened out. Sleep took her, and her heart slowed.

CHAPTER 12

HAUNTING MEMORIES

She rolled onto her back under the warm blankets. The early sunlight was peeking through the windows, giving the room a soft purple glow. Aili's heart raced. Today was the day, her first official mission with them.

Andvari was already at his desk, going through the papers there. "Wash up and change. Breakfast is coming to us today."

Aili took her day clothes and went to the bathroom. She washed up and braided her hair. Food smells wafted over to her. Aili sniffed the air. Pancakes? Fresh rolls, for sure. Her stomach growled. She could smell the fresh fruit in the rolls, and knew there would be nuts inside, too.

When she opened the door, Andvari and Kyson were already eating at the desk. Aili narrowed her eyes at that chair he made—out of nothing, she might add. No, not nothing, air. Still, how did that even support a man as big as him?

Andvari pointed at her plate, sitting on the corner of the desk. "Come and get it."

Aili tossed her night clothes on her bed and snatched the plate from the desk. Her mouth watered. She sat on his trunk and dug into her food, starting on the pancakes before moving on to the lightly spiced rice and beans.

"I've done the morning checks. Once she's done, we can go." Andvari nodded at the pile of gear by the door.

"I've done mine, too. I'll meet you at the stables. You've got the maps?" Kyson set his empty plate on the tray.

Andvari nodded. "I taught her to pack like a Scout, so any of us can find anything in any pack." He downed the last of his tea in one swallow.

"Smart." Kyson stood.

Aili set her empty plate on Kyson's. She moved to her trunk and looked over her gear.

"Don't forget that medicine pouch of yours. It's better stocked than the ones we carry."

She held it up and showed Andvari. "Got it." Aili slipped the pouch under her shirt and fastened the strap around her shoulders. With a last glance at everything, Aili gathered her gear in her arms.

"Grab your gear. Time to ride." Andvari collected his own armful of items, slinging the heavier packs over his shoulder for her.

"See you in the stables." Kyson strode from the room.

Aili rebalanced her gear. This was more than she ever took anywhere before. She shifted again and nodded to herself. Andvari grabbed her last bag from her trunk and added it to his pile. They headed to the stables, through the quiet and empty halls.

Jordi had Leya, Charger, and Trickster groomed and tied in the aisle, waiting for them. Trickster already had his saddle on. The other saddles and gear were on racks outside the stalls, ready to go.

"I've had her fitted. This'll do you well." Jordi gestured to a Scout saddle on the rack beside the pony.

"Go over Leya one last time, and Jordi will help with the saddle." Andvari set his gear along the wall. "After that, I'll do one last inspection. We've got more gear than I think you're used to, since we're going into potentially hostile territory."

Aili set her packs down near Leya and stepped beside the pony. She ran her hands over Leya, stopping to scratch her favourite spots. Leya huffed at her each time she moved on.

"I know, girl. We've got somewhere to be, though. I'll scratch more later."

Jordi lifted the saddle from the rack and handed it to Aili.

"It's so light." Aili admired the leatherwork.

Jordi smiled. "It's got a light frame to spread the load. The leather is soft and light, spelled for durability, and has concealed places for things like your sword. See?" He lifted the saddle flap and showed Aili leather straps underneath.

He helped her hide some equipment in the saddle and showed her how to tie the packs to the rings. By the time they were done, half her gear was concealed by the leather, including her sword.

"Clever." Aili ran her fingers over the saddle.

"You're welcome." Jordi grinned.

Aili raised her eyebrow. "You made these, or did you design them?"

"Both."

"It's part of his duties, and he's very good at it." Andvari lifted Charger's saddle onto his back. "He knows horses well and can design gear that helps keep them healthy and happy while meeting our needs."

"Do you want me to help her with the main packs?" Jordi picked up the large saddlebags.

"If you have time." Andvari fastened his gear to the saddle, concealing much of it.

Jordi placed the packs behind Leya's saddle, showing Aili how to balance them, and ensure the weight was spread evenly.

Aili fastened the straps around the rings. "It's been a while since I've felt like a beginner like this." She tightened the straps around her bedroll and tarp.

"Learning new things is good for us." Jordi rested a hand on her shoulder. "It reminds us what other people feel like when they learn something new and reminds us to have compassion if they're struggling."

Aili nudged him with her elbow. "You sound just like Darik." Her chest felt tight, and Aili pressed a hand to her heart.

"Not surprising, since he trained me." Jordi nudged her back.

"Right, he was a Scout, wasn't he?"

"Not just any Scout, either. He had Andvari's job. He was one of the best."

Aili looked up at Jordi. "What happened? He never talks about it."

"I'll tell you soon." Andvari stepped beside Leya, looking her over. "You look ready."

Jordi nodded. "She is."

Andvari ran his hands over her gear and nodded. "Bring her out and mount up."

Aili slipped Leya's bridle on and led her down the aisle behind the others. Jordi followed her out and gave her a leg up. Aili glanced behind her at the packs. Vaulting on was out of the question with the gear in the way. Jordi showed her how to adjust the stirrups, giving tips on doing it from the saddle.

"Thanks." Aili smiled at him.

Jordi rested a hand on her knee. "Be careful out there."

Andvari waved. "We'll be fine. See you soon."

Aili guided Leya behind Charger. Kyson and Trickster followed behind. They weaved through the camp, heading east. Leya needed two steps for each step the big horses took. Aili patted her smooth, glossy neck. Leya was fit. She'd be fine.

She blinked back a tear. The camp disappeared in the hills behind her. It was home, and she was leaving. How long would they be gone? When would they come back?

Andvari led them across the meadows, pink and gold light shining as the sun rose. The grasses turned to shrubs, and finally to trees as they entered the forest. She'd spent the last few weeks playing tracking games here. Over there was the first time she actually caught up with him, in fact. Aili smiled.

"What are we looking for once we cross the border?"

Andvari turned in his saddle, letting Charger choose the path. "We're looking for anything out of the ordinary, or any traces of magic. If we can find something, we can use spells and figure out what happened. We need to be close, though. You can help with that."

"Sure." Aili shrugged. "How can I help?"

"You feel magic. We can sense it with spells, but you don't need that. Your senses and abilities seem to work even when ours are affected. You said it was like a tingle or a vibration, right?"

Aili nodded. She balanced as Leya stepped onto the path to the border, still behind Charger.

"How far away can you detect magic?" Kyson steered Trickster up beside her, since the path was wider and clear of trees.

"That depends on how strong the magic is, and how old. I can already feel the border, even this far away. Regular spells are a few hundred yards, usually. For small magics, I might need to be within a few horse lengths, unless I'm actively looking." She shifted the reins in her hands, holding them loosely.

Andvari slowed Charger, letting them catch up. "Do you know how long you can feel magic once it's cast?"

Aili smiled. "Big magics, a long time. Normal magic, probably about a week, I think. Little magics might fade within a day."

"Once we get across the border, start looking for any traces of magic. We'll look for physical signs of the Scouts."

She peered down the path, the trees blocking the weaker morning light and leaving the path in shadow. "We'll need to get away from the border first. It's such a big magic it overwhelms everything else."

"I wonder why the University mages couldn't detect her ability to feel magic." Kyson rubbed his chin and looked down at Aili from Trickster's tall back.

The magic from the border made her skin prickle already, though she couldn't see the shimmer yet. It got easier to see magic now that she wasn't surrounded by it all the time, like in the city.

"I didn't even know what I was feeling until I left home. The capital is so full of magic it all blurred together. Besides, I felt it my whole life. I didn't know nobody else felt it, or that I was special that way. What do you see and feel at the border?" Aili glanced between the men.

Andvari smiled. "Nothing. If it weren't for the markers on the trees, I'd never know. What about you?"

"I see it like a massive shimmering translucent curtain that dances in the breeze. It glows, even though I can see right through it. It's more like I see it with my mind, and my eyes let it appear to me. There it is." Aili pointed ahead on the path.

Andvari and Kyson exchanged a look.

Kyson shrugged. "You should do a writeup on this. Get it published in the University papers. You could be famous."

Andvari snorted his laugh, his hand pressed over his mouth. "I'll pass." He pointed at a marker on a tree. "Time for your next adventure. Let's go save the world."

Kyson laughed. Aili blinked. He actually laughed? Kyson?

"Dramatic, don't you think?" Kyson raised his eyebrow.

Andvari grinned. "Maybe."

Aili focused on taking slow and deep breaths. Her chest felt tight, like someone wrapped a giant hand around her and was squeezing. She was at the border. Fortunately, being around the magic in camp so much and playing games so close to the border, Aili had grown used to the sensation a bit. It no longer seemed like a million tiny needles piercing her skin, but was more like the charge of a thunderstorm many miles away.

She sighed when they crossed and the discomfort eased, though she felt it for a few horse lengths after crossing. Leya flicked an ear at her, sensing Aili's tension, but not experiencing her discomfort. Aili shifted and stretched her muscles out, relaxing her body.

"What do we do if we encounter someone on the road?" Aili glanced up at Andvari, high above her on the tall horse. She kept her voice low and hushed.

The forest was dark, oppressive, and unwelcoming. The trees seemed younger and wilder somehow, like trees in her country were used to people and talked with them, and these trees might never have seen a human, or didn't like them if they did.

"Stay close and let us do the talking. We know how to act."

How could Andvari be relaxed about all this? She shook her head and looked down the road. The border magic faded. She felt the smaller magics scattered around the area. Did Scouts pass through here a lot? Aili closed her eyes and opened her senses.

"That way." She pointed into the woods, where the strongest tingle of weak magic was.

"Magic?" Kyson shifted in the saddle and peered through the trees.

"Recent enough to feel easily, but a few days ago, I'm guessing. Maybe more."

Andvari nodded. "Single file. Follow me. Aili, stay between us."

He steered Charger from the path. Tree branches brushed against them as they weaved their way among them. Aili kept Leya close behind him. Kyson followed her.

"Slightly left." The trail grew stronger and faded again. Aili checked again; her eyes closed as Leya followed the big horse. They were definitely going in the right directions. "Wait, it's gone."

Andvari stopped Charger, and Leya stopped, tilting Aili in the saddle.

"Gone? Any ideas?" Kyson cast a spell.

Aili recognized the pattern of his spell, seeking magic, but she didn't feel it settle anywhere. She checked again. "Maybe they had to stop casting their spell, or something happened to them."

"Check again. Take a moment and settle first, so you can look as far as possible. Let me know if you feel anything at all." Andvari turned Charger to face her.

She closed her eyes and sunk into herself, calming her heart and mind. Leya stood still, not even swishing her tail. Aili opened herself up to her surroundings. There wasn't much magic here, hardly anything left at all, and it was fading fast.

Something pulled at her from the distance, like an echo of magic, but twisted and dark. Aili pointed towards it; her eyes open. "I don't know what that is, but there's something over there that doesn't feel right."

Andvari raised his eyebrow. "Magic?"

Aili shook her head. "I don't know what it is. It feels like magic, and not. It's big, though, and not close."

Andvari and Kyson exchanged a look. What were they thinking? She frowned and looked down at Leya's mane. How long would it take her to know them well enough to read all those silent looks?

"We'll check it out. It's in the direction the Scouts reported going before they disappeared. Keep an eye out for any magic. Tell me about anything, no matter how insignificant. If someone magicked a tissue for their nose, I want to know." Andvari turned Charger.

"Road?" Kyson pointed.

Andvari nodded. He guided them back to the road. He signalled Aili to ride beside him, and Kyson took the lead. She let out a breath, having them around her like this. Aili wrinkled her brow. Since when did she need anyone in the woods? Forests were her home, and she'd never been afraid before. Since she had people around her she could depend on, who were just as skilled in the bush as she was or more, she realized. She wasn't alone anymore.

Aili looked up. Her heart raced. Two men were walking towards them. They dressed in the same clothing and had swords on their belts. Aili glanced up at Andvari, who watched them with narrowed eyes. The men watched her group just as attentively.

"Be calm. We're just travellers," Andvari muttered.

The men spread out and blocked the road. They drew their swords. Both men had dirt clinging to their skin and clothes, like they'd been farming or in a mine or something. Dust fell from their clothes as they moved.

"What are such unusual travellers doing on this road?" The man stared at Aili.

"We're heading to Rindell." Kyson's voice held no emotion. He sat straight, but relaxed.

"You're not traders. What business would you have there?" The man narrowed his eyes at Kyson.

"She has family." Kyson gestured at Aili. "We're escorting her."

The men grinned at each other.

"Have fun." The men stepped aside.

Aili pressed Leya a little closer to Charger as they rode between the men. She shivered at the horrible breath of the one near her, turning her face towards Andvari instead.

"Such a cute thing. I wouldn't mind escorting her myself."

Her cheeks burned. Her fingers went white as she clutched her reins. They rode past the men and left them behind. Aili didn't relax until that feeling of being stared at passed.

Andvari glanced behind him. "They're gone. Think nothing of it. This country treats women differently, but we'll protect you." He grinned at her. "Besides, I've seen you with a sword, and without one. You can protect yourself just fine."

Aili pressed her hand to her mouth, stifling her giggle. She'd read about other countries, but this was only her second time across the border. That first time hadn't been all that great, either. There were some advantages to being a mage. If a woman didn't like how a man spoke to her, she could set his pants on fire, or do something else equally fun.

The road was deserted. Not even a sound from another human reached them. They found a sheltered spot off the road for some lunch, tucked into a clearing in the trees. The horses grazed as they ate a fast meal of ration bars. Aili located edible berries right nearby to give their meal a fresh burst of flavour.

She re-tightened Leya's girth and swung up into the saddle. The leather was comfortable, and she had solid support. With her used to riding, she shouldn't even get sore by the end of the day. Aili kept Leya beside Charger on the road again. She kept sensing for other people, but there was no one around. This forest was empty. Too empty.

Andvari looked up at the sun, dropping fast to the horizon. "Look for a campsite. We'll shelter in the forest, away from the road. I don't know how strong our wards will be, so we'll use low-impact camping and standard concealment."

Kyson nodded. He guided Trickster into the trees. And-vari nodded to her, so Aili went next. The shadows grew darker and longer, getting more menacing as they went deeper into the trees. Kyson finally stopped and slipped from his saddle, landing lightly.

"Settle your horse in first, and we'll set up camp after that." Andvari dismounted Charger behind her. "You can check and groom the horses. Bed them down for the night."

Aili nodded. Her leg was stiff as she lifted it over the saddle and packs. Had she ever ridden that long without getting off and running a bit as well? She gripped Leya's mane as she landed, holding herself upright. She unfastened Leya's saddle and lifted it from her pony's back, setting it beside the others under a tree.

She took her brushes from her pack and wandered over to Leya. Aili pressed firmly with each stroke, massaging her back muscles as she brushed. Leya looked good, no heat or swelling, and her hair lay flat as it should. Leya grazed, stopping when Aili found a pleasurable spot to brush.

Aili put Leya's brushes away, and she grabbed Charger's brushes. She went over to the big horse, stretching to reach the top of his back. He and Trickster were both healthy and ready for another ride tomorrow. She set up a highline between two trees, a spot with plenty of grass below, and tethered the horses to it.

The men had camp nearly set up, including dark tarps rigged as shelters. Kyson stretched a cloth out and kneeled beside it. He stacked kindling and logs on it, preparing their campfire. Aili closed her eyes and explored the tarp with her senses. The magic in the cloth was still powerful, ready for use.

"What is that?" Aili kneeled beside him and touched the cloth. It was stiff and felt like nothing she'd ever touched before.

"It's a portable fire pit. It'll safely contain any fire, no matter where we put it. Blowing sparks won't leave the protective area, they'll fall back into the fire harmlessly. We can even use this in dry conditions without risking a forest fire."

Andvari sat across the fire pit from her. "Get comfortable. We're going to practice useful magic for camping and outdoor situations."

Aili shifted and crossed her legs. She flinched when Kyson knocked sparks from his flint. He leaned down and tended the fire, and soon the kindling burned. The fire flickered up and over the logs. She stared at the flames for a long moment, before looking up and meeting Andvari's gaze.

"There are times you need to cook, or need to warm up, and you don't want to risk lighting a fire. A campfire can give away your position. There are other ways to make heat." Andvari leaned back on his hands, his gaze on the fire.

She sighed and rolled her shoulders. Aili knew how to make fires. Darik taught her, but she preferred not to. She knew which plants were edible raw.

"I'm getting the impression Fire Magic might be the last you learn."

Aili glanced up from the flames. He held her gaze. Did he know? No, he couldn't. The corners of his mouth curled into a slight smile.

"What are we trying?" Aili smiled weakly.

Andvari smiled wider. "The easiest way to stay warm or hold heat is with large rocks. You'll need a heat source. We use a spell to heat a rock when we want, but you'll need to find heat from nature. Where might you look?"

Aili leaned back against her hands. "The sun. That'll work when I can sense it. Hmm, at night I could use—" She stared into the trees, her mind on natural heat sources. "There's heat deep in the ground. I could bring that up. If it was safe to make a spark, that might work, too. Hot springs are another way, if we're in the right spot."

He gestured to the fire. "For your first attempt, you can use the fire, since it's right here. When you're ready, heat that rock up."

She reached over and picked up the large rock. It was bigger than her hand and hard to grip. She set it down in front of her. The cold surface was rough, much different from the heat on her skin from the fire. How might this work?

The air around the fire nearly shimmered with the heat. Aili reached out with her abilities and stirred the air, swirling it around. The fire glowed brightly, the flames reaching higher into the air. Aili pulled the air around the rock and pressed it against the surface. The heat seemed to dance from her grasp. How could she hold something she couldn't see?

The rock warmed under her hand, not enough to cook with, but was pleasantly warm to the touch. Aili frowned at the rock. Water and Earth Magic felt so easy. If she was supposed to be equally powerful in all magic types, why was this so darned challenging? Air Magic seemed to have its own rules or something.

Andvari touched the rock. "Well, it would help warm you in an emergency. Try another heat source."

She felt down, deep below her within the planet. Her senses almost hummed as she sunk into the soil. Aili called to it with her will. The heat wanted to rise. She guided it up with her abilities, right into the rock. Aili yanked her hand back from the intense heat.

Andvari's hand hovered over the rock. "That's how you do it." He smiled at her. "Soon you'll be able to control how much heat you use."

Aili dropped her chin in her hand. "Air Magic is hard," she whispered.

Andvari watched her, his head tilted like the stable dog used to. She could almost imagine him with one ear perked up.

"Fire bothers you. Would you tell me why?"

Aili looked down at her rock. Her fingers ran over the stitches in her pant leg, and she gripped the fabric. "I was with father at the University that day." She hated how her voice shook, how she couldn't talk about it, even now, after all these years.

"You survived the fire?" Kyson rested a hand on her back. "Only a handful of people made it out."

Aili nodded. "We were on the ground floor. Father was meeting with the man who led the Fire Mages back then." She looked up, blinking rapidly. Deep breath now. She wasn't in any danger now.

"Take your time." Kyson's voice was low and soft. Magic flowed through his hand and into her back, a soothing presence.

"We were in his personal library. I was reading, resting on a sofa. It had a pattern that looked like little flames. The fabric was scratchy." Aili swallowed. Her throat wanted to close up. Her hands shook, and she pressed them against her legs.

Andvari came around the fire and sat beside her, facing her. He took her hands in his and magic tingled in her hands as he connected with her. Aili felt herself being pulled from her thoughts and back to the forest, to the chilly night air. She could do this. He deserved to know.

"I just got into a book on Fire Magic theory. An alarm blared through the tower. It sounded a lot like swords clashing." Aili swallowed and took another breath. She blinked back the tears. "A student had been experimenting without permission, looking for the best magical fuel for a fire. It got out of control, they said. It didn't behave right, either."

Kyson rubbed her back. "You must have been young. Maybe only eight years old or so."

"Seven."

Andvari wiped the tears from her cheeks with a cloth from his pocket. "What was it doing that was different?"

Aili tilted her head and thought back. "It moved down like fire normally moved up. Normal fire eats cloth and paper, organic things. This ate magic. The tower was full of magic." Her voice faded to a whisper. She took another breath and let it out slowly. "It spread in minutes over the whole tower. It burned with a purple flame."

"How did you get out?" Kyson asked.

"It came into the library under the door. We couldn't get out that way. The Fire Mage tried to control it with magic. It spread faster." Aili gulped. "The sound was horrid, deafening, like a roar that filled the whole place. I didn't even hear the window break, when father hit it with the chair. He grabbed me and leapt out."

Tears streamed down her cheeks. She brushed them away, and more took their place. She'd told no one before, not even Darik. Her heart pounded. She could still feel the heat from the fire if she thought about it. Her body shook and felt frozen all at once. Sweat beaded on her back.

Andvari shifted beside her and tucked her under his arm, her head over his heart. She leaned against him. They sat quietly, letting her breathe and calm down as Kyson tended the fire. Aili took deep breaths, slow and controlled, just like Darik taught her.

"So, no purple flames while we practice Fire Magic?" He wiped her cheeks and handed her the cloth.

"Nope." Aili managed a shaky smile. "Other colours should be fine."

His body shook slightly with his quiet laugh.

"How long did it take you to get comfortable starting fires?" Kyson prodded a log with a stick, shifting it in the flames.

"Oh, I'm still not comfortable. I can do it, though. Took Darik years to convince me to try, and we still didn't start until I was older. Not many years ago, even."

"It's brave to try. You work with normal fires well. We'll go slowly as you start and help however you need. There's no rush, and we can start fires without magic, too." Andvari took the damp cloth and tucked it back in a pocket.

Aili giggled. University mages would never brag about anything non-magical. She never belonged there, in their world of magic and spells. Doing things without magic was beneath them, or so they pretended.

"Go check the horses if you like. We'll cook supper." Andvari moved his arm.

Pony time sounded like the perfect cure to a shaky mood. Aili shifted and stood. "Sure."

Leya was grazing beside the big horses, just beyond where they stood tethered. Aili joined her and ran her fingers through the pony's thick and soft hair. Aili leaned against her, feeling the heat from her skin through the hair. She took a moment before greeting Charger and Trickster, too.

"Supper." Kyson held a bowl up.

Aili wandered over and took the bowl. She settled on the grass beside them, balancing the bowl on her lap. Her hands trembled. Why did she have to remember? She picked at her food, barely tasting it, as they ate quietly together.

Andvari took her empty bowl. "Go get some rest. We'll clean up."

She stumbled to the shelter and crawled into her bedroll. Aili stared out into the forest, the shadows deep and the silence almost indescribable. Where was all the birdsong? Did the birds avoid this place, too? The trees were so thick she barely noticed the sun was still up as she closed her eyes. The red light of sunset would not help this forest feel welcoming.

***

Breakfast smells pulled at her, easing Aili from sleep. The sweet roots and berries brought a smile to her face. Aili stretched and blinked, gazing up at the shelter over her through sleepy eyes. What time was it? She eased herself from her bedroll and stepped from the shelter. Her muscles ached. Aili stretched again, reaching for the sky, before folding and touching her toes.

They had the camp mostly packed up, just the shelter and Andvari's kitchen tools still out. She sat with them at the campfire and ate another quiet meal. Once she finished eating, Aili rolled and packed her bedroll.

Kyson dismantled the shelter and added it to the packs. He moved to the middle of camp and stood; hand stretched out. He chanted under his breath as he turned slowly. Aili watched with wide eyes as grass sprang back up where they pressed it down while sleeping. A log rolled back to where they found it, no longer needed as a chair. She couldn't tell anyone had ever been here.

Andvari pulled a small white stone from a leather pouch that nearly glowed with magic. He walked around the camp. Any traces of spells they used were pulled into the stone. Aili blinked and rubbed her eyes. Was she seeing this? A spell fragment zipped past her and into the stone.

"Where did you get that?"

Andvari held the stone out and let Aili look at it. "All field Scouts take one on missions."

Aili held her hand just over the stone and opened her senses. She could feel it slowly, incredibly slowly, pulling magic from Andvari's body. No wonder the leather pouch had such strong protective magics. She lowered her hand, and he tucked it back in the pouch. She'd seen one of these before in the University, kept in a special room with other artifacts and tools.

"This is a good place to test if our tracking magics still work, and how strong they are." Andvari glanced around. "We're well hidden among the trees. Kyson will guard the horses and supplies first, then he'll try things while I stay."

Aili shifted from foot to foot, her fingers twisted together. "What would you like me to do?"

"You can find your way back here no matter what, even in these thick woods, right?" Andvari held her gaze.

She grinned. "I can find my way back to Leya, no matter where we both are."

"Great. Now, just like in practice, go out on a circular path and end back here. Don't worry about concealment as much, but know there could be people around, so be careful. I'll follow using magic, testing all the different types I can use and see how well each works right now." Andvari raised his hand and Aili felt the magic gathering at his fingertips.

"Okay." Aili slipped into the bushes.

She set out through the trees, a living shadow among the darkness of the forest. Aili walked calmly, quietly, staying low. Bushes were thick and close, and the trees were dense. The forest pressed down on her. Aili pressed her lips together. She'd never experienced fear in a forest before, not of the forest itself.

Aili straightened up and stuffed her fear down. It's caused by magic, she reminded herself. She rolled her shoulders and loosened her muscles. Darik was right. Act confident, stand tall, and it gets easier to face scary things.

The terrain gave her a lot to work with, and Aili slipped into a low area snaking around the campsite. If his magic worked, he'd have no difficulty following her path. He should even catch up to her at this pace.

Her muscles stretched and loosened as she moved. Aili let her senses out, brushing her awareness against the trees. They weren't so different from the trees across the border, younger, and the same species. These trees weren't used to people, though. People came, cut them down, and left again.

Aili focused on a tree ahead of her, blanketing it with her senses. She snuck over to it and placed her palm on its trunk. It shivered under her touch, barely perceptible, but Aili felt it all the same. It had never spoken to a human before.

Was that why the forest was unwelcoming? Had the magic amplified the trees' emotions, giving it form to scare people with? Who set those spells? They felt old, incredibly old, and powerful. Ethala Minis? Her friends?

Aili shuddered as images flowed into her from the tree, healthy trees cut down, burned, stripped of bark while still alive, and more. She brushed her tears away with her sleeve. She poured feelings of friendship into the tree, sharing memories of mages working with trees, taking donated wood with the trees' permission.

The forest brightened around her, just a little more light getting down to her, and the oppressive feelings passed.

Aili straightened up and sent a last burst of her love for the forests out, touching every tree she could reach.

She pulled her awareness back fully into her body and focused on where she was. She needed to get moving. Her bones ached, her body sensing some kind of vibration that threatened to tear her apart. Aili clutched her head and collapsed, her knees hitting the soil, and she fell to her side. Breathing was a struggle, the air not wanting to reach her lungs.

The ache stopped, gone as quick as it hit. Aili rolled to her knees and pressed her hands against the ground. Her stomach rolled. She took a slow breath, and the nausea eased. With a hand grasping the tree beside her, Aili pulled herself upright, her body shaking.

A hand pressed over her mouth and an arm lifted her from the ground. The bushes closed around her as they held her to the forest floor. Someone large and strong kneeled over her, pressing her down. Aili knew that smell, that light soap scent. She looked up and met Andvari's gaze. He lifted his hand from her mouth and pressed a finger to his lips. She nodded.

"They must be around here somewhere." A rough, gravelly voice sounded from their left. The bushes shook as someone moved through the thick undergrowth.

"They must be camped near here, unless they moved all night." Another man spoke, somewhere close to the first man.

"Nobody walks in these woods but us. We'll circle around and look again."

CHAPTER 13

SOMEONE TO HEAL

Aili remained still as the voices went silent and the snapping twigs faded. Were those bandits out to rob them, or soldiers like on the road? She glanced up at Andvari. He stared after them, his deep frown so foreign for the cheerful man.

Andvari held his hand out and helped Aili up. He lifted his hand and circled his first two fingers around. Aili knew that signal, it meant return to camp immediately. She felt for Leya, a burning spot of brightness in her heart, and homed in on her. Aili turned and slunk back to camp, silent as a mouse. Andvari stayed with her, a hand on her back, a solid and comforting presence.

The horses stood tacked up and ready to go. Kyson sat on a log, watching over the animals. He stood when they burst from the bushes and darted to the horses.

"We have to go. They're looking for us," Andvari whispered. "Mount up. We're cutting through the woods and going that way." He gestured with his thumb.

Aili put her foot in the stirrup and Andvari swung her up over her pack, into the saddle. Her body still trembled, though it was easing off. She gripped Leya's mane and held the reins loosely. The men swung up into the saddles and Andvari set off. Leya fell into step behind him, Kyson and Trickster staying close on her tail.

They rode through the forest, keeping to low areas and away from trails. The sun was high overhead when they stopped in a clearing.

Andvari turned Charger to face her. "What happened back there? You crumpled and fell and couldn't get up. Are you alright?"

She twisted her fingers in Leya's mane. "I don't know. It felt like powerful magic, but not like at the border. The border isn't hostile. This flooded me and overwhelmed me like I've never felt before."

Kyson rode up beside her. "Hostile?"

Aili closed her eyes and let the memory wash over her. "Maybe more like hurting? Like an injured animal lashing out."

"Do you know what was hurting?"

She opened her eyes and looked at Andvari. "The forest, maybe? No, not the forest. Something big. I felt the forest's fear before, but that's gone. It's something else."

Kyson arched his eyebrow at her. "Could you explain that? The forest's fear?"

"Oh, yeah, sure." Aili told them about her conversation with the tree, and how she shared memories with it. "It stopped being afraid. It was after I ended that connection when I got overwhelmed by the feeling, whatever it was."

Andvari shook his head. "My student talked to a forest."

"Well, it's more like feelings and impressions than a conversation with words." Aili squirmed in her saddle. "It's like talking to animals that way."

"Do you think her openness to magic in that moment made her more vulnerable to whatever it was, or maybe it's the different way she interacts with magic?" Kyson rubbed his chin.

Andvari shrugged. "Maybe either, or something else entirely. We'll keep a close eye on your magic use and let me know if you feel anything odd at all, no matter how small. If you are more vulnerable when you use larger magics, we'll need to be careful what you do and when."

Aili nodded. Fabulous. I'm powerful, but also vulnerable. What if I have to choose between using magic and collapsing, or letting one of them get hurt? Why can't life be simple?

"We keep moving and stay off the path. Have you ever felt anything like that when scanning for people or magic around you?" Andvari turned Charger around again.

She shook her head. "I've been fine that way."

"Good. Keep an eye out for us, but stop immediately and tell me if you feel off."

"I will," Aili promised him.

Andvari guided Charger through the forest, Aili behind, and Kyson on rear guard. They dropped into a gully and snuck their way along. The horses picked their way through the scrubby brush. The deeper shadows in the gully made finding good footing more challenging. Aili glanced up. Someone would need to be sitting right above them, looking down, Aili realized. Otherwise, they were away from view.

Her lungs ached. She let out the breath she didn't know she was holding. Aili opened her senses and scanned the area as far as she could manage. People moved about above them, not too far from the edge of the gully. Her heart raced. They'd get trapped down here. Aili gave the signal, two fingers held up, and pointed to where they were. Kyson nodded and whistled so softly; Aili was surprised Andvari heard it.

He held a hand up and signalled a halt. Aili willed the horses to be still and silent, touching them with her abilities. A single hoof stomp or snort and they'd give their position away. The horses stood so quiet she could mistake them for statues.

Aili tracked the men above with her senses. They were approaching, aimed just past where the three waited below. She clutched her saddle with one hand, still pointing so the Scouts knew where they were.

Andvari slid from the saddle and nodded to Kyson. Kyson nodded back. Andvari held a hand up and lowered it in front of himself. Aili followed the tingle of magic draping over him down to his feet. A silencing spell, she realized.

He moved to the gully edge and crept up the slope. Not a sound from his movement gave him away, not a snapping twig or dislodged rock. Aili blinked and shook her head. He climbed, slow, steady, and silent.

Snaps and cracks of branches above now let her follow the men without her abilities. Andvari crept up near them. Aili took slow breaths, not too loud now, don't give us away. We're not defenseless, and they still have magic, too. We'll be okay.

Andvari crouched in the bushes at the top, his gaze fixed on where the sounds were coming from. The footsteps approached. Aili tensed in the saddle, ready to spring up and help him. The footsteps turned and passed, going the way her group came from.

He crept back down the slope and moved to Charger. Andvari tapped his cheek, a signal everything was okay. He swung up into the saddle and they headed off again. Aili tried to recall the map. Would the gully flatten and rise soon? They couldn't climb the sides easily with the horses.

With a wave of his hand, Aili rode up beside him. "Anyone else?"

Aili searched again; her eyes closed as Leya kept up with the big horse. Deer, small mammals, birds of every variety she could think of, but no people. "Not within my senses. They're still moving away."

He turned in the saddle to face Kyson. "Those were soldiers. There was a path just above us back there."

The gully turned, following the nearby cliffs and taking them deeper into the forest. That spot of wrongness was still up ahead and off to their side. Aili pressed her lips together. Hiding in the forest was a fun game as a child, but this was nothing like that at all. Her fingers tightened on her reins.

The gully rose gradually, and the shadows weren't as dark. Trees thickened. They were heading back into the flatter forest.

"People?" He glanced back at her.

Aili scanned their surroundings. She shook her head.

He let Charger pick the easiest route back up into the trees. The gully flattened out and Aili sighed. It was too confining down there, and she didn't want to do that again. Andvari slowed and waved her up. She rejoined him.

"Can you still feel the wrongness?"

She nodded. "It's that way." Aili pointed through the trees.

The sun marched across the sky, relentless as they rode towards their target. Aili scanned every few minutes, even though she could feel for nearly a mile out here. She couldn't shake the twitchy feeling, the fear of being snuck up on. Despite scanning the map carefully before they left, she didn't remember any path back there. What else didn't they know about?

Her heart hammered in her chest and her palms sweat. Adrenaline surged through her, giving her the shakes. This wasn't like the trees or whatever the thing ahead of them was, though its emotions were strong. Aili slumped in the saddle and looked around as best she could. It wasn't human, but it was close. There, that way, she felt stabbing pain and fear.

"Stop." She pulled Leya to a halt.

Aili dropped from the saddle and darted into the bushes, her legs shaking as she ran. Someone needed her help. Someone was calling to her, somehow. Aili pushed through the thick underbrush, her abilities helping ease her way as the bushes parted for her.

Something lay on the ground ahead. Pain flashed through her again. Aili dashed to it and kneeled beside the furry pile. She lay her hand on the neck of a small deer, collapsed in the bush. It looked up at her, lifting its head as high as it could. Pain flooded Aili.

She let her senses flow through the deer. There, in the back leg, she felt the stabbing sensations the strongest. Aili leaned over its back and looked closer. Deep gashes tore into the hind leg, the skin ripped by sharp teeth.

Aili took a few slow breaths, still connected to the deer with her senses. She sent calming through her hands, a promise to help. Crouching low, Aili moved back to the hurt leg, staying near the deer's back where she wouldn't get kicked.

"Aili?" Andvari's whisper cut through the brush, tight and sharp.

"Sorry. Hang on." Aili focused on the bushes and eased them apart for him.

Andvari came over beside her and looked down at the wounds.

Kyson joined her behind the deer's back. "That's not good. She'll need immediate help. She's already weak and tired."

Andvari smiled at Aili, calm as ever. "How would you usually help her?"

Aili chewed on her lip for a moment. "I could use lotions and potions, but those take days to work. I'd have to move her somewhere safe while she healed."

"As Scouts, we have options. We protect the forests and all life within it. That includes healing injured animals. We have spells, but it's time you learned more serious healing than scrapes and minor cuts. Are you ready?" Andvari stroked the deer's soft hair.

Aili grinned. "You bet. I'd love to do more than remove ticks and ease pain."

"We can heal her, but it will drain us to do a wound this severe. You can heal her using less energy, and still have us to protect you if you're tired. With time you can heal this without a second thought. This time, though, look for a source of energy, some extra life from the forest. You'll need it."

Aili closed her eyes and meditated, connecting herself to the forest around her. Energy filled everything, but it gave life to whatever it was in. The trickling stream nearby was too slow and gentle to have anything extra, either. Aili frowned and kept looking.

"Anything I take, I weaken or kill something else," she whispered.

"How about taking a little energy from a large group of trees? They're resilient, and can replenish their energy from the deep soil, especially if you bring up more ground-water for them."

Aili smiled. That might work. "Would they mind?"

He grinned. "You can talk to trees, right? Ask them."

She grinned and shook her head. It seemed so obvious now that he said it out loud. Aili closed her eyes and felt around, letting her senses rest against the deep roots beneath her. Their roots branched widely. A cluster of the oldest oaks stood nearby, strong, and full of vitality.

Aili settled her senses over the trees, touching their essence with hers. The trees were old, and their rhythm was slow. Their life force pulsed far slower than her heart and being in contact pulled her body with them. She needed to be quick before she passed out.

Using pictures in her mind and her emotions, she tried to express what she wanted, but how do you imagine that? She shared her love of the forest and life within it, pure and strong emotion. That was the best she could do. Aili pulled back a bit, leaving the edge of her essence against the trees, and waited.

'We agree.' Aili felt it in her bones, more a sensation than words, but the meaning was clear.

Aili pulled strands of life energy from the trees, just a bit from each, and spun them together. She brought the energy to the deer and stared down at the wound. What now?

"Think of stitching the wound closed using the magic like a thread. Start in deep and work your way out." Andvari petted the deer, a tingle of calming magic flowing into her through his hand.

With both hands on the deer's hip, Aili probed the wound with her senses. She could feel the tears and rips, but the bone was intact. The life energy slipped through the tissues with her guidance, and Aili gently pulled until the edges of the wound were together. It took care to line the muscles up, and the veins were tiny, but Aili didn't stop or lose focus once. The deer depended on her.

She braced against the deer's hip and her head drooped. It was done. The deer shifted and raised her head, her legs curling beneath her, bending normally. Andvari moved around and wrapped an arm around Aili. With her weight off it, the deer sprang to her feet. She lowered her head and licked Aili across her cheek. With a flash of her white tail, the deer disappeared into the bushes.

"You did good, Kid." Andvari helped her stand. "We need to go."

Aili clung to his sleeve and walked beside him. "My brain is tired."

"I know." He scooped her up in his arms. "You did an amazing job for your first serious healing magic. Your focus was better than I've ever seen it, and your brain needs to rest. Healing magic is the hardest magic for anyone. Many mages never master it."

She closed her eyes and rested her head on his shoulder.

Andvari carried her through the bushes and set her on Leya's back. "Can you sit on your own?"

Aili opened her eyes and met his gaze. She clung to Leya's mane. "Yes. She'll take care of me."

"Let me know immediately if you need help or feel unwell." Andvari walked to Leya's head and took hold of her rope bridle. He stared the pony in the eye. "You take care of her, too."

Leya snorted. Her head dipped down and rose again.

"I'm talking to a pony," he muttered, letting go of her bridle. "She's actually talking back to me." He stroked her nose. "Stay close."

Leya moved beside Charger and waited, standing closer than normal. Charger didn't even flick an ear at the pony in his personal space.

Andvari swung into the saddle. He reached down and touched her shoulder. "Close your eyes and rest your brain. We'll stay on lookout."

Aili closed her eyes. Leya's movement rocked her, a soothing and familiar motion with a steady rhythm. With each step, she felt stronger and less tired. Maybe only a few minutes later, Aili opened her eyes and looked up at him. Leya was still right beside Charger. Kyson was leading with Trickster this time.

Andvari smiled down at her. "How do you feel?"

"Still tired, but just my brain. My body feels good again." Aili patted Leya's neck.

"When we use magic, we get body tired. You're recovering quickly, though. Are you hungry?"

Aili smiled sheepishly. "I'm starving."

He pulled an energy bar from his pants' side pocket and handed it to her. "Eat this now. We'll stop for lunch soon."

"There's water ahead. We can stop there and take a break, if it's drinkable." Kyson pointed ahead and to the side a bit.

Aili closed her eyes and listened. The stream sounded small and shallow, but active and fast flowing. They reached it in minutes. The water was wide and clear. The bottom was rocky, and the stream bubbled as it flowed around the bigger rocks.

Kyson rode to the stream bank and slipped from the saddle. He kneeled beside the flowing water and held his hand out. Kyson chanted under his breath. "It's clear and safe."

Aili eased herself from the saddle and stretched. "Is magic limited?"

Andvari dismounted Charger. "What do you mean?"

"I mean, is there only so much magic, and we'll eventually run out of it, or is there always more energy to cast it with?" She joined Kyson at the stream's edge and kneeled.

Kyson shrugged.

"I don't know for sure, but I've never heard of anyone running out of magic permanently before." Andvari rubbed his chin. "We can tire ourselves out and need to rest, but we get stronger as we get older and more practiced. We also live longer than the non-magical folk, so I doubt it's shortening our lives at all. What're you thinking?"

She scooped up water in her hand and soothed her dry mouth. "Well, I'm doing magic with what I find around me. I'm limited to what's available, but it never seems to run out, as there's so much power of different varieties around me. Are spells similar?"

Leya ambled to the short and sweet grasses beside the stream, where the sun beamed down through the thinner trees.

Andvari took metal cups from his pack and handed one to Aili. "Not like you mean, I don't think. I can cast a spell to start a campfire as many times as I want until I pass out, but that's my limitation, not the spell. Nobody has ever mentioned fire starting spells just quitting after a while."

She scooped up a cup of water and downed it. Aili stood and looked around, turning slowly. "It's such an enormous world, so full of life and energy." She peered up through the leaves at the sky. "If I take energy from a living thing, though, I weaken it. If I'm not careful, it can die."

"You can sense that?" Andvari kneeled beside her and collected a cup of water.

Aili stared down at the flowing stream, watching a leaf float past. "I can use water without harming anything, as long as I don't drain a water source. Rivers and waterfalls are the best. I can pull energy from the ground or breeze, too." She pulled Leya's reins up and tied them out of the pony's way.

Kyson hobbled Trickster and Charger and let them loose to graze. Andvari pulled the fire cloth from a pack and set it out. Aili took another drink, watching quietly. He had his thinking face on, that slight twitch to his eyebrow and the corners of his lips turned down a hair.

"How does healing feel to you, especially when dealing with minor wounds?" He stacked the tinder and a few small logs, just enough for a quick fire. Andvari struck the flint with the knife and the sparks landed in the tinder.

"I can take energy from the injured person if I don't need a lot. They can rest and sleep or eat to get it back." Aili set the cups beside the fire cloth to dry.

"You have both advantages and disadvantages, then. Nature Mages can harness the power of oceans or volcanos or storms, when they're focused and strong enough mentally, but they need the power around them and the focus to do it. I can cast a spell as many times as I want using nothing around me, but it'll always be limited by my strength, unless I enhance that somehow. With enough fuel, I can grow a fire to any size, but it'll always start as a small flame." He blew on the little flames, and they grew, spreading through the kindling.

Kyson sat beside Aili. He handed the rations to Andvari. "Can you use the sun for energy?"

Aili tilted her head and considered his question. "I think I do. Anything I do in the sunlight, it's stronger and easier. I don't need as much energy from whatever I'm working with, either."

"Is that how you kept the magic going at the waterfall?" Andvari shifted a log, and the fire spread.

She smiled. That was a fun day, and one she'll remember for a long time. "It might have been. It wasn't entirely coming from the water, and I wasn't taking it from the land."

"Sit and rest. We'll have this cooked in moments." Andvari set large rocks in the fire and lay the food on them.

Aili leaned back against her hands and watched him cook the food. He wasn't using magic. Could he still, or was he being careful with it? He soothed the deer, so he still had some magic available. Kyson stood and disappeared among the trees, quiet as a ghost.

She watched the smoke rise a few feet before it just dissipated. The cloth glowed in her senses, so Aili looked closer. The patterns were within the cloth itself, woven into it permanently, and holding the magic set inside.

Kyson reappeared, a cloth bundle in his hands. He kneeled beside her and gave Andvari the cloth. Andvari opened it and sorted through berries, leaves, and roots, setting some on the rocks and putting others aside on the cloth.

He held out a double handful of berries to Aili. "Here, eat. Get some more energy back."

"Thanks." Aili popped a berry into her mouth.

"I found this for you, too." Kyson held out a delicate thin green plant with little white clusters of flowers. "Eat this first."

Aili grinned and took the plant. She bit into the sweet leaves and the juices coated her mouth. Energy rushed through her body. She no longer needed a nap. Aili chewed the plant and ate it, licking her fingers clean of every bit of juice. "Thanks for the Corbina Weed."

Kyson waved at her; his mouth stuffed full of berries. They all ate their berries as the roots cooked on the rocks.

Andvari pulled roots from the rock and set them on a cloth. After smearing some crushed herbs on the roots, he passed the cloth to Aili. "Careful, they're hot."

She sniffed the air and smiled. The herbs grew abundantly in her forests, but it was soothing to find them out here, too. Ilia used many of them on magically depleted people. Aili devoured her roots, licking her fingers clean after.

Cleanup took little time, and they were back on their way, no sign they'd ever been there. They remounted the horses and continued on, Aili keeping them on track.

"This forest feels empty," she whispered.

Kyson rode up beside her. "There should be farms scattered around this forest. Can you feel any of them?"

Aili shook her head. "Just deer and small animals. Nothing like livestock anywhere, and no people I can feel."

Andvari turned and frowned. Why did he need that frowny face? Aili took a slow breath. No, it would be okay. It had to be. But Kyson had a dark expression, too.

"What?"

Andvari nodded at Kyson before turning and watching, guiding them on.

"Back home, people mostly live in cities and settlements. The forests are untouched and wild like you're used to. Only Scouts, and you, I guess, roam the forests and spend a lot of time there. We don't even live there, though. Here, the land isn't as vital and lush, and people live everywhere. They need more land to grow enough food, but there should be farms everywhere." Kyson glanced around.

"What about the predators, though?" Aili closed her eyes and opened her senses. "There are deer everywhere, but there should be wolves or something. It's not balanced."

"Another mystery," Andvari whispered.

The sun moved across the sky, slowly dropping towards the horizon. The hills eased into rolling land, tough and rugged, with plenty of rocks in the otherwise soft ground. Andvari led them on, skirting hills wherever they could, and staying in cover.

Aili scanned the forest. People were way off in the distance, at the edge of her range, together in a group. Birds circled overhead or flew between trees, searching for food. Something else tugged at her, though.

Andvari stared off in the direction she felt it, whatever it was. His shoulders were tense, and he was listening, his head cocked to the side. He raised his hand and signalled a halt. "Six?"

Kyson closed his eyes and listened. "Maybe seven."

"Too fast for humans."

"Wolves." Aili clapped a hand over her mouth and cringed.

Andvari frowned at her. After a long moment, he smiled and shook his head. "You're sure?"

Aili nodded, her cheeks burning. "Positive. You never forget wolves and how they feel. They have their own magic."

"How do you know that?" Kyson peered into the trees.

She shrugged. "I've felt it. The pack in the woods regularly ranged where I played. I've met them many times."

Andvari's jaw dropped. "They never attacked or drove you off?"

Aili twisted her fingers in Leya's mane. "No."

Kyson shook his head, his eyes wide. "Those wolves protect the heart of the forest. They keep people away from the middle of the woods. They protect the Mother Tree."

She pressed her lips together and stared up at Kyson.

Andvari moved Charger beside her and reached a hand down, resting it on her shoulder. "Aili, have you seen the Mother Tree?" His voice was barely a whisper, and the corners of his mouth turned up into a near smile.

"Y—yes?"

The Scouts stared at each other for a long moment. Kyson looked like Aili had just slapped him, open-mouthed and stiff. Andvari's hand twitched.

"What's gotten into you both?" Her voice shook. Were they okay? Had she said something wrong? Should she have lied?

Kyson focused ahead towards the wolves. "They're coming closer."

"Can you talk to them?" Andvari squeezed her shoulder lightly.

"I think so. Wolves are different, but they're smart." Aili squared her shoulders and straightened in the saddle.

"Great. We don't want to fight them. We just want to pass through."

The wolves shone like beacons in her senses, coming closer each moment. They circled Aili and her friends, darting around in the bushes just out of sight. A calm settled over her. Aili slipped from the saddle and stepped forward, sensing for the pack leader. She kneeled and stretched her hands out, opening herself to the wolves with her awareness.

"What are you doing?" Andvari hissed.

A massive wolf stepped from the bushes; his nose high as he sniffed her. No, it's a she, Aili realized. The wolf stalked towards Aili. Their eyes met, the gold and the green. She led this pack, Aili knew. She's the leader.

CHAPTER 14

WOLVES AND STORMS

L eya dropped her head to the grass and tore a mouthful off, ignoring the wolves completely. The pack emerged from the bushes, watching the small group. Aili touched the horses with her abilities, sending calm to them. Charger snorted and blew out a breath, his head lowering. Trickster grabbed a mouthful of grass, ignoring the wolves as well.

The big she-wolf stared at Aili.

Aili lowered her gaze and waited. Paws padded through the soft soil, just a faint sound. A cold, damp nose brushed over her forehead and touched her palm. She smiled at the smell of damp fur.

"Aili?"

"It's fine," she murmured.

The cold nose pressed to her forehead. Images flashed through her mind. Darkness surrounded a hill, despite the sun being up. Men chased the wolves with torches and weapons, axes glinting in the sun. Purple lightning hit the hill, and the ground shook. Fear and dread rushed through her, a clear memory from the wolf. Last, an image of her and her group.

Aili shared images of her home in the camp, her and Andvari exploring the woods as he taught her new skills. She showed brief scenes from the battle, and the men who tried to invade. Aili let her sense the danger and how she was heading to the wrongness. How was she supposed to show the wolf they were here to help? There was a limit to thought pictures.

The wolf licked her forehead. She turned and trotted into the bushes, disappearing without a sound or the rustle of a leaf. Her mate stood and stretched before following. The pack melted back into the bushes, gone like phantoms in the night.

"Care to explain before I give the lecture on safety and communication, or after?" Andvari looked down from Charger's back, his arms crossed over his chest.

"Sorry." Aili stared at her boots as she rose and walked back to Leya. "I'm not used to needing permission to do things."

Andvari sighed and ran his hand through his hair. "It's not that you need permission. I'm responsible for your safety. We work around wolves and know them. They won't usually attack without a reason, but when they do, they're deadly."

She eased herself back into Leya's saddle. "I knew I was okay."

"Tell me that, next time." He finally smiled. "I know the rules are different with you because your magic is different. Remember that we can't sense and feel what you do or know things the way you know them. Aili, look at me."

She swallowed and clenched her teeth. Aili met his gaze, ready to face the disapproving stare she knew so well from childhood. Most mages used that look on her.

He smiled. "What did she have to say? You had quite the conversation, didn't you?"

Aili rolled her shoulders and smiled back. "We're heading the right way. It's in a hill, and it's affecting everything around it. There are men with swords and axes guarding it. They chased the wolves away."

Kyson tilted his head, his chin resting on his hand. "She treated you like a pup."

"She's old and revered. The pack loves her. In wolf terms, you're both younger than her by many years." Aili grinned at him.

Kyson shook his head. "She's in excellent shape for an old wolf."

"You like wolves?"

"All Scouts like wolves." Andvari stretched in the saddle. "They keep forests healthy. Kyson studies them every chance he gets."

"When we get back and have time, would you show me the pack in the western woods?"

"Sure. I can introduce you." Aili nodded.

Kyson straightened up and almost smiled.

"Let's go." Andvari turned Charger. "We need to find a campsite before nightfall."

"She said humans don't come around here. That's why they came." Aili guided Leya behind the big horse. "The other humans left a while ago, when the hill changed, and nobody has been back since. Not for half a day's trot, as the wolf runs."

"What else did she say?" Andvari waved Aili up to ride beside him. "That's useful to know."

Aili traced the front of her saddle with her fingers. "Sorry, I'm new to this teamwork thing." She wiped her eyes with her sleeve, blinking to resist the tears.

"I'm sorry, too. You're capable, and I forget you're not a Scout. It's unfair to expect Scout discipline from you."

"Really?" Aili straightened in her saddle and glanced up at him.

"Really. Your bushcraft is as good as younger Scouts, and you're at home out here. In base camp you seem a little out of your element, more like the first-year mage you are, but out here you thrive. Sometimes I forget and expect too much." Andvari smiled at her.

She pressed her hand to her chest, over her heart. He wasn't disappointed in her? Aili smiled, though it felt shaky. No, he marvelled at her progress, and her abilities, even if she was a new mage. The slight chill she felt since crossing the border eased just a little.

"Over there." Kyson pointed through the bushes. "A good campsite."

Aili peered through the trees. Yes, high shrubs sheltered it, she could sense the water nearby, and the grass was dense enough to keep the horses fed all night.

Andvari nodded. "Good choice. Lead us in."

Kyson guided Trickster through the bushes, letting the horse pick his way in. They emerged into a clearing large enough for everyone. Aili slid from Leya's back.

Andvari dropped to the ground beside her and rested his hand on her shoulder. "Look after the horses. We'll do the camp setup. After we eat today, we practice Drill and meditate, since we have some privacy."

Aili nodded. Everyone untacked their horse and set their packs aside. Aili grabbed the brushes as the men went through the packs, collecting what they wanted. She set to work on Leya first, checking her over and brushing firmly as they set up the tent and got a fire going.

Charger grazed calmly as Aili checked him, running her hands over him and looking for heat or swelling. He felt good, healthy and relaxed, so she collected his brushes and set to work. She had to reach up as high as she could to get his back properly. His sides heaved as he sighed.

Trickster stood nearby, just as calm. Aili ran her hands over him and stopped at his left front leg. His tendon burned with heat under her hand. She can't let him go like this, or he may not stay comfortable for long.

Aili pulled out her herbalism kit. "Trickster has some inflammation here. Probably from that soft soil earlier."

Kyson strode over and kneeled beside Trickster, his hand over the spot Aili pointed to. "You've got something for him?"

She smiled and nodded. "Absolutely, and it'll work in under an hour on this. Ilia helped me make it, so you know it's strong."

Kyson stood and stroked the black horse's long nose. He rested his forehead against Trickster's as he patted the thick neck. "Thank you."

Aili opened her kit and selected a small container of lotion. She scooped some out and rubbed it between her palms. With firm pressure, Aili rubbed the lotion into his hair. He snorted and swished his tail. Her eyes watered and her nose stung. Her palms tingled.

"I know, big guy. It'll feel weird, and it stinks, but it'll help." Aili tucked her kit away and wiped her hands on her pants.

Kyson scratched the big horse's chin. Trickster leaned into the touch, his head against Kyson's shoulder. Aili smiled up at the pair. She closed her eyes and sent a touch of healing into the tendon, to help the lotion work better.

"Supper's ready." Andvari held two bowls up.

Aili wandered over and took a bowl from him.

"Let it cool first, unless you can treat burned mouths." Andvari smiled.

She settled on the grass near the fire and held the bowl up to her face. The sweet smell of herbs soothed her nose. The mash of roots and rations with berries mixed in smelled wonderful, and she could see the little flecks of spice he added from their supplies.

"Oh, being fancy with actual dishes," Aili teased.

"Only the best, for such fine accommodations." He raised his metal cup to her.

Aili scooped up a small spoonful and blew on the steaming meal. "Mm, this is good."

She scrunched up her face and smiled. The pepper gave a burst of heat to the meal, and the herbs brought extra colour to the pale roots. Berries burst in her mouth, a tart juice to offset the sweet herbs.

Andvari chuckled. "You've been in the bush too long. It is good, though, isn't it?"

She closed her eyes and tasted the roots on her tongue, mixed in with everything else. A quick check confirmed nobody was around, and Aili let herself get lost in the meal. Her muscles relaxed and the knot in her shoulder released as she rolled it.

Aili stared into her empty bowl. "I'll help clean up."

"Ever use magic to wash dishes?" Andvari raised an eyebrow.

Aili giggled. "Of course not. My magic teacher is lazy and lets the camp staff do all domestic tasks."

Kyson snorted into his cup. He sputtered and coughed, his face turning red. Aili buried her grin in her hands and Andvari laughed out loud, throwing his head back as he leaned back against his hands. Maybe, just maybe, everything will turn out okay. If they can still have fun, things can't be that serious.

Kyson wiped his chin and took a slow breath as he set his cup on the ground. "Good luck teaching this one discipline and the chain of command. The respect part still needs work." He cleared his throat and wheezed again.

Andvari took his canteen and opened it. He set it propped up against a rock. "Call the water and direct it across the plates. See if you can create a powerful stream and blast the food loose." He set the bowls and cooking pot beside the canteen.

Aili focused on the plates and reached for the water with her mind and senses. All that practice is paying off, she thought. She pulled the water from the canteen and directed it into the first bowl.

She twisted the water and swirled it around, giving it speed and strength. That's the simple part, she sighed. Aili guided the water around the bowl, pushing it over the bits of food stuck to the sides. Berry juice and bits of rations blasted off, gathering in the pool of water in the bowl's bottom.

The bits of roots stuck stubbornly to the side of the bowl. Aili spun the water harder, narrowing it into a funnel. She scoured the sides with her water funnel until all the roots and debris were loose. With a quick hand motion, Aili grabbed the bowl and dumped the food debris in the grass.

"Show off," Andvari teased. "You're doing great. Keep going." He beamed at her.

"This is so slow, though."

Aili collected more water from the canteen and started on the second bowl. A quick swirl with the loosened funnel cleaned most of the food, and she tightened the funnel down to pressure wash the sticky roots again. The last bowl was even easier and faster.

The pot was a challenge, with its vertical sides and sharper corners at the bottom. A blast of water shot up and sprayed a fine mist until Aili pulled it away from the corner. She focused harder on the food debris, and not spraying them with the sharp water jet she needed to clean the pot.

"Wouldn't this be faster without magic?" Aili glanced at Kyson, who wiped the last utensil dry with a cloth. She glanced at the clean cups lined up in front of him, washed and ready to be put away.

"It is right now, but you're still learning. When you started with a sword, how long did it take you to go through the first form?" Andvari crossed his arms over his chest.

Aili smiled. "It felt like forever. Maybe twice as long as forever."

"And now?" He leaned back on his hands.

"I can almost keep up with you two perfectly."

Andvari nodded. "With practice, you'll get a lot better with your Water Magic, too. Taking the time to learn to clean dishes, you're getting more practice in, and you'll improve your control for all your magic, too. In a few years, you'll send a single blast of water across the dishes in about a second and they'll be completely clean."

"At the rate she learns, that could be in a month." Kyson set the last spoon down with the others, clean and ready to be tucked away.

Aili glanced between the men.

"That's true." Andvari stood. "Grab your sword. We have forms to practice, and you're ready for the next few moves of the fourth form."

Aili leapt to her feet and ran for her saddle. She slipped her sword free of its hiding place and held the smooth scabbard in her hands. It felt warm and light, almost weightless, like it belonged in her hand. Was that the bonding magic? His sword didn't feel light like this to her, the one time she put it away for him.

Andvari collected his sword from his saddle. "Ready?"

She fastened the belt around her shoulders. The leather was soft and curved around her, fitting her perfectly. Aili nodded. She followed him past the firepit, to the area with no trees in the way. Was this why they tucked the tent among the trees?

"Bare hand one." His voice was quiet, blending into the hooting owls and gently rustling leaves.

Aili followed him through the forms, just like at camp. Her body flowed through the motions. The stretching and bending relaxed her body and eased any tightness from travel. Her mind settled, muscle memory guiding her instead of thought. Aili opened her senses and touched the forest, one with nature, as she meditated while moving.

She shut out the sensations of the wrongness in the distance, blending her awareness with the healthier forest around her. She kept up easily as they gradually sped up, following his quiet count. It seemed no time had passed when she finally stood still, warm and breathing hard after the third sword form.

"Come. We'll work here, and Kyson will do his own speed practice over there." Andvari shifted closer to the bushes. "Ready to practice sword form four?"

Aili grinned and bounded to his side. She absorbed every correction she could, moving slowly and letting her body get a feel for each movement. He led her through as much as she knew many times until the sun dropped low enough to scatter deep shadows through the trees.

"Anybody nearby?" Andvari rested a hand on her shoulder.

She closed her eyes and relaxed. "No. My range is longer than ever, and it's just us and the animals."

"Great. We'll do a few minutes of sitting meditation and get some sleep after that. I'll take first watch."

Aili tucked her sword beside her bedroll and settled beside the firepit again. It still radiated heat, though the fire was already out. The men joined her, and Aili shifted into a meditation position. She practiced a quiet meditation Darik once taught her for relaxation and sleep, focusing on an image in her mind and her slow and steady breathing.

She followed Kyson into the tent and tucked herself into her bedroll. Andvari walked around the edges of the campsite, the tingle of his warding magic flowing around them. Aili closed her eyes.

***

"Are we still alone?" Andvari's voice pulled her from sleep, his hand on her shoulder gently shaking her awake.

Aili rubbed her eyes and sat, her brain still slow and fuzzy. What was she doing? Right. Look for dangers. Aili opened herself to the surrounding forest. "We're alone." She covered her wide yawn with her arm.

"Great. We can have a hot breakfast, and you can light the fire. The sun is up, so you have a heat source." He nudged her shoulder. "Come on. Get it ready when you are."

She glanced down at her rumpled clothing. This should be easy. Aili smoothed her hands over her clothes and the dirt fell to the ground. The wrinkles from sleeping vanished. Clean, pressed, and ready.

Aili gathered kindling and fresh wood from around their campsite. The sun peeked over the trees, energy and heat beaming down on the forest. Not too much. She nodded. She could work with this. Probably. She stacked the wood and prepared the fire.

Now, not too much, and don't let it linger. Pass the heat through and don't burn yourself, she muttered as she focused on the wood. Smoke rose from the spot she stared at. Tiny flames appeared and spread over the kindling. Aili let go of the power completely and sat back. She pressed her palms to the ground and let any lingering power go into the soil.

"That was smooth." Kyson settled onto the grass beside her.

"The hard part is controlling the energy I use, and only channelling what I need." Aili wiped her forehead with her sleeve. "I'm still figuring that part out."

Her body still felt charged. Her heart beat fast and her nerves tingled slightly. She took a slow breath and calmed herself, tuning into the energy of the planet instead. After not seeing the sun properly for a while, she smiled up at it with her eyes closed. This was what being alive felt like.

Breakfast was quiet and leisurely. She helped them clean up without magic, taking her time and enjoying the warm breeze. They packed camp, each taking some tasks. Aili pulled the strap snug around the tent. Would this be her last moment of peace on this trip?

Leya relaxed as Aili groomed her, her back hoof cocked and her head low. Charger dozed beside her, and Trickster chewed the grass. Aili tacked Leya and set her packs in place. They mounted the horses and rode on, back into the thicker trees and the darker undergrowth.

"What's on your mind?" Andvari fell back beside her, slowing Charger.

"How do you keep from getting moody and miserable on these missions into dark places?" Aili peered up at slivers of blue sky through the trees. "I was feeling down without the sun. If it weren't for this morning, I'd be exceptionally grumpy right now."

"We train for it." He smiled at her wide eyes. "Really. We pick people who can handle being alone, like I know you can. We also meditate to deal with strong emotions and work in pairs so we can help each other. Don't be afraid to apologize, either, as we've all been grumpy at some point. Lean on your partners, as we can keep each other going when it's tough."

Aili giggled. "Meditation. That's the Scout answer to everything, isn't it?"

"Of course. Also, we keep our moods up by torturing students with lessons and more meditation. Keeps my mood high and keeps me busy." Andvari reached down and lightly poked Aili's shoulder. "Did Darik ever teach you the mind and emotion meditation?"

She smiled and nodded. "First one he taught me." Memories flashed through her mind, her as a lonely child with tear-stained cheeks, and Darik sitting in meditation with her.

"Do some now, just for practice. Leya will look after you. Won't you?"

Leya turned her head slightly and snorted.

Aili suppressed her laugh, a hand over her mouth. It warmed her through, getting to laugh again. She rested her hands on her legs, the reins loose between her fingers. Aili felt for the sun, opening her senses up this time instead of out. She hovered her awareness in the leaves and soaked in the warmth and light.

Her body filled with energy again, controlled this time. With her this relaxed, she could really sense her surroundings. The forest was peaceful around and behind her, but something felt off.

"Andvari?" Aili whispered.

"Yes? Meditating?"

Aili opened her eyes and met his gaze. "Yes. Something is happening up ahead."

He brought Charger to a halt. "What is it?"

"The people ahead, there's a lot of them. I think they're taking cover. Possibly from a storm. The sky is awful dark over there." Aili gripped her reins and straightened in the saddle.

"Let's have a look. There are some hills just ahead we can probably use." Andvari turned to Kyson. "Map?"

Kyson steered Trickster beside Charger. He pulled the map from the pouch and unfolded it. The horses stood relaxed, ignoring the map spread out over their necks. Aili waited as they debated and pointed. Kyson folded the map and tucked it away. They turned and headed up the slope, towards the top of the highest hills.

Aili took a slow breath and rubbed Leya's neck. The air seemed charged. She knew that feeling. A distant roll of thunder broke the silence. They crested the hill in time to see the sky light up ahead. A thunderbolt flashed from a massive hill in the distance to the sky above.

Andvari slid from Charger's back and handed the reins to Kyson. Aili landed on shaky legs and gripped Leya's mane for support. The lightning was purple. It shouldn't be purple. Why purple? How was he so unconcerned, staring off at the storm like that, all relaxed and curious? Her fingers tightened on Leya's mane.

She handed Leya's reins to Kyson and followed Andvari to the edge of the bushes. Her hands shook and her mouth was dry. Aili gripped a tree and held herself upright.

Andvari wrapped an arm around her shoulders. "What's wrong?"

Aili pointed. "It's the hill the wolf showed me." Her throat ached with each word.

"Sit." He lowered her to the ground, and Aili leaned on him. "Can you sense the energy from the lightning?"

She nodded, her jaw trembling.

"Can you tell where it's going to strike next?"

Aili closed her eyes and opened herself. Her awareness brushed against the edge of the storm. The energy swirled around, threatening to suck her in. Aili lowered her awareness to the land below the storm, energy building in the soil. Power gathered in one spot and Aili pointed. Light flashed through her eyelids, blinding white with a touch of purple.

"Good. The next one?" His hand squeezed her shoulder. He was still so calm. How did he do that?

"It's coming closer. Can we go?" She opened her eyes and blinked back the forming tears. "Please?"

"You can feel its path?" He shifted and kneeled beside her.

Aili nodded. She pointed. The lightning flashed. "Please?"

"Come on. Let's find shelter."

He slid his arm around her and helped her up. Aili stumbled along as fast as she could go, each step shaky. He lifted her onto Leya's back, and Kyson gave her the reins. The wind picked up, whipping at their clothing and rustling the bushes.

"That's not a normal storm. We need shelter now." Kyson handed Andvari Charger's reins.

They mounted the big horses and Andvari led them down the hill. He kept Charger beside her. Halfway down, the rain started, heavy drops pelting against her skin.

"With lightning, don't control it." He raised his voice over the wind. "It's too powerful for anyone, including a Nature Mage. You can use your knowledge and abilities to keep people away from it, though."

Aili nodded. She shivered in the chilly wind; her clothing was already soaked with the rain. Even from this far away, the lightning overwhelmed her senses. She patted Leya's soaked neck. "Thank you, girl," she whispered. "You stayed calm."

Kyson took the lead at the bottom of the hill and scanned the surrounding land through the thick rain. Aili trembled as the rumbling thunder approached. The air hummed with energy, and her nerves felt like they were on fire.

"There," Kyson yelled, pointing ahead in the gloom.

A few steps later, Aili could make out dark shadows ahead, large buildings in the gloom and downpour. The place was silent, no animal noises, no one running around taking livestock in or protecting crops, nothing at all.

"Well?" Andvari nudged her lightly. Water dripped from his nose, yet he still smiled.

Aili blinked in the rain. "Right." She smacked her forehead. This close, her senses easily covered the farm, and it was devoid of any farm animals or people at all. A few small mice scurried in the rafters, but that was it. "No people." She raised her voice over the driving rain and wind.

Kyson led them into the yard, the large barn ahead blocking some of the wind. She eased her frozen body from the saddle and pulled the reins over Leya's head. Andvari handed her Charger's reins. She held the big horse as he opened the large door a crack and slipped inside.

The door creaked open wide, and he stood there, grinning. "This is lovely. Come on in."

Aili brought the horses in, Kyson right behind her with Trickster. Small balls of mage-light hovered around the barn. It was dry inside, with no wind to batter her stiff body. She stumbled forward, leading the horses deeper in. Water pooled harmlessly at their feet, collecting and flowing through channels in the floor. She walked through a thick layer of hay. Wind hammered the wall, shaking the building.

"It's stable." Andvari took Charger's reins from her. "It'll stand through this."

She focused on herself and the horses first, pulling the water from her hair and clothing. Leya dried before her eyes. She rubbed the smooth forehead. Aili cared for the horses before she turned to the men and dried them as well.

They unsaddled the horses and turned them loose in the end, where a massive pile of hay reached for the loft above. Aili shivered as she watched Leya dive into the pile, teeth first. She needed her cloak. With all the loose hay around, they couldn't use a fire.

Andvari draped her cloak around her shoulders as Aili looked around again. The ceiling was high, with sturdy beams holding the roof up. A non-magical wagon sat at one end, harnesses on the wall beside it, ready for horses. Tools and cutting implements hung on the opposite wall. Why hadn't they taken any of this with them? Did they take the animals, or did something else happen to them?

He wrapped a blanket around her as well. "Don't get cold."

Andvari and Kyson gathered a mound of hay together and they spread a blanket over it.

"Come on over." Andvari waved for her.

Another bolt of lightning flashed, close this time, and Aili scampered over. She dropped to the blanket and huddled in the middle, her body shaking. Andvari lay beside her. Kyson settled on her other side and draped a blanket over everyone. Aili sighed in the warmth of her blankets, cloak, and their body heat. She closed her eyes and curled up on her side.

"You're small, and don't have the muscle mass we do. You'll get cold easily, and we don't want hypothermia. It can be deadly on a mission like this." Andvari rubbed her back.

How many storms had she spent like this, curled up on a hay bale outside Leya's stall, as Darik sat with her? The familiar sound of horses chewing hay, unconcerned by the storm, soothed her. No, she was safe and warm, and Leya wasn't panicking. Things would be okay. Aili drifted off, only her nose poking out of the blankets.

***

A sharp crack of thunder yanked her from sleep. Aili flinched, her body tensing. Where was she? Right, the storm. She glanced around. Andvari lay beside her, his eyes closed. He didn't move at all. How could he sleep through this? Wait, did he always have those worry lines on his forehead? No, those were new, she was sure of it.

Aili rolled slowly. Kyson reclined on her other side, alert and watchful. He nodded and tapped his head, the signal for safety. Aili nodded. If it weren't for the noise of the wind slamming into the building and the rain smashing against the roof, this would be fun. At least she was finally warm.

She rolled and watched the horses. Leya's hindquarters were all she could see, the pony's head buried deep in the hay mound. Charger was flat on the hay, fast asleep, his head propped up on the hay pile. Trickster lay on the hay, eating around himself. Not one of them seemed bothered by the storm. She settled on her back and stared up at the roof above her. If they were relaxed, she could relax.

Light flashed. A crack rang out seconds later. Aili jerked, the blankets holding her somewhat still. She glanced at Andvari, still fast asleep. How did she not wake him, pulling on the blanket like that? Aili closed her eyes and focused on her breathing. Steady now. Safe and relaxed.

The storm eased. She passed the time meditating. After a while, who knows how long, Andvari stretched and opened his eyes. He nodded to Kyson. Kyson rolled onto his side and closed his eyes. His breathing slowed. Did he seriously just fall asleep that quickly? Was this a Scout thing? She glanced at Andvari.

He smiled. "You learn to rest when you can and trust your partner," Andvari whispered. "On missions like this, it's another way to keep your mood up. Stay well rested."

With him on watch again, Aili let her body relax. The thunder grew more distant with each passing minute. She let her head roll against his shoulder. He was always looking out for her. What might it have been like to be caught out in this storm, though? How much time had passed?

It was still dark out, with no light through the cracks between the window shutters.

Kyson woke as the rain eased. He sat up and stretched. Andvari shifted from their makeshift resting place and slowly paced, easing the stiffness from his body. Kyson got up and retrieved some rations and saved berries from their packs.

Aili sat, still wrapped in the cloak and blanket. They sat on the blanket with her and ate quietly, listening to the sound of the rain against the barn. She opened her senses and explored around them. The rain was moving on and would be gone soon.

A loud rumble made Aili jump and turn. Charger shifted and snored, a deep vibration that filled the barn. She covered her mouth with her hand and hid her laugh under another snore.

"He can make a racket, can't he?" Andvari chuckled.

She popped another berry into her mouth and glanced at the shuttered window. It was easy to see the outlines of the windows now. "Daylight." Aili leapt to her feet and dashed to the nearest window. She peered through the glass, between the wooden slats of the shutters. "The clouds are passing."

"Well, time to get going." Andvari walked over to Charger.

"You'll have to wake the big guy up." Kyson stepped beside him and looked down at the massive horse stretched out on the hay.

Another window rattling snore sounded as Charger's side heaved up and lowered.

"Anyone around, Aili?" Andvari moved behind Charger's back and kneeled beside his horse.

Aili closed her eyes and felt again, this time looking for people. "No, not within my range."

She gathered her blanket and rolled it up. Aili tucked it back in her pack. Leya was laying next to Trickster now, her chin on the ground. Aili patted her rump and pushed on her. Leya turned her head, pinned her ears, and rolled her eyes. Aili ignored her and nudged her again. The pony shifted and got to her feet.

"I know, girl. It was a good rest, wasn't it?" Aili scratched her neck.

They saddled the horses and went over the gear. Everything was in good shape and ready to go. Aili grabbed a warmer pair of pants and slipped them on, stuffing her lighter pair in the pack. Andvari pulled his cloak out, and Kyson changed into a warmer shirt.

"Wait here." Andvari moved to the door and slipped through it.

Aili glanced at Kyson.

Kyson checked Trickster's girth. "He'll be back."

CHAPTER 15

THE INTRUDER

How can a single minute feel like an eternity? The barn door slid open. Light shone in around him, hiding him in the glare. Aili raised a hand to her eyes and smiled at the warmth from the sun. Andvari stretched his hand out and Charger ambled over to him. Aili and Kyson led their horses outside, and Andvari closed the door behind them.

She glanced up at the sun, already across the sky and sinking toward the horizon. It must have been hours since they took shelter, snug and warm in the barn. They'd be looking for a campsite soon, if Aili was any judge of time.

Andvari held his hand palm up, his fingers bent to the sky. At the signal to mount, Aili swung herself up into Leya's saddle. The air was still damp and felt charged, like after any rain, cool on her skin. Aili pulled her cloak around herself snugly.

Andvari circled his hand around. Aili nodded. She closed her eyes and searched. The wrongness was closer and pulled at her. The charge in the air seemed to amplify the sensations. Something dark was ahead, calling to her. Aili pointed. Andvari nodded and took the lead.

Scouts had an amazing sense of direction and training, so they didn't get lost no matter where they went. He must know what direction they needed to go, she pondered, letting Leya carry her behind Charger. Maybe he wants to be sure it's not moving? What if the wrongness is affecting his ability to sense directions, like it affects his magic?

Andvari waved to her, and Aili eased Leya up beside him. "Keep checking regularly and let me know the instant you feel anyone is around."

Aili nodded. She let Charger go ahead as Andvari turned into the trees, away from the path. Water dripped from the branches. Aili watched the drops roll off Andvari's cloak in front of her. Each little droplet landing on her felt like a tiny burst of energy and power. Whoever made the spells that waterproofed the cloaks, she really needed to find them and thank them. Branches brushed against her and the horses, sending water cascading down to the soil below.

The sun dropped lower, and the shadows lengthened. Aili dried the horses often, keeping them more comfortable.

"People are coming out and moving around again."

Andvari turned in his saddle. "Can you tell what they're doing?"

Aili searched for them, reaching her senses as far as she could. "I think they're patrolling. They're moving parallel to each other, scattered around the hill. There's nobody else around. No farmers or loggers, nobody."

"Maybe they're doing something military here and moved the locals out," Kyson suggested.

"The hill is still the source of the disturbance?"

She nodded. "It feels like magic, but not like magic. I can't really explain it."

"Try," Kyson insisted.

Aili closed her eyes and let her senses brush against it. "It has a tingle like magic, like incredibly potent magic, but also something else. It feels wrong, like the magic is sick. That's the best I can explain."

"Halt for a moment," Kyson requested.

Andvari stopped and Leya stopped beside him.

Kyson rode Trickster up beside Aili. He reached down and placed his fingers on her temple. "Breathe and focus on that feeling. Relax and let me in."

Aili opened herself and let him join her in her head. She explored his presence, letting him link directly to her abilities. *This is so weird. It almost tickles, but not.*

'The feeling?' Kyson nudged her inside her mind.

Aili grinned. She turned her attention to her senses and focused on the hill. Kyson followed her attention. He wandered through her senses for a few moments.

Kyson pulled himself back from the link and lowered his hand from her head. "What the—?" He shook his head. "Here." He reached out to Andvari, stretching easily over Aili.

She watched them, sensing the magic flowing between them above her. *This is wild. I never knew magic could do that.*

"I don't know what to make of that, either." Andvari rubbed his chin. "Find a camping spot. We have little daylight left."

Aili searched the forest, probing with her abilities. "This way."

"Lead on." Andvari held his hand out.

She steered Leya through the bushes, feeling ahead to keep on track. *It was here, just up ahead. Don't let them down now. I know I felt it. The trees were so thick, though. Had I sensed it wrong?* Aili reached out again. *No, there it was, right up ahead.*

Aili touched the trees with her essence and whispered to the trees and bushes. Thick branches shifted, moving aside to reveal a small clearing. Aili rode inside and slid from the saddle. The ground was soft under her feet, springing back as she stepped. Had anyone been in here in ages?

"This will do nicely. Fast camp, no fires." Andvari dropped to the moss beside her.

Bedrolls only. I can work with that. Aili looked after the horses as Andvari rigged a tarp and Kyson cooked. She checked Trickster's leg. The tendon felt cool and strong. He's healed, and she was going to keep him that way. The other horses were still strong, no issues, either.

The men sat on the moss nearby, dividing up stored food they foraged and rations. Aili settled beside them and took her share. They ate quietly together and settled into their bedrolls.

"Anyone?"

Aili reached out. "No, not nearby. There are fewer people out now, maybe a third of earlier, and they're all close to the hill."

Kyson shifted up to his elbow. "Should we be planning a night infiltration?"

Andvari looked at Aili, his brow furrowed. Was she a burden? Without her here, they could do whatever they needed. It's not like they can just leave her somewhere and complete the mission. What if someone else found her? Aili closed her eyes tight and took a slow breath.

"Not tonight, for sure. We need rest. We'll scout the area tomorrow and see what we learn."

Kyson lay down and stretched out. Aili closed her eyes and rolled to face the horses. Tears rolled across her face and fell on the pillow. Maybe she'd feel better tomorrow, when the sun was out. Being with people was great, but feeling like a burden made her chest ache.

She took deep and slow breaths and focused on the meditation for calmness. Be still inside, calm, just like the surface of a smooth lake. There. He hasn't said he's disappointed, or sorry I'm here. I won't assume he is.

Her heart slowed and her tears stopped. Aili drifted off, wrapped up in her bedroll.

***

The sun shone down on her face, still dim from rising and being filtered by the trees. Aili stretched and opened her eyes. The horses napped, Leya and Trickster still down as Charger munched on the grass beside them.

She rolled onto her back. The soft ground had made the most comfortable mattress she had since they left camp.

Aili opened herself to the sky and touched the energy from the sun directly. She smiled to herself. That's more like it.

Aili glanced at her other side. Kyson still slept. Andvari sat on his bedroll between them, his eyes closed and his breathing slow.

Andvari opened his eyes and smiled at her. "Good morning," he whispered. "Feel better?"

She grinned. Aili slipped from her bedroll and stretched again. "Sure do. He had the late watch?"

Andvari nodded.

Aili kneeled on her bedroll, her fingers twisting around in front of her. "Am I slowing you down? Am I in the way?"

He held her gaze, his expression calm and hard to read. Would he answer?

"Yes, and no. We'd never have gotten here so fast without your help. We're moving slower because of the rugged terrain and the thickness of the forest. If we had to track this with our magic and skill, we might have lost the trail soon after the border."

Aili frowned. That wasn't an answer. Well, it was, but not to what she wanted to know. She glanced over at Kyson as he rolled and sat up. "I am slowing you down, though."

Andvari smiled slightly. The corners of his mouth turned up. "I need to be mindful of how tired you are. You're not used to long missions like this. When you're tired, you're more likely to make mistakes with magic, and right now we're depending on your help. Everyone makes mistakes when tired, not just you."

Kyson reached into the packs and grabbed some ration bars. He tossed one to Aili, and she caught it. Aili opened the rations and nibbled on the dense fruit and nut filled bread, flavoured with herbs. They were depending on her? Was that better or worse? What if she did mess up? Was she both a help and a hindrance? Well, at least I'm not just a burden.

She helped pack up, and they saddled the horses. Leya pranced and snatched at the grass, making Aili move with her to fasten the packs. Aili smiled at the perky pony and scratched her between her front legs. Leya lifted her head and stuck her lip out, going still and leaning into the touch.

Andvari whistled softly, barely audibly. Aili spun. He waved her over, so she joined him beside Charger. Andvari gave a signal Aili didn't recognize, and Kyson nodded. The massive man moved into the bushes, silent as a shadow. Aili glanced up at Andvari, but he shook his head, a hint of movement she barely saw. She remained still beside him, her palms sweating.

He leaned down, his mouth beside her ear. "Breathe. Settle and search again. See what you feel."

Aili pressed her palms against her pants. She closed her eyes and relaxed, letting her awareness spread slowly. The hill tugged at her attention, like an itch she couldn't scratch. Her surroundings felt normal enough, but seemed a little fuzzy.

The hill pulled at her again. Something in the feeling there slithered around, just beyond her grasp, just out of her reach. Was it even magic? Aili focused on the sensation. Deep inside the cloud of whatever it was, there was something that wasn't moving. Something was waiting. Everything else flowed around it.

She opened her eyes. "It's growing."

The bushes shook, the leaves rustling. Andvari stepped between Aili and the bushes and grabbed his sword from the saddle. Someone was approaching. She could hear the footsteps. Aili ducked around Charger and grabbed her sword. She planted herself in front of the horses.

A man burst through the bushes and stumbled, tumbling down towards her. Aili raised her sword. He fell, his body lurching at Andvari, and Aili saw his hands tied behind his back. Kyson grabbed him, stopping him before he hit the ground. He pulled the man to his feet and held him. The man slumped to his knees, Kyson slowing his fall.

"A spy or advanced watch, sneaking around the camp here." Kyson towered over the man. He crossed his arms over his chest.

Andvari stepped in front of the man. He stared down into his eyes. "Who are you, and where are you from?"

"None of your business." The man spat on Andvari's boots.

Andvari was behind him before Aili could blink. He placed a hand firmly on the man's shoulder and pressed down. The man curled up and winced.

"Interrogate him." Andvari's voice had an edge Aili had never heard before.

She hugged herself tightly. Did she want to see this? They'd always been kind, men of honour. Was she about to see a side of them she wouldn't like? She'd trusted them. Would she see something she'd never forget?

"I'll never tell you anything." He snarled up at Andvari, his teeth bared like an animal.

Kyson stood immediately behind the man and set a hand on his forehead. He chanted softly, a steady murmur, as he set the spell. Aili felt the tingle, sensed the growing power, and watched as the man's face relaxed completely.

What was she watching? Was Kyson controlling him, or doing something else? The pattern was unimaginably complex, and she couldn't fully understand it. The man sat still, so still he could have been a statue, and Kyson stood unmoving behind him, his eyes closed.

Long moments passed. Aili made herself breathe. Andvari watched over them, glancing around occasionally as well.

Kyson opened his eyes. "He's an outer guard for a machine. He doesn't know much about it. It taps power from the planet and they're experimenting with it. They want to power their towns and grow their technology."

Andvari frowned. "Their technology is basic. How can they possibly take power from the planet?"

Kyson shrugged, his hand on the man's shoulder. "He doesn't know much, but saw a picture of the machine. They discovered one line of power running through the planet, and the machine was supposed to exploit that. He's never seen the machine, but it's his job to help guard the hill where they're hiding it."

"What does he know of the attacks on our border?" Andvari slipped his sword back in the scabbard in Charger's saddle.

"I learned a lot about that. The outer guards discovered the border weeks ago, but it was still too strong then. It's been growing weaker in a few areas, and a couple of men slipped across. They didn't stay long. The border guard chased them back, but they told of a land full of resources and bounty. They wanted it."

Andvari walked over to the man. "How do they know where it's weak?"

"At sunrise and sunset, it can be visible as a faint shimmer in the air, like Aili described. Those areas grew larger as time passes. I think it's a safe assumption the machine is responsible." Kyson pressed down as the man shifted. "Maybe it's drawing on the magic in the border, or the land itself."

"He's never been close to it? We need to learn more." Andvari paced.

Kyson pointed. "It's in the hill. That's all he knows."

"Anything else?"

Kyson shook his head.

Andvari stared down at the man. "We can't let him go like this, and we can't leave him behind. We're not taking him."

Aili's eyes widened. Her jaw dropped.

He glanced over and laughed, his blue eyes shining. "Relax. Kyson will wipe his memory of us, and we'll send him home. He'll forget all about the military and his duty."

The man let out a breath and slumped. "Thank you, Sir."

Kyson pulled him upright, a hand clamped around his shoulder. "This will go quicker if you don't resist. I've seen it all, anyway. Stay relaxed and I'll leave all your memories of your home and family. Struggle, and I risk wiping everything. You'll sit here, drooling on yourself."

"Yes, Sir." The man had wide eyes and his jaw clenched.

Andvari joined Aili at the horses and set a hand on her shoulder. She leaned against him. Maybe she could borrow his strength and confidence.

Kyson rested his hand on the man's forehead. Aili waited, watching the magic as Kyson sifted through his memories. The patterns changed, glowing brilliantly in her mind, though her eyes saw nothing. Within minutes, Kyson removed his hand and stepped back. The man opened his eyes and looked around.

Andvari kneeled in front of him. "What's your name?" He nodded, and Kyson untied the man's wrists.

"Jeb. Who are you?"

"Just some travellers." Kyson folded the tie and tucked it back in a pocket. "You tripped and hit your head. We stopped to help. Where are you headed?"

Jeb rubbed his temples. "Home. I'm a long way from there. How did I get here?"

"That blow to the head must have been bad." Andvari offered him a hand and helped Jeb stand. "You should take it easy. Be careful as you go."

Jeb nodded. He brushed his clothing off, and damp soil fell to the moss. "Thanks for the help. I'd better start back. I have a long way to go."

"Safe travels." Andvari walked him to the edge of the clearing.

Aili followed him through the bushes with her senses. He walked straight, headed for wherever, not stopping or slowing for a moment. How had she missed him earlier? Was the hill affecting her ability to focus? She should have sensed him. Aili chewed on her lip lightly.

"Okay, let's go."

Aili patted Leya, her mind still on what she'd seen. "What was that? Memory magic? That's incredibly rare."

Kyson shrugged. "My specialty. Always have been good at it. Got out of trouble as a kid a lot." He chuckled.

"Everyone in the Scouts has a specialty. We choose partnerships and who goes on which missions, all with those skills in mind." Andvari checked Charger's girth.

"Yours are concealment and tracking magic." Aili smiled.

Andvari grinned. "Mainly, yes. Kyson can extract knowledge from people we encounter, leaving them unharmed, even if they resist. He's that good."

Aili spun and faced Kyson. "But you told him—?"

Kyson chuckled. "What I said is technically true, though not likely. It's easier and faster when they don't resist, and we want to get closer before dark. They're almost done testing the machine, and we don't want it turned on to full power."

"Mount up." Andvari swung into his saddle.

"One more thing." Kyson mounted Trickster.

Andvari turned his horse. "What?"

"I barely managed that. It's my strongest magic, and it was all I could do to finish the spell. I can't even start fires right now. How are you?"

Andvari frowned. "I have some concealment. That's about it. You?" He turned to Aili.

"My focus is shaky, but my abilities are fine." She mounted Leya. Well, fine, except for missing Jeb there. How did I not feel him there?

"Just do your best. We have plenty of skills that don't need magic at all. We'll get by and be okay." Andvari eased Charger into a walk and headed through the gap in the trees.

Her fingers tightened around Leya's reins. If she could miss someone that close to camp, what else was she missing? How could she possibly be of any use if she wasn't dependable? Aili kept Leya beside Charger, moving up once they were free of the clearing. She fidgeted. Leya swished her tail and smacked Charger. Charger pinned his ears.

"Sorry," Aili whispered, touching the horses with her senses. She took a slow breath and focused on calming her body.

The forest thinned out. Half-dead trees, missing leaves or needles, made walking among them easier. Aili pressed a hand to her forehead. Some trees were as good as dead, their bare branches drooping, while others sported brown leaves despite it being spring. Bushes weren't in any better shape, some brittle and bare and others halfway there. Even small groundcover plants had dried up and shrivelled.

She reached out, searching for how far this blight extended. "Guards approaching." Aili pointed.

He stopped and signalled a dismount. Aili slipped from Leya's back. Being low made them harder to spot. She smiled at the remembered concealment lessons he gave her back in camp last week. Those were fun. Could she use the information now, when it mattered?

They skirted the base of the hill, darting from cover to cover. Aili signalled the patrol again, just over the rise now. Their cover was barely adequate, and they needed something better. Aili searched. There must be something, anything at all. Wait, that would do. She tapped his arm and pointed.

He nodded, and they dashed for the better cover, a thick cluster of bushes still holding their leaves. She touched the bushes and an opening appeared. These bushes grew thick but had space between them, even for the big horses. Aili led them deep into the cluster. She closed the bushes again, the leaves overlapping and hiding them from sight.

"We wait," Andvari whispered, his hand on her shoulder. "Don't move at all. The leaves will move, too."

Aili rubbed Leya's forehead. Please, girl, don't move. Don't swish a tail or snort. She touched the bigger horses as well, asking for stillness. Aili tried to calm herself, tried to breathe slowly, but her legs wanted to shake, and she gripped Leya's neck to stay upright.

He wrapped an arm around her and let her lean on him. Aili clung to his shirt. Why did she want to cry so badly? Where were these emotions coming from? They couldn't be hers, could they? We're okay right now, she reminded herself. He's not that worried. I don't need to be, either. Calm and collected, I can relax.

Bright colours moved closer, the red standing out between the small gaps in the leaves. That's an odd choice for a group in the forest. Aili pressed her lips together. Something tugged at a memory, but it was just out of her reach.

"That was an awesome bar fight."

"I heard it took him an hour to wake up. That kick to the head nearly killed him."

"Well, he shouldn't have challenged the captain. No one has ever beaten the captain, especially not while drunk."

Aili wrapped an arm around her stomach. What kind of people were they? Did she have to hear this? She covered her ears. Muffled voices kept talking, but at least now she couldn't understand them. Andvari hugged her closer and rubbed her back. She stayed motionless beside him until he touched her hands. She glanced up and slowly eased her hands from her ears.

"They're gone. Sit." He kept a hand on her arm until she settled.

She curled up and lay her head on her knees. Stomach, please settle. Andvari sat beside her and rubbed her back.

"Here." Kyson kneeled in front of her and held a small piece of dried root out for her.

Aili took the root and chewed on it. Tangy sharpness filled her mouth, but her stomach settled as she slowly turned the root around in her mouth. Her temples stopped aching, and Aili could see straight again.

"We'll protect you. This is a rough culture, but you'll be okay." Andvari held her gaze.

"I know that colour pattern, the red and blue and yellow. I can't think of where, but I know it." Aili's jaw trembled and her words were shaky.

"Relax your mind. It'll come to you, but not if you force it." Kyson patted Aili's knee.

"Kyson?" Andvari gave a hand signal.

He shook his head. "It's worse, closer to the hill. I'm effectively without magic now."

Andvari rested a hand on her shoulder. "What comes to mind when you think of the colours? Are there smells or sounds, or maybe an image?"

"Old books and chanting, and mage-light lamps." Aili shook her head. "The University? That can't be right." She scrunched up her nose and explored the images in her mind.

"Another mystery." Andvari took her hand. "Can you ride?"

Aili nodded. Walking might be difficult on unsteady legs, but she could ride. Andvari stood, keeping Aili close, and walked her to Leya's side. He lifted her into the saddle and Aili picked up the reins.

"Can you feel anyone else?"

The men had passed and were already two hills over. No one else felt close. Was she feeling everyone this time? Aili thought so. She shook her head. A touch of magic eased the bushes apart. The bushes trembled like her body did. Andvari and Kyson led their horses back out from the bushes, Aili between them.

"Let's go," Andvari whispered. His hand waved forward, a signal to ride. "Scan as we go. We're watching, too, but you give us more time to hide."

They mounted and rode on, through the dying forest and towards the hill. Leya stayed between the bigger horses as Aili rode with her eyes closed, scanning constantly. The sway of Leya's walk soothed her, distracting Aili from the feelings of decay and death that pulled at her. Focused like this, she steered them around two more patrols and safely closer to the hill. See, she could do this.

Andvari stopped in another cluster of bushes and signalled a lunch break. Aili looked around and nodded. They were in a tree stand with thicker bushes, between two hills and back from a path. She dismounted Leya and took rations from her pack.

He sat on a dead tree and patted the trunk beside him. "Keep your energy up. How are you feeling?"

Aili sat beside him and unwrapped a ration bar. "I'm okay." No, I'm a moody mess and don't know why.

Her stomach rolled again, threatening to empty itself. Aili tensed her muscles to overwhelm the trembling. Maybe it's a good thing she never made it to the tavern when she first tried. Could she get those voices from her head? Aili never wanted to hear a conversation like that again.

"Here. Chew this." Andvari tucked a tablet of crushed herbs in her hand. "You know what it is?"

She glanced at the little green tablet and nodded. It dissolved in her mouth, breaking apart into a fine powder. Her muscles relaxed, and Aili's stomach calmed again.

Her hands were steady. Aili smiled. She helped Ilia make hundreds of these one day. They helped with shock and trauma, including emotional trauma.

"Better?"

Aili grinned. "Better."

"When we get back, we'll help you deal with everything. The first mission is usually the hardest. We're here for you." Andvari tore a bite out of his ration bar.

They finished their meals, and he gave her a leg up onto Leya.

Aili sent out her awareness. "There's one last patrol ahead." She shared what she saw, and where she thought they might be heading.

"Kyson."

Kyson handed Andvari his reins and slipped from the bushes. Aili stroked Leya's smooth hair as the pony grazed. She followed Kyson with her senses.

"Your chewing will give us all away," Aili whispered.

Kyson appeared beside them again, silent and unseen, until he stood. "We have enough cover to get past them. After that, we need a new plan if we want to remain unseen."

"Your magic is still alright?" Andvari touched her arm.

Aili nodded. "The herbs helped. I feel more focused again."

The men mounted their horses, and they rode from the trees. Aili kept her senses out and ready. The land around her felt increasingly lifeless and without energy, and the trees were bare of leaves. Even the last cluster of bushes they took cover in were barely alive.

Andvari signalled a halt, and everyone dismounted. The guards were close. She could feel it. At a signal, the tall horses lay down, shaking the ground just enough for Aili to feel as they landed. Andvari kneeled next to Charger and stroked his neck. All that separated them from the guard was a rise in the hill. Aili crouched beside them and Leya lowered herself to the ground.

She strained to hear anything. A steady and rhythmic sound stood out from the silence. Footsteps, she realized. This group was marching together, not the haphazard walking of the other groups. Aili watched them in her senses, all moving together like a single being.

The footsteps passed and faded. They disappeared around the hill. Andvari waited a few minutes before he got Charger up. Leya rose to her feet with a grunt and shook herself. Aili clung to her mane and stroked her sleek hair. Leya pressed her head to Aili's arm.

"Are you okay?" Andvari was at her side in an instant. He rested a hand against her back.

Aili nodded. If she was this scared with a tablet calming her, what would she feel like without it? A steady breath helped, and her hand stopped trembling.

"Anybody else?"

"Not too close. They're all over the hill, though, mostly moving in and out over there. There's a spot halfway up the slope that might be an entrance."

Andvari crossed his arms and shifted from foot to foot. "Can you feel for another way in?"

Aili leaned against Leya and closed her eyes. She tried to slow her breathing and meditate. A leaf fell and crackled against the dry grass. Trickster exhaled loudly. Focus. Aili rubbed her temples.

Andvari moved behind her and set his hand against her back. His fingers were icy, even through her shirt. Aili focused on where his hand met her body and took a slow breath.

"That's it. Slow and steady, just like you've practiced. I've never connected with you without my magic, but our bond of teacher and student might still work. Let me in."

She felt his energy against her skin and opened herself to it. Aili slowed her breathing until it matched his. His fingers warmed up. Andvari joined her in the link, a presence in her head.

'Great. I can use your magic if you relax. Focus on the breathing and let me do the rest.'

'This place is full of magic and anti-magic.' Aili scratched her nose. 'It makes my skin itch.'

'Focus on the breathing. You're making this harder.'

Her cheeks burned. Aili pushed a sob down and settled on her breathing. He didn't need her making this difficult. As she felt her breath flowing, Aili relaxed. Hey, now she could sense what he was doing.

He turned her attention into the hill, down below the surface. Tunnels crossed the soil, tangling among themselves. Three came to the surface. Two had people in them, but the third was empty. Did they forget this one?

Andvari pulled himself from her awareness and back into his own body fully. Aili sensed his fatigue, felt his lack of energy. His strength was being pulled away, a bit at a time, just like the land around her lost its energy.

"Near the base of the hill, a third of the way around." Andvari pointed. "A quiet entrance."

"Unsafe? Is it clear?" Kyson folded his arms over his chest.

"It didn't feel unsafe. It's not in use, so there may be a reason I couldn't detect, or maybe they forgot about it." Andvari patted Charger.

"It's our best chance," Aili whispered.

"Mount up." Andvari leapt onto Charger, showing more energy than she knew he had.

Aili pulled herself up onto Leya. Her legs felt like heavy metal, stiff and awkward. She couldn't vault if she tried. Was the anti-magic sapping her focus, or was the magic interfering? She didn't know. He struggled to focus when they linked, and she couldn't help much, but it wasn't just her being affected. How was he even still walking with how weary she knew he was?

He signalled for her to keep watch. Aili trusted Leya to stay with them as she closed her eyes. Leya followed them through the remaining cover as they skirted the hill, circling around. The path was longer, but they might remain hidden. Maybe.

Aili felt the entrance. In her awareness, mist shrouded the hill. It was thick, like a black fog that coated the land and suppressed magic. Something lay in the fog's heart, dark and secret, hidden from her. If she got too close, her focus slipped, and she slipped from the hill completely.

Maybe I can dispel the mist with some light magic? I only see it in my mind, so maybe I can use it in my mind, too. Aili pictured a large ball of light around herself, free of the mist. Her eyelids glowed and her skin felt warm.

"What are you doing?" Kyson hissed.

"Stop. We need to hide." Andvari's concern pulled her from her senses.

She opened her eyes and saw a ball of light around them, shining brightly and eliminating shadows. Oh, no. Everyone for miles will see this. Aili tried to extinguish it, tried to pull it back in herself, but the light shone on, undimmed. Her palms sweat and the reins slipped through her fingers.

"People are coming. Everywhere." Tears poured down her cheeks.

"Hide. Head for the bushes." Andvari waved her off.

Aili stared at him. How could she leave when they're in trouble because of her? Her body froze, and her limbs wouldn't move. They needed her. She failed, but they still needed her. She couldn't let them die.

"Go!"

She turned to Leya, and the pony danced around under her.

"Too late." Kyson shifted Trickster in front of Aili.

Andvari glared at her. "Next time, listen immediately."

Aili hung her head. She didn't want to see the men circling them, weapons drawn. Rough hands pulled her from the saddle and yanked her arms behind her back. Her shoulders protested and her body ached. A cord wrapped around her wrists, rough and chafing, and they shoved her to her knees.

'Run. Take them and go.' Aili pushed her will on the horses, especially Leya. Could they feel all the fear and hope she willed to them?

Leya bit the man holding her reins and tore herself free. She kicked out and spun, scattering the men. Charger broke free and bolted towards Trickster, who dragged the man holding him for a few feet. The horses galloped across the hill. Horses always knew the way home. Aili would see them again. She had to.

CHAPTER 16

CAUGHT

"Just passing through, are we?" He glared down at Aili, his arms over his chest. "I didn't believe you then, and I won't believe you now. So, you discovered the machine? Now you can help us power it. Bring them."

Someone hauled her up by her tied arms. Pain shot through her, and she cried out. Andvari turned and charged towards her. Another man grabbed his arm and pulled him down. She cried freely when the sword hilt hit him and Andvari crumpled to the ground. Dust rose around his body.

"Enough. You want to carry him back?" The leader spun and glared at Andvari.

The man sheathed his sword and snapped to attention. "No, Sir."

Men dragged Andvari to his feet. He swayed and his legs buckled, but they hauled him up again. Her heart ached to watch him stagger along, barely upright, between the soldiers holding him. Aili choked and coughed. Swallowing was almost impossible, and her throat was tight. How was she going to get him out of this?

She stumbled along beside the man with the iron grip on her upper arm, into a cave entrance big enough for four people abreast, or a large wagon. The air was dry and burned her lungs. Torches line the wall. An oily residue settled on everything near the light. The darkness between let her breathe, but the dark closed in on her.

The area around her buzzed and tingled. Was it magic, or that anti-magic, or both? Her nerves were hot, and it was hard to tell. Normally, soil was full of life, insects and plants throughout, and even caves had a variety of animals living in them. Not this place. People were the only life she could feel.

The wrongness throbbed around her. Her brain ached. Loose rocks underfoot threatened to send her sliding down the tunnel. Andvari was behind her, and she heard him struggling to walk. Pebbles pelted the back of her legs, where he dislodged them and shuffled through them, kicking them away with each step.

They turned a corner into a cavern. Aili blinked rapidly. A bright light shone from the ceiling, hurting her eyes. It wasn't torchlight, but something she'd never seen, not once. It vibrated and pulsed, but not the slow and steady vibration of the planet. No, this thing pulsed out of rhythm and her body ached from it.

She blinked again and looked up. The cavern ceiling was rough, and crystals reflected the light like tiny stars. Wait, were the crystals glowing?

"Him first. He looks strongest." The leader gestured at Kyson with his thumb.

Her breath caught in her throat. Two men dragged Kyson to a massive machine at the far end of the cavern. It took up most of the space, taller and wider than the manors she lived among. Dark liquid flowed through large tubes connecting parts of the machine. A vertical cylinder of glass opened, and Kyson stumbled in, shoved by the guards.

He hit the floor and groaned. His wrists bled from the ties. Aili growled and charged forward. The hand on her arm yanked her back and held tight. Her bone protested and Aili cried out, dropping to her knees.

Kyson shifted and wriggled to his knees. He met Aili's gaze. Tears flowed down her cheeks. They lined the cylinder floor with the crystals that suck in magic. She met his gaze. They both knew what that meant. His own eyes were bloodshot, and his body trembled.

Andvari staggered as he tried to straighten up. She had to help them, had to save them both. The machine throbbed in time with the crystals. Her energy swirled around in her body, out of its normal circulation, and she couldn't think straight.

They dragged her to cages along the wall near where Kyson remained trapped. They dropped Andvari into the end cage and left him on the floor where he landed.

"You two will be next." The leader kneeled beside her and raised her chin with his finger until she looked up at him. His breath nearly knocked her out right there. "With your power, we'll have everything we need. The machine will power up completely, and that barrier around your land will be gone."

Her gaze flitted around as the cage door closed on her. No, slow down and think. What can I use to help? Her focus was gone, that incessant throbbing disrupting her abilities in a way nothing else had. The cavern was rock, and the floor had some sand and gravel. More cages lined the opposite wall. Two people lay inside, unmoving. They wore Scout clothing. Aili focused hard, as hard as she could, but felt no life energy from them.

Andvari panted as he shifted to his knees, his forehead still on the ground. He needed care. Aili tried to focus, turned her full attention to him, but she couldn't hold his life energy in her mind or senses.

Men moved around the machine, adjusting dials and reading gauges. The leader stood and paced, his arms over his chest as he grinned at the machine.

Do something, she screamed to herself. Focus. Her body wouldn't respond. What caused that infernal throbbing? Could she stop it somehow? She opened herself, just passively watching. It was magic, but it blended with the wrongness. The throbbing pulsed in time with the liquid spurting through the tubes. It was the machine, for sure, but how could she stop it?

"He'll be drained within the hour. We can begin after that." A man pressed a button, and the crystals below Kyson glowed.

"Alright, men, good job. Drinks for everyone." The leader stalked off behind her, his footsteps covered by the cheering.

Aili closed her eyes at the echoing cheers. After the silence of the forest, the noise sent stabbing pain through her skull. She curled up and pressed her head to the sand.

The men left, leaving one man standing watch. He grumbled, muttering something under his breath as his gaze wandered the room, resting over Kyson and Andvari briefly. He looked at Aili and smiled. She shuddered at the way he glanced at the door, making sure they were alone.

"Such a pretty young thing." He stalked towards her. "If you're going to die anyway, what's the harm?"

Thick fingers pulled a keyring from his belt. Aili trembled and shimmied back into the corner. The key slid into the lock and turned with a click. No, this can't be happening.

How can things get worse? She curled up tight in the corner, the metal bars pressing against her body.

He kneeled beside her. A dirty finger touched her hair. "This won't take long."

Anger surged through her. For a moment, the throbbing was gone. Her thinking was clear. Only her heart pulsed inside her, racing as adrenaline filled her body. Aili focused on the ropes around her wrists. The rope exploded, fragments flying everywhere.

"Wha—?" He stared at a piece of rope beside her.

Aili shifted and sprang up, her elbow swinging towards him, fuelled by anger and fear. Her elbow collided with his jaw. She felt his bone break. She was going to bruise, but she smiled anyway. Aili spun and whirled her elbows around, striking repeatedly before ending with a round-house kick as he stumbled away. He hit the floor. She grabbed the keys and dashed to Kyson and the cylinder.

"It's on the control panel, but I don't know which button." His voice sounded distant through the thick glass.

She ran to the controls. The front of the machine was filled with panels of buttons. Which one? It might take weeks to try them all. The humming throbbing crept back into her awareness, and her bones ached again. What else could she do?

A toolbox sat on the floor near the doorway. Would they see her? The door was partly closed, with bright light flooding through the opening. She had to try. Aili darted to the toolkit and shuffled through it. A hammer, a screwdriver, a large metal bar with a hook. Her hand paused on the bar. It was heavy, heavier than she thought possible. This just might do it. She gripped the bar and ran back to her friends.

Aili dropped the bar near Kyson and darted back to the cage where Andvari kneeled. She fumbled with the keys, dropping them in the sand. Aili picked the keys up and stood quietly for a moment, calming herself. Slow and smooth, she reminded herself.

The first key slid into the lock but wouldn't turn. The next two wouldn't even go in. The fourth slid in. Holding her breath, Aili turned the key. The lock clicked, and the door swung open. She darted inside and kneeled beside him.

She held his chin in her hand and inspected the deep gash on his forehead. His eyes stared ahead, not taking anything in. This was not good. Her hands trembled as she pulled her healing kit from under her shirt. Her fingers ran along the vials, and she pulled one free, knowing them all by touch.

The cap came free with the flick of her thumb. She dabbed some of the thick oily liquid on her fingers and ran it over the cut, before smearing more over his forehead. He groaned softly and panted at the pain.

Aili stroked his hair gently, just like he did for her when she felt scared. "You're going to be okay. This'll take the pain away and make you feel better. Don't worry. I'm looking after you."

She tucked the precious vial back in the kit and slipped it back under her shirt. The link wasn't working, and the vial would not refill, but she had some left. She wouldn't be able to make more right away. Aili had to preserve what she still had. It wasn't like she was without healing potions, but that one worked on absolutely any injury, no matter how bad it was.

It took both hands to grip the end of the heavy bar and hold it up. Aili moved to the cylinder and stared at it. Would this be enough? Was she strong enough? She hauled the bar over her shoulder and swung with all her strength. Her muscles burned with the effort and her hands cramped.

Clang! The bar vibrated in her hands, sending shock waves up her arms. Her hands went numb. Aili swung again and again. The cheering and talking from the other room better be enough. She swung again, and the bar bounced off the cylinder, hitting the sand with a thud. She wasn't strong enough. She couldn't do it.

Kyson pressed himself up to his knees again, his hands against the glass. At least she freed his hands earlier when she freed her own. Wait, her magic worked earlier. She stared at the fragments of rope scattered around Kyson. Could she do it again?

Anger did it. Anger freed her of the machine's hold. Aili focused on her rage, on the people who hit Andvari and who were going to kill Kyson. She burned at the way they treated her. She snarled at the selfish people who didn't care how they were hurting her forests; they were greedy and lacked compassion.

She picked up the bar and felt into the dirt and rock below her, feeling for the strength of the planet. It was there, the power of earthquakes and tides and more, ready for her to borrow. Aili swung again. The glass cracked. The hook stuck in the glass. Aili blinked. Almost there.

The bar fought her attempts to free it. Pieces fell from the hole as she wiggled the bar. She pulled the bar free. Kyson looked pale, a shocking sight for the usually dark-skinned man, and he was too weak to stand. Her anger burned over how they treated him.

Aili turned to the tube connecting the cylinder to the machine. The black oily substance had a purple tinge now, with a hint of light blue in it. She raised the bar and smashed it down with all her might. The bar plummeted down onto the glass.

Black sludge sprayed out, hitting the machine and the cylinder. Smoke poured from anywhere the liquid landed and Aili held her nose. She darted back away from the spray. The cylinder wall cracked and grew cloudy. Gears ground to a halt and she covered her ears at the noise.

"Hide. Go." Kyson waved at her and pointed to the exit.

She stuffed the bar through the hole she made earlier. Kyson grabbed the bar. Aili spun and ran. Where to hide? She scrambled around the machine and into the shadows, where she felt a tunnel hidden behind some rock.

Yelling men poured into the room as she tucked out of sight. With the machine disabled, Aili could think and feel again, though her pounding heart drowned out the world around her. The machine let out a low hum, just enough to blur the cavern in her senses, but not enough to stop her. Aili darted into the tunnel and ran with all the speed she had left.

The yelling faded as she ran, the tunnel sloping up as it wound around on itself. Her legs wobbled. She needed to rest, needed somewhere safe to hide and regroup. Please, let this lead me to safety. Aili wiped the tear away and kept running.

A thin glowing line appeared on the ceiling, a faint brown warmth that pulled at her. It gave just enough light for her to see and brightened up a few feet in front and behind her, moving with her. Her legs gave out and Aili hit the sand, her knees protesting.

She forced herself to her feet, her hands on the rock wall, and pushed on, following the light. The door ahead got her attention, and the light turned and passed through it when she arrived. Was this it, a place to hide and regroup?

A glance down the tunnel showed her footprints leading off into the dark. Aili frowned. With a touch of focus, she called a breeze down the tunnel towards her. She slid down to the sand as she sent the breeze down, blowing her footprints away and hiding her passing.

Aili reached up and turned the metal handle. The door swung open. She crawled inside and nudged the door shut with her foot. The light led her on, deeper into the room. Tall shelves of rough-cut wooden planks filled the room, each one stuffed with crates of supplies. Dust coated the crates. How long had they been here? How long did it take to build the machine?

She dragged herself to a corner and collapsed. Her light disappeared, leaving Aili in the total dark. Tears filled her eyes, and she curled into a ball. She hadn't saved them. They were still trapped and weak, wounded and drained. Andvari needed time for the healing to work, and that was the best healing potion she had. Leya and the horses wandered the forest, where anything could happen. She didn't know where she was, and had no idea how to fix any of it.

Memories of camp life flashed through her mind. How could she have found a home, a proper home with adopted family and friends, only to lose it all like this? Life in camp was everything she longed for. She had belonged with them, and for the first time in her life, she had a purpose. She even had magic.

Now she might lose it all, because some people wanted more. Here she lay, covered in dirt and sand, surrounded by people who wanted to use and kill her. Two people she cared about, her adopted family, were about to be killed, might even be dead already. How could she save them? Could she save them at all?

Think, Aili, she scolded. What is it about the machine that affects me so? What was it doing? She thought back, searching for the feeling. Images of Andvari laying there, helpless on the floor and bleeding, pulled her thoughts away. Seeing the fear in Kyson's eyes still shook Aili to the core, and that memory wouldn't let her go, either. She left them both behind.

Silent sobs wracked her body. Aili covered her mouth with her hand. Sand adhered to her lips, dry and cracked skin like the sand that clung to it. Sand stuck to her wet cheeks. Everything she cared about was in danger. Life wasn't fair, she knew that better than most, but this was a new level of unfair she didn't know existed.

They wanted to destroy the barrier. Were they going to invade? It sounded like it. A year ago, she might not have cared. She had no magic and no future she could see. Now her heart burned at the thought of losing it all: her forests, her country, the people she loved. Now she cared. She cared with her whole heart. With something to lose, her heart ached worse than she'd ever felt before.

It'll take days for Leya and the others to get back, and for the Scouts to know something went wrong. Would it be too late, or had she damaged the machine enough to buy some time? She must have. Aili pulled together every ounce of courage she had.

Sure, she had no idea where to go. Her teacher and his partner were in the hands of murderous enemies. She had no idea what to do next. Nothing was going to stop her from trying. If she had to do it scared, she'd do it scared, but she was going to save them. That was step one.

If they succeeded, step two was to escape, regroup, and form a plan. Andvari was a master sneak, and with his lessons, Aili was, too. He made sure she had the skills, and she was going to use them. Darn it all. She could do this.

Aili held her hand palm up before her. If brand new mages can do this, so can she. Aili focused, and a tiny ball of light shimmered into existence. She grinned. Nothing like mortal peril to encourage new magic use.

She opened the door a crack and listened. Aili peeked out. Silence met her, and darkness. If they were still yelling, she couldn't hear it from here. She eased herself out into the tunnel.

What was that? Aili crouched and held her light down. Footprints in the sand passed up, heading for the tunnel exit. She knew those boot prints. After all the games in the forest, she could even tell which boots belonged to which man. Kyson must have been supporting him with the way the tracks scuffed the dirt and gravel, but he was up and moving. His healing was working.

Aili ran up the tunnel, ignoring the burning in her legs from the sand and loose gravel. She felt ahead, but the tunnel was empty. It meant they might have made it out, though. Aili grabbed that hope and ran on. Nothing was going to stop her now, not when she needed to find them.

The path spiralled up, rising quickly. Light appeared ahead, faint at first, and growing brighter as she ran. Daylight, she grinned. It reflected off the rock walls and deeper in, but the warmth was unmistakable.

The footprints faded and disappeared. Aili smiled. His magic must be returning. If he was hiding behind a ward somewhere in the forest, it would be harder to feel him. His magic might blend into the mess of energy around the hill. Still, she knew his magic.

She slowed at the tunnel entrance. Were there guards? She couldn't feel anyone. Why not, though? Were they not watching this tunnel at all? Why not? Had they forgotten about it?

Aili huddled inside the tunnel and opened her senses. There was nothing nearby, no animals or people, no signs of life. She was on the far side of the hill, away from that large entrance tunnel.

With hands clasped in front of her heart, Aili wished with all her might. "I could really use some help." Was there anyone there to hear her? Ilia told stories of ancient spirits of the land that helped or hindered people, but nobody believed those anymore.

A breeze swirled up around her. Leaves lifted from the dead grass and blew around, following the breeze as it headed out into the sunlight. A tendril of wind clung to her, pulling at her hair and shirt. Aili followed the breeze, scampering down the hill and into the forest of dead tree trunks.

She stopped with the wind, huddled behind a thick cluster of bushes. The branches were so dense she couldn't see, even without the leaves to hide her. She eased her way deep into the middle of the bushes and sat, hidden and protected. With a slow and steady breath, Aili opened her senses and searched her surroundings.

Pairs of people moved around the hill. There was no way to tell which were her friends and which were soldiers. Her heart sank. She knew this wouldn't be easy, but why did everything have to be so darned difficult?

Wait. Over there. Was it? Three large animals moved through the trees, one shining like a beacon in the forest. Leya. She was alive and unharmed. Had she kept the others safe? There were no people close to them. Why hadn't they gone back to camp?

Feeling filthy, her skin was dry and itchy, and with a thirst she couldn't believe, Aili pushed herself up and slipped from her hiding place. She set a course towards her pony, letting her senses keep her safe and away from people. Small plants and herbs still grew under trees, away from the hill, and some bushes had leaves that weren't dead yet. Aili scanned for plants as she walked.

There, behind those bushes, Aili found what she was looking for. She picked the low groundcover, the tiny purple flowers wilted already. The plant pulled from the soil with little resistance. Aili chewed the stems and fluid flowed into her mouth. The sweet fluid gave her a burst of energy.

Aili weaved her way through the forest towards the horses. She knew the moment Leya sensed her. The horses approached, far too slowly, though. Why? Aili picked up the pace, dashing between cover and staying low.

The soft whicker greeted her. Aili burst through the bushes and wrapped her arms around Leya's neck. Leya pressed her head to the girl's chest. She ran her fingers through the thick mane, gripping tightly.

"I am so glad to see you," Aili whispered, tears dropping into the pale mane.

She stepped back and examined Leya. Her pony was in good shape, other than the mud. Trickster looked good, though his tendon needed more liniment. Aili rubbed the liniment into his leg, taking a moment to heal him with her abilities as well.

Charger stood behind the others. His head was low, and his breathing was shallow and fast. Aili froze, her eyes on the big horse. His eyes were glassy and unfocused. She felt him trembling when she touched his shoulder.

Aili flowed her senses into him. His back end was weak, and pain flooded her through their connection. An arrow stuck from his left hindquarters. The big horse rested his toe on the ground, his weight shifted to his uninjured leg.

"Easy, boy. I'm here to help." Aili rubbed the big horse. "Stay still and I'll have you fixed in no time."

She moved back to his hip, her hand on his side. Aili stood beside the wound, a hand on either side of the jagged cut, the arrow sticking out between her hands. She flooded the area with soothing magic. The big horse lowered his head and let out a deep breath.

"Sorry, boy. This might not feel so good, but you'll feel better afterwards. I'll be as quick as I can."

He snorted softly and closed his eyes, his head down near his knees. Aili pulled her healing kit out and selected a potion to numb the area. She spread it around his wound. The sharp knife had been sterilized and wrapped, ready to go. Aili pulled the knife from her kit and a pair of metal tweezers.

"Steady, now." Aili rubbed his hip with her forearm, since her hands were full. "Just hold still and I'll have this out in no time. Stay quiet, so nobody finds us."

He sighed and flicked an ear back at her. Aili spread the skin and eased the knife in along the arrow shaft. With a touch of magic, she guided the muscles apart, making space to pull the arrow out without catching the sharp barbs. She pulled slowly until the arrow slid free.

The lotion worked and Charger remained still, not feeling the pain from her efforts. Aili tossed the arrow aside and slid her knife free. The wound closed when she released her magic. She tucked her tools back into the cloth and placed a hand directly over his wound.

Ali sunk her awareness out across the area and pulled a bit of energy from each living plant she found. She stitched his muscles and tissues together, burning out any microbes as she went. His skin sealed together, and the wound closed.

She tottered back to his head on shaky legs. Charger stood a good chance of recovering now. Aili pulled out the last of the Cure-All and looked at the nearly empty vial. She couldn't make more, not here without ingredients, but she had other potions, too. He needed this.

Aili rubbed the last of the potion into his forehead. He drew his lip back at the sharp medicinal smell. Aili smiled. She felt that way about it, too, but this stuff was amazing.

"Okay, Leya, I need some Corbina Weed for him." Aili rubbed Leya's chin. "You know the stuff. Small flowers and it grows below trees and shrubs. You love it, but don't eat it. He needs it more than you. Andvari and Kyson are out there, somewhere, so keep an eye out. Soldiers are out there, too."

Leya snorted and trotted off into the trees. Charger needed rest and time for the potions and lotions to work. Aili stood beside him, her own body spent and shaky after healing him. She stroked his neck.

Charger collapsed, shaking the ground as he landed. He let out a long breath. Hurry, Leya! Tears rolled down her cheeks and fell on his nose. First Andvari, and now Charger? She kneeled beside him and poured more healing into him, more than she had to give, but she had to try. Would Leya find the weed? Aili had seen it, knew it was in the area, but was any close enough to help?

She watched the sun drop and the sky turn from blue to purples and reds. Darkness would hide them, but how much longer would Leya be? Had something happened to her? Charger wasn't getting worse, but he wasn't improving quickly, either.

The bushes rustled. Leaves dropped off from the shaking. Aili grabbed a camp knife from Charger's packs. Leya? Maybe, but she was too tired to check. Her energy was as low as Charger's now. She stood ready, knife out, and she slowed her breathing.

The bushes parted.

"Leya." Aili dropped the knife and dashed over to the pony on wobbly legs.

Leya gripped the plants in her teeth. She walked over to Charger and dropped them in front of the big horse.

Aili patted her pony. "Thanks, girl." She dropped to her knees and picked up the Corbina Weed. Aili held it to Charger's lips. "Come on, boy. This will make you feel better. Eat up."

He nibbled at the plants, but struggled to chew them.

"Come on. You can do it. Try again."

"Maybe I should try?"

Aili spun. She grinned, her heart warm and hopeful. Andvari walked over, still leaning on Kyson, but looking steadier than she expected. His eyes were bright, and he was alert, his focus on his horse. Kyson brought him over and Andvari sat beside Charger.

Charger lifted his head and whickered.

"Alright, buddy. You know what to do." Andvari took the weed and held it to Charger's mouth. He held Charger's head up. "Chew."

Charger lipped the plant from his palm and chewed. After about a minute, the big horse swallowed.

"That's my boy. Have some more." Andvari fed him the rest of the Corbina Weed.

Charger shifted to his belly, holding his head up on his own now. He took the herb and chewed with more energy, showing genuine interest in the food this time. Aili pressed trembling hands against her legs and smiled as the big horse munched on the plant. Andvari took a bite as well and shared the last plant with his horse.

Once Charger had eaten, Andvari shifted to near his hindquarters. He inspected the wound with his physical senses, his hands moving gently through Charger's hair. Andvari held his hand out to her. "You did an amazing job."

Aili took his hand, and he pulled her in for a hug. Aili sobbed and wrapped her arms around his neck.

"You're fine." Andvari rubbed her back. "A lot has happened, but you gave us a fighting chance. You also saved my horse."

"I was so scared, and I couldn't help," she whispered, mumbling into his shoulder. His shirt grew damp with her tears. "You were both dying and now I'm a weepy mess."

Andvari chuckled. "We're not dying now. You saved us both and gave us every chance to get better. Now we even have some magic back, so why don't we make a camp and rest properly? We'll come up with a plan and figure it all out."

"You have some magic?" She lifted her head and peered up at him.

"Some." He nodded. "When you damaged the machine, I felt a little magic come back. They have it partially repaired, but you did a good job on it. The cylinder won't work, at least. I can't call for backup yet. Something is still interfering."

"Where's that magic coming from, though?" Kyson sat beside them.

"A person," Aili whispered. "It has to be."

"No mage would be involved with this. We'll figure this out." Andvari straightened up and let Aili lean against his side.

"Even weak, your wards are better than mine." Kyson waved vaguely around the campsite.

Aili turned and inspected Charger's wound; fresh pink skin surrounded by hair now. Andvari stood and slowly walked around the campsite, setting basic wards and concealing spells. When he was done, he staggered over to Charger's side and collapsed against the big horse. Andvari leaned against Charger's back. Charger closed his eyes and let out a deep sigh.

"I hope you included a silencing spell." Aili patted Charger's shoulder as the horse let out a deep snore. "The sleep will help the potions work. Hopefully, by morning, he'll be good as new."

"The same stuff?" Andvari tapped his forehead, where the residue still left a light brown streak across his skin.

Aili smiled. That oil would linger for days. She nodded. "He's worth it."

"He sure is. Thank you." Andvari stroked Charger's neck.

'Now, don't anybody get any more potentially fatal wounds. I still have powerful potions, but no more of that stuff. You've been warned." Aili yawned.

Andvari suppressed his laugh, and Kyson grinned.

"Come here." Andvari held his hand out to her.

Aili settled next to him, under his arm, and curled up beside Charger. Charger's side vibrated with each snore. "He could wake the capital city with that noise."

Andvari chuckled. "I set the silencing spells with the wards. He sure can make a racket, can't he?"

She tilted her head back against his arm and stared up at the sky, the stars easily visible through the barren bushes and trees. "It's a big old world out here."

The moon rose over the trees, casting shadows across the ground.

Aili sighed and closed her eyes. "I didn't want to leave you both."

Kyson sat on her other side. "You did the right thing."

"Funny how the moon feels magical." She opened her eyes and stared up at the moon.

"You use the energy of the sun. The moon reflects that light. We should all get some sleep." Andvari closed his eyes and tilted his head back.

"Who's going to keep watch?" Aili nudged him in the ribs lightly. "You've always set a watch before."

"He will." Kyson gestured to Trickster.

Trickster snorted and bobbed his head in the air. Aili covered her mouth and giggled. His hearing was better than theirs, and he'd notice anything far sooner than they would. In this light, with the moon shining, his night vision was as good as theirs, too.

Leya lay down near Aili, close to Charger and Andvari. She landed with a quiet thump. Aili curled up along her back and rested her head beside Leya's. Her body was sluggish after all the healing. She closed her eyes.

"Help us." Who was that? It sounded distant and ethereal, almost otherworldly.

"Where are you?" Aili listened, straining to hear the voice among the odd echo around her.

"We're dying." The voice faded.

Aili sprang to her feet and searched the forest. She opened her senses, but only felt her friends, though she couldn't see them. The trees loomed over her in the dark, sick and withering, and unfriendly. She wrinkled her nose at the smell of rotting vegetation. Aili headed off into the trees. If someone was in trouble, she was going to find them.

Leaves dropped from the trees at a steady rate, falling straight down instead of drifting down slowly. Aili stopped and listened. Running water bubbled nearby, off to her left. She followed the sound. The trees had more life closer to the water, but were still like shades, remnants of a forest dying slowly.

She found the stream flowing fast in a depression. The black sludgy water ate away at the banks, leaving a shadowy fog where soil used to be. Aili recoiled and backed up.

"We're fading. Help us." It was barely a whisper now.

"I'll help, but I don't know what to do."

Aili ran as the black sludge in the stream surged towards her, overflowing the banks. She stumbled and fell, landing on the parched soil and dead grass. The sludge washed over her, covering her like an oily blanket.

She couldn't see. All sounds disappeared, like the sludge absorbed them. The reek of death and rotting filled her nose. Which way was up? Aili thrashed, trying to feel anything around her, even the soil beneath her.

"Time—up." A distant voice, one she knew well, pulled her from her panic.

Aili opened her eyes. The sludge was gone, and so was everything else. Something nearby shone through the darkness, something she could feel but not see.

"Time to get up." Andvari's voice penetrated her hazy brain, pulling her from her sleep.

She hoped it was sleep, anyway. Aili felt the sun on her eyelids and sensed light. She opened her eyes and saw the forest, her friends sitting beside her, and the horses dozing around her. Aili reached for him, her insides feeling cold as ice. Andvari pulled her into his arms and hugged her tightly.

"Are you alright?" Kyson rubbed her back.

"Yeah," Aili mumbled into Andvari's shoulder. She rubbed her eyes. "I just need a moment, and my cloak."

Kyson went to her packs and retrieved her cloak. He draped it around her, and Aili pulled it on, pulling it close about herself.

Andvari pulled a ration bar from his pocket and un-wrapped it for her. "Here. The food will help."

Sweet herbs filled her nose, dispelling any memories of the smells in her dream. Her stomach settled and warmth flowed through her fingers and toes. Aili distracted herself from how she felt by listing the herbs she could taste, a potent blend for mages under stress.

She nibbled the bar, letting the cloak keep her warm. Sweat soaked her clothes, and she'd need to change, but whatever that nightmare was, it was leaving her finally. Andvari got her some dry clothing as she finished her breakfast.

"Thank you." Aili wolfed down the last of the ration bar.

She took her dry clothing and changed, using her cloak to cover her and keep her warm. Ah, dry clothing. Was there a better feeling out in the woods? Aili stuffed her wet clothing in her pack. She could clean it later.

"We've had a chance to plan while you slept." Andvari unwrapped his own breakfast, a regular ration bar full of dried fruits and nuts. His skin was back to the healthy pink, with only a fading scar left on his forehead. "Here's what we're thinking—"

CHAPTER 17

A New Plan

"It's agreed, then. We send the horses back with a message, now that Charger can run again, and we go destroy the machine." Andvari propped himself up with his hands. He watched Charger browse through the dried grasses, looking for anything edible.

"How do we get back in?" Kyson crossed his arms over his chest.

"The path we came out wasn't guarded. We just have to scour the hillside and find it again." Aili stared off towards the hill, though the trees hid it from sight. She could still feel it.

"That's not a problem. I'll find it before we leave."

Aili stared at Kyson, her mouth partly open. "How? Did you become an Earth Mage overnight?"

"Mind Magic." Andvari chuckled. "He can tap into our memories and create a mental map of everywhere we've been since leaving the tunnel."

"There are still guards wandering the hillside. I can guide us around them out here, but what if they're in the tunnel?" Aili played with the top of her boot, her fingers sliding over the smooth leather.

Kyson grinned. Aili shivered.

"It's weak and not working now, but there's a sleep spell on the border. It affects all non-magical folk when they try to cross, usually. We have a personal version of the spell, though we have to be close to use it." Kyson rubbed his hands together.

"How close?" Aili raised her eyebrow.

"In contact, touching their head." Andvari lifted his fingers. "It works nearly instantly. If we can sneak up on them, they won't even know what happened. Magic or not, we're sneaky. I can give us an edge there, too."

"Are you sure you're ready?" Aili narrowed her eyes at him. "You were dying not even a day ago."

Andvari shrugged. "I'm not at my best. I have limits to my magic and strength, but I have skills and experience to compensate. You still have full magic?"

Aili nodded.

"Okay, we'll make some plans for you now, so you don't find yourself mentally stuck if we get into a fight. What can you already do? List it for me." Andvari held her gaze.

"I can use small breezes, like when I cover my tracks. There's not a lot of breeze down there, though." Aili rubbed her chin. "The air is humid in the cavern, and I can get a small amount of water from it. I could also influence things like their clothing or supplies."

Her heart sank. There wasn't much she knew how to do yet. There weren't any plants or animals to ask for help from, and she'd not done much with rock, though she'd seen a few spells. Maybe she wouldn't be much help after all.

"I know you can sneak and use shadows. If you get any breeze at all, lift sand up at them and get it in their eyes. They can't hit what they can't see," Kyson offered.

She nodded. They will take her, so they must think she could help. Were they on some impossible mission? No, they thought they could manage, so it must be possible. "How do we destroy the machine for good?"

"The glass tubes?" Kyson ran his hand through his hair.

Andvari shook his head. "That, too, but the machine itself needs to go. You heard them. They have replacement glass, and lots of it. We'll brainstorm as we walk. Let's go."

Andvari went to his pack and pulled out a parchment and quill. Aili watched the quill as he wrote, scratching a message to whoever. He hung the note on Charger's saddle, fixed in place with a quick spell. He added an identical note to Leya's and Trickster's gear.

"Get your swords and anything else you want or need. We may run and fight, so choose wisely." Andvari pulled his sword from the hiding place and strapped it around his waist.

Aili retrieved her sword and stuffed more ration bars into her pockets. She double checked her medical kit and nodded. She tacked up Leya, packing the bridle instead, and checked the girth. Leya was ready to go, too.

Andvari looked at her. Aili nodded. Kyson wandered over, cloak on and sword at his side.

Andvari stepped in front of Charger and held the big horse's face with both hands. "Help."

Charger snorted. The horses turned and headed into the forest, straight for the border.

"What was that?" Aili watched Leya disappear into the distance.

"He'll lead them back to camp. Jordi will get the messages and send help. The horses will wait in camp for us, where they're safe. Now, let's get moving." Andvari nodded to Kyson.

Kyson stepped in front of Aili; his hand raised. "Relax and let me in. Think about the entrance. I'll get the details. You don't need to remember anything except the entrance itself."

She nodded and closed her eyes. His cool fingers rested against her forehead. Aili recalled the entrance and the bright light shining down the tunnel, nearly blinding her until she was outside. She remembered the trees, thick and sickly, with a few dead leaves hanging from their twigs.

"I got it." He lowered his hand from her head. "I know where to go, at least close enough."

"Great. Let's get moving." Andvari gave the hand signal to move out.

Kyson turned on his heel and headed through the trees. Aili followed him, walking beside Andvari. She kept her senses open. The horses were already out of range, beyond where she could feel them. She glanced at Andvari often, but he was moving okay, almost like his old self again.

"Guards," she whispered. Aili pointed through the trees.

They ducked into the bushes, her magic easing their way, and hunkered down. Andvari brushed a hand over them, and Aili sensed the spell settling over them, silencing any noise they might make. Her heart pounded.

The guards passed nearby, the sound of crunching dead leaves under their feet giving their position away. The footsteps faded. They were alone again. Aili looked down at her boots. The magic must still work, as she didn't remember hearing their own footsteps making all the noise the guards did.

They slunk from the bushes, and Kyson picked up their path again. Aili searched by feel as the men looked around and cast the occasional tracing spell. How had she made it so far from the hill yesterday? She didn't remember running that long.

"Two guards, standing together ahead," Aili whispered. She pointed. "That might be the entrance."

Andvari nodded to Kyson. He rested a hand on Aili's shoulder. Kyson snuck away, disappearing through the trees. Breathe, she reminded herself. They had the advantage. Would Kyson be okay? She reached out with her senses to follow him, but he was already on his way back.

Kyson appeared between some bushes. He signalled silence, a finger over his mouth, and for them to follow. Aili kept close to him, and he led them up the hill to a cluster of bushes and a fallen log. She crouched between them behind the log and peered over, looking down at an angle at two guards in those brightly coloured uniforms. There was no missing them in this forest. They stood out against the brown bark like a beacon in the night.

Kyson brought his hands up and gestured. Plan? Andvari frowned down at the guards below, completely unaware they were being watched. Aili cast about with her magic.

What might help? Squirrels darted about, searching for stored food. They were too busy. A deer wandered past, heading across this desolate wasteland to the forests beyond.

She looked again. What about him? She rubbed her chin. Yes, he might be willing if she could motivate him.

Aili raised a finger and tapped her temple, signalling an idea. Andvari locked his gaze with hers. He stared for a few moments before nodding. Aili sent her awareness out and brushed her essence against the massive snake. She suppressed her shudder. Snakes and ponies didn't mix, and she had to agree with the ponies on this one. Still, desperate situations called for desperate actions.

The snake turned its head to her, feeling her essence around him. Aili opened herself enough to communicate and showed him an image of him resting on a large and warm rock. She sped the image through the seasons, ending with him still there on his rock, snow around him but a warm and dry rock under him.

The snake shifted and uncoiled. He was interested. Aili showed him a picture in her mind of the two men near the tunnel entrance. She let her imagination take control, and pictured the snake slithering over, chasing the men away.

He coiled tightly and withdrew from her. Was he not interested, after all? He blinked and uncoiled again, slithering towards the men. Aili smiled. Warming a rock was easy, and she'd happily do that for him if this worked.

A guard leapt to the side and pointed. "Rock Viper." He turned and clawed at the boulders around the entrance, scrambling up the hill.

His buddy startled awake and scampered away, climbing a tree nearby. He clung to the tree trunk and pulled his sword, pointing it at the snake. The snake crept after the first man, slithering up the boulders as he chased him over the hill and out of sight. The other guard scampered down the tree and took off through the forest the other way.

Andvari curled up beside her behind the tree trunk, his hand to his mouth and his shoulders shaking. He took a deep breath and turned to her. "Brilliant. How'd you get it to agree?"

"I offered a trade. That big flat rock might be ideal." Aili pointed down the hill.

A quick search with her senses showed the men still running away. Aili darted down to the rock and kneeled beside it. She glanced up. Even when the trees recovered, it would get the afternoon sun. She could do better than that, though.

She pressed her hands to the rock and felt deep below her, searching for the warmth within the planet. Aili pulled the heat, guiding it to the rock, and filling the rock with warmth. She kept going, making a permanent channel for the heat, until her hands were comfortably warm on the rock.

Andvari and Kyson moved to the entrance. He waited outside while Kyson snuck in. Aili waved at the snake and pointed to the rock. It slithered towards her, over the side of the hill. She darted over to Andvari's side and followed him into the darkness.

She glanced back once inside. The snake curled up on his rock. He lifted his head. Did he just wink? Aili shook her head and followed Andvari deeper into the tunnel. She must have imagined it.

They stopped around the first bend, where the light grew dim. Andvari passed his hand over her eyes and chanted under his breath. Aili blinked. She clearly saw their outlines, shapes in the dark. Night vision? Enough for her to see by, anyway. She also saw the edges of the tunnel, as well as the occasional torch, sitting in brackets along the walls, cold and dark. They weren't burning, so that was a good sign, right?

Andvari did the same for himself and Kyson. Kyson led them down, Aili right behind him. She let her senses out and searched. The vision spell was fine, but she could see farther this way. Aili followed quietly until they reached a corner.

She tapped Kyson twice on the shoulder. He stopped and crouched. Kyson nodded. Two guards ahead. He set off slowly, staying low this time. Aili smiled, remembering the discussion she and Andvari had about staying unseen.

People don't look down, so being low gives you the advantage. They peered around the corner.

Two men stood against a wall, on either side of a door. Torches illuminated the area. The tunnel was open and bare, no cover for them to sneak in with. She glanced up at Andvari. He grinned and nodded to Aili, making the hand sign for torch and breeze.

Aili raised an eyebrow. She closed her eyes and searched for a breeze. There was a slight breeze, but not enough to extinguish the torches. Never mind, that was not her only option. Aili reached out with her abilities and pulled the air away from around the torches, spinning it into a shield around the sputtering flames. She sucked away air from behind the shield and the flames went out.

Andvari and Kyson were already moving. He gave her the signal to wait as they disappeared around the corner.

"Relight it, you fool."

Someone let out a stifled cry. Silence. Aili pressed her hands to her thighs and rolled her shoulders. The Scouts were fine, she was sure of it. Andvari appeared at the corner and waved for her to follow. Aili bounced to her feet and dashed after him.

Kyson stood over the guards, sleeping or unconscious on the dirt floor. He held a hand up to the door and chanted. "It's locked. I can't get in."

"We need somewhere to put them." Andvari set his hands on his hips and looked at the door.

"There's a storage room back there," Aili whispered, pointing back up the tunnel.

Andvari grabbed a guard's ankles and dragged him through the sand, back up the tunnel to the door Aili showed them. Kyson had the other guard. Aili opened the door and called a tiny ball of mage-light, though their vision spell let them see where all the shelves were. They dropped the men behind some crates and looked around, their own balls of mage-light out now.

"How did you know about this?" Andvari picked a metal part from a bin and examined it.

"I hid in here last time, on my way out." Aili touched a sheet of glass stacked in a pile on another shelf.

"It's been used by more than you, and recently." Kyson pointed at large footprints near more crates in another corner.

"What's worth guarding?" Aili stared out the door, into the tunnel.

"Let's find out. It might be important." Andvari led them from the room and back down to the door. "Can anyone feel anything?"

Aili placed her hands flat on the door, against the rough wood. The door shone with magic, and she could feel beyond it. "There're no people in there, but I felt the wrongness inside. It's like the machine, but smaller."

Andvari turned the handle, but the door remained locked tight. He let go and jumped back, shaking his hand as he grimaced. "Spelled shut, by a Master Mage, at that. But who?"

He and Kyson shared a look. Andvari's brow furrowed, and Kyson frowned. It was odd seeing their expressions through the vision spell. There, but not there. Where did the magic come from?

"We'll destroy the machine and come back. Remember, this is also our best escape route." Andvari glared at the door.

Kyson tilted his head towards the way down. Andvari nodded. He took Aili's hand. She sensed his pain and flowed healing into his hand, relieving the stinging from the locking spell. Aili curled her fingers around his hand and walked with him down towards the machine. He walked slowly and guided Aili as she closed her eyes, searching ahead for them.

"Nobody, path," she whispered. "Can't feel cavern well."

"Machine working?" Kyson whispered, moving close for her to hear.

Aili nodded. "Barely. Waiting."

"For?" Andvari squeezed her hand lightly.

She shrugged. It wasn't alive, and she couldn't sense any motives from it. It was just a machine, and one with twisted magic, at that.

They stopped around the corner, the cavern just ahead. Andvari let go of her hand and stood back. He gestured to himself, his fingers moving, and Aili watched with her senses as the spell settled over him. She waited with Kyson while Andvari crept around the corner and into the cavern.

He was back in moments. Andvari held up two fingers and pointed to their location. He held a hand up to her, palm out, and she nodded. They didn't need her in the way, not with only two guards. This time, she would listen and do what they asked. No more stray magic in enemy territory.

Aili crouched and pressed herself against the rock wall. The silence bothered her, though it also meant her friends were safe. She followed them with her senses instead, two glowing forms approaching the guards. Aili played with the hem of her shirt. He wasn't fully healed yet. Would he be okay?

They snuck up on the guards, despite the light in the cavern and the open space. It felt so odd, seeing the Scouts crouching, creeping across the room, and the guards completely unaware. In moments, they were laying on the ground. One of them walked back to the tunnel.

Kyson's dark shape waved her over. He was broader in the shoulders than Andvari, though just a little shorter. Aili couldn't help but crouch, despite him walking tall and confident. Why can't there be more shadows? Those crystals didn't feel warm and friendly like the stars, but felt harsh and unnatural.

Aili shielded her eyes with her hand. In moments, the spell adjusted for her, and she could see again. She scanned the room, turning slowly and searching the shadows for anything at all. Something inside pulled at her, whispering about something waiting for her. What, though?

Spare parts lay strewn about the machine. Torches sat in holders, lighting spots where panels sat nearby, revealing the machine's inner parts. Aili could see gears and tubes and lights from the switches. Where had the repairmen gone? The machine hummed, dim and almost inactive, but still there, still pulsing in that unnatural way.

"Any ideas?" Kyson folded his arms over his chest.

Andvari stared at the machine, his hand on his hip. The thing towered over them.

"What's powering it?" Aili took a step towards it.

"The heat and energy of the planet."

Where was that voice coming from? It seemed to echo around the cavern. She knew that voice. Where from? Aili spun and crouched, her hands up and ready.

His staff clunked against the gravel and sand with each step. His robes billowed around him as he walked, the fine fabrics almost floating. A memory rushed through her mind, those robes and the colours, a crest on a wall in the University. She knew him.

"What are you doing here?" Aili stepped beside Andvari and braced her hands on her hips.

"I should ask you the same question, magicless child." He stared down at her as he approached. "Magicless no more, I see."

"You know him?" Andvari set his hand on her shoulder.

"Orlo Mindar. You're from the University."

"That's Master Mindar to you, student." He glared at her; his lip curled back in a snarl.

"The specialist in magic research that went missing?" Kyson moved up beside Aili, partially shielding her with his presence.

"Not missing, apparently." Andvari pulled Aili back a step. "Why would you be interested in a machine that drains magic?"

Orlo Mindar rolled his eyes. "Typical. No understanding. It doesn't drain magic. Well, it does, but only to gather it. We can use that gathered magic to power spells stronger than anyone has ever seen before. The University refused to research the lines of power. We came to learn more."

He walked towards the machine. Andvari pulled Aili out of his way and back. She wrinkled her nose at the smell of burning torch and decay that oozed from his clothing.

Orlo Mindar stopped in front of the machine, his eyes raised to its heights. "If we can gather the power from the planet, directly from the lines close to the surface, think of what we could accomplish. We would have strength like this."

He spun and raised his staff. Aili shifted closer to Andvari, and he wrapped an arm around her. Orlo chanted, his voice growing louder with each line of the spell. Warriors made of summoned water hovered in the air, circling around him, all facing the Scouts.

"I'll distract him. Seal the door behind us. His backup is there," Andvari whispered.

Aili moved behind him, her hand on his shirt. She closed her eyes and opened her senses, feeling for the door. People gathered beyond, drinking and resting, some sleeping on benches. Aili sunk herself into the rock and let her essence seep inside it. The rock was hard and brittle, just like the mountain Dinna worked. Aili smiled.

"Your machine is weakening the border around our home," Andvari called. "They're planning an invasion."

"They will never succeed." Orlo laughed. "The Border Patrol and Scouts will see to that. The magic is old and strong."

"They crossed once already, a large group of them. We barely chased them back. You're draining other mages of their power." Kyson stepped towards him and shook his fist.

The rock shifted under her will, like clay in her hands. She pulled it across the doorway, narrowing the entrance a bit at a time. How long could they keep him busy? At least he couldn't feel magic the way she could. Aili would need every advantage she could get.

"Nonsense. They don't have magic. They're nothing compared to us. How could they threaten the greatest race in all the world?"

More time, Andvari, just a little more.

"How does the machine gather magic?"

Yes, keep him busy. Right, he could feel her using magic, since he was her teacher. He knew she wasn't done. Just a little more now. She grabbed the last bit of rock and closed the doorway completely. Aili relaxed and lay her hand flat between his shoulders. She was done. It was just them and Orlo Mindar.

"The machine attracts it, somehow, like a magnet. The liquid in the tubes stores it. It can hold magic. I can tap into it and perform miracles like this." Orlo Mindar spread his hands wide. The water warriors floated around the cavern, circling the group.

She grimaced. Aili wiped her forehead with her sleeve. Seriously. Teachers. She shook her head and stepped around Andvari. "You don't really know how it works, or who you're hurting. What kind of researcher ignores that? How could you?"

Andvari pulled her back and kept an arm around her shoulders. Aili watched the familiars floating around them, waiting. Many mages could conjure one familiar, possibly two, if they were good, but how could he focus on so many at once? A quick count and she guessed at twenty. There was no way the three of them could fight all at once.

"All research carries risks. When we get everything working, I can transfer the power into crystals and take them with me." Orlo brushed his fingers over the crystal at the end of his staff. "Then I can take my rightful place as head of the University, the position that should have been mine years ago."

A warrior floated towards Aili; its translucent hand extended towards her. Her heart hammered in her chest. She felt inside and touched her inner core. Aili's abilities exploded from her, flinging the creature back. It spattered against the wall and collapsed, water droplets spraying the machine. Steam rose and gears screeched as the water dripped into the open panels.

She grinned. She could affect them. They were actual water, conjured normally by a mage, and she could use that. Water was one of her favourites.

Orlo stared at the warrior, or rather, where it dissipated.

"Playtime?" Aili raised an eyebrow at him.

"Keep him busy, but be careful," Andvari whispered.

"I got this." She took a step forward, her arms crossed over her chest.

"You insolent little—" Orlo's face burned bright red. "You can't have magic like that. Weeks ago, you had nothing at all."

"You're right." Aili stretched her hands out and widened her stance, flowing into the first bare hand fighting form, collecting her energy between her palms. Her movements were slow and fluid, like water. The steam and droplets from the warrior zipped over to her, collecting in her hands. "I understand magic and water, though. Possibly better than you do."

She formed the water into a ball between her hands, still moving through the form, using it to power her focus. Surface tension held the ball together, with a touch of her power to strengthen it. Aili stretched the ball out into a rope, spinning it and strengthening it more.

With a flick of her wrists, Aili tossed the rope out. Her magic and gestures shaped the rope, moving it around the other warriors, gathering them into the rope and making it thicker. The rope lengthened, responding to her will, and weaved its way around the room, towards the red-faced mage near the machine.

His body trembled, and he snarled at her. Orlo muttered a counter spell. With the help of the fighting form, her focus was strong, stronger than his. She didn't have a spell for him to counter, and his magic fizzled out.

"There's no way you're more powerful than me," Orlo screamed.

Aili shrugged. "You're right. I can't actually cast a spell to save my life."

She coiled the water rope around him loosely. Aili pulled tight, and the rope snapped close around him. She risked a glance over to the Scouts. They were on the machine, opening panels and searching for something. Aili sensed Orlo muttering a counter spell. She spun the rope and twirled him around. His spell dissipated.

If he could form water familiars, he was an elemental mage. Markings on his staff confirmed this. He could create more familiars and control them, but she worked with the water itself, and could overwhelm his control spells. Would he try again?

Water blasted away from him, spraying the machine. Steam rose from the hot metal. Her clothing was damp, and the air felt thick. The pulsing from the machine grew erratic. Could he sense it, or was it like magic, and only she knew?

"A child with no magical skill will not taunt me." He stalked towards her, robes dripping wet, staff held high. Water dripped from his nose, falling to his shoes. His hair hung limp and his beard was a scraggly mess.

Aili burst out laughing.

A fireball rushed towards her. Aili's breath caught in her throat. She dodged behind a boulder, her legs pumping as hard as she could manage. Heat burned her skin, and the fireball passed over her, within inches of her. It hit the wall and flashed out.

She curled up behind the rock, her body shaking. She glanced up. Andvari was at the corner of the machine, a metal bar in his hands, jammed down inside the workings. He gestured at her, signalling a shield. He pointed at the water.

Aili took as slow a breath as she could manage. Yes, water absorbed heat. She could do this. Aili pulled the water towards her and gathered it in her hands. She formed it, stretching it and flattening it into a shield.

She stepped from behind the boulder, the shield still forming in front of her. He raised his staff, and another fireball formed at his fingers. Aili focused on her shield, keeping her breathing slow and controlled.

He drew his hand back, ready to throw the fireball at his fingertips. She wasn't ready! It was too thin and not firm enough yet. The fireball hurled at her. She tossed her shield in front of her and drew her sword, swinging it through the flames as she rolled away. The fireball disappeared and her sword was hot in her hand. The blade shimmered with a dancing light, small flames flickering along the edges.

He glared at her, waved his fists, and stamped his feet. Aili chuckled to herself. He reminded her of Silla, before the girl started spending time with horses. He pointed his staff at her. The crystal glowed, filling the room with a bright light. A fireball formed at the tip, larger than anything she'd ever seen a mage conjure before.

Now what? She stared at the growing ball of flames with wide eyes. Wait, science and sorcery. She could do this. Fire needs oxygen, heat, and fuel. His fuel was magical. Could she cool the flames or smother them? Her Air Magic wasn't strong and practiced yet, but she could smother him.

Aili sheathed her sword and dashed across the room, as far from Andvari and Kyson as she could get. She gathered all the water she could, holding it in a ball in her hands. Aili put herself in front of the machine, right by the main control panel. Her friends were still on the machine, dismantling it. Were they safe from his attack? She knew she wasn't.

Orlo tracked her with his staff, the tip still pointed at her. The fireball glowed and burned, almost as tall as he was. Aili spread her hands and the water ball became a water disc. The fireball zoomed towards her.

She dodged, keeping the water between her and the fire. The water absorbed much of the heat, turning to steam. Her skin still ached, despite her protection. Flames roared past over her head. Aili rolled along the sand, grimacing against the pain.

The fireball hit the machine and spattered, spraying flaming sparks everywhere. The controls melted and fused.

"I didn't want to do this, but you leave me no choice," he bellowed.

The air tingled with magic, but stronger. It felt like—her eyes widened—like right before a lightning strike. She raised her hands and signalled hide and cover to the Scouts. They leapt from the machine and ran for the boulders. Think, Aili. You have seconds to live, at most.

Power grew beneath her feet. Electricity loves water. She gathered any water she could, even vapour from the air. Aili rooted to the spot, forming the water into a trail, right to the machine. She set her magic and ran, darting for the nearest boulders near the cages. Her feet tingled now, not just her senses, and she ran faster.

Lightning arced across the room. Aili opened her mouth and covered her ears, tucking into a ball as she landed and rolled. The hill shook and a deafening bang made her ears ring. Something was burning. All she saw was white, even with her eyes closed.

She groped around, but her skin tingled from the burst of magic, and she couldn't feel anything. Something hard pressed back against her. The floor, she realized. Aili opened her eyes and blinked furiously. She could see shapes. Shapes are better than whiteness.

Aili slipped her medical kit from the harness under her shirt. It felt intact. Wait, she could feel again, at least a little. Using her diminished sense of touch, Aili counted the vials and selected the one she wanted. She knew what each vial was and where in the kit it was and didn't need to see to get the right one.

The vial was heavy. She hadn't needed this one yet, and it should be full. A flick of the thumb opened the cap, and she dabbed some on her finger. Aili smeared the liquid over her eyelids. The pain eased, and the whiteness diminished more. She blinked. Shapes were clearer. Now she could see colours a bit, too.

She tucked that vial away and took another out. This little vial had a dropper, and Aili tilted her head. She dropped some oil in each ear and shuddered at the cool sensation. The hum eased off, though with oil in her ears she wouldn't hear well anyway. Aili tucked the vial away and put her kit back under her shirt. Great, she could sort of see, and kind of hear, though not well. At least the hum was almost gone now.

Aili peered around the boulder. The machine was a melted mess of twisted metal, with oily black liquid pooling on the floor. It sat quietly, other than the steam rising from it. The pulsing hum was gone. Flames flickered out from an open panel, black smoke rising from the spot.

Where was he? Was he sneaking up on her? Aili glanced around, flicking to the platform first. There was no platform anymore, just a pool of the black sludge and twisted metal. Wait, was that—? A burned pile of robes still smouldered, and part of a staff lay broken on the ground, the crystal missing completely. She looked away.

Where were her friends? Her heart sped again, and she wobbled to her feet. They ran that way, she guessed. Aili stumbled towards the boulders, her body stiff and unresponsive. Was that movement behind the boulder? She forced her legs to go faster.

A blurry silhouette moved towards her. Blue mage-light sparked to life and brightened the surrounding area. Aili blinked rapidly; her sore eyes overwhelmed by the light. Arms wrapped around her and clung to her. Her sore and raw skin screamed at her, but she hugged back as hard as she could. They were alive.

"Quickly. We have—destroy—crystals." Andvari guided her over to the cylinder, the melted remains still partly intact.

Aili stared down at the glowing crystals. Her mind was as numb as her body.

"Draw—sword. I'll help—together."

She grasped her sword and drew it from the scabbard. Her hand shook. Andvari wrapped his hand over hers, holding the sword in her fingers. Her grip steadied with his help.

"Together."

She let him guide the movement, focusing on feeling the power within her sword. She could feel his energy through their hands and channeled his intention along with hers into her sword. The flames along the blade roared to life, glowing and flickering as they raised the sword.

He brought the sword down on the crystals. The flames and her abilities joined, melting the crystals where the blade struck. They shattered like glass, the edges melted smooth and charred black. Power burst from them with each strike.

The walls shook. The rock shifted above them.

"We have—leave." He steered her across the room towards the tunnel.

Her skin screamed at her again, pain lancing through her body. Aili whimpered and tears cascaded down her cheeks. She forced her body to stay upright and her legs to carry her. Kyson appeared on her other side and took her arm, supporting and partly carrying her. Their boots pounded the sand, stirring dust as they ran.

"Keep going." Andvari helped her into the tunnel. "We'll treat the burn once we're out." His voice sounded distant still, but she heard each word that time.

The ground shook. Shard of rock fell from the ceiling, pelting Aili's damaged skin and causing fresh cuts and bruises. She ran on with them, up and around the winding tunnel. Aili slipped, but Kyson pulled her up and hustled her along.

She flushed with relief at the light ahead, safety just a few yards away. Aili stumbled along beside them, running with everything she had left. They burst into the daylight, dodging the snake sunning himself on the rock.

Aili cried out at the sun in her eyes and slammed her eyelids shut. Andvari pulled her to a rock and sat her on it. She sat quietly as he examined her skin, her body still shaking.

"Here." Kyson placed a hand over her eyes and chanted.

The sun dimmed in her senses, and she could see again, though her eyes needed more time to recover. "Thanks," she managed between whimpers.

Andvari slipped her healing kit free and opened it. He checked the vials. "Here it is. Everything is full again. You can use this."

He dabbed some of the oily brown liquid on his thumb and wiped a line on her forehead. Her pain eased and she could breathe without struggling.

"That one." Aili pointed at a vial with yellow ointment. "Burns, please." She hissed at the sleeve scraping over her burned arm as she moved.

Andvari nodded. "Kyson?"

"Sleep." Kyson's fingers touched her temple.

Everything went dark.

CHAPTER 18

HOME AGAIN

Aili knew those smells. Fresh hay and sun-warmed horse. Chewing, she could hear chewing. Leya? A cooling breeze blew gently over her arm and face. Something soft covered her. A blanket? She was laying on something soft. Aili rolled towards the sound and smell of horse and opened her eyes.

"Leya," she croaked, her voice sore.

She lay on a cot beside a paddock, back in the camp. How did she get here?

"She's awake!"

Aili winced at the shriek, grateful it grew distant and faint rapidly. She rolled enough to see Silla tearing across the grass and disappearing into the stable, her voice still audible as she called for someone. A woman dashed from the stable, followed by a man. Wait, that's Nali and Kyson. Aili smiled.

She rolled. Her limbs were stiff. How long had she been laying here? At least her body was listening. Nali sat on the edge of the cot and slipped a hand under Aili. She helped Aili sit.

Kyson kneeled beside her. "He'll be right here. How do you feel?"

Aili held her hand up and bent and straightened her fingers. "Odd, my nerves are supercharged, but I'm okay. Everything is louder and brighter than it should be."

Nali pulled Aili's tunic down slightly at the back and checked Aili's skin. Her skin was still raw, but it no longer hurt, it was just sensitive. She no longer wanted to cry at the lightest touch.

"Your nerves still have some lightning in them. We don't know how long you'll be like that." Nali held her gaze.

"It might be permanent?" Aili whispered.

Nali shrugged. "We don't know."

Leya lifted her head and stared towards the stable. Aili turned and looked over. Andvari was running towards her, dust rising from the path as he passed. He didn't slow until he was close, and he stopped beside her. Kyson moved and Andvari kneeled next to Aili.

Andvari took her hands in his. "How are you doing?"

Aili smiled. "I'm okay."

"He didn't leave your side the whole time since you came back until the Commander threatened him if he didn't shower and have a proper meal." Nali pointed to a bedroll on the ground beside the cot.

Aili grinned. He was family. That's what family did. They stayed with you when you needed help or care. "How did we get back? When?" She looked down at her hands, fresh pink skin instead of burns. It was days, not hours, she bet.

"Two days. That a lucky healing time for you or something? Kyson kept you asleep while they treated your burns so you could rest and not feel the pain." Andvari squeezed her hands lightly.

"Thanks," Aili whispered.

Kyson leaned over and reached his hand to her forehead. She sat quietly and let him scan her, the magic tingling more than usual with her supercharged nerves.

"She feels better, though her nerves are still more active than they should be." Kyson took his hand away.

Aili glanced at the small paddock, where Leya chewed on a pile of hay. "How are Charger and Trickster?"

"They're fine. They're in the stable, resting." Andvari glanced over his shoulder at Leya. "We healed both horses and they're ready for anything. Leya wouldn't leave you, magical locks on her stall or not, so we came out here with her."

Aili giggled and smiled at her pony. Leya snorted at her, her ears perked towards Aili.

"Once we got outside the hill, the mirrors worked again. I contacted Dinna once you were asleep. She flew out to get us right away." Kyson stood and stretched.

"Don't worry, you slept through the entire flight." Andvari chuckled.

Aili grimaced, her nose wrinkling. "Thanks."

Nali rested her hand over Aili's heart, over the soft tunic. She chanted low and soft; a healing spell Aili recognized from Ilia. The old woman used it on a lightning strike patient when Aili was little. Camp noises quieted and her eyes stopped watering in the sunlight. Her skin no longer prickled where the cloth touched her. The smell of horses faded slightly, sadly, but she'd be grateful when she was around more people, like during Drill when they were all sweaty. Aili didn't want to think about that.

"That should help for now. Let me know if you need the spell again." Nali lowered her hand. She stood and walked back to the main building, past the stable.

Andvari sat on the cot beside her. "Thank you for everything."

She smiled, despite the tear rolling down her cheek. "Is it really over?"

"Our part is. Dinna headed back with a Scout team and some Border Guards. They're scouring the ruins of the collapsed hill." Kyson paced slowly, stretching his body as he walked. "They're still searching for the source of the magic we sensed, the one from the locked room, but everything is a mess over there."

"The three of us have time to rest and recover. You've never been through anything like that, I'm guessing, and you need time to let it sink in and process it. Besides, you've almost learned sword form four, and need time to practice that." Andvari stretched his legs out.

Aili pressed her hand hard over her mouth, holding back the laughter that bubbled up. "We nearly died, many times in a single day, and he's worried about my training?"

Andvari pulled out his mirror and held it up for her. "Have a look."

She searched her reflection. Those final crystals in her band glowed a faint red. She hadn't mastered Fire Magic, not by a long shot, but she must have started with the flames trapped in her sword. Three gold strands threaded through the mostly silver band. Small cubes appeared between the clusters of crystals, each bragging about one of her magical accomplishments. One even had a little lightning bolt.

"Wow." Aili touched her band, her fingers brushing over the little cubes.

"Wow, indeed." He tucked his mirror back under his shirt.

Tears poured down her cheeks. Memories flashed before her, gone as soon as they appeared. Andvari, bleeding and hurt on the ground, Charger collapsing in front of her, smoking robes and a broken staff, and more.

Andvari draped an arm around her shoulders and let her lean against him, her head over his heart. He held her and let her cry until her tears dried on their own.

"What about the door? The wrongness?" Aili wiped her face with her sleeve.

Kyson and Andvari looked at each other.

"Dinna led some powerful Earth Mages in, and they're still searching. They have found nothing and haven't gotten deep in that tunnel yet." Andvari stared off at the forest past the paddocks, his eyes distant and not focused on anything.

"Thanks for getting me out," she whispered.

"I put you in danger. His voice cracked. He brushed his arm over his eyes. "I should have refused."

Kyson kneeled in front of Aili. "He wanted you to stay here, where it was safe. The Border Council figured you could help, and you are his student, so they all voted for you to go."

"I wanted to come." Aili touched his shoulder.

Andvari laughed. He relaxed a little beside her, his arm no longer so tense. "Yes, you sure did." He wiped his eyes with a cloth from his pocket. "Rest. Soon, the three of us go back to the capital. Ilia assured us she can get your nerves back to normal, or at least make you comfortable again."

Aili grinned. If anyone could fix her, it was Ilia. She shifted and rested her head on his shoulder. They sat together and watched the sunset. Leya stayed near the fence, grazing on the hay and some grass. Tomorrow was another day. For now, her loved ones were safe, and she could rest. That was enough for her.

SNEAK PEEK - FACING THE FIRE

CHAPTER 1

Andvari's large and warm hands rested on her shoulders. He locked his eyes on hers, filled with concern for her. "Are you sure you're ready? We can wait a few more days."

Aili brushed a lock of her brown hair back behind her ear, a lighter brown than his hair. Small strands escaped her braids and tickled her face. She smiled up at her magic teacher, knowing he was also her friend and he cared about her.

"I'm ready. It'll be a quiet and short ride, and you'll be there."

She held his gaze, willing him to see how much she'd healed. Aili rested this last week, cared for by a few Scouts who could help her heal. Did he still see the little bolts of lightning that flashed across her eyes occasionally? They disrupted her vision, but didn't hurt, just tingled a little.

"Alright we'll go tomorrow like we planned. We'll pack and prepare today after meditation." His brow furrowed. He still hesitated, but she couldn't heal completely here. They both knew that.

"Can we meditate with the fighting forms? It makes my nerves tingle less than sitting does."

Andvari frowned. "You're still having that much trouble?" His gaze ran over her from head to toe and back.

Aili giggled. "You can't see my nerves through my skin. I'll be fine. Besides, the point of travelling is to see Ilia. She'll fix me up good as new, right?"

He pulled her to his chest and hugged her. Aili discovered the first day she woke up back in camp that firm pressure on her skin helped her nerves calm, after falling asleep leaning against him and under his arm. The camp seamstress sewed her a special blanket with weights in it she could drape over herself, and her friends gave her firm hugs regularly.

She rested her head over his heart, listening to the steady beating. He rubbed her back through the soft shirt, which protected her still raw and healing skin. Aili was incredibly sensitive to any stimulation now. Even the light breeze from a window could irritate her. She hoped Ilia, a Master Healer and Herbalist, could fix her. Aili used to love sitting in a breeze.

"Hay barn?"

Aili grinned. "Beat you there."

She tore from the room, turning to the window in the hall. Aili slid it up and leapt through, tucking and landing on the shed roof below. She dashed to the edge and leapt into the hay bales. She could hear him behind her, slowed by the small window as he eased his large body through.

Aili rolled from the hay pile, landed on her feet, and darted around the hay barn to the open side. Her body felt good, ready for the challenge. His long legs carried him past her into the hay barn. Aili jogged into the building and stopped beside him. She felt better after her run. Her burns healed well, though the new skin was still tender, and the creams and lotions kept her comfortable.

"Does that mean you're doing the planning and supply list?" he teased.

"Oh, please, you know I'll do a better job." Aili shifted her feet through the ankle-deep hay, testing her footing.

"You, a mere student of a couple of months at most, think you can organize better than me, a highly trained Scout, and expert at travel and covert movement?" He raised an eyebrow at her. "Challenge accepted. I want to see that list by supper time."

"Consider it done. Now, were we going to meditate or not?"

"Fine, if you feel that good, we'll begin with the first form. We won't stop until all four are done, slowly and with excellent technique."

She turned and faced the open side with him, a few feet apart so they wouldn't hit each other by mistake. He called the commands, preparing her, before leading her through the movements. She cleared her mind and calmed her body, opening herself to her surroundings. Aili looked like his tiny shadow, matching his movements almost perfectly.

Aili could feel the camp, sense each resident, and knew where the horses were. She hadn't tried any active magic since returning, worried about controlling her abilities, but the passive listening was still comfortable. She could even feel Leya, her pony, relaxing in a stall in the stable.

The sun cast a soft glow over them, light filtered through the trees near the edge of the camp. She was grateful for the shelter and shade now. The brighter midday light still hurt her eyes. She loved the fresh smell of hay and horse. Camp life, here on the edge of the Eastern Border Woods, was way better than the capital city where she grew up.

Andvari settled into the closing position of the third form with her. "Excellent. Ready?"

Aili nodded. She pressed her hands to her thighs and steadied herself. She'd only been working on form four for a short time now, and she wasn't feeling confident yet.

"I'll talk you through it. Prepare."

She straightened her body and slowed her breathing. Aili cleared her mind. This was the first advanced form the Scouts used, and she needed to pay attention. Her heart raced at the memory of Darik teaching her the first three forms years ago. No, focus, she reminded herself. Think later.

Andvari waited for her to settle. How did he always know when she was thinking? She took a deep breath and let it out slowly, imagining her mind like a calm pond without ripples.

Aili followed him through the form, grateful for the commands to help her. She remembered more than she hoped, letting her body carry her through the form without thinking. Aili faltered on the last few moves. He slowed the pace and let her correct herself.

"Excellent progress. You learn so quickly. Ready for lunch?"

"Can we eat…"

"Room, stable, or field?" His eyes shone. He didn't bother hiding his grin.

Aili laughed. "Will you stop that?"

Andvari shrugged. "What can I say? It's a gift."

"Stables?"

"Go. I'll get us plates and meet you there."

Aili walked to the rear stable door nearby, sticking to the shade between buildings. Most horses were out in the paddocks to graze and enjoy the sun. She could hear them blowing softly to keep their lungs clear, though they were on the other side of the stable near the trees.

Leya's sharp whinny echoed through the barn, greeting her eagerly as she entered the stable. Aili walked down the aisle to her stall, Leya's nose barely poking over the half-door. She rubbed the pony's soft nose, laughing at her little nostrils vibrating with a pleading whicker.

"Okay, an apple it is, you manipulative little thing." She stared into Leya's soft brown eyes. "You're using your cute against me."

She grabbed an apple from a treat bin in the feed room, hesitated for a moment, and grabbed two more for Charger and Trickster. Aili returned to Leya's stall. Leya's head was straining to get over the door, her white mane flopping around with the effort.

"Here." Aili reached her hand over the door and offered the apple on her flat palm.

Pale lips sucked the apple in, the red fruit disappearing quickly. Leya crunched the apple, chewing it easily with her powerful jaws. Aili rubbed the pony's golden forehead. Leya gulped the apple and stared at Aili, her upper lip curled up as she sniffed the other apples.

Aili moved to the next stall. Charger, Andvari's massive gelding, ambled to the door to greet her. He sniffed her, reaching easily over the wooden half-door, and pressed his head to her. She rubbed the long dark nose before offering him his apple. Charger slowly took the apple from her, his whiskers gently brushing over her palm.

"At least someone's a gentleman," Aili teased her pony.

Leya stared at her through the upper stall bars, her eyes fixed on the last apple. She whickered softly.

"You had yours. You have plenty of hay."

Aili moved another stall over to Trickster, Kyson's horse. Trickster took the treat from her before going back to his hay, ignoring her presence completely. Aili grinned. She scratched his favourite spot, under his belly, between his front legs. He stretched his neck out and bobbed his head up and down, delighted with the attention.

She scratched for a minute before running her hands down Trickster's front leg. His tendon felt good. She healed him on their last mission, but she'd always check him from now on. Since Kyson was Andvari's Scout partner, she'd see both him and Trickster regularly.

"He's looking good."

Aili looked up and saw Jordi leaning against the stall door, watching her.

"You did a great job with him. I've been helping him strengthen that leg since he got back." Jordi smiled.

"Is he up for the ride?" Aili felt the leg again. No heat or swelling. She couldn't even tell he'd ever injured it.

"He's right as rain," Jordi assured her. "While you were being healed by Kyson and Nali, I tended him. He's doing better than you are."

Aili's grin twisted. "Thanks for reminding me. I almost forgot about the lightning strike and my nerves being crazy."

Jordi chuckled. "Any time. Joining me for lunch?"

"Don't mind if we do." Andvari held a plate up for Aili.

She left Trickster's stall, latched it behind her, and took the plate. Aili moved back to Leya's stall and sat on the hay bale, leaning against the stall wall. Leya's nose poked over the door, sniffing the carrots on Aili's plate.

"Those are for her, you greedy little thing," Andvari scolded. He sat on the hay bale beside Aili. "You can have a carrot from the feed room later."

Leya snorted.

"Be right back. That smells good." Jordi disappeared down the barn aisle.

Aili picked up the fresh roll, still warm, in her hand. The herbs smelled sweet and inviting. Aili's stomach rumbled. She bit into the roll, steam releasing from inside, and she tasted the dried fruits as a burst of sweetness on her tongue.

"I missed these." Aili smiled, holding the roll to her nose, and breathing in.

"There's a pan-fried version we can make over a campfire." Andvari held his roll to his nose. He sniffed and his eyes closed. A smile spread across his face. "They are amazing, aren't they?"

"That is one advantage to staying in camp." Jordi floated a hay bale over and sat with them. "Fresh rolls whenever I want them." The hay bale shifted under his weight as he settled, flattening slightly under the massive man.

"Ilia and I used to make different varieties, depending on what her patients needed. She had a blend of herbs for nearly everything." Memories of countless days baking in Ilia's workshop filled Aili's mind. She could still smell the herbs and flowers mixed with baking bread.

"I wonder what blend she'll use on you?" Andvari teased.

"Knowing her, I might have a diet change. Lifestyle and herbs over magic, to let the body restore itself." Ilia had told her that many times, not once deterred by Aili's lack of magic back then.

She chewed her carrots, cooked perfectly with just a hint of crunch, in a light sauce with spices. A touch of sweet, a touch of mustard, perfection. Aili fingered her neckband, lost in the memories of her and Ilia.

Everyone had a neckband. It's colours and decorations showed a mage's status and abilities, as well as notable accomplishments. Aili glanced at Andvari's neckband. His band was platinum, showing his status as a Master Mage. The crystals along his band were an emerald green, the colour of Earth Magic. Small cubes with inscribed pictures told of many deeds he did, magic spells he created, and incredible magic he had performed.

Aili wondered what magic made the bands work. She'd read a lot as a child, more than anyone else she knew, but no books or scrolls ever mentioned how the bands worked, or even where they came from. Everyone just had them.

"Yours is still the same." Andvari somehow seemed to know when something was on her mind. It seemed as magical as the bands some days.

Her band only changed colours weeks ago, a couple of months at most, when she became his student. Before that, it remained the dull bronze of a baby or small child. She still secretly feared she'd wake one day, and her abilities would be gone, her band bronze again.

Everyone else in her country had their magic assessed and identified around five years old, the occasional child being six, but nobody went past seven without their band turning silver and them being placed with a teacher. Nobody except Aili, that is.

"So, ready to go back to the capital?" Jordi asked.

Aili shook her head. "I'm looking forward to seeing Ilia and Darik, but that's it." She scooped up a little rice with lentils in it. A burst of orange filled her mouth. She closed her eyes and savoured the taste. The mages in the kitchens were amazing with flavour.

"We'll be stopping by the University. I have a meeting with the Commander and the Grandmaster about what happened in the cavern. You'll come with me unless you'd rather explore the University grounds?" Andvari offered.

Aili shook her head. "Can't I stay in the woods?"

"We'll be camping there, but we still need to go into the city. It's a business trip, as well as a chance to get you healed. You've never seen Headquarters, have you?"

"Not inside, no."

Jordi set his fork down. "You don't want to stay with your parents?"

Aili frowned. "I'd rather be in the woods."

"When you make the supply list, make sure there's camping gear. Don't worry about meals. We'll get food and ingredients from the city." Andvari grinned.

***

"Come. There's a lecture for students I think you should watch."

Aili looked up from her list.

"Don't worry about that. I'll finish it." Andvari opened the door and waited.

"A lecture?" Aili shifted from the bed near the window.

"You'll love it. It's very science based. Kyson, as our highest-ranking Air Mage, is teaching advanced students something you'll love. Come on."

Aili handed him the list and slid her boots on. He led her down the hall, scanning the list as he walked.

"This is a great start. I'd almost think you were a Scout, not a student."

Aili grinned. She followed him down the stairs and outside. He headed into the fields around the camp to the West.

"Since you're still recovering, I don't expect you to take part unless you want to." Andvari glanced down and met her eyes. "You can if you feel up to it. Judge that for yourself."

Kyson sat on the grass with a couple of students about Aili's age, advanced students nearing the end of their training. She hadn't met them yet, though Aili had seen them around. Andvari led her to the group and sat with them. Aili sank to the grass beside him.

"Here." Kyson handed her a cloth and a crystal.

Aili nodded and took them.

"We can use these crystals to see how light behaves. It's made of many wavelengths, and we can use that when we want to make something invisible, or otherwise change how people see an object." Kyson held the crystal up and shone the sunlight on the cloth, separating the light into its colours.

Aili listened as he discussed how light behaves, and how to bend light around objects to make them appear invisible. She watched with wide eyes as the cloth in front of him disappeared. She could still see the grass bent down under the cloth, and feel the cloth with her magic, but the cloth was invisible to her eyes.

"Remember where you left the cloth, or whatever other object you made invisible. Otherwise, you'll need a detect magic or locate the unseen spell to find it again." Kyson cast a detect magic spell, and the cloth showed up as a faint shimmer in the grass. "Still, it can be useful if you want to hide something, and no one is actively seeking it. Try now."

He talked them through the spell, making sure the students knew the gestures, words, and mental focus. Aili played with the prism, shining the light around her. She didn't feel ready to work out a method for herself yet, with her nerves all haywire, but she watched the others.

The girl focused and chanted, her fingers moving over the cloth. Aili watched the cloth shimmer and lose its colour, appearing translucent, like a ghostly outline. The boy tried. He squeezed his eyes shut tightly and cast the spell. His cloth turned green.

"Good effort for your first try, both of you." Kyson pointed to the cloth. "You bent the red light away, so don't give up. It'll come easier to her as a Fire Mage than to you as an Earth Mage. You'll do other things easily that she struggles with, too. Keep practicing."

The young man nodded and smiled. "Thanks."

Aili played with the prism again, beaming the light around. She aimed for the list in Andvari's lap, scattering the light over where he was writing.

"Getting bored?" Andvari grinned.

"Not with the theory, just with my current limitations. It almost feels like not having magic again." Aili wiped a tear away as her voice shook.

Andvari set the list aside and hugged her firmly. "We leave tomorrow. Ilia will help you. You'll get your abilities back."

"The healers don't know that," she whispered. "You sound so sure."

"I am sure." He brushed a lock of her hair back behind her ear. "I know you, and I know that old woman. She won't quit until you're well. Now, do you need an advanced lecture on light bending to ease your boredom?"

"Can I?" Aili glanced at Kyson.

Kyson chuckled. "Go ahead. Ask anything." He ran his hands through his dark hair and straightened up.

"Challenge accepted." Aili shifted and faced him.

She left an hour later with her head full of new knowledge and her brain aching from concentrating.

***

Aili checked Leya's gear again, her hands running over straps and feeling the balance. The saddle was in great shape. Her pack spread the weight over the pony's back.

Leya could carry her and her equipment comfortably for the trip.

They weren't carrying much this time, mostly the supplies for camp like a tent and bedrolls, and cooking equipment and basic food supplies. Being so close to the city, they could get what they needed daily if they wanted. It made the horses' lives easier, not carrying heavier food items.

"Ready?" Andvari led Charger into the aisle.

"Sure am." Aili followed with Leya.

He glanced over at her packs and nodded. After her last mission with him, he knew she could pack for travel efficiently and safely for both herself and her pony. He trusted her to pack her own gear and look after Leya.

"Great." Kyson led Trickster behind her. "It's been too long. I miss the solitude of the bush."

Aili giggled. "It's been a week."

Kyson nodded. "Way too long."

Andvari smiled and shook his head. "Mount up."

Aili vaulted onto Leya, her physical energy and fitness recovering faster than her magical abilities. She was grateful Leya was short, and she wasn't given a taller horse instead. Leya grew up with her, being fifteen, only a few years younger than Aili. Darik, her father's Stable Master, trained Leya for her and taught her how to train horses when she turned twelve.

They set off from the stable through the sprawling wooden buildings of the camp. Aili sighed happily, pleased the sun would be behind them for the ride. Her eyes still struggled with the bright light. The sun peeked over the trees behind them, casting a red and purple glow over the peaceful meadows.

Andvari turned in his saddle and looked back at her, letting Charger steer through the camp. "Let me know if you get tired or feel off. We can take a break any time we want."

"I will." Aili guided Leya behind him, single file on the narrower paths between bunk houses and storerooms.

She watched people moving around, freshly awake and preparing for the day or heading for bed after a long night shift. Horses had the right of way, but they still considered it rude to ride over someone, especially if they were tired. Aili smiled and nodded at people who greeted them.

The road widened and Aili moved Leya up beside Charger. The air was crisp and cool. Fall was approaching quickly, summer was ending. Aili admired the rolling foothills. Mountains to the Northeast stood tall over the skyline, delaying the sunrise for camp residents until it was higher in the sky. The journey was mostly downhill through farmland, along well tended and wide packed dirt roads.

"Why do they call them the Western Wood, when they're really in the middle of the country?"

"With all that reading as a kid, you didn't read the history books?" Kyson guided Trickster up beside her.

"No, she was too busy reading advanced magic books," Andvari teased.

"Seriously," Aili rolled her eyes. "You're my teacher. Teach me something."

"The border moved a few hundred years ago. We gained more land to the West when the war was going badly for Haramot. They were burning the forest and cutting it down for war machines. We chased them off and rebuilt the forest. We added the buffer zone to the West to protect the land."

"We stole it?" Aili raised an eyebrow at Andvari.

"I think you can rule out a future for her in politics and diplomacy," Kyson snorted.

"Hey, if it protects the land, especially my forest, I'm good with it," Aili defended.

"That area has changed hands many times over its history. It was ours and sometimes given away before. Ownership is not so clear cut there." Andvari scanned the road ahead.

Aili glanced around her. The meadows were passing behind as they entered the farming belt. Crops, orchards, and vineyards would soon line the road for many miles. Aili's heart sank. She preferred the wild places, the forests and meadows, and the untouched land where animals roamed freely. Riding back to the city felt like walking towards a cage.

Despite her preference for wild places, Aili delighted in seeing the plants growing, tended, and cared for, the fruits and grains ready for harvest. Last time she was on this road, she was running away. She didn't stop to appreciate the many shades of green and gold, the colourful fruits splashing colour in the fields. Sweet fruit smells filled the area, ripe produce ready to be eaten.

She enjoyed the quiet during their travel. This road was quieter, as it only led to farms and to the camp near the border. They greeted the occasional farmer passing by and waved to people harvesting fruits and crops near the city.

Aili noticed the University towers first, light reflecting off the white stone like a beacon. As they crested another rise, the city slowly appeared over the rolling hills. The old city spread South, gradually turning to the shorter buildings in the outer neighbourhoods. The path carried them closer, right to the city's edge.

"Wait." Aili stopped Leya in the middle of the road.

Andvari stopped Charger and turned to look at her. Trickster halted moments later.

"We can go around the city completely. There's no need to cut through." Aili pointed down another road. "This northern road skirts the entire city, and there's a game trail from it right into the woods. I know a great campsite that's only a quick ride to the city."

"I defer to your judgement." Andvari waved a hand to the alternative path. "These are your woods. Lead on."

Aili sighed. Her shoulders relaxed. She guided Leya down the path to the North. Grain fields and oil seed crops bordered the road, the city just beyond it to their left. She could feel the energy in the plants, vibrant and healthy, waiting to be harvested.

The road turned West again and passed between the forest on their right and the buildings on their left. Copper roofs over stone manors stood high beside them. The University ahead towered over everything else. She shuddered. So much stone, so many walls. Aili was glad to avoid it all. The only redeeming quality in Aili's eyes was the ancient trees that shared the streets and inner parks. They towered over all but the manors and University.

She turned her attention to the woods on her right. This forest, her forest, was the oldest forest in the country. It was full of the ancient magic of nature, wild places and animals that ran free and lived with little human influence. The Scouts cared for the forest like any other, helping injured animals and watching for signs of diseases. The Mother

Tree lived deep in the forest, the first tree that brought all the others into being.

They passed the back wall of the University, thick white bricks that shimmered with protective magics. Students didn't always have excellent control, and the spelled walls would keep stray magic contained. Her nerves ached. Aili grimaced. It felt like being struck by lightning again, though not quite as strongly as the first time. She swallowed hard, ignoring the tightness in her chest, and rode on.

"Here." Andvari handed her a medallion on a chain, a heavy thing, but Aili loved it.

Aili took it gratefully and hung it around her neck. Her nerves calmed to their normal buzzing, and she could breathe again. Ages ago, he loaned her this medallion to help her cross the magical border. Back then, he explained how it can cancel magic for the person wearing it. They didn't use them often, but Aili appreciated their abilities.

"Better?"

She smiled at him and nodded. "Better."

"What is it?"

Aili stared at the white wall to her left, the words of the protective spells weaving across the stone in her magical awareness. "I feel the magic in the wall is so much stronger since I've spent so much time away. It's like I was numb from its constant presence when I was here all the time."

Aili always figured everyone else could feel magic the way she could when she was growing up. It wasn't until a passing comment she heard somewhere that she learned it wasn't normal. Besides, growing up around such powerful magics seemed to make her senses dull, as it wasn't until she got away that she learned to detect individual spells from the mess of magic in the background.

"How am I going to survive this?" Aili whispered.

"Magic shield?" Kyson met Andvari's eyes.

"Maybe." Andvari stared down at her, his sharp blue eyes assessing her. "How does our magic feel to you? We've cast it on you before. Was it okay for you?"

Aili nodded. "It feels familiar. I trust you both. Your magic is fine."

"When we get to camp, we'll see what we can do for you."

"It's not far," she promised.

Aili left the road and onto a path among the long grass, barely visible, and only if you knew what to look for. Deer used this game trail, followed by coyotes. Aili steered Leya between the trees, letting the pony pick the best path. Aili removed the medallion and handed it back, feeling more comfortable away from the wall.

"Thanks."

"You're okay now?" Andvari placed the medallion back in its protective pouch and pocketed it.

She nodded. "I never realized how strong the protective barriers around the University were."

"They have to be, with all those students running around and setting things on fire," Kyson explained.

Aili shivered, the memories coming back. She took a deep breath and calmed herself as the lightning flashed across her eyes.

"My apologies. I didn't mean..."

"It's fine," Aili assured him. "I'm learning to deal with it." She gave him a warm smile, using another deep breath to relax her body.

Aili grinned at the thought of Kyson with a student. He was an excellent teacher, but having someone underfoot all the time? No, he loved the forests too much. As a Master Mage, he was qualified to teach, but he was also a demanding teacher, even with his patience. She was pleased Andvari was her teacher. He let her have more freedom and explore things as she wanted.

Aili turned and guided Leya West again. She knew these woods, having grown up playing in them. Darik taught her how to navigate and survive out here. She led them around the city and across the southern edge of the woods, ignoring the trails they crossed.

"You've spent more time here than anyone else I know. Where do you recommend we set up camp?"

Aili turned and glanced back at Andvari. "I know the perfect place."

She followed a small stream to a pond. The running water kept the pond fresh and both the stream in and out of the pond were shallow and clear. The trees stood back from the water, leaving a large open area to set up the tent and move around. The horses had plenty to graze on here. Berry bushes grew just North of the pond. Bushes hid them from the edge of the forest and the farms beyond it. They were now on the West side of the city.

Kyson whistled. "Beautiful. Everything we need, right here."

Aili laughed. "I camped here with a blanket, tarp, and knife. That's all. This forest provides everything else if you know where to look."

She glanced around. The tart red berries were still in season, and the smaller blue berries were just forming, ready to eat soon. Aili knew where to harvest roots nearby and plenty of herbs grew in the area. Large trees at the edge of the clearing gave shelter and she could hang tarps among them or set up a high line for the horses if she needed. The leaves hadn't started to turn and drop, but it wouldn't be long now.

Something tugged at Aili, a whisper in her being. She closed her eyes and breathed, opening herself to the surrounding forest. The campsite felt normal, all was well here. No, it was in the woods to the Northwest. Something was affecting the plants there.

"What's up?" Andvari rested a hand on her shoulder, reaching down from Charger's back.

Aili shook her head, opening her eyes and scanning the trees. "Something's different. The energy has changed."

Kyson dismounted Trickster. "In what way?"

"I don't know. It mostly feels normal, but there's a touch of not normal beneath it. It's like from behind the door in the tunnel. Magic, but something else, too."

She chewed on her lower lip. The men exchanged a glance.

DEAR READER,

If you enjoyed my book, please consider leaving a review. It helps other people find my books, so they can enjoy them, too.

You can find more information on all my books at www. aliings.com. Sign up for the newsletter for bonus content and scenes, tips and facts, book information, and more.

THANKS

Books don't magically appear from nothing, and it takes more than the author to bring them into existence. To Brian, who did the early horse care each day so I could write uninterrupted, thank you. You believed I could do it when I suddenly decided to be an author. Your editing skills were appreciated.

To my dear friend Rod. You encouraged and supported me, shared my excitement at each milestone, and believed in me.

And to Irene, who gave the editing process a boost. Thank you all.

ABOUT AUTHOR

Ali spends her days with her horses and ponies, dreaming of adventures and magic. She enjoys martial arts, especially swords and edged weapons, though she practices for self-improvement. She also practices meditation, both sitting and moving varieties.

ALSO BY

Forest Guardians

Runaway Magic

Facing the Fire

Healer's Strength

Scout's Honour

Shadow Hunter

The Last Dragon

Apprentice Scout

Chasing Shadows

Legends of the Mountain

Phoenix Rising

Other Books

Rogue Magic